LUCY MARTIN

the
choice

LUCY MARTIN

the
choice

WELBECK

Published in 2022 by Welbeck Fiction Limited, an imprint of
Welbeck Publishing Group Based in London and Sydney.
www.welbeckpublishing.com

Cover design by Simon Michele
Cover photographs © Lyn Randle / Trevillion Images

A CIP catalogue record for this book is available from the
British Library

Paperback ISBN: 978-1-78739-773-6
Ebook ISBN: 978-1-78739-774-3

Printed and bound by CPI Group (UK) Ltd, Croydon, CR0 4YY

10 9 8 7 6 5 4 3 2 1

PROLOGUE

The men in the room have lit their cigars. Someone leans over to offer her one and now the others are all crowding around her, telling her it won't do her any harm to try one puff. She takes it and inhales, but the smoke seizes her by the lungs and the next second she's coughing herself awake.

Her eyes snap open and the men have vanished. The smell is putrid, chemical. Smoke is filling the space like hot water in a cold bath, seeking her out and billowing in opaque clouds towards her makeshift bed. Her heart leaps from sleeping to racing in a second, thumping so hard she thinks it's going to escape her body.

She pulls the blanket off her face for just long enough to shout 'Hello? Anyone there?' before her words are drowned by the hiss and crackle of fire from the other side of the wall. But there's no one there. Not even to tell her to *sshhh*, that she mustn't make a fuss, that it will be over soon. Smoke engulfs her and she's coughing again, eyes stinging, throat burning.

They've done what she knew they'd do, eventually. It was just a matter of time before she became a liability, before the curiosity of neighbours or a visiting tradesman made the whole thing unravel. She's been living on borrowed time. She should have thought of something, made a plan . . .

Don't panic. Find water. She knows you need to be low down. Heat rises. Smoke rises. One or the other. She edges off the bed, crouches down on hands and knees and crawls across the floor to the far wall. Holding one end of the sheet over her face, she feels around for the tap over the basin. She turns it one way and another until a trickle of brown water drips uselessly on to the sheet. Precious seconds tick by as the pipes try to gurgle into action. They've turned the water off. But they've done worse before.

She leaves the pointless tap dripping as she gets back down low, the barely damp sheet pressed up against her mouth and nose. She dares to breathe, tiny shallow breaths because any more and she'll be dragging the poison into her lungs and it will all be over. There's a sudden crack as a beam snaps and falls and she crawls a little faster towards the door, the one that leads to freedom, the one that's always locked and bolted from the outside. She's praying harder than she ever has before. Only a miracle can save her now, but she suspects that God abandoned her long ago.

She's almost as far away from the bed as the chain will allow her when something sharp pierces the heel of her left hand. She inhales sharply with the stab of pain and her lungs fight back in protest as she fumbles to find what it is. It's much bigger than a splinter of wood, smooth on one side, ridged on the other. She turns it over in her fingers and the realisation has barely hit her before she's forcing the tiny key into the padlock attached to the steel cuff on her wrist. One small turn and the metal breaks apart. She shakes her hand free, momentarily too bewildered by freedom to move or think.

Her head is fuzzy, her thoughts too muddled to focus, but she knows the flames will be upon her in seconds if she can't get out. She tries to tie the sheet more tightly around her face but she loses balance and the room spins. She mustn't give up, not now, inches away from the door.

She reaches for the handle and reels back in shock as she touches it. It's burning hot. She uses the sheet to protect her hand and tries again, eyes closed tight in prayer once more. If it's locked, she dies, if it's not, she has a chance, just a chance . . .

CHAPTER 1
Ten years later

'Glad to see you're unpacking at last.' Ronnie surveyed the scene before her from the doorway. Shards of morning sun had crept around the closed curtains, throwing a harsh spotlight on the chargers, cables, paperbacks, flip-flops and bikinis that decorated the carpet like a holiday collage. The fragrance of coconut after-sun lotion mingled with another that could only be described as *teenage bedroom*, while Tilly, the desolate queen of her ravaged domain, lay half-propped up on pillows, cocooned in her duvet, eyes fixed on her phone.

'Mmm?'

The heat was stifling. Ronnie picked her way through the wreckage, pulled open the curtains and lifted the sash window. Glass glided over glass, and she leaned out to smell the morning. Higher than the tops of the highest trees in the park below, their third-floor apartment was drenched in sunlight, and the sky was a cloudless blue.

'That's more like it.'

'Mum! Too bright,' Tilly protested, reaching down for a pair of sunglasses before going back to her screen.

It was hard to resist snatching the phone off her, but in Ronnie's experience, coaxing and cajoling was the way forward with the twins, every time. She forced a smile that she hoped looked encouraging.

'Back to school tomorrow, remember? We need to put a wash on, dig out the pencil case, clean out the mouldy rucksack, you know the routine.'

'I know. I just . . .' Tilly sighed a deep sigh that said *have you got all day?*

Ronnie stepped over the spilt contents of a washbag and sat down on the bed.

'Talk to me.'

Tilly shuffled sideways to make space. Her eyes were puffy from crying and lack of sleep.

'I miss Jake.' Her words came out in a whisper, like a confession that couldn't be held in.

Ronnie's heart ached in sympathy. *You're only as happy as your unhappiest child* was suddenly and horribly true. 'I know you do. I know how it feels.' She gave her hand a squeeze but it was unresponsive.

'You don't. How can you possibly know?' The teenager forever misunderstood, thought Ronnie, always thinking they're the first person in history to suffer the torment of being in love.

'Because I've been there, believe it or not.' Ronnie's first holiday without parents had been a trip to Mallorca with school friends, each of whom came home starry-eyed over some boy they'd met at a club and never saw again. In the weeks that followed, tans and memories faded. Without the instant-messaging technology that controlled the lives of today's youngsters, they had all moved on, put it down to experience, and most had gone on to make the same mistakes a few dozen more times before compromising with suburbia and a Ford Focus. Holidays were a parallel universe that sucked you in and spat you out when your time was up. They weren't the real world, but perhaps living in the real world wasn't a lesson Tilly was in a hurry to learn.

'What if he's the one? What if I've just met my soulmate and then we never see each other again?'

Ronnie's reply was automatic, the instinct of a mother trying to rescue her child from pain. 'If you want to, you'll find a way. You have your whole life before you. There are plenty more fish . . .' She stopped herself before any more clichés came out. Love had nothing to do with logic, she knew that, and children didn't listen to their mothers on the topic because, as Tilly had just pointed out, what did *they* know?

'Do you think he feels the same way about me? Do boys feel the same as girls about this stuff?' She sniffed, pulling out a tie-dye sarong from under her pillow and wiping her eyes with it.

Ronnie had no idea how men felt about love any more. Since her divorce, she had felt relieved not to have to grapple with the question, but right now Tilly needed some sort of answer, so she had to come up with one.

'Not exactly the same. I think they feel things differently, they can compartmentalise better than we can, and that's not such a bad skill to have. Helps you get on with the rest of your life. Stops you completely going to pieces.'

'I'm worried that's happening to me. I'm going to pieces.' Tilly pulled the sarong off her face and stared at it as if it was to blame for everything.

'Is that the one he bought you in the market?'

That only made the tears come in torrents. 'God, Mum, what am I like? I don't recognise myself.'

Ronnie pulled her into a hug and tried to find words of comfort.

'Once you get back into your routine, it will pass. You can make plans to see him again. It's not over . . .' She stopped again, mid-sentence. There was no point in promising anything she couldn't deliver, and she had just done exactly that. She was out of her depth here and there was no manual to hand about how to manage teenage heartbreak. It was like being in an exam facing a question you hadn't prepared for, and the world was watching how you dealt with it. Parenting issues were the sting in the tail of divorce. If the children lived with you, then how they turned out was down to you. There was no blaming the other any more. 'You'll get through this. You're strong and brave, beautiful and kind. You're a warrior queen.'

'A what?' Tilly pulled back, aghast.

Ronnie just stroked her hair and wiped tears from her cheeks. 'I don't know. I like the sound of it though, don't you?'

It had always been her priority to try to instil resilience into the twins. But the journey to true grit was an uphill

4

one, as she had discovered. Simon's hasty departure and swift acquisition of a new girlfriend had left her questioning her value, not only as a wife (because she'd been so quickly replaced), but as a detective (because she'd failed to spot all the clues he'd left) and today as a mother too. If her daughter was this devastated over a holiday romance, then maybe she wasn't doing the parenting properly either. She didn't remember being this upset about any of her own teenage love affairs, but then time had a way of erasing memories of pain.

Just as the question *Am I good enough?* took root in her mind, so did an image of an exasperated Serena rolling her eyes in despair. '*You were just the same when you were younger!*' Her fearless sisterly support didn't allow for self-doubt. The same could be said for Susie Marshall, the best of best friends, just a little more gung-ho. While Serena was Ronnie's psychological rock, the human diazepam, Susie brought the champagne and fired up the barbecue. Where were those two when she needed them?

A cough from the landing broke the spell. Tilly broke away and leaned over to plug in her phone. 'Sorry, Mum, I'll get up.'

Ronnie's shoulders untensed in relief. The storm had passed. She hadn't failed. Not this time.

'Good. And in the meantime, let's get this cleared up before Auntie Serena arrives. Looks like we've been burgled.'

It turned out she had Eddie to thank for bringing the crisis to an end.

'How long have you been hovering in the corridor?' It was getting harder to admonish him now that he towered six inches above her. She could have sworn she was taller than him before the holidays. It must be true that children had their growth spurts in summer, and when they were asleep, because he spent a ridiculous amount of time in bed these days. How he had managed to get a tan on holiday was a mystery.

'I could hear Tilly howling. Wanted to find out what all the fuss was about.'

'Really?' Whether he had any intention of offering Tilly comfort was doubtful. Although the two of them were friendly enough most of the time, Eddie would never miss a chance to torment his sister, especially where *boys* were concerned. 'She's fine now. Missing Jake, but give her time and she'll be saying *Jake who?* But, more to the point, how's your unpacking going?'

Taking him by the arm, she led him back to his room and watched him gather up the entire contents of his open suitcase, scrabbling in vain for the last sock, which he finally managed to hold on to by a thread.

'Ah, OK, so pretty well then. Can I help?'

He smiled hopefully around his bundle.

'Washing?'

CHAPTER 2

Ruth jolts awake. Another nightmare slides away into the shadows as her eyes adjust to the day. The sun reaches through the slats in the blinds to tap her on the shoulder and drag her back into the real world. She turns to look at the clock on her bedside table, which says six thirty, as it does every day when she opens her eyes. She can't train herself to lie in, even on a Sunday, can't let go of the conviction that sleep is a dangerous place. She focuses on the ceiling for a few seconds, tracing the crack that wavers along its border with the far wall, like her path through life, from the darkness to the light.

Morning brings some kind of relief but for the first few seconds her heart is racing, so she breathes deeply in and out, and in her mind, she goes over what she's achieved, the progress she's made. It's supposed to reground her, stop her mind wandering to dark places.

She starts by mentally listing the friends she's made in the last ten years, but it's not going to be a long list. There's Gemma and Phil next door – strictly speaking, her landlords, or landlord and lady, which sounds odd because they're so down to earth. They hadn't just rented out their cottage to her but had welcomed her into their lives like a long-lost friend, invited her to supper, brunch and lunch, to watch the Cup final, even to Ollie's first holy communion. She had politely declined the last one. She wouldn't feel comfortable in a church, but Gemma and Phil didn't need to know that, or why. Choose your battles, she tells herself. No point in going too far and spoiling everything.

Then there's her job with Madison's Nurseries. *Gardens, not children.* That's what she has to say every time someone asks what she does. She doesn't want to be around children, but planting flowers gives her hope, because it's working with nature to make beautiful things that survive harsh winters and live to see another summer. They are survivors, like her.

Madison isn't exactly a friend, but she behaves like one, always saying caring things and asking how you feel. She seems to want her employees to be as American as her, urging them to shower the clients with insincerities – how often do you really need to tell someone to have a nice day? And *please know* that they should get in touch with any questions *or* queries. What was the difference between a question and a query? Or a worry and a concern? Why did people use so many words where just a few would do?

The other staff are kind and let her be herself, they don't insist on her joining them at nights out in the pub, and they seem to get that she's, well, different. She's the only female van driver on the team, and that pleases her, because it shows that whatever they think of her, she can do what men do. She's a match for them.

Whether she's a match for Finnian Macaulay is another matter. Her heart gives a little jump at the thought of him. He seems like a good man, the kind she should have met long ago, if things had been different, if her life had been normal. And he's handsome. The kind of fairy-tale handsome that promises wedding bells and happy-ever-afters.

Landlady Gemma was the one who made her go online and start dating. She helped her put the profile together and showed her how easy the whole swiping thing was. 'Makes me wish I was single again,' she giggled, and Ruth felt sad suddenly, because of course Gemma was joking. Nobody would say that and mean it.

It had taken her months, well, more like years, if you really counted, to work up to it, and then the 'it', the moment of pressing the button, letting it all go live, was an anticlimax, and a risk. She was putting herself out there on the internet for all to see. If *they* found her there . . . She brushes the thought aside. It isn't going to happen.

She went through with it in the end because the emptiness she felt inside had become all-encompassing, inescapable. For a whole decade, she'd kept herself out of the limelight and under the radar, because that was where she was safest, but there had always been something missing. When she dared to imagine filling that void, it was like seeing a flicker of light at the end of the tunnel. She imagined having company on dark nights instead of lying awake in unexplained terror, convinced she'd heard a noise. She'd have someone to go to places with, because she rarely ventured further than work or the reservoir these days. The person she found wouldn't have to know the real her. Online they didn't do background checks. Nobody needed to know the truth about her past.

Her dating profile gave nothing away. She was vague about where she lived (Home Counties) and what she did (horticulture), and the photos were sufficiently blurred and distant to make her almost unidentifiable. Gemma tried to persuade her to use a bikini shot, but she didn't want to admit she didn't have any bikinis, or that even if she did, she didn't know if she could actually do that. She won't look at herself in the mirror unless she's fully clothed, even now, just in case she sees scars that she's forgotten about.

For one agonising second, she's back there in the cabin, Nate's breath heavy in her ear, one calloused hand holding her wrists behind her head as she tries to separate mind from body because it's the only way. She focuses on the world outside, a world she can barely remember.

When she wrestles her way back to reality, she realises she has forgotten to breathe again. *Breathe, Ruth, breathe in for four, hold for three, out for five.* Or was it six? She panics, before remembering it doesn't matter, just a longer breath out than in, because that's the poison coming out.

Fighting the thoughts that pour into your head is like pushing away the sea, scooping water out of a leaking boat. That's how dreams work. They find loopholes, gaps in your defences, and flood your mind with reminders of unfinished business, fears you think you've left behind long ago. Every time you come up for air, they just drag you back down to the depths and tighten their hold until, one day, that long outbreath, however many counts it might be, will be your last.

It takes a minute or two for the wave to subside. When she's sure it's over, she slides her feet into slippers and pads into the bathroom, where her reflection in the mirror above the basin is testament to her broken nights. Darkness circles her half-open eyes, her skin is blotchy, her lips are dry. She makes a mental note to go back online to get better sleeping pills. In the meantime, a hot shower, caffeine and fresh air will have to get her through the day.

She takes her coffee outside and sits on the bench under the magnolia. The oldest tree in the world, she read somewhere, dating back to twenty million years ago. Gemma and Phil planted it when they moved in and Phil had complained ever since because nobody had told him it was basically a pollen factory and would make him cough and splutter for six months of the year. Then Ruth showed him how to infuse steam with the magnolia petals as a remedy for the hay fever and all the badness was cancelled out. Phil was sceptical but at least he wasn't coughing and sneezing any more.

Their house and hers stand side by side like big and little sisters, at the end of Lime Close, half a mile from West Dean village, and hidden behind wooden gates which slide open at the flick of a switch. At the front, Ruth has planted roses and camellias, buddleia and lavender, so there's colour all year round, and that's where she sits under the canopy contemplating the day.

There's transition in the air. August has been swallowed up by the hungry beginnings of autumn, the sun is already lower in the sky but there's a heaviness all around, the threat of a storm which will come down like a curtain at the interval to allow the change of set for the next act. Seasons are like life. There's a time for planting, a time for harvesting and, outside the rush of activity, there's a time for pruning – cutting back the weary stems that have done their job, letting the plant conserve its energy for new growth.

She examines the roses and is busy with her secateurs when the gates buzz open and Gemma's Porsche Cayenne crunches into the drive. A Porsche is supposed to be a sports car, but this one is a giant spaceship that tells the rest of the world, *We are sports car people but we're serious about parenting*. It makes Ruth happy to think that some children get to travel in cars like this, but it's the kind of happiness that's tinged with envy.

Gemma jumps down like a jockey leaping from a stallion and, now she's outside it, the car dwarfs her. Ruth imagines people must think the same when she gets out of the Madison's Nurseries van. Often they do a double take, expecting a man, and she still gets a twinge of amusement from giving them a surprise.

'That's a bit of a busman's holiday.' Gemma is heaving her shopping out of the boot.

Ruth puts her secateurs down and rubs her hands, checking for thorns. She should have worn gloves.

'I suppose you're right, but it's hardly a chore.'

'You have a nurturing instinct. It's a good thing.' Gemma puts the bags of shopping down on the front step and sinks down next to them. She ties her long hair back in a scrunchie, turns her head to the sun and pushes her sunglasses back on her head, closing her eyes. A plane passes overhead, a reminder of the bliss of escape, but Ruth imagines her vision of bliss is different from Gemma's. She doesn't need a bright white beach and swaying palm trees. What she has right here is more than enough.

'Thanks.' Ruth turns her attention back to the rose bush. She picks up the secateurs again, looks for the five-leaf growth on the stem and cuts just above it, swiftly, deftly, leaving the plant free of its dead parts, ready to grow again. 'I can do the back garden if you like, while you're on holiday?'

'That would be great. Thanks, Ruth.' Gemma pauses, looks at Ruth as if trying to assess whether it's safe to go on. 'By the way, how did you get on with your online dating? I keep meaning to ask. Living vicariously through you – shame on me.' She glances conspiratorially over her shoulder. 'Phil's a sweetie, bless him, but a girl can dream.'

'Oh.' Ruth reddens out of instinct, before her brain takes over and reminds her there's no need. She is safe here. She exhales to expel the tension and smiles with what she hopes is confidence. 'Actually, it's going well.' But Gemma's expression indicates she wants more, so Ruth flounders on. 'I mean, it depends what you mean. I don't have much to compare it to.'

Gemma nods. 'Well, that sounds good enough for me. I'm happy for you. Hopefully it blossoms and you have more news for me when we're back from Cayman.'

'How long are you going for?' Ruth is glad to change the subject.

'About a month. Give or take. And looks like we're just in time to escape the change in the weather.' She shades her eyes and looks skywards. 'Hard to believe this summer's almost over.'

Ruth is still processing her words. 'A month?'

'It depends how Phil's job goes, and how the boys settle in at boarding school.' Gemma trails off and Ruth feels a pang of confusion. She can't fathom why anyone would send their children away. Gemma reads her mind, or her face perhaps, and offers justification. 'They're looking forward to it, you know. Have been for a while. And it makes sense with all the travelling Phil's doing now. Gives them stability, and the schools round here are a bit, well . . .' She drifts off, and Ruth imagines she doesn't want to say anything bad. Gemma never says anything bad about anyone or anything, even wasps and the government.

She nods in an attempt at reassurance but she doesn't know why Phil can't travel alone. He's a big boy. Gemma could stay at home and give her children what they need, which is a mother. She forces a smile and says, 'Absolutely' with all the bravado she can muster.

On cue, the front door is opened wide by a grinning Phil, with his trademark jolly wave. He's dressed smartly from the waist up. A crisp shirt and tie, combed salt-and-pepper hair, but the incongruity of his shorts and trainers makes him look like the final picture in a game of consequences.

Consequences was Ruth's favourite childhood game. She and Martha would play it at the kitchen table, usually

14

while they were waiting to go to Assembly and sometimes in the actual Assembly Hall before prayers, or after it was all over and the grown-ups were chatting, then again every evening when Aunt Esther was in the kitchen making dinner. Martha would cut a piece of paper longways down the middle. She and Ruth would start by drawing a head, then they'd fold over the paper to hide what they'd done and pass it to the other, who would draw the body and pass it back, then the legs. When you unfolded it, the absurdity of mismatched body parts and clothes was the funniest thing imaginable, until one day when Martha drew something rude on hers and Uncle Nate saw it when he came home. Then there really were consequences.

Ruth remembers the first punishment as if it were yesterday. A smack on the cheek, being sent to bed with no supper, with the door locked from the outside. That was when they were still allowed to go to school and were taught Latin by strict old ladies in black robes. Nate gave them a warning, *No more drawing.* So they would play consequences with words instead – so-and-so met so-and-so at so-and-so place, he said blah, she said blah and then *this* happened. What happened in the end, the actual consequence of all the *he said, she said* was the funny part, because it was so disconnected from the rest of it. Martha would write things like *the king arrived and killed all the monsters.* The king was always the outcome. He was a reminder that random good things happened out of nowhere, because of nothing, and you had to be ready for that. And he brought a happy ending, not the

Armageddon Uncle Nate would threaten them with. Everyone needed a king in their life.

The word games didn't get them into trouble as much as the pictures had because Aunt Esther didn't bother reading the whole unfolded paper – either that or she couldn't read their handwriting, which was deliberate, because they didn't want her snooping in on their secrets anyway. It never occurred to them that she couldn't read. Not till many years afterwards.

Ruth tunes back in to the present. She doesn't know how long she's been out this time. Her face must have gone blank with the memories, but her neighbours don't seem to notice. Phil is saying something about how long the weather will stay warm enough for shorts. He works mostly from home, which is why he's only ever dressed properly from the waist up. Ruth wonders what happens when he has to get up and fetch something, close a door, open a window. Then he'll give the game away. But he must have thought of that. After all, they like him enough to send him on business trips to places Ruth has barely heard of. When he's not travelling, he and Gemma play golf together on a Friday morning and then go out for lunch, returning after school pick-up with the boys in the back, rejoicing that it's the weekend again. It's a life Ruth finds captivating and repellent at the same time, if those feelings can co-exist.

He asks how Ruth is, admires her rose pruning and says he doesn't know the first thing about flowers, then he carries the shopping bags inside. Now Ruth's conflicting feelings merge into a pang of jealousy, because Gemma has everything she should have had, and Phil is her king. He's the kind of husband Ruth should have found, if things had been different, if she hadn't spent half her life hidden and the other half on the run.

CHAPTER 3

'Nice tan, sarge. Good holiday?' DC Baz Munro peered round his computer screen as Ronnie backed through the heavy office doors laden with bags.

'It was wonderful. But those stairs are steeper than I remember.'

Pausing to get her breath back, she took in the reassuring scene before her. Everything at Halesworth CID, staircase aside, was as it always had been – the early-morning aroma of coffee and aftershave, the low chatter of voices punctuated by phones buzzing and the occasional siren from outside. The traffic noise was constantly being weighed up against the need for fresh air and Ronnie had always made her views clear. She noted the venetian blinds banging in the breeze and nodded approvingly. Baz followed her eyes as he pushed his chair back and leapt up to help her with her bags.

'Ah yes, we're all freezing to death but didn't want to disappoint you on your first day back,' he grinned. 'What's in here?' He peered inside. 'Pressies?'

'A few Greek treats for the team. Hands off.' She reached out to grab it from him and he raised his hands in defeat.

'So, how was it? Sun, sand, sea and . . . sangria? Or is it ouzo over there?'

At least he hadn't left her hanging on too long for the fourth 's' word. She sank into the chair opposite him and leaned over to pull a bottle out of one of the bags. 'Ouzo doesn't travel well, but don't tell the others that.'

'You mean you've bought us second-rate souvenirs?' Baz exclaimed in mock horror, taking the bottle off her and frowning at the label.

Ronnie slapped his arm. 'Shut up, or I'll show you my photo album.'

'Maybe just give me the key points. Briefing time in five.'

'Sun, sea, sand, ouzo, just as you correctly guessed, and some quality time with the kids, until Tilly fell in love and spent the rest of the week starry-eyed and useless.'

'That doesn't sound surprising. We've all been there.'

'I think I've blocked out the bad memories of unrequited love. But what I want is a new-improved version of me, not a reminder of my teenage self.'

'Stop! You've put me off having kids already. Is it that bad?'

Ronnie had an image in her head of how bad it was and wondered how to express it without seeming ungrateful. 'Watching your children grow up is like that scene out of *The Sorcerer's Apprentice*. You want them to be independent, but you still want to have some sort of control, and they have other ideas about that.' She scanned the piles of papers, envelopes and folders that littered Baz's desk. 'So, how have you managed without me?'

'Barely survived, sarge, it's been absolute chaos. The suburbs are awash with bandits.'

'I'm glad I'm still indispensable,' she smiled. 'Did you and Amber get away in the end? Not taken her back to St Petersburg to visit the folks?'

'Not in a hurry to do that; saving up the annual leave for a bit of winter sun, and someone had to hold the fort in your absence.'

'Of course. Talking of which, where are we with the dating-app conman?'

'Not sure where that's leading to be honest. Nothing much to go on, just a distraction for the silly season. It's always the same around this time of year.'

'I see. So case closed, then?'

'Yes. The DI's orders. We hit a wall, and with no evidence to speak of, we're on a hiding to nothing.'

'Tell me anyway. What did you find out? I'm interested.'

'Really? I don't want you going round thinking all men are like him.'

'I want to know everything.' Ronnie nudged him. 'We've got a few minutes. Did you ever get an ID on the guy?'

'Not as such. He's either using multiple identities or we're looking at a gang of them. But the tactics are similarly underhand, and you've experienced some of those.'

He was talking about the night at Hemingway's a few months earlier when they had come so close. If she'd known the man sitting next to her, the one who had spiked her drink and tried to force her to go home with him, if she'd remembered his face enough to ID him, that would have drawn a line under things. There might not have been any more 'victims'. Or at least they could have been sure that this new catfish wasn't the same man.

'Almost had him, didn't we?'

Baz hung his head. 'We almost did.'

'Not that my drink-spiker was necessarily the same guy, of course,' Ronnie added.

'You're right. In fact, there's nothing to link these reports with that guy, apart from being bad to women.'

'What linked the recent reports with each other, in terms of MO?'

'Just the love bomb. You know the story – flattery, flowers, *I've never felt like this before about anyone else.*'

'Creep. Then he goes in for the kill?'

'He goes in for the *money*. Susses them out first, lots of openness, talks about his second home on the Costa del Sol, his boat and the fleet of sports cars squirrelled away at the family's country pad – which he's got plenty of photos of, by the way.'

'Stock photos, I'm guessing.'

'Yes, easy to find online. No surprises there. And the obligatory dog, of course.'

'A *dog?*'

'Golden retriever. This one.' Baz flipped open his laptop, googled the breed and scrolled down a few inches. 'Ta-da. It's officially the key to getting a woman to swipe right, apparently.'

'OK, and same pics for every woman?'

'The dog is the same. We think. Only one of them took a screenshot of the photo from his profile.'

'What about the other photos? Do we know he's using the same ones with each woman he gets his hands on?'

'Again, they all get a bit tearful when they describe the stately home in Yorkshire and the view from the balcony in Puerto Banús, but we don't have hard evidence. All the pictures were on the app or on his phone and, of course, he's not on the app any more. And before you ask, no we can't get hold of deleted profiles.'

'Have they made a complaint to the app? Which one is it?'

'It's called Sidekick, a newish one, all about being mates first and foremost, the importance of getting that chemistry right rather than hook-ups, so a great angle, but it's based on the same swiping principle as the others.' He paused for breath before carrying on. 'And yes, they have raised it with the site but by the time they do, he's gone. Then a few days later, we presume he's back on there looking for a new friend.'

'What do the women have in common? What's his target market?'

'Seems to specialise in women of a certain age looking for love second time around.'

'Aha, so really narrowing it down then. Plenty of fish in that pond.'

Baz laughed and opened one of the files on his desk, pushing it towards her. 'There they are – the three women we've got so far.'

'Who were seduced by his shaggy-dog story and Spanish love nest.' Ronnie looked hard at the photographs. They looked to be in their early forties, heavily made up, thin, sad-looking. 'Could there be more victims out there? I'm guessing yes.'

'If there are, I can imagine they're taking time to come forward out of some sort of shame that they have actually fallen for the scam and handed the money over to him.'

'Nobody with half a brain hands over cash to a virtual stranger any more, do they?'

'Sadly, it would seem that their vision is so clouded by the fog of infatuation that they will believe anything.'

'What's he telling them to make them give him money?'

Baz seemed almost embarrassed to answer. 'He's lost his online banking device. Needs to pay a supplier ten thousand pounds by the weekend.'

'Seriously? They have that much cash sitting around? And they actually go through with it?'

'Oh yes, and of course it's hard to prove months later that the money wasn't voluntarily handed over. And when it comes to their own motivation for doing it, there's a holiday to the Mediterranean on the horizon, the use of the family yacht. Got to be worth ten grand in itself.'

'I bet they never even make it to the airport.'

'Correct, last-minute change of plan, business emergency. Needs to jump on some other plane and do more important things the day before.'

Ronnie held up her hand. 'Let me guess, that'll be the trip he mysteriously never comes back from.'

Baz nodded. 'Got it in one.'

'Did the women have any photos they'd taken themselves?'

'That's another thing. He's not keen on them taking photos of him. He does all the selfies himself, keeps them on his phone because he's going to make an album of their relationship for her birthday. Another one said he just pulled on the shades or made some kind of excuse. So . . .' He flipped open another folder and scrolled down to some pixelated images that left everything to the imagination. 'We're left with a couple of distant ones, shades on of course, so could be the same guy, might not be.'

Ronnie looked closer at the picture on the screen. 'That's not much to go on. I see what you mean about case closed. Anything else?'

'Conflicting reports about the car he drives.'

'Well if he's got a fleet of them up at the stately home, that's not surprising, and with his access to other people's finances being what it is. Nationality?'

'Irish, says one of his conquests, but the second said American, until we got her to listen to a bunch of accents and she didn't know one from the other.'

'And none of them smelled a rat?'

Baz grinned. He liked his idioms, and this one seemed to please him. 'No rats were smelled, until the money and the man had disappeared.'

'Something wrong with our education system if grown women are falling for this stuff.' Ronnie found herself speaking someone else's words, echoes of her mother's familiar head-shaking diagnosis of society's ills. It didn't actually surprise her that it was going on. She just wished it wasn't true, because if it was happening to other women, then it could easily happen to her. And it nearly had.

'Schools are probably all over the dangers of online scams these days, but the internet wasn't even invented when these women were there, remember? And perhaps it's the dream come true for some of them, the righting of wrongs, the happy ending that makes them realise it was just a question of waiting for Prince Charming.'

Ronnie suppressed a smile. Tilly would take him to task for saying that, telling him that women didn't think like that any more, that *Prince Charming* had long ago been deleted from the lexicon of youth and had no place in assumptions based on gender. But then again, she had proved just yesterday that she could be very much the lovelorn Disney princess when the situation presented itself. Perhaps Baz had a point.

'Fair enough. I just despair of where we've got to sometimes. We should have gone beyond this by now.'

'But then again, I suppose that's why we do this job,' said Baz, clapping his hands together decisively. 'Because there will always be people who think they can get away with it.'

There was a tap on the half-wall that separated Baz's desk from the rest and Jules Mayer appeared, the new DC in the station everyone was talking about. 'DS Delmar?'

Ronnie nodded to Mayer and turned back to Baz. 'They can't. And they won't.' She straightened up and checked her phone. 'Monday-morning briefing. Can't say I've missed it much.'

CHAPTER 4

The sky is darkening above the warehouse when Madison comes out of the Portakabin and hands her an envelope full of cash. Ruth smiles and tucks it into the inside pocket of her coat, zipping it up carefully.

'Thank you,' she whispers. It's not illegal, she's sure of that, but it feels odd, and she knows it's not the normal way of doing things, but she can't open a bank account, so she has no choice. She glances around out of instinct, but nobody's watching. The others are busy taking equipment out of Davor's van, hauling it into the dark recesses of the giant shed, laughing about something or other. She's used to them sharing jokes she's not a part of, but it reminds her who she is, where she stands, always on the outside of things.

'You still good for tomorrow's deliveries?' Madison glances upwards. 'It looks like we're in for some weather.'

Ruth nods vigorously. 'Of course.' It's important to show willing, and she is more than willing. She is more than grateful.

She watches Davor and Eva unload the machinery from her van and reload it with trays of plants. *No tools are left in here overnight* it says on the back door. The sign's been there ever since the burglary, before Ruth's time, when Madison lost her livelihood and almost her mental health. She reminds them of this regularly. It's an American thing, being obsessed with therapists. Madison says she's always had one. Finn laughed when she told him about it, his great guffawing laugh that made her feel safe but a little bit scared.

Davor brings the last of the trays for the next day's drop-off, slides it in and slams the door shut. 'It's all yours,' he says without making eye contact. 'If the rain's heavy, use the gazebo for the planting. I'll do the school visit.' Then he raises his eyebrows at Madison, in a kind of silent question that she is expected to understand. Ruth wonders whether they're in a relationship. There's something between them that even Ruth can see, and she isn't used to noticing things like that.

Madison smiles and hands her the keys. 'Go well, Ruth.' It's a weird thing to say, but then Madison is weird. Then, as if it's an afterthought, she adds, 'You got plans tonight?'

It's only a question, but Ruth feels suddenly cornered and her heart beats faster. She keeps herself to herself and doesn't understand why anyone would want to know what she does in her private life at all, let alone a Tuesday night. But it's polite to reply, so she should think of something. She's letting a long breath out, and she's about to answer, when Davor rescues her. He's probably keen for her to go so he and Madison can be alone. He says something about the time, and having to get back. So Ruth just smiles and takes the keys. She climbs into the driver's seat and starts the engine. Madison waves, and within seconds, Ruth is swinging out of the yard and heading for home.

She's still feeling anxious as she pulls away from the lights at the first crossroads. Her heart is still beating its way out of her chest. She tries the breathing again, but it's hard to do while driving. She should pull over and compose herself but she wants to get home before the storm comes. It's beginning to rain, just drizzle, but she sets the windscreen wipers to the lowest setting and it calms her, watching them bow in unison to an off-stage ruler. As a child, she used to let herself be mesmerised by them from the back seat of the car, imagining the endless list of tasks they were agreeing to perform. It made her feel lucky. Perhaps things aren't so bad. Her list isn't actually endless. Just two deliveries, some shrub planting and a collection from a job they'd finished the previous week.

The rain and the wipers are working their magic and her pulse returns to normal. She turns on the radio and the DJ is introducing a song for everyone driving home in the bad weather, as if he knows what she's doing. She changes station and lets a song she doesn't know play itself out. She turns on to the dual carriageway that takes her out of town towards West Dean, and that's when she has an idea.

Ideas are a new thing. Ideas used to be frowned upon, the devil finding work for idle hands. Ideas meant breaking away, because the real ideas, the acceptable ones, had already been had. Having a new one was like saying the old ones weren't enough. It was like saying things needed changing.

This idea is allowed though. It's allowed because everything is allowed, in this new world where you can put bikini photos on the internet. Her mind races to shut it down, just out of instinct, but then she remembers, she's free now. It's OK to think things, and do them.

Finn lives in Wakehurst, just one junction before West Dean. She doesn't know where exactly, but she can call him, say she's passing by, ask if he's in. Her heart swells at the thought of it. Can she do it? Or will the past, the habits of long ago, stop her in her tracks, pull her finger back from touching the call button on her phone?

'*Nice girls don't do that.*' In her head, Nate is taunting her, the trace of a smirk on his face. '*So what does that tell me?*' He's touching her, tilting her chin up towards him with his finger, leaning forward to whisper in her ear, his stubble brushing her face. She shuts him down. That whole part of her life is over. A new chapter has begun. She indicates left and heads for the village.

It's a prettier village than West Dean, that's for sure, but then Ruth doesn't mind too much where she lives. Gemma calls their neighbourhood *a pensioners' paradise.* Most of the houses have grab rails and ramps up to the doors, pansies in the flower beds and cars with blue badges in the drive. It makes Ruth feel safe. Nobody will go looking for her there.

Wakehurst is different. It's what they call *up and coming*, or *bijou*, apart from the caravan site of course. But the twenty-somethings who come flocking to set up home in the renovated maisonettes don't notice that until after they've signed on the dotted line. Then it's too late. The place is full of upwardly mobile couples commuting to London using what the estate agents call *convenient transport links*, but which are regularly cancelled. Leaves on the line. Planned engineering works. If they make it back, there's a gin bar, a gastropub and a Little Waitrose. A mile or so outside the village, there's the Wakeley reservoir, a popular spot where the locals walk their Labradors and mutter about the *blot on the landscape* that they call the new wind farm. Ruth likes the wind turbines, giant spinning blades that remind her of the power of nature and what it can deliver when properly harnessed. It's an old site where some of the turbines have four blades rather than three, but they still seem to spin at the same speed. She goes there after work most days, parks the van by the water and wonders at the irony of it all. They tower over humanity like giant windmills marching across the hills, but they are the servants of man. Power is just an illusion.

She asked Finn where he lived the second time they met but he just laughed and shook his head and said, 'Easy, tiger,' which made Ruth blush. She should just phone him, not prowl around like a tiger. That's the right way to do things.

There's a queue at the traffic lights, which only seem to be letting a couple of cars through at a time. She's holding her phone and her finger trembles over his name, but she does it, she touches the screen and her heart speeds up again as the ringtone sounds. After five rings, she hangs up. He must be busy. She should go home. She turns left into a residential street, then into a side road because there's a car behind her getting impatient. The sign says Blyth Road. It reminds her of a holiday they took to the Northumberland seaside when she was small. Her grandparents on Pa's side lived there and that was where he and Ma were heading when their car went off the road. She tenses at the memory. She imagines them with her now, telling her to be careful, and she's about to do a three-point turn to retrace her route when she sees him.

He's smarter than she remembers, dressed in a suit and shiny shoes. He makes a dash out of a single-storey red-brick building, a newspaper held over his head to keep the rain off, and now he's climbing into a blue Golf, the one with the scratch down the passenger side. She remembers it from their first date when he dropped her home. 'Kids, you know what they're like,' he said, then seeing her face, quickly added with a grin, 'Not mine, don't worry!' and she smiled. Sharing humour was one of those things that made relationships work. She had read about that, and Gemma had told her to put it on her profile, *looking for someone funny who makes me laugh*. It had seemed an odd thing to ask for. Surely both of you needed to make each other laugh? It wasn't just one person's responsibility to be the comedian.

Ruth doesn't duck down, just watches the Golf rev into action and disappear down the road. He drives right past her but doesn't see her, probably doesn't expect her to be there, driving a white van. He probably thinks she's a delivery driver – Evri, Amazon. They are everywhere these days after all, pandering to people's daily whims.

She is brought back to earth by another van hooting at her. She can see the male driver in her wing mirror, holding his hands up, mouthing something she would rather not hear. She hurriedly pulls into a space a few doors down from where Finn came out. The van passes, accelerating through a puddle, and a small child walking down the pavement screeches and clutches on to his mother. Ruth watches him with a dull sense of longing and regret. The rain is still spattering on the windscreen and she doesn't want to go home. She wants to be part of one of those families, pulling the curtains on the gathering dusk, tucking a toddler into bed and settling down to supper and a film. She imagines that life often, but here it is, so close she can almost touch it.

The house Finn has come out of stands lower than its neighbours, a single-storey sixties build nestling between unremarkable semis and set back a bit from the road, with a few potholed parking spaces in front. A Jacksons For Sale sign marks the border with the next property. It looks lost and out of place; the brochure probably says it's *ripe for development* or *an investment opportunity*. The windows are intact, but streaked with grime, the porch roof is splattered with bird poo and the pillars that hold it up are green with moss and mould. It looks abandoned – so what was Finn doing in there?

Magnetised by curiosity, she crosses the road and glances left and right in case anyone's watching, before making her way along the cracked paving that leads down the side of the house.

If he hadn't left the side gate unlocked, everything would be different – she'd turn round and go back to West Dean, the whole episode forgotten. But she pushes it and meets no resistance. The door behind it is stiff but easy to force open with a foot pressed against the bottom and a hard thump to the middle. Her heart is pumping with fear and excitement as she pulls it shut quietly behind her.

The first thing that strikes her is how empty the place looks, as if the people who belonged there were suddenly removed. The kitchen worktops are littered with opened envelopes, half-spilling out their official-looking contents. A printer sits dormant in the corner, its mouth half open, a few uncollected pages lying on its grey plastic tongue. Whatever was happening here was suddenly interrupted, like at Sleeping Beauty's castle. Ruth wonders what the interruption was, and where Finn was going in such a rush, and so smartly dressed. A thought comes into her head that fills her with dread and makes her stomach turn. She doesn't want to think about it, but it's the only reason she can come up with that he wasn't answering his phone.

She banishes the thought from her mind with a flurry of comforting logic. There's nothing she can do if Finn wants to see other women before he decides who it's to be. She will wait for him to do that, because nobody wants a Prince Charming who hasn't made his mind up yet.

Through the other door, she can see a wide hallway, with a bathroom opposite. There's a sign on one door for men, and another one for women further up. It might have been a school or a community hall. There's a smell of bleach and mothballs and a hint of damp. The floor is mottled lino, the walls neglected magnolia. It all feels so familiar, but she can't retrieve the memory. It's buried too deep.

At the end of the entrance hall are double doors with panels of bevelled glass she can't see through. She pushes them open just a crack. It's the main room, the reason people come here – or came here, because the thick layer of dust on the floor and broken window blinds tell a story of obsolescence. Wooden folding chairs are piled against the walls at the sides of the room but some have slipped down and lie like wounded soldiers abandoned in the field. She lets the doors swing back shut and goes to leave through the main entrance but the door is obstructed by a scattering of post, letters with angry red writing demanding to be opened, takeaway menus on shiny paper offering half-price Tuesday and free garlic bread and, underneath them all, a crumpled newspaper – one of the local rags, Gemma calls them, that get stuffed through letter boxes and put straight into the recycling.

That's when she catches sight of something that makes her blood run cold. But she can't unsee it. She gasps for breath as adrenaline floods her body.

Run.

But she's frozen to the spot, and the rain is hammering so hard now on the skylights above her that she hasn't heard the car pull up on the drive or the footsteps on the gravel outside. She doesn't see him come in through the open kitchen door, doesn't hear his roar of fury, until it's too late.

CHAPTER 5

'Hello? Can you hear me? Can you tell me your name?'

Ruth feels the world come back into focus as someone close to her face is telling her his name and asking for hers, how long she's been there, among other things, but she can't keep up and she can't remember. Her head is pounding and they give her a mask to hold over her nose and mouth.

'Martha,' she says. The lie is automatic.

'OK, Martha, I need you to breathe deep slow breaths for me now.'

They lift her on to a stretcher and into an ambulance. Beeping sounds, something is being wrapped around her arm, squeezes tight, then releases. The mask comes off and they want to know where the pain is, then they want to know who did this to her. She finds her voice and tells them the pain's in her shoulder, her head, her cheekbone and the answer to the other question she doesn't know. She didn't see his face, and when the hard blow struck her head she blacked out. They don't ask for more, but they tell her she needs to speak to the police. The thought makes her shiver, her teeth start to chatter and they give her more blankets. They say the word 'shock' and the siren blasts as they gather pace towards the hospital.

The hospital staff want to know more things – who her GP is, and they don't believe it when she says she doesn't have one. They assume she's lost her memory and say, Not to worry, there's plenty of time to fill in the forms. The ambulance crew tell the doctors that they searched the place where she was found but it was empty, so whoever had attacked her was long gone.

They wheel her into a brightly lit cubicle where she is left with the curtains open, watching doctors and nurses hurry back and forth. Eventually, one of them stops at her bedside, pulls the curtain closed and peers at her over his glasses. Ruth stiffens in response, until he introduces himself as 'one of the doctors' and her mind settles. She's safe, for now.

He tells her she's had a head injury and that she needs to be admitted for observation because she might have a concussion. A kind nurse brings her water and pills and she falls asleep but she can hear them through her torrid dreams talking about 'whoever did this' and 'domestic violence'. All she wants is to go home and be invisible again.

She's woken early in the morning by phones ringing and the hum of chatter outside the ward. For a second, she panics, not remembering where she is, but the kind nurse comes back and tells her she must stay in hospital until she's well enough to leave. The nurse's name is Cathy. She says she has a daughter Ruth's age, and Ruth suddenly wants to cry, because she doesn't have a mother any more, which is a stupid reason, but she can't stop herself. It's like all the sadness is pouring out at once in a tsunami of tears. The other patients avert their eyes. Cathy brings more water, pulls the curtains, then when it passes, she helps Ruth to the bathroom, and Ruth forgets, just for a second, but it's long enough for Cathy to see, and gasp at what she sees. She lifts up Ruth's shirt and then the next minute she wants to see the rest of her stomach, and her back, and when Ruth is back in bed, she hears her on the phone asking something about safeguarding.

They've told her she needs to wait to be discharged but she can't stay there another second. She waits until the woman at the desk is on the phone and finds out that it's easy to leave hospital without being asked any questions. The doctors are too busy looking at files of notes and writing on clipboards. The nurses are pushing trolleys and asking old people in loud voices how they're feeling this morning. When the automatic doors slide open to release her, she breathes deeply and closes her eyes for a second to drink in her freedom.

Her van is still in Blyth Road, which is a half-hour walk from the hospital at the most. She walks with her head down, looking a few paces ahead, keeping her hair pulled around her face to hide the bruise on her cheek. She catches sight of herself in a car window and her heart misses a beat. She has become old, washed up. Her body is bent over in defeat. She tries to stand a little more upright to draw less attention to herself. It's a rainy Wednesday morning and nobody's interested in her, she tells herself. She's anonymous. She will get her van and go home and wash her face, put make-up on over the purple swellings and go about her day. Finn Macaulay will be forgotten. She pauses under a bus stop to get her phone out and block his number.

But when she turns the corner into Blyth Road, her blood goes cold with the memory of the previous night, what she found in Finn's house, the blow to her head that made it all go dark. *Escape*. She panics, feels in her bag for the keys and can't find them. She checks her pockets, then her bag again, tipping its contents on to the pavement, forcing a jogger to step off the kerb into a puddle. She thinks back to the night before, tries to focus on what happened when she saw Finn come out to his car. She doesn't remember getting out of the van, doesn't remember locking it, or even shutting the door.

Just as her thumping heart is about to explode in her chest, she sees it. Hidden between two removal lorries, it looks smaller than she remembers. Relief floods her body. As if on cue, she hears a jangling in her coat pocket. Her keys weren't there before, but they are now. She thanks a God she doesn't believe in any more, climbs in and sits for a minute, waiting for her head to stop throbbing.

What she does next is more on autopilot than through conscious thinking. Her brain must still be half asleep, or is her brain the one that's taking over from her unconscious mind, overriding the part of her that says, *Run away, take cover*? Whichever it is, a minute later, she finds herself pulling out of the tiny space, performing a U-turn, and then she's on the A road out of Wakehurst, heading for Halesworth Police Station.

CHAPTER 6

'DS Delmar, how can I help you?'

Detective Inspector Lydia Burnett was a formidable woman whose voice could still make Ronnie feel like a naughty child with her hand in the cookie jar. She clasped her hands in front of her, half supplicant, half assertive executive. Lydia could read into it what she wanted to.

'Sorry, just wanted a quick word, ma'am.'

'Did you, now?' Lydia looked mildly exasperated. 'Can't it wait till I've finished my meeting?'

Ronnie resisted the urge to roll her eyes. 'I'm not sure, ma'am. Probably not, if I'm honest.'

Lydia exhaled and leaned one arm on the nearest desk. 'OK, what is it?'

'A woman has just come into the station, completely distraught, saying she was assaulted by some man she met online. I'm going down to talk to her now. Interview room three.' She looked over to where Baz was sitting opposite Lydia's giant desk. He was flicking through a folder. Ronnie couldn't quite make out what it was. 'Unless DC Munro is free to do the interview?' Her voice trailed off as she willed him to turn round, reveal the contents of the file that he and Lydia were having their secret meeting about. 'I mean, it could be our catfish she's just met, and I know Munro's been running the case.'

Lydia appeared to ponder for a second. 'Turning violent now is he, this catfish?' she mused. 'Must have met with some resistance, or has this one rumbled him, I wonder, threatened to blow the whole thing apart?'

'I just thought, since DC Munro is leading the investigation on that—'

'Firstly, we have closed the catfish case, with no reliable witnesses and no evidence that would pass muster with the CPS. Secondly, DC Munro is in a meeting with me which will take a while longer, but I'm sure you can handle this on your own, or see if DC Mayer is free?'

Ronnie nodded. 'Presumably we can reopen the case if we have good reason to?'

'It would have to be a very good reason, DS Delmar. I can't afford my detectives to be wasting time on women who should know better.' She turned to go back into the office, then looked back, reading Ronnie's mind, the trace of a smile on her face. 'We're discussing the sergeant's exams, in case you were wondering.'

'Of course, great.' Ronnie turned away as she replied in case her expression gave her away. Since when did they reserve their resources for victims of crime who had passed an IQ test with flying colours? Lydia's dismissive tone had made it clear that on this occasion she was more preoccupied with Baz Munro's rise up the ranks; but there was no need for verbal retaliation, and as for reopening the catfish case, it all depended on what the woman in interview room three had to say.

Room three hadn't been Ronnie's choice. Windowless and airless, with stained ceiling panels and the home of half a dozen storage boxes, it was a claustrophobic's nightmare. Baz always said that when he was forced to use it, he tried at least to be grateful he wasn't buried alive, hammering on the roof of his coffin, and today the comparison seemed particularly apt. A second batch of storage boxes had been lined up against the wall, shrinking the remaining space by another couple of feet. Ronnie tried to summon up some of Baz's gratitude and failed.

'I'm so sorry about this room. I'm afraid it was the only one available.'

The face across the table from her smiled a tiny smile that disappeared the second it surfaced, as if the pain was too much. Ronnie wanted to take back her words. They made it sound as if the station was heaving with criminals.

She glanced down at the notes from front desk and back up at her witness, who looked more like a suspect in a drugs raid than the victim of a brutal attack. But Ronnie was probably just too used to seeing young girls dressed up to the nines and Instagram-ready. Tilly would spend hours in front of the mirror before stepping outside her bedroom, even on a beach holiday. Especially on a beach holiday, in fact. The woman before her was the very opposite – beaten up, hollow-eyed, haunted. She clasped her hands in front of her on the table.

'Ruth Jones? I'm Detective Sergeant Delmar. Why don't you tell me what happened, from the beginning?'

As Ruth spoke, Ronnie studied her face, her clothes, her mannerisms. She looked older than her twenty-eight years, a good ten years older, and it was hard to pinpoint why. She was dressed in a plain blouse, trousers and a black hoodie, with no concession to fashion or flattery. There was a nasty bruise spreading across her cheek and red marks were visible on her wrists and forearms until she pulled her sleeves back down. She wore no make-up and a mass of unruly dark hair overshadowed her face. Her features were striking, almost beautiful, but under cover. She was hiding from the world.

'I shouldn't be here, I'm sure it was nothing.' Her eyes darted from the plain grey walls to the stained ceiling to the piles of boxes, then back to her hands that gripped the table before her.

'You were right to come,' Ronnie said. 'Now, tell me what happened. As much as you can, from the beginning.' She poured water into the plastic cups and pushed one towards the other woman. Ruth took a sip before replying, then fixed her eyes on the middle distance.

'It started with the dating app. I knew I shouldn't have gone on that thing, but I thought it might help me, and Gemma, she's my neighbour, she said it was fine, that everyone does it.' Her voice was jumpy and disjointed.

Ronnie did her best to dispel her anxiety with soothing words. 'It's the way most people meet these days.'

Ruth seemed calmer then, as if she had been spared a punishment, and her first confession had been swept under the carpet.

'Which app was it?'

'Sidekick.' She bit her lip, eyes down in submission like a repentant sinner. 'I know, not very romantic, but I wasn't sure I wanted romantic, not at first. I think it's better to get to know someone before . . .' She trailed off. 'Is something wrong?'

Ronnie readjusted her expression. The impact of Ruth's words had registered too obviously on her face. 'No, not at all. Please carry on.' She scribbled the name of the app in capital letters, underlined it and sat back in her chair to give Ruth more space.

'I met a man, called Finn, or Finnian, that's his real name, and we went out twice. For a coffee the first time, then for drinks, but I don't drink, so it was a coffee again.'

Ronnie carried on scribbling on the pad as she listened, then looked up. 'Did you get a surname?'

Ruth's eyes widened with fear, and Ronnie put her pen down. 'Don't worry about that. Take your time. I'll try not to interrupt.'

'It was when I went to his place.' Ruth's voice was faltering now. She wrung her hands, then hid them under the table out of sight. 'I'm not sure he even lives there. It didn't seem much like a home. I know I shouldn't have been there, but he wasn't answering his phone, and then when I saw him leave, I wanted to see inside the place. I wanted to know where he came from, what he did, because he was so secretive and it was the only way I was going to find out.'

'That must have been frustrating, not knowing, and especially getting no answer on the phone.' Ronnie kept her eyes on Ruth, willing her to get to the part where they might get the detail they needed.

'So I let myself in. It wasn't locked, not properly, and I was looking around, trying to work out where I was, and that's when he came home . . . I think it was him, but I didn't see because he came up behind me, and he was angry.' Her words became whispers, then a whimper that Ronnie could barely make out, in between gasps for air. 'But it was what I *saw*.'

Ronnie leaned forwards, holding her gaze. 'What did you see?'

Ruth's lips tightened as if to stop the answer escaping.

'There was something. It made me scared. And now . . .'

'And now what? Ruth, you can tell me.' She glanced at the clock on the wall behind Ruth, wondering how long Baz would be.

Ruth screwed her eyes tight shut. 'I shouldn't say. I don't know what to do.'

'You're doing fine so far, Ruth. You're in the right place. You're safe here at the police station.'

Ruth's forehead furrowed with doubt.

'And I'm here to help you, but you have to tell me what happened,' Ronnie coaxed. 'Was it because of what you saw that he attacked you?'

Ruth seemed confused. 'I don't know. I didn't see him.' She wrung her hands and closed her eyes tight. 'He's coming for me. That's all I know.'

'You mean Finn? He's coming for you?' Ronnie's head was pounding with frustration. 'Ruth, I need you to explain so I can help you. Can you tell me the address where this happened?'

'He'll find me, I know he will.' Panic was mounting in Ruth's voice. She touched her neck, where a bruise on her collarbone was turning a dark shade of purple. Her voice returned to a whisper. 'He'll find me, and he'll hurt me.'

Ronnie inhaled deeply and met her gaze with as much compassion as she could muster. Ruth was one of the few that came forward, and needed careful handling, but she seemed to have hit a brick wall. She tried to adopt a gentler tone.

'Ruth? Can you tell me what it was that you saw in Finn's house?'

'It was *him*.' Ruth had drained her drink and was crunching the plastic cup in her hand.

'Do you need a minute? I can go and get us some more water.' Ruth could take as long as she wanted if she was going to lead them to their man. The important thing was to let her feel secure again, which was going to take more time than Ronnie had imagined.

There was a knock at the door. DC Munro's head appeared in the square window. Ronnie stood up, gave him a nod and turned back to Ruth.

'I'm just going to have a quick word with my colleague. I won't be long.'

Stepping into a side room with Baz, Ronnie briefed him on the story so far. It couldn't have taken more than a minute to relay the conversation, but it was long enough for Ruth, because when they returned to the interview room, she had disappeared.

'You let her walk out of the station, just like that? Didn't anyone see her leave?' DI Lydia Burnett was less than impressed when they stood before her like schoolchildren caught smoking behind the bike sheds.

'There's no security between room three and the front desk.' Ronnie was telling Lydia what she already knew, and her eyes were rolling. She had never been behind the idea of converting the receptionist's kitchen into *a more productive space* but the shrinking budget had forced sacrifices at all levels.

'Front desk had a queue of people, so nobody saw her go,' Baz offered, in half-hearted support.

Lydia waved away his excuse. 'Well, that settles that one – another flaky witness just confirms my view that we were right to close the catfish file.'

'But ma'am, surely it's worth another go. I mean, she was physically assaulted by this man, which could mean, as you suggested earlier, that he's turning violent, or she rumbled him, found something out about him she shouldn't have. She's been to his house apparently, so we're closer than we ever were before.' Ronnie paused for a reaction, but Lydia's face remained impassive.

'Have you got an address?' she asked eventually.

'For Ruth, not her attacker. But I'm not sure it's the right move to go piling round there. We don't want her to feel trapped. She's traumatised enough already. If she's scared of him finding out she's been to the police, we need to win her trust before anything else.'

Lydia seemed to be giving the thought some consideration, and tapped her fingers on the desk as she composed her reply.

'Can I just begin by reminding you that this is strictly a one-off and if nothing comes of it then we move on? None of the women who have come forward have done anything but muddy the waters. Almost as if they are in league with this catfish of theirs and bent on wasting police time.'

'Ma'am—' Baz interjected, presumably anxious to defend the case he must have spent several weeks on over the summer, but Lydia raised her hand to silence him.

'Leave it till the morning. See if you can persuade her to come back, or at least give a statement, and see if you can get her to give us an address for our man so we can get over there and see what he has to say for himself.'

'Yes, ma'am. And if it *is* him, we're killing two birds with one stone,' Munro offered, throwing a glance at Ronnie. 'What do you think, sarge?' For a minute, she thought he was asking her about his apt use of an English proverb.

Ronnie was still stunned by Lydia's acquiescence to any follow-up at all. 'I think we treat the matters as separate, given the different MOs, and it's a bonus if the two birds come in for the price of one.'

Baz looked delighted. Lydia just nodded and waved them away as she picked up the phone.

Ronnie was halfway down the corridor when Baz caught up with her.

'Sarge?'

'You OK to go over there first thing?' Ronnie slowed her pace to ask the question, but didn't stop.

Baz overtook her and stopped slightly in front, at an angle, hand on the door frame of the main office.

'Is everything OK?' His expression was one of genuine concern. Ronnie couldn't help but notice.

'Yes. Why do you ask?'

'I thought I'd done something. You've been off with me all day.'

Had she? It was true that Ronnie's head was full of jumbled, conflicting thoughts. She tried to make sense of them before answering, because something had rattled her. Before her stood her second in command, a highly capable young DC, just trying to climb the ladder as anyone in his position should. And there she was, DS Veronica Delmar, with her own blossoming career and no reason to worry that it might be snatched away from her. And yet it was there, that flicker of insecurity. The same insecurity that had once driven her and was now driving her daughter to swoon and weep over a boy from a beach holiday, and there was no room for it in her life, least of all her working life.

'Not at all – lots on my mind. And with Ruth Jones running off, I suppose I feel a bit shaken up. I didn't mean to be unfriendly.' The words were easy to say, and seemed to give Baz the relief he needed.

'Phew, glad to hear it, and no offence taken.' Baz's smile returned and he pushed the door open with a flourish.

'How about I take you through our catfish witness statements? Just in case you can see any parallels with what Ruth told you.'

Ronnie managed a smile in return as she ducked under his arm and pulled a chair up to his desk. 'Good plan. Show me what you've got.'

CHAPTER 7

Ruth leans on the side of a car to catch her breath. She shouldn't have gone. What was she thinking? No one would believe her if she told them the truth. They'd want proof, witnesses; they'd say she was delusional. And all it would take was for someone to recognise her, put two and two together, for someone in the police to be one of them, looking out for her. She's made a decent effort to disguise herself, wearing a different wig from the one she wears to work. The hair is easy, but she can't change her height or her build, the shape of her nose, the line of her jaw. There are plenty of things that can give a person away. She takes a few long breaths in and out, tries to weigh up the dangers before her, but she can't get there. Panic is rising in her chest and she has a vision of Finn as she turns and he's towering above her, bringing back memories that make her legs give way beneath her. She can't let that happen again. She must fight it, but the nightmare is all around her. Fear has her in its tight grip and it's not letting go. She disobeyed, she went behind his back, and now she's in trouble like before. And there will be consequences.

A police car passes, siren blaring. She must be right that they're all connected. The police are on his side, working for him to find her. She holds her breath, crouched behind a car with rain dripping from her face. Her trousers are soaked through now but it's quiet again and she stumbles on. Her van is only one street away. She can make it.

The rain is pooling in puddles on the pavement and the road. A passing car splashes her and she jumps with the shock, looks up in panic, feeling her heart pumping, but it's not him. She pulls her hoodie more firmly over her head and focuses her gaze a few feet ahead of her, occasionally glancing up to check the road signs. It's still sore where he hit her, she doesn't know what with but it felt like an iron bar.

As the scene comes back to her, tears sting her eyes and some escape and get mixed up with the rain on her face. She wipes them away but all she can think of is how much she wants her mother to come back and take her away from all this, make everything all right again. She thinks about little Rex, who must have finished primary school by now. The thought of him and Martha makes her heart ache, while her brain, the part of her that keeps her safe and alive, shouts, *Stop, stop* . . .

She unlocks the driver's door with trembling fingers, climbs in and sits at the wheel, but she feels too exposed, even with the rain lashing the windscreen. She pulls off the wig and puts on the baseball cap that sits on the passenger seat, pulls it down low over her face, tucking her hair under her collar. Now that she feels the relief of anonymity, the panic lifts and evaporates. She indicates right and pulls out on to the road, forcing her mind back to the tasks that lie ahead in her day.

There are the deliveries and two planting jobs to do between her and Davor, as well as checking up on the sensory garden at Holly Lodge. Davor will take the second van. Eva will clock them in and out when they register the jobs as completed. The list is flexible. What she can't do, he will take on and vice versa. They are a team.

The traffic is light despite the rain. She sets her satnav to the first destination, then realises that Holly Lodge, the second job on their list, is on the way. She's literally going to pass by the entrance, then after that, her work will be done and she needs to get home to safety.

It crosses her mind that the van will give her away. Perhaps she can drop it somewhere, far enough away to leave a false trail, but with the keys in it this time so someone takes it and leaves even more of a trail to make her impossible to find. She'll get back home by bus. She messages Davor to tell him she'll do the school job, then spots another police car and quickly drops her phone in her lap. That was close.

CHAPTER 8

Serena had only been at the flat for a few days, but she fitted in as if she'd been there for ever. The twins loved their favourite (and only) auntie, and she seemed to go some way to filling the gap that Simon had left, balanced out the family to an even number again, with the right adult to child ratio.

'Morning. Can I make you a coffee?' She was already in the kitchen when Ronnie appeared in her dressing gown, the surfaces were sparkling, a scented candle burning on the table.

Ronnie stopped in her tracks, a smile spreading across her face as she inhaled its scent.

'Let me guess, bergamot and grapefruit?'

'Spot on. And don't look so surprised. I'm just showing gratitude to my hostess. I don't know where I'd be otherwise.'

'At Mum's?'

'Even with her away on holiday, it would be weird. She'd still be there in spirit, tutting at my odd habits.'

'Hardly odd, just a bit alternative. And you're more than welcome to stay as long as you like while the builders are at your place. No point going back before they've finished.'

Ronnie pushed open the French windows that looked over the park below and leaned out over the balcony. The sun was rising later every day now, but the temperature wasn't dropping. The weather forecast was for a storm that never seemed to arrive, but autumn was trying to make its presence felt. Three floors below, the lawn was strewn with the first flurry of fallen leaves and the trees that lined its perimeter were already sporting the new season's shades, nature's actors changing costumes for their next scene. September was the month that the acer and the horse chestnut, alongside maples and rowans, all vied for the prize of most Instagrammable foliage.

'Do you ever experience those blissful moments when you just appreciate everything you have?'

Serena came up behind her with coffee. 'It's not like you to come out with things like that.' She handed her one of the mugs. 'Flat white for you, detective?'

'Thanks. I have a feeling I'm going to need it. I'd got too used to the holiday timetable of snooze, swim, snooze, booze, repeat.'

The park was filling up. Dog walkers were gathering for their early-morning chat, long shadows stretching away from the sunrise. The twins had always wanted a puppy but they would have to enjoy the sight of them from afar for a little longer while they were in a flat. Another reason to hang on in there for a few more years, perhaps.

'And now it's back to grim reality.' Ronnie took a sip of coffee. 'Wow, that's good.'

'What's happened?' Serena frowned. 'You were all gratitude a second ago.'

'A moment of amnesia must have overwhelmed me, because, as it turns out, the Surrey suburbs aren't the Garden of Eden they are perceived to be.'

'Anything you are at liberty to divulge?'

'While I was away, we were fumbling around in the dark, looking for someone who was making a bit of a name for himself online. Targeting middle-aged women, making off with a fair bit of money and disappearing.'

'Hmmm. Catfish? Isn't that what they call those guys?'

'That's what we're calling him, since the other names he goes by seem to vary according to who you ask.'

'Apparently, it comes from when they used to put catfish in the tanks with the cod on their way from Alaska to China. The catfish would chase the cod around, stop them getting bored and keep them tasty.'

Ronnie winced. 'So at least he's stopping us getting bored and keeping us tasty. Lucky us.' She followed her sister back inside. 'And talking of tasty, why does coffee taste so much better when someone else makes it?'

'Because this someone uses proper beans, not your instant stuff, probably.'

Serena had a point. Ronnie had never got round to reading the instructions for the built-in coffee maker that Simon had insisted be included in their state-of-the-art kitchen.

'Anyway, the witnesses that came forward to tell us about this guy turned out to be flaky and there wasn't any real evidence to build a case, so Lydia decided to call time on it. And she had a point, but then yesterday a new witness came forward. A woman who'd been beaten up by some guy she met on the same app as the other women had met the catfish.'

'Do you think it's the same guy?'

'Well that's the weird thing about the police mind, isn't it? You end up looking for a connection where there might not even be one, just to make the pieces of the puzzle fit.'

Serena clapped her hands together. 'I know exactly what you mean. It's so much easier to make sense of life when the mysteries are neatly resolved.'

'It would be easier to assume that the catfish and this woman's attacker are one and the same, but with nothing at all to go on except coincidence, I'm up against it, especially as Lydia doesn't want us wasting more time on a case that has so far delivered precisely nothing.'

'I see where you're coming from. Stubbornly refusing to let go of the case that's all about women being taken for a ride, and doing whatever it takes to make this new one fit the profile.'

'You know me too well,' grimaced Ronnie. 'And, now I've got the bit between my teeth, I can't let go of it. And don't tell me to do daily meditation. That's another stubborn refusal of mine.'

'I wasn't going to say that at all.' Serena looked affronted. 'What I was actually going to say was practise detaching from the narrative.' She flicked her hand as if casting a spell. 'Sometimes we need to untie ourselves from its shackles and rewrite the story.'

'I'll do my best.' It was a lot to take in just before a day at the office. 'But it sounds like a lifetime's work. In the meantime . . .' She looked around for her jacket and swung her bag over her shoulder. 'I'm going to shackle myself to my desk for the next few hours.'

Her mind was already back on the catfish. Detaching from the narrative in his case meant the list of his possible motives going from manageable to infinite. For Ruth Jones, the possibilities would have to include that her injuries were the result of self-defence by the innocent party she was attacking, or even that they were self-inflicted. It was impossible to keep all the scenarios in her head at once. For now, Ronnie might just carry on assuming things were as they appeared to be.

She drained her mug and picked up her bag, just as Eddie exploded into the room, dropping his rucksack on to the floor.

'Mum, have you seen my football boots?' he asked, rubbing his eyes. 'I overslept. Oh, hi, Auntie See. Did I just interrupt something?'

'Not at all. Now what do footballers have for breakfast? Can I make pancakes?' Serena hopped down from the stool and rubbed her hands together.

Ed grinned at his mother. 'Err, can she stay for ever please?'

CHAPTER 9

Baz was climbing into his Vauxhall Astra as Ronnie pulled into the overflowing car park. Like the interview rooms, it seemed to have been requisitioned for things with no connection to its original purpose. A stack of pallets took up two of the CID spaces and an overflowing skip straddled two others. The internal refurb that had seen off the staff kitchen and enforced a new cheek-by-jowl work ethos was making its presence felt. She gave Baz a thumbs up. Jen Connolly was in the passenger seat and gave her a wave. She was a good PC, aspiring to move over to CID, and had the enthusiasm and the grit to make it work.

Baz's window slid open.

'Great timing, sarge. Just off to see our friend Ruth Jones in West Dean.'

'Go easy, won't you? Don't scare her off. We need our witnesses confident and clear-headed.'

'Of course.' Baz revved the engine and pulled away.

Ronnie watched them leave, wondering what Ruth would make of the police turning up at her house. Most likely she'd be terrified, but there was no other way if they wanted to find the truth behind her story. She climbed the stairs to the office with heavy, weary steps and a dull sense of foreboding. Perhaps she should have been the one to go with Baz. Ruth might react better to a familiar face, but Lydia had the last word on that, and all Ronnie could do was wait and see how things worked out.

Morning briefing was the three-line whip that day. Lydia took her position before the assembled staff, some of whom had spun round from their desks, while others leaned against the wall or perched on a windowsill, notepads at the ready. She glanced at her watch, then at the clock as if one of them was lying. Adjusting her glasses, she shuffled and reshuffled the papers in her hands, before gazing around her audience with the air of a military commander readying the troops for battle. There was something about her that was different from the previous day. Her aura of calm control had been replaced by one of seriousness that Ronnie didn't often see. She cleared her throat.

'I think we should start. Latecomers will have to catch up, and their lateness duly noted.' Her eyes rested on the empty chairs, then settled back on her notes. 'I won't beat about the bush. Yesterday afternoon, Wednesday third September, a seven-year-old boy called Liam Buckley went missing from Holly Lodge primary school, just outside Wakehurst.'

Ronnie did a double take. Had she heard right? Child abductions were hardly run-of-the-mill police work in the suburbs. She looked around the room and was met with shocked faces.

'It was a premeditated abduction, as far as we can see, and an unusually complex one, by all appearances.'

Lydia's eyes cruised the room, settling on Ronnie, who had no trouble staring right back, unblinking. 'His grandmother, Dawn Buckley, was on her way to collect him from school, but she was persuaded at knifepoint to get into a car, which took her some five miles away and dumped her in the street, leaving her to make her way back.'

'Unharmed?' a voice asked from behind a computer screen. Jules Mayer was a new DC who had recently moved over from uniform and was taking to it like a duck to water. She had already established her reputation as a stickler for squeaky-clean procedure and a campaigner for the kind of policing that the public wanted to see.

'Unharmed.' There was a hint of surprise in Lydia's voice as she re-examined the notes in her hand. 'It would appear they wanted her out of the way so the coast was clear for the abduction to take place. The family is living temporarily in a caravan on the Coopers Lane estate while their flat is being made fit for habitation.'

'Bloody estate kids. Probably running a drugs ring.'

It was another voice from the back of the room, mumbling but audible. Lydia's eyelids flickered with irritation but Jules Mayer had already identified the source and was staring at him incredulously, the words 'Are you serious?' on her lips.

'I don't care if they live in a tree house. A missing child is a missing child.' Lydia paused and resumed her characteristic composure before continuing. 'We are assuming that whoever abducted Liam's grandmother, who by the way was restrained and blindfolded so unable to ID her kidnappers, then drove back to the school to collect Liam.'

The scenario was getting more bizarre by the second. 'The teacher just released him to a stranger?' It was Jules again.

Lydia inhaled sharply. 'It would appear so, but let's delay our judgement of her, and anyone else, until we have the facts.'

Ronnie played with the scenario in her head for a second. The few times she had been there at home time when Tilly and Eddie were in primary school, the procedure had been pretty chaotic. It was easy to imagine a teacher might have to turn away for a moment to deal with a crying child, a lost bag, the cry of *miss, miss* . . . Lydia had a point.

'You can imagine,' she continued, 'that in the first week of school, the teacher isn't familiar with all the parents' faces, they all arrive at once, she's exhausted, relieved it's the end of the day. Added to that, in this case it's pouring with rain, and if Liam runs off towards someone in the playground, she might, however wrongly, assume that was who he was supposed to go home with. But as I said . . .' She paused for effect. 'Our investigations will reveal the detail.'

'When did they call it in?' Jules again. When Ronnie was new in CID she had always left the heckling to the old hands, and usually to the men. If there had been a question to ask, she'd have put it to one of her peers afterwards rather than shout it out to the boss mid-meeting. It had taken her a good year or so to find the courage to speak up. This was interesting.

'Thank you, DC Mayer. That brings me to another issue,' continued Lydia. 'As I mentioned, the caravans are being used as temporary accommodation by several tenants of the Coopers Lane estate who had to vacate while the cladding was replaced on their block, among other issues – damp and dry rot being just a couple. The council offered to rehouse them on the other side of the borough, but they chose to stay put and they've been there ever since. As you might imagine, with the re-cladding issue followed by the failed rehousing attempt, they have lost all trust in the authorities, and that includes the police. Public services are their enemy. The icing on the cake is that the council is about to turf them off the land and hand it over for private redevelopment. It's hardly surprising they didn't want us involved first off. So, in answer to your question, DC Mayer, Liam disappeared yesterday at 3.20 p.m. but we only got the call this morning.'

The room was silent apart from the scribble of pens on pads. Looks were exchanged. Then all eyes were back on Lydia, whose face was decidedly downcast. It wasn't often she looked beaten.

'So, I don't need to emphasise the urgency of the situation. DS Delmar, I'd like you to take the lead. DC Mayer you're on this too. We need to speak to the teacher, the teaching assistant, the head, anyone working at the school yesterday, the other parents, any visitors to the school, and obviously Liam's family, neighbours, relatives, friends, the lot. We need uniform going house to house in the immediate area, we need CCTV and anything you can get on the vehicle that was used to kidnap Liam's grandmother. I want all hands on deck.'

'Yes, ma'am.' Ronnie exchanged glances with Jules Mayer. From their brief spell working together before the summer, Jules had struck her as the type who saw things others didn't, picked up on what wasn't said as much as what was. If anyone was hiding something, then she'd be the one to uncover it. She had a rare ability to read people, to listen, observe and absorb in a way that most officers were in too much of a hurry to do.

Lydia was on her way back to her desk when Ronnie caught up with her, notepad in hand, questions on her mind. The previous day's events seemed to have been eclipsed by the news of Liam Buckley.

'What about Ruth Jones?'

'What about her?' Lydia frowned. Ronnie remembered why she never used to challenge higher-ranking officers. They could kill with a look.

'We're almost there, if we get her in. If anyone has a relationship with her, if there's anyone she trusts, it should be me.' She paused, then seeing that Lydia seemed to be expecting more, she carried on. 'I mean, this is a uniform job on the missing boy, first off, getting statements from the family and witnesses.' She regretted her tone instantly. Now Lydia regarded her with something like amusement, the lion playing with the mouse. Perhaps it was just a matter of sitting through the lecture. In fact, the DI surprised her, and she surprised herself.

'DS Delmar, I was expecting your protest, but Munro and Connolly are over at Ruth Jones's place now. They can bring her in, get the address for the man that hurt her and then check the ID with the other witnesses. Worst-case scenario, we question him in relation to the one-off assault, but she may not even want to press charges. Best case, he's our catfish and we wrap that case up once and for all. But, either way, all that takes second place to finding our missing child. Think of the consequences of a second's delay on this. The force has a troubled enough reputation as it is. Uniform were on the scene first thing but we need to get down there to manage the situation because they will only be an antagonising presence. Am I making sense?'

A huge amount of sense, Ronnie thought. Munro and Connolly would bring Ruth in and they'd have their man in front of the magistrates in no time. Lydia might be right. She let the thought settle and gave what she hoped sounded like a convincing response.

'Completely, ma'am. A missing child comes first.'

CHAPTER 10

In nearly ten years of working at Halesworth, Ronnie had never had reason to visit the Coopers Lane estate. The ex-council tenants were to all intents and purposes a peaceful bunch, living, with the local authority's agreement, on a field behind the disused flats that had been their home for decades. A quick online search told her that the flats had initially been declared unsafe when a tenant went to the press with details of mould growing in her asthmatic baby's bedroom, and the council had no choice but to throw their hands up in surrender. Most of the tenants had gone willingly elsewhere, but a minority had fought the decision and set up home in what was effectively their own back garden. With a purpose-built sanitary block and hook-ups for electricity, it wasn't an unpleasant life.

It was only half an hour after Lydia's briefing that Ronnie and Jules Mayer approached the Buckleys' caravan, but the word itself did nothing to describe the luxury mobile home that they found themselves in front of. It looked more like a 1970s bungalow, complete with a freshly painted veranda and overflowing pots of geraniums.

It stood in a cluster of similar but less well-kept structures surrounding a patchy area of dry grass and sand where a group of barefooted children chased each other around a football goal, its netting sagging and ridden with holes. They screamed with what could have been fear or delight, while a scrappy-looking terrier yapped at their heels. One of the children swung on the far post, screeching as she was caught by her pursuer, who wrestled her to the ground. She lashed out, screaming now, calling for her mum, who was nowhere to be seen. The dog barked even more loudly, trying in vain to restore order to chaos.

Ronnie stood and watched the scene for a second. Jules sighed and gave her a look.

Ronnie turned to her in surprise. 'How do you know what I'm thinking?'

'Your face, sarge.' Jules smiled and Ronnie straightened her expression before knocking on the door.

The door was opened by a thin woman in her late fifties, eyes hollow and sleepless, dressed in loungewear and a pink faux-fur gilet which she pulled tightly around her as Ronnie showed her badge.

'Mrs Buckley? I'm DS Delmar and this is my colleague DC Mayer.'

'Dawn Buckley. I'm Liam's nan. I live next door.' She jerked her head towards the adjacent caravan. Standing in the doorway at the top of the steps, she towered over them and didn't seem in a hurry to change the power dynamic.

'May we come in, Mrs Buckley?' Jules asked.

'You can call me Dawn.' She was still blocking the door. 'Shouldn't you be out looking for him, not coming round here for a chat?' Her eyes darted from Ronnie to Jules and back again. It was the usual response, and so was Ronnie's answer.

'Absolutely, and we have a team of uniformed police officers out there right now searching the area, but it's also important that we talk to Liam's parents, get a picture of him, the kind of boy he is, so we can understand how he might behave.' She was careful to use the present tense. She'd seen others caught in a spiral of furious accusations after talking about a missing person as if they were long dead.

Dawn Buckley seemed satisfied, and held the door open wider.

'Come in then, but don't stay long, you need to be on the streets trying to catch him, whoever's responsible.'

She stepped aside, making way for Jules and Ronnie, who nodded their thanks and took in the scene. The inside of the caravan told a different story from the shiny exterior. It was the smell of damp that hit Ronnie first, a fusty odour that reminded her of the contents of Eddie's rucksack after cadet camp. It must have been hard keeping a place like this fresh and dry. A glance up at the ceiling showed a yellow patch where the rain had come through. A bucket stood beneath it to catch the drips. It was empty. If this family had moved out of the frying pan into the fire, at least someone was trying to keep on top of the housework.

'You can sit on the sofa.' Dawn moved a pile of papers to the floor – among them, a child's drawing of a rocket.

Dawn plucked it from the pile and handed it to Ronnie. 'He drew that yesterday morning, before I took him to school.' She half-turned, wiping away a tear she didn't want them to see.

The colours spilled over the outline, making the image hard to extract unless you looked at it without focusing. Ronnie was reminded of the optical illusions Eddie used to present her with, challenging her to see a woman's face in what appeared to be nothing more than a haze of swirls.

'Can I make us some tea?' Jules's voice was kind, mothering almost.

As the kettle boiled, Ronnie looked around the room. Aside from the leaky ceiling patch, things seemed to be perfectly in order. Sparkling kitchen surfaces, plump sofa cushions and dining chairs pushed in neatly under the table. 'Are Liam's parents around?'

'Cara's in there.' Dawn pointed to the far end of the room, where two doors at diagonal angles to each other presumably led to the bedrooms. A sign that read *Mum and Dad* in colourful crayoned letters was Blu-Tacked to it at a jaunty angle. Little Liam was quite an artist then. 'Steven's out there looking. Where you should be.' Her last words came out in a whisper.

'Can we see her, do you think?'

On cue, the *Mum and Dad* door opened and a figure emerged, sleepy-eyed and bedraggled, a blanket draped around her shoulders, furry slippers on her feet. Jules turned to her and proffered a mug of hot tea, which she took without a word.

'Cara Buckley?' The question was routine, like the nurse checking a wristband in hospital every time medication was given. It couldn't be anyone else sitting in your bed, you weren't going anywhere, but there seemed to be an assumption that you had escaped and an impostor had taken your place.

Cara placed the mug on the table and sank into the sofa. 'Yes. I thought we'd been through all this.'

'Hello, Cara. I'm Detective Sergeant Ronnie Delmar, and this is my colleague Detective Constable Jules Mayer.' They took their seats opposite Cara.

A trace of a smile spread across her face.

'Boys' names, both of you.' Her voice was different from Dawn's. Softer, better spoken.

Ronnie caught Jules's eye and smiled. 'I like to tell people we have to pretend to be men to climb the career ladder. But actually it hasn't been quite that bad. Ronnie and Jules are short for Veronica and Julia – but it can cause confusion, I admit.' It was a good sign that they could talk like this, smoothing the sharp edges of grief with the emery board of humour.

She opened her notebook and clicked her pen. She had scanned the page of information that uniform had provided, but it was never the same as hearing it first-hand. Witnesses were apt to divulge different information according to who they were talking to, as if particular personalities allowed them to reveal particular things. The facts could be efficiently recorded by fact-seeking interrogators, but it was observing nuances of mood, eye movements, patterns of speech, the way someone held their cup of tea, that added flavour and substance to the bland soup of note-taking.

'Can we start by just asking you about Liam, what kind of boy he is, what he likes doing?'

'He's a good boy.' Her voice choked, but she cleared her throat and went on. 'He likes drawing.' She picked up the rocket picture and let her eyes rest on it for a second, then blinked the tears away and looked back at Ronnie. 'He's always been good, never questions anything, does what he's told.'

It wasn't the most promising of starts. In an abduction case, you'd rather have a child that made a fuss, made things difficult so that they'd be released by the captor before any harm was done. If he had gone obediently with whoever it was that took him from the playground, that was half the battle over for his kidnapper.

'And you and your mother-in-law alternate with the school pick-up, is that right?'

'That's right,' Cara whispered. 'Dawn was collecting Liam because I was working. It's a cleaning contractors. Yesterday was an end-of-tenancy clean. They can take all day.'

'I can imagine. What time did you get back?'

'I got home at six, and nobody was here, so I just assumed Dawn had taken Liam out. Then she turned up a bit after six, without him. When she told me what had happened, I felt sick.'

Ronnie was about to ask why on earth they hadn't called the police there and then, but thought better of it. They had their reasons.

Jules had taken the seat next to Cara and touched her arm. The lightest of touches. She had an instinct for where the boundaries lay. 'It must have been a horrific shock,' she said.

Dawn was leaning against the Formica worktop, her expression softer but still guarded. It was interesting that she hadn't chosen to sit with the rest of them. She was hard to read. Ronnie caught her eye.

'Can you tell us what happened when you went to collect Liam? I know you've been through it once already, but sometimes there are details that come out on the retelling that you didn't remember first time.'

Dawn took a breath and blinked hard, refocusing her gaze on the middle distance. In the window behind her, the sky had cleared and the sun was creeping out from behind a bank of clouds at last.

'I left here at the usual time, two forty-five. I like to be early, you know, don't want the little lad feeling we've forgotten him.' She adjusted her furs as if to confirm her liking for order, getting things right. 'School finishes for the little ones at three twenty, so I had plenty of time.'

'Did you have anything with you? A phone? A bag?' Ronnie scribbled on her pad and looked up again.

'I was wearing a raincoat. My phone was in my pocket, but I remember seeing when I left here that the battery was dying. They barely last any time these days. I think it's a ploy to force you to buy the latest model, and I'm not doing that. Sorry, that's not relevant is it . . .' She glanced around nervously. 'I had a Penguin biscuit in my other pocket for

Liam. Cara doesn't like him having chocolate, but what's a grandson for if not for spoiling?' She tried to smile at Cara, who didn't meet her gaze. 'I was just around the corner from the entrance to the school, walking past the bus stop on Orchard Lane, must have been about ten past three, when this car pulled up next to me.'

'Can you describe it?'

'It was a black Land Rover. The driver leaned out of the window, asked me directions to somewhere, or that's what it sounded like, and I went closer because I couldn't hear properly. And the next thing was the back door opened and there was someone yanking me inside with a knife pointing at my face, telling me to get in.'

'That's all? Get in? Nothing else?'

Dawn hesitated, her hands grasped the overhang of the worktop and squeezed tight. 'I think that was it. It happened so fast. I think they said, "*if you don't want to get hurt*". I can't remember the words exactly.'

Ronnie exchanged glances with Jules. Dawn was gripping on tightly for a reason.

'So all this, in broad daylight. Was there anyone else around that you could see? Any witnesses at all?'

'I wasn't aware. I mean, I don't remember. There could have been, but it had been drizzling all afternoon and when people are holding umbrellas, they only look two feet in front of them. They might have thought I was getting a lift or being rescued from the downpour.'

'What did the driver of the car look like? Did you see them through the window before they pulled you in?'

Dawn blinked, as if she didn't understand the question, or was playing for time. Her eyes flicked upwards, left and right, looking for clues.

'I mean, were they white, black?'

'White. He was white. He wore a baseball cap pulled down over his face and a scarf pulled up over his mouth. I remember thinking it wasn't cold enough for a scarf. And glasses. Little ones, the sort you don't imagine working very well because there's so much around the outside of the frames that you're not going to be able to see properly. A dark jacket, a puffer jacket I think.'

She was on a roll now, and Ronnie was struggling to keep up. Her grip on the countertop had loosened, as if she was relaxing into the story, or *her* story, whichever it was. The fact she was remembering thoughts as well as observations made what seemed a very unlikely story more credible.

'What sort of age?'

She made a face. 'I couldn't say. I'm not good at ages. Middle-aged. My age.'

'And the woman you mentioned when you called the station? What about her?'

'I couldn't tell her age, but she had kind eyes.'

'Kind eyes?' Ronnie repeated the words because they didn't fit the story at all.

'I know. It didn't match what she was doing, or what she was saying.' Dawn's expression changed. 'It was like she didn't want to be doing it.'

Ronnie's pen hovered above the paper. 'That's interesting. Anything else on the woman's appearance?'

'No, it was too quick.' Dawn appeared to lose her breath for a second, as if the memory of it all was too much.

'And once you were in the car? What happened then?'

'The woman, the one with the knife, she told me to handcuff myself to the handle above the door, and I tried to do it, but I've never seen handcuffs before, so she had to help me. I thought about trying to get the knife when she put it down but . . .'

Her expression looked pained, as if she'd done wrong.

'It was probably best to do what she said,' said Jules in a soft voice that seemed to smooth over Dawn's agitation.

'And then she blindfolded me, but I kept saying, "I need to collect my grandson. Let me go." And she just said, "Don't you worry about him. He'll be fine."'

'It was a woman with the knife? You're sure about that?' It was interesting that Dawn was suddenly remembering the conversation word for word.

'Yes, I was shocked. I mean, you don't expect it.' She looked apologetically at Jules and Ronnie. 'But maybe you do, in the police?' They nodded encouragement and she took up the story again. 'She slammed the door, then another door opened and shut so she must have got into the front, and then we drove for what seemed like hours, but it was probably only half an hour, and there was all the school traffic.'

'You didn't have any way of checking the time at any point, even after you were released?'

'The phone was dead by then, which is why it took me so long to get back from where they dumped me. I couldn't phone for help. I couldn't even pay for a cab. I walked for over two hours. The man gave me a bottle of water when he let me out. It was like he felt sorry for me, like he didn't want me to suffer.'

Ronnie held her hand up to interrupt. 'A water bottle? Do you still have it?'

Dawn looked panicked. 'I threw it away. Sorry, I didn't think . . .'

Jules looked alarmed and, after a nod from Ronnie, took over the questioning. 'Carry on, Dawn. You were saying he didn't want you to suffer. Did he say anything that made you think that?'

'Nothing, just mumbled, "You can find your own way home now," and then drove off. Did a U-turn in the road and disappeared out of sight.'

'Did you stop anyone? Tell them what had happened so they could get a message to Cara or ring the police?' Ronnie interrupted. 'You must have been so worried about your grandson at this point.'

Dawn looked at her as if to assess what she was trying to say. 'I knocked on the doors of a few houses but got no answer. Then when I found a shop and persuaded them to let me use the phone, I couldn't remember Cara's number.'

'But what about calling 999?' Jules gave Ronnie a pained look. Perhaps she should drop it. Lydia might be right about the breakdown of trust.

Dawn looked as if she was blinking back tears. 'I know, but I was OK. I just thought maybe Liam was too. I thought . . .' She broke off completely and came at it from another angle. 'I went straight to the school and they said Liam had been collected on time, which made me sick to my stomach, because Cara and Steve couldn't have known what had happened to me. They couldn't have made it there before me even if they *had* known. When I got back home, I was just hoping against hope that Liam would be here, that a miracle had happened, or it was all a dream, but it was just Cara, and, oh my God, her face, when she saw me on my own, I'll never forget.'

Cara's head was in her hands as she relived the moment her world had collapsed.

'What did you do first, Cara, when you realised what must have happened?' Ronnie watched them both now as Jules went through the questions.

Cara gathered herself to answer, lifted her head slightly and took a breath. 'I called Steve. He was at work. He does casual building work around the village. They're working on a refurb at the moment. We're hoping to move there when they throw us out of here but the sellers keep putting the price up. They know we're desperate, you see.' She looked up. 'Sorry, that's not relevant, I can't think straight.'

'Cara, you're doing great. Everything is relevant,' said Jules. 'Carry on.'

'When I called him, he came straight away and went out looking for Liam, with a few of the others.'

'Others?'

'Men from the site.' She hesitated. 'I know what you're going to say. We should have gone straight to the police.'

Ronnie wanted to scream, *If you'd done that we might have got him back safely by now*, but she kept her mouth shut and let her DC continue.

'What stopped you?' Jules asked, her expression all sympathy, unchallenging.

Cara looked up. Ronnie saw her eyes properly for the first time, full of fear and uncertainty, glancing at her mother-in-law and then towards the window, as if she was about to divulge the deepest secrets. Dawn was biting her lip, eyes down.

'Nobody trusts the police round here.' It was a barely audible murmur. 'It's not just because of what happened with our flats. It's everything else. You know, you read stuff in the papers every day.'

Ronnie did know. It was an uncomfortable truth that public trust in the force wasn't what it used to be.

'What changed your mind?' Jules reached for her tea, took a sip, defusing the intensity of the question.

'We've got nothing to hide. We need help. You'll find him, won't you?'

'We'll do our best.' It was never an easy question.

'Steve doesn't know I called you,' Cara added, partly in afterthought, partly explanation.

That would explain the anxious glances at the window.

'You did the right thing calling us. And we aren't here to investigate anything except Liam's disappearance. You'll have to take my word for that.' Ronnie hoped her words sounded as they were intended to, but the look on Jules's face said otherwise. Ronnie let her take up the reins and find more palatable words.

'We will have to talk to everyone, but not because they are suspects in Liam's disappearance, it's just to get a better picture of him, of his life, and of all the events that led up to his abduction.'

Cara seemed satisfied. Even Dawn managed a smile and a nod.

'So, what other family members are there? Do you have siblings? Does Steve?' Ronnie looked from one to the other. Cara glanced at Dawn. 'I'm an only child. I bet they wish they'd had more now. One who lived up to their expectations, maybe.' Her eyes teared up for a second before she regained her composure. 'And Steve . . .' She looked back at Dawn. 'Steve has one brother, Joe.'

Dawn stiffened, then plastered a smile on her face. 'He doesn't come around here much any more.' Her eyes flicked to Cara and back to Ronnie. 'How about I show you Liam's room?'

Ronnie stood and followed her to the bedroom end of the caravan. Next to the *Mum and Dad* room was another door bearing Liam's name in giant crayoned letters.

Jules moved across to sit next to Cara, who was scrolling through her phone. 'I've got some more pictures of him I can send you,' Cara said, momentarily distracted. 'They've got the school one, and one of the three of us – Steve, I mean.' She glanced apologetically in Dawn's direction, but she was out of earshot. 'Here you go, this is him on his last birthday.'

'He's a cute little boy. You can see where he gets his looks from.'

Liam's room gave nothing away they didn't already know. Superhero duvet cover, a bumper set of coloured pens on a desk alongside a pad of paper and a pile of comics. A novelty clock on the bedside table. Stickers on the front of the drawers that housed his clothes – a mixture of jeans, shorts, T-shirts and sweaters that you might find in any child's closet. A box of Lego on the floor, half pushed under the bed. It took Ronnie back to when her own children were his age. All those toys, all those activities they used to enjoy, and now they needed little more than a screen and a Wi-Fi signal. She picked up a Lego structure from the box.

'It's a hospital,' said Dawn, by way of explanation. 'He wants to be a doctor when he grows up.'

'Anything missing, that you know about?'

Dawn was standing so close that Ronnie could feel her breath on her neck.

'Nothing. He was in his school uniform. So at least you should find him out there easily. Blue blazer, yellow and blue tie.'

Ronnie didn't tell her that in most abduction cases, the first thing they would do was change the child's clothes, cut their hair, make them unrecognisable to even their own family.

'Did he have a phone?'

'Lord, no. Steven wouldn't hear of it. No need, and it addles their brains, these youngsters. Cara lets him play on her iPad for an hour after school, but there's no more technology allowed.'

Dawn shut the bedroom door behind them and ushered Ronnie back to the others. She looked at Jules, then at her watch. 'Right, I think I've got everything I need.'

Ronnie held out her hand to Cara, who shook it, and then to Dawn, who didn't. 'DC Mayer will stay on, she's leading the house-to-house on the encampment, then further afield. We will of course be in touch as soon as we have any news at all.'

'One more thing.' It was Cara. An afterthought, or perhaps something she had been itching to say all along but hadn't found the words or the courage.

'Yes, of course. What is it?' Ronnie had one hand on the door handle and the metal felt refreshingly cold under her fingers.

'Should we be offering a reward for his return?'

'*Can* you offer a reward?' This didn't seem the type of family with a fortune stashed away in the bank. Who would live in a caravan if they could afford to pay for a building with a roof that didn't leak?

'My parents might.' Her voice came out in a whisper, with another furtive glance at Dawn, who was busying herself with putting the washing-up away. 'We don't speak very often. My mother is sick and my father never approved of Steve. Said I was basically running away to the circus and that it would all end badly. They cut me off financially, but now I think he'd put up the cash just to prove himself right.'

It wasn't an unfamiliar story, parental disapproval of a marriage choice, but clearly Cara's parents had taken it to a whole new level. Perhaps the offer of a reward was the first step in persuading their daughter to come back to the fold. Nothing could be more powerful than the argument that they had saved Liam's life. But the whole issue needed careful handling.

'Rewards can work like a dream if there's someone out there who's unsure about coming forward, but there's a downside in that it can lead to a whole load of time-waster calls into the station, and a few wild goose chases. So, by all means talk to them if you can, and if they want to, we can have another conversation, but it's not the magical solution you might think it would be.'

'Would you consider doing a public appeal for information in the meantime?' Jules interjected.

'How does that work?' Cara seemed hesitant. 'I'm not sure if Steve would agree, but I'd be happy to do it.'

'We get you in front of the cameras and let the public hear you talk about what happened. It can be very powerful in terms of public engagement.'

She thought for a millisecond before replying. 'How soon can we do it?'

'Tomorrow?' Ronnie exchanged surprised glances with Jules. Most parents were too traumatised to go for the TV appeal so quickly. 'Would you be up for that?'

'Yes, anything.' Her voice was back to its normal volume now as she shook off the nerves that were holding her back. Dawn had retreated to the other end of the room. Ronnie wondered whether the two things were connected.

'Here's my number.' Ronnie handed Cara a card. 'When your husband gets back, have a chat with him, give me a call and we can make a plan.'

Cara nodded. 'I'll call you. I want to do it.'

Jules said her goodbyes and headed off to check on how they were getting on with the house-to-house. The scrappy dog and its friends had disappeared when Ronnie shut the door of the caravan and made her way to the car. The sun had sunk behind a cloud again and the air was humid and heavy. Autumn was fighting for its turn at the seasonal wheel and summer wasn't giving up yet.

Ronnie cast an eye around the rest of the site. 'Where are you, Liam Buckley?' she whispered into the damp, still air. 'Who's taken you? And why?'

CHAPTER 11

'What do you mean you couldn't find her?' Ronnie was perplexed. All she could think was that if she'd been the one to go looking, rather than Baz, there would have been better news than this.

'No answer at the address she gave us. No sign of life there, either.'

It took a feat of self-control to hide her exasperation. 'Did you try the neighbours?'

'Actually, yes.' Baz was eyeing her warily. 'Her house is like an appendage to a bigger house, like an annexe with its own entrance. So I went to the main house. The woman there said she didn't know, but Ruth had probably gone to work.'

'And did she tell you where she worked? I didn't manage to find out yesterday when she came in.' Ronnie put her head in her hands. But it wasn't over yet. Baz seemed to be saving something up till last. She knew that look.

He opened his notebook. 'She said Ruth works at a local nursery, but also spends time with her sister in Sussex, might have gone up there. She was obviously in a hurry, bags in the hallway. Looked flustered, like she was about to go off somewhere, so I didn't get much more out of her than that.'

Ronnie sat back in her chair, put her hands in her lap to stave off the frustration and managed a smile. 'Good observation. I like it. Did you follow it up, what she said about Ruth's work?'

'Of course.' There was a twinkle in his eye. 'Turns out it's not the sort of nursery I had in mind.'

'Children or plants?'

'Plants. Planting, landscaping. Clearing rubble. You name it, they do it.'

'And was she there?'

Baz shook his head, but his expression was all confidence now, which brought Ronnie relief.

'She wasn't there, *but* she wasn't expected to be in till Monday anyway. She was on deliveries yesterday, and they were all completed on schedule so no panic there. If she has a day off, she often keeps the van because she doesn't have her own car. Looks like we can relax, sarge.'

Ronnie let the mounting stress melt away. 'So, where's she gone, if she's not at home?'

'To see her sister in Sussex? I don't know, but I don't think we need to worry, do we, sarge?' His tone was bordering on exasperation. 'I mean, it's up to her if she wants to pursue the complaint, whatever it was, so let's focus on the missing boy until she shows up again.'

'Or doesn't.'

'Or doesn't.' Baz exhaled, resigned or annoyed, she couldn't tell which. 'Let's cross that bridge when we come to it.'

'Oh, and Baz, check the hospitals.'

'What?' He slapped a hand on the door frame and spun round. 'I didn't know she'd been to hospital?'

'I don't know either but it's worth a try. See if anyone matching Ruth's description came in on Tuesday night or Wednesday morning. Even better, if she was collected by ambulance, we'll get the address we're looking for.'

'All right, sarge. I'll get on to that, but I'm sure she'll turn up.'

He left the room with one hand holding the back of his neck. It was a pose you wouldn't adopt naturally, unless someone had triggered you, dislodged a part of your body into a position that it wouldn't normally be comfortable with.

Ronnie stood for a second watching the spot where he'd been standing. It was the news she'd least wanted. To choose between two missing-person cases on the basis of risk was like assessing where to drop a bomb by measuring likely collateral damage. Don't drop the bomb at all. Don't choose between two victims of crime. If less time and money was spent on chasing cannabis-smoking teenagers, they might not have to make this kind of choice at all. But the rules were the rules, and resources were not unlimited, as she was constantly being reminded.

'Sarge?' It was Jules, leaning around the thin partition that separated their desks and ranks. 'Just back from the camp. Have you got a second before I go round talking to Liam's classmates?'

'Of course, what've you got?' Ronnie shook off her discomfort and beckoned her to sit down.

Jules glanced over her shoulder before sinking into the chair opposite Ronnie and speaking in a low voice. 'Nothing concrete from anyone I've spoken to so far. Not that keen to talk, if I'm honest. Have you heard anything on Cara's parents and the depth of their pockets?'

'Not yet. Did you meet Steve Buckley?'

'I did. He came home just as I was about to leave.'

'What did he have to say? Is he on board with us?'

'I let Cara explain who I was, and then I tried to keep it businesslike, which seemed to work. He seemed to be fine with our involvement as long as we prove our commitment, which I think I convinced him of. I'd say there was a bit of male ego stuff going on there – the father's responsibility to keep the family safe, you know what I mean?'

'I do.' It was a common enough scenario, a woman asking for help where a man might feel too uncomfortable to do so, and especially when dealing with two female police officers.

'Anyway, we have his statement and the alibi checks out. No surprises there.'

'What did you get from the neighbours?'

'I'm not sure what to make of the set-up in that place.' She pulled her chair closer. 'It's just, when we went round the other caravans, I mean saying they weren't keen to talk is an understatement. Several officers had the door shut in their faces earlier in the day. I thought I stood a better chance out of uniform but the minute they knew who I was, it was total shutdown.'

'Disappointing, but not entirely surprising,' said Ronnie. 'Did you get anything at all?'

'Eventually I got something, from a woman who seemed to have a real problem with the Buckleys. She was the only one who gave us anything at all, but it could be important.'

'Oh yes?'

'Linda Carter. Early forties, divorced, lives alone apart from the dog. Definitely not a big fan of Steve Buckley. Seemed to know he'd gone out searching with some of the other men, wouldn't say who they were or where they'd gone, but she might have genuinely not known.'

'And what was her golden nugget of information?'

'She said one thing before she slammed the door on us.' Jules flicked through her notebook and nodded. 'OK, so, in her own words: *That family's not all they appear to be, let me tell you.*'

Ronnie raised her eyebrows. 'And she wouldn't go any further?'

'Unfortunately not. Hard to believe she couldn't summon up some empathy for a family with a missing child. Anyway, uniform is still out there doing house-to-house and Cara's agreed to let the liaison officer sit with her, at least while Steve's out. We could get them to probe her for more details on what it is that the neighbour might be taking exception to.'

Ronnie flicked through her notebook to look back at Dawn and Cara's answers to her questions. 'There could be something there. I didn't quite know what to make of her relationship with her mother-in-law for a start. It seemed a little tense. What did you think?'

'Hmmm, yes, definitely tense, and . . .'

'And what?' Ronnie always thought that a revised comment was never as worthy as the one it was replacing. She wanted the first words that came into Jules's head, not the edited version.

Jules inhaled and exhaled again before speaking. 'It's just a hunch, but I'm not sure I believe a word of what Dawn told us.'

Ronnie bit her lip and scanned the pages of notes. 'I have to admit, I actually felt the same. I'm glad you agree.'

'But now I'm just not sure how much of it has surfaced since that Linda Carter said what she said. Are you sure we're not being dragged into what might be just idle gossip?'

Ronnie nodded and stared at the notes before looking back up at Jules. 'Actually, yes, I am. Dawn wasn't telling us everything. It was in her body language, the way she stood, the impatience to get rid of us. She's hiding something.'

Jules seemed to appreciate the certainty. *Conviction is the first step to a conviction*, Baz had declared after the last case they'd worked on went to trial and resulted in a hefty prison sentence. He was so proud of his new motto he'd stuck it on a Post-it above his desk. But conviction needed evidential support and a bit of sober reflection, not just a hunch and a gut feeling.

'Well, let's find out what that something is,' said Jules brightly.

'Start by checking out the shop that she stopped at on her way back. See if they can confirm that she came in. And Joe, Steve's brother. Find out where he is and see if you can talk to him.'

Jules scribbled a note on a Post-it while Ronnie looked at her phone to check the time. Staring out from the home screen, there was a message from Simon asking whether they could change his weekend with the twins. That was something that used to set her on edge, the assumption that she would change her plans to suit him and his new twenty-something girlfriend, but this time it washed over her. *Detach from the narrative.* She wasn't attached to her free weekends, since they were mostly filled with paperwork and admin, so maybe she didn't need to feel triggered by the words on the screen. It was the first time that the possibility had even crossed her mind. She looked back at Jules, invigorated suddenly.

'Right, we need to get going with all this. When you've checked the shop, get those interviews done with the kids while the school day is fresh in their minds. And while you're doing the rounds on that, I need to talk to Lisa Blake at Holly Lodge and check their CCTV.'

Jules turned to leave with a grin and a thumbs up. 'Can't wait to hear how that teacher explains herself.'

Holly Lodge was the kind of name that gave a school a head start in its popularity with young parents. You'd half-expect the Famous Five to come skipping out of the gates clutching their picnics and lashings of ginger beer. In reality, it was little more than a classic Victorian mansion, extended to the back to accommodate a gym and some new nursery classrooms. The separate signs for boys and girls were still visible above the original entrances, but between them a new glass door leading to a comfortable reception area announced to the world that it had graduated successfully to the twenty-first century. The bell summoned a bespectacled purple-haired woman who took Ronnie's name and gave her a lanyard.

'Chloe will escort you, detective.' With semaphore hands, she indicated a small blonde girl, and Chloe's eyes widened.

'Detective? As in police?'

'Ask for Miss Blake.' The older woman took care to enunciate each syllable so that there could be no confusion.

Ronnie had forgotten what it was like inside a primary school. It smelled of a mixture of cabbage and poster paints. The walls along the corridor and up the stairs were crammed with exquisitely curated displays of children's art and photos of key events in the calendar – international day, Black History week, National Smile month, all of which had been notably missing from her own education. When did they manage to do any maths and English?

Lisa Blake was staring out of the staffroom window, nursing a cup of something in clasped hands. She turned around as the door opened, wiping her face with her sleeve.

Chloe slipped away, looking over her shoulder as she headed back to class to tell everyone that she'd met a real-life lady police officer. If she only knew the reality of the job – head ruling heart, the drudgery of rigid compliance with procedure – she might not have been quite as starstruck.

'You're the detective they said was coming?' the teacher asked. 'You're not taking me away, are you?' A look of alarm spread across her face.

Ronnie flashed her badge. 'DS Ronnie Delmar. Don't worry, we can do this here. There's no need to come down to the station. I just need to ask you a few questions about what happened yesterday. Is there somewhere we can talk?' She glanced around at the clusters of onlookers pretending not to listen. She didn't want this to be a side show at a fairground.

'Of course. Follow me.' Lisa put down her mug, led Ronnie down the corridor and opened a door labelled 'Pastoral Care' in comic sans font with a swirly border. 'We can go in here. Abbie's gone home now.' She gestured to a shabby sofa that looked as if it had seen better days and Ronnie sank into it, immediately feeling disempowered by the sagging springs and coffee stains on the arm. If this was where troubled pupils came for comfort, they'd be facing an uphill struggle.

Lisa perched on the swivel chair at the cluttered desk. Her hands hovered in her lap, presumably missing the prop she had left in the staffroom. 'I expect you want to know what happened, in my own words. I've seen these things on TV enough times.' There was something about her manner that made Ronnie uneasy. She brushed it off. She was being oversensitive, but it was hard not to feel irritation at someone who could release a child to a stranger and then nonchalantly predict police procedure as if it was a murder mystery weekend. She smiled, to ensure her thoughts had no outlet into her facial expression.

'Exactly. And if you like your crime thrillers, you'll know I'm about to pull out a good old-fashioned notebook,' she replied. The pad was on her lap in a second, pen poised. 'First I just need to confirm your name and address.'

Lisa recited it like a child reciting their five times table, blankly staring out of the window.

'How long have you been teaching at Holly Lodge?'

'It's my first week. I'm straight out of college. But it's not my first time in a school. I mean, we had loads of teaching practice, and induction here too, and I have to hand in all my lesson plans. It's not like I'm just . . .' She drifted off, bit her lip and looked at the floor. 'Sorry, I didn't mean . . .'

'That's fine, don't worry, I'm sure you have had the best training. Why don't you start by telling me about Liam, what he's like at school?'

Lisa brightened slightly. 'He's a sweet boy, much better since I moved him to the front of the class.'

'What was he like before?'

'Oh, you know, messing about at the back, thinking I couldn't see him.' Lisa's face tightened, as if in reaction to confessing to a lack of discipline skills.

'What kind of messing around?'

'Just the usual. Anything but focusing on his work for the first two days of term, barely took any notice of what was going on. But yesterday was different.'

'Because you could keep an eye on him?'

'Maybe. He's just concentrating more. Less distracted. It happens.'

'No learning difficulties? No processing issues as far as you're aware?'

'None that I've been made aware of. He's right where he should be in terms of his age, according to his teacher from last year. I don't know him well enough yet, but nothing has been picked up as far as I know.'

'What about friendships?'

'It's early days, beginning of term, hard to say.' She was vacillating, as if the answer would inculpate her somehow.

'Does he have a friendship group, or any particular boy or girl he's close to, do you think?'

'Not really.'

Lisa looked glum now. It was time to change the subject, but Ronnie made a mental note to come back to the friendship issue. It seemed that Liam wasn't a very happy boy and yet nobody wanted to explain why.

'Let's move to what happened yesterday. How do you manage the pick-up, when you're new and don't know the parents, or even the children, very well? How does it work? What's the protocol?'

Lisa brightened up momentarily. 'Well, we follow the school procedure, so the parents say who they are here to collect and then they take them.'

'What about the children? Don't they have to say they know this person? And do you have a list of authorised collectors?'

Lisa's unease had returned as quickly as it had lifted. She took a breath, as if to prepare for a rehearsed speech. 'Yes, of course, they say things like, "There's my mum," but a random stranger wouldn't know their names, and the children don't go off with someone they don't know. They just wouldn't.'

Ronnie thought about every single child abduction she had been involved with and gave Lisa a weak smile. 'If that was true, my job would be a lot easier,' she said. 'What about the list? Who was authorised to take Liam home?'

'His mother, Cara Buckley, or his grandmother – Dawn I think her name is. They alternate.'

'And who were you expecting yesterday, Dawn or Cara?'

'I'm not sure. I assumed one or the other.'

Ronnie inhaled and let her breath out slowly. Her instinct was to scream at this young woman before her, *Don't you realise the position of responsibility you have here?* But instead she nodded and stroked her chin. 'So, Lisa, tell me, on the basis that it wasn't his mother or grandmother, do you have any idea who Liam went home with yesterday?'

Lisa's face went blank, her shoulders slumped and her hands gave up their fidgeting. Her tone lost all of its edginess. She was broken down, ashamed, unable to meet Ronnie's eyes. 'I don't remember, not exactly. I remember him running to someone.'

'A man or a woman?'

'I couldn't be sure. I mean, you can't always tell, can you, with coats and umbrellas and hoods up in the rain. It could just as easily have been a man or a woman.'

It was frustrating not to get the basics, but Ronnie tried another angle. 'OK, are there any details at all that you *can* remember? Height, hair, clothes, build, did you hear a voice calling his name at all that might have given them away as a man or a woman?'

Lisa was silent for a second, eyelids flickering as she focused her thoughts. 'I can't remember. I mean, at the time I thought it was his granny. I was sure I'd seen a flash of pink fur and that's what she always wears, although it was raining, so that would have been weird, and that makes me think I'm muddling it up with other memories of her being there. Do you know what I mean?' She looked up for reassurance, her eyes pleading to be understood for their clumsy misidentification. 'Liam went running across quite willingly. I just assumed. Oh my God, I hate myself for this, you have no idea.'

Then the tears came, in a torrent of regret and helplessness, making Ronnie's own eyes sting as she stared at the stained carpet to calm herself. She had been there once, tormented by regret at not having done what she was supposed to do. It was the worst torture, not being able to go back and do things differently.

'Take your time, Lisa, you're doing so well.'

'*Well?*' she sobbed. 'I've never done so badly, I've never let anything like this happen before. I'd do anything to have yesterday again.'

'Listen.' Ronnie put down her pen, leaned over as best she could from her sunken seat and met Lisa's eyes. 'We don't know where Liam is, but he may very well turn up safe and sound at any moment. Children mostly do. We're talking to other parents from the class, as well as Liam's family and neighbours. We're checking all the cameras, CCTV, eve-rything. These things don't always end badly, with a body being dredged from a river, whatever Netflix tells you.'

Lisa wiped her eyes with her sleeve and managed a small smile. 'Thank you,' she murmured. 'I couldn't bear to think of anything bad happening to that little boy and it being my fault.'

'Here's my number. If there's anything else that occurs to you, let me know, straight away.' Ronnie pressed her card into Lisa's hand and got to her feet. 'You have given us something to go on. But anything, literally anything, how-ever irrelevant it may seem to you, could be instrumental in helping us find Liam. I know you've heard that line before too, but I mean it.' She opened the door to find another young woman standing in front of her. She jumped back, as if she'd been caught listening in on their conversation.

'Sorry, I forgot something from my office earlier. I didn't realise.'

Ronnie moved to let her pass, and heard Lisa exclaim, 'Abbie, sorry, we used your room, thought you'd gone.'

'No worries.' Abbie was flouncing out again before Ronnie had got much further. 'I hope you find whoever took Liam,' she called over her shoulder, before pushing through the swing doors and disappearing into the car park.

'Pastoral care? Are you sure?' Ronnie wondered aloud.

'Yes, she's great with the kids,' sighed Lisa. 'Believe it or not.'

*

The debrief at the station seemed to last an eternity, with very little headway made. The search of the area was widened, house-to-house extended from the site all the way to Wakehurst village and back out to the school, but nobody had seen anything. The residents of Orchard Lane had nothing to say about a black Land Rover picking up a fifty-something woman at the bus stop, presumably having better things to do than stare out of their rain-spattered windows at passing traffic. The parents of Liam's classmates didn't recall who'd collected him, blaming the inclement weather for the most part, but it was clear that they barely knew who he was. Even the more careful parents were of little help, and their views very thinly disguised by carefully chosen terminology. 'Ah the little boy from the Coopers Lane estate. Yes, we know who he is. I don't think he and our son are great friends, but I'm sure he's a lovely boy . . .'

The site manager was happy to go through the CCTV of the school gate as many times as it took, but the combination of the rain, the umbrellas and the hoods made it impossible to identify Liam in the crowds of children leaving. Most of the children had let go of any hands they were holding by the time they reached the exit; many had run ahead and some lagged behind the parents in charge. It was a minefield.

Visitors to the school that day were being followed up individually by a team of officers led by DC Mayer. The list was longer than Ronnie expected. There were social workers, catering vans, a handyman, a school governor and a couple of student teachers doing classroom observations, but Jules was confident she'd have their statements on her desk by the weekend. And the best news of all was that, although the reward hadn't been agreed as yet, Cara Buckley had agreed to do a TV appeal. That would capture the public interest and engagement the way nothing else could, and they needed all hands on deck, as Lydia had said.

It was almost eight o'clock when Ronnie got home and pulled up next to her sister's car. Serena drove an MG whose interior was somewhat worse for wear and, at that moment, getting a drenching from the relentless rain that hadn't let up for two days. She rarely remembered to close the roof and had only recently agreed to Ronnie keeping the second key so she could help prevent further damage. Serena was a law unto herself but Ronnie secretly admired her for it. Damp seats were a mere inconvenience, not even worth a second thought. Ronnie could do with taking a leaf out of her sister's book. Sweating the small stuff only made you blind to the things that really mattered. And there were plenty of those right now.

Before going indoors, she collected her thoughts on the day's events. A child was missing, had been for over twenty-four hours now, and someone had gone to great lengths to orchestrate the abduction. Intercepting Dawn Buckley would mean not only knowing who she was but also when she was likely to pass by that exact spot. Taking Liam from school relied on Lisa Blake allowing him to leave, as well as Liam going voluntarily. But if the teacher shared the prejudices about children from the council estate that some of the Wakehurst parents had shown, it might well be possible that Lisa was less attentive to who collected Liam, and the abductor knew that.

If what she had said was to be believed, Dawn had been driven some distance before being left to trek back to the school, and so it would have been impossible for the Land Rover to make it back there in time to take Liam. If the Land Rover kidnappers were the orchestrators of the abduction, a third person needed to be in on the plan to carry it out. Was it a paedophile ring or a revenge abduction? Was there a gang involved or an unhappy neighbour with a point to prove? And where did he or she take Liam? Did the Land Rover come back for them? Did they have another car waiting? In either case, Liam could be a very, very long way away by now, and time wasn't on their side.

Ronnie made a quick dash from the car to the building, holding her bag above her head to keep off the rain, and took the lift up to the third floor. The children were already tucking into Doritos, and pushed the bowl away guiltily as she came through the door. Eddie looked up and spotted her disapproval but had his defence at the ready.

'Mum, Auntie See's doing some meditation yoga stuff and we're starving hungry. What's for dinner?'

She set down her bags on the worktop and whipped away the crisps before the next hand could reach for the bag.

'No spoiling your appetites. You will be fed. Now, who wants to help cook?' Those were the words guaranteed to make the twins disappear into thin air. Ronnie poured herself a glass of rosé, told Alexa to play some Rolling Stones and switched on the oven.

'I can't get no satisfaction,' the first line belted out from the speakers.

Alexa was a mind reader.

CHAPTER 12

Cara Buckley looked exactly right, Ronnie thought, watching her take her place in front of the crowd of reporters on Friday morning. Just enough make-up to restore her humanity, an outfit that did nothing but clothe her body, discreet jewellery that even a seasoned detective wouldn't remember five minutes later. She looked calmer than Ronnie expected, which must have been partly due to the presence of DC Mayer at her side offering last-minute words of reassurance. Jules laid out the facts of the case, introduced Cara with the briefest of words, and the room went silent.

'Please,' Cara said, holding up Liam's photo and gazing wide-eyed round the room before finding the camera again. 'Please, if you know anything at all about our little boy, if you have any information, however irrelevant you think it might be, please do come forward. The police are awaiting your call. Thank you.' She sat back while Jules fielded questions. Yes, they were going house-to-house throughout Wakehurst and beyond; no, there had been no ransom demand. Then came the question of whether a reward would be offered for Liam's safe return. Jules said, 'No reward.' But Cara sat forward again, and said it was under discussion.

Ronnie put her head in her hands. She'd done her best in the corridor outside the press room as they were waiting to go in, but even seconds beforehand the discussion was still heated. Dawn had expressed utter disapproval of the idea, saying it would bring the wrong sort of people out of the woodwork. Cara had countered, in a rare display of bravery, that Dawn had never forgiven her parents for their disapproval of the marriage, but she and Steve had no time for pride getting in the way of finding their son. Ronnie urged her to consider the offer of a reward very carefully indeed. The station would be swamped with time-wasters within minutes, making it harder to sift the good information from the bad.

'Please let's have this discussion with Steve before we go in all guns blazing,' she had implored. But Cara had taken matters into her own hands.

When it was over, Cara had been escorted away by uniformed officer and the last of the press had shuffled out of the airless briefing room, Lydia made a brief victory speech to no one in particular.

'I think,' she declared, brushing imaginary media-dust off her jacket, 'that despite the loose cannon of reward talk, it was a success. I was worried they were too anti-authority.'

Ronnie had been wondering the same thing but said nothing. Jules spoke her mind, though, as she left the room in a flurry of indignation. 'If the Buckleys are anti-authority, it seems to me they have every reason to be.'

'She's been well trained,' observed Lydia, the trace of a smile on her face. 'Very underdog-aware.'

Ronnie felt an urge to defend her DC, then thought better of it. In any case, Lydia was on her phone already, waving Ronnie away with a nod and a thumbs up. She was dismissed.

The phone lines buzzed for the rest of the day and were answered by a team led by PC Overton, which gave Ronnie the confidence to turn her attention back to Cara and Dawn. There was every reason for her to accompany Cara back home, and there was every chance that if she did so, she might find out a little more about the family, and whether the door-slamming neighbour Linda Carter was right about there being more to the Buckleys than met the eye.

Dawn had taken herself home when they got back to the caravan. Hardly surprising, given their dispute at the station. The sparkly cleanliness of it all struck Ronnie again, and she wondered who did the housework there. She couldn't imagine Dawn discarding her furs to get busy with the Domestos. Cara read her mind. 'I gave it a quick going-over this morning. Couldn't sleep, needed to be busy.'

'I'll put the kettle on. You sit down and relax.' Ronnie found mugs and teabags and a tin of shortbread in the cupboard.

'Liam's favourite,' Cara said, but reached an arm out to stop Ronnie putting them back. 'Don't worry, I'm OK. No point falling to pieces when my boy needs me to be strong.'

'If you're sure. And they are my favourite as well as it happens.' When the kettle had boiled, Ronnie sat down and put the tray on the table between them. 'So, how did Steve feel about you doing the appeal?'

Cara's face brightened. 'He was fine about it. He's on a deadline with the building work if we're going to complete on the purchase by the end of the month, and he said I'd do a better job myself. You don't think it was a mistake, do you?' She looked at Ronnie in sudden wide-eyed panic.

'Not at all. There are no rules for these things.' Whatever she thought, there was no point in letting Cara go down the route of regrets now. Ronnie poured the milk into the mugs and gave them a stir. 'Sometimes you have both parents there and it seems to dilute the message. The audience gets sidetracked by inventing flaws in their relationship. They read things into their mannerisms and imagine all sorts of things, mostly because they've watched too many TV dramas.' She imagined Lisa Blake drawing her own amateur-sleuth conclusions. It was all conjecture, but if it gave Cara some comfort it was worth it.

'So I haven't made things worse by going it alone?'

'Not at all. So, tell me, what's life been like since you moved out of the flat?'

'You know the council have plans to move us off the field soon? Well, there's that, and so much more . . . How long have you got?'

Ronnie sipped her tea and listened. She was impressed with Cara's ability to speak the difficult truth without a trace of the resentment that must have lain beneath it. She talked about her falling-out with her parents, her worry that her mother would die soon, Steve's struggle to find work,

Liam's struggle to make friends, as if these were nothing more than potholes in life's road. The less she made of it, the more Ronnie felt engaged. *Self-pity feeds on itself*, her mother used to say when she or Serena had felt the need to vent their woes more than she considered necessary. Cara had none of that, but then again, she seemed resigned to things that piqued Ronnie's interest.

'Why do you think he struggles to make friends?'

'Living in a caravan. People make assumptions. That we're travellers for a start, and everyone has something to say about them. They assume we're poor, that we aren't putting our child first. Lifestyle choice brings so many consequences you wouldn't have thought of.'

'Liam's teacher said there had been some behaviour issues in the first few days.'

'I know. I don't know if it was a bullying issue or what, but she said she was moving him to the front of the class. I never found out how that went.' Her voice faltered and she put her head in her hands.

Ronnie let her thoughts settle. There was something trying to piece itself together in her head that wouldn't quite fit. In the meantime, sympathy was the way to keep Cara talking.

'Sounds like you're up against it at every turn.'

'And now they've issued us with a legal notice to leave, we've got to find somewhere else to live.'

'That's a lot to deal with, on top of this.'

'The place Steve's doing up now, he's hoping he can get a good deal on it for us and a couple of the other families.'

'You're going to move in when he's finished the work?'

'If it all goes through, yes, that's the plan, and if he can get the basic work done to make it habitable in time. But then there's the money. We're still a few thousand down and there's no way to make up the shortfall. No way that we can see, anyway. We agreed one price, then they put it up as soon as they knew we were keen. I wanted to ask Mum and Dad, but Steve wouldn't let me. He said if they offered, he might change his mind, but he wasn't going cap in hand.'

'I can imagine, his pride would have been hurt, if he's not exactly the apple of their eye. Hard for him to ask.'

'I'd rather take my chances without being in their debt, but then, it's not just about me. It's . . .' Ronnie could tell she was about to say Liam's name, but tears welled up in her eyes and stopped her.

Ronnie tried to lighten the mood with a focus on the future. 'So who else is moving into the new place?' Her mind was on the door-slamming neighbour Linda Carter. Presumably she wouldn't be on the list.

'Not sure yet.' Cara reddened and took a gulp of tea, hiding her face with the mug for a second. 'It's been difficult with a few of them round here recently.'

She was getting closer to something now. 'Any particular reason?' she asked. 'It seems like a solid community, from what I can see.'

Cara took a long breath. 'I think I know the reason but it's hard to talk about it. Dawn wouldn't approve.'

Ronnie felt a twinge of impatience, imagining Dawn's footsteps padding closer and closer to the front door, while Cara deliberated on the ramifications of spilling the beans.

'Well, she's not here, and there's no reason she needs to know you've said anything, but it might help the investigation to tell me what it was all about. It's surprising what turns out to be important.'

Ronnie didn't have to wait long, and neither was it the kind of explanation she had feared – some complex family feud dating back to time immemorial. It was much simpler than that. Cara came out with it in a single short sentence in between sips of tea, as she might comment on the weather, or a button coming loose.

'Steve isn't Liam's real dad.'

Ronnie did her best not to react, just let it sink in before asking her next question.

'And who *is* his dad?'

She fixed a blank expression on her face, the result of years of habit, Ronnie assumed. 'Joe. Steve's brother.'

'The one that makes everyone go quiet when you say his name?' No wonder Dawn had bristled so visibly at the mention of him if he was at the root of a family scandal.

Cara nodded slowly, avoiding Ronnie's eye. It must have been easy to produce the first few words, but much harder to go back further, dust down and lay out the facts that she was so used to keeping locked away. 'That's why it's so difficult with Dawn. You must have noticed we

107

don't get on that well. She disapproves of me anyway as an outsider. I'm sure she thinks Steve could do better, and then with this on top, it's a lost cause.'

'She disapproves of you having had a relationship with both men?' Ronnie could imagine it hadn't been easy for any of them.

Cara's eyes were firmly downward, her mouth hardened. 'It wasn't a relationship.'

'Oh, I'm sorry, I didn't mean to suggest . . .' Ronnie wished Jules was there. She'd find the right words.

'No don't worry, you didn't know. I was with Steve at the time, we were courting. Steve is quite old-fashioned like that. Then he went away for a few days with the lads, some seasonal work on the coast, and that's when Joe turned up, out of the blue, demanding to meet me.'

'OK. Take your time.' Ronnie braced herself for what was coming. 'So, you'd met him before then?'

'Briefly, but only when he was moving his stuff away. He left after some sort of big row, saying he could do better and that his family was an embarrassment. Didn't want any part of it.'

'But he came back?'

Cara took a deep breath and focused outside the window, on the sentinel trees that separated their field from the lane. Above them, a plane cut through the sky, leaving a white plume in its wake.

'He said I'd regret it living with these people, that I'd be better off out of there.'

'And how did you react?'

Cara looked back at Ronnie now, emboldened some-how. 'I told him to leave. I told him I was marrying his brother, and that I wasn't going to change my mind.'

'And then?'

'And that's when it happened.' She bit her lip and closed her eyes briefly. 'The thing was, I didn't . . . It wasn't . . . what's the word?'

Ronnie waited till she found the word, but it was on the tip of her tongue before it escaped Cara's lips.

'It wasn't consensual. He forced me to have sex with him, in our flat, where I was staying on my own just for a few days.' Her face clouded with the memory. 'I should never have opened the door to him.'

'You weren't to know what he was going to do.'

'Then he disappeared the next day and I never saw him again, not even at our wedding.'

'Ashamed of what he'd done?'

'Maybe. He hardly ever contacted Steve or his mum again, as far as I know.'

'Does he know he's Liam's father?'

'Yes, he knows. I think Dawn told him at one point, maybe to get him to come and visit. And Steve knows too. He was furious when he found out.' She hesitated, as if she'd gone too far and she needed to reel it all back in. 'But now he loves Liam more than any father could love a child. More than Joe could have, that's for sure.'

'I see.' Ronnie absorbed the facts as Cara had told them. 'That's quite a big thing to live with, for you all.'

'Yes, but you get used to it,' said Cara. 'I just wish all the other families felt the same, but some of them seem to think I'm some kind of – well . . .'

She trailed off. Ronnie drained her mug of tea, which was going cold.

'How did they find out?'

'He was drunk in the pub, told one of Steve's mates, who told everyone else. Most of them have moved to the new flats now, but it was another reason we wanted to stay here.'

'But you said they aren't giving you an easy time even here.'

Cara sighed. 'They might have known all along and just not worried about it, but now they're just looking for someone to blame. If Liam's been taken, it must be my fault somehow.'

'Well, that's their issue. If they knew the truth, they would be ashamed of themselves.'

Cara grimaced. 'I'd rather not tell everyone what happened.'

She was right. The world still blamed women for being abused by men. An image of Ruth Jones flashed into Ronnie's mind and she felt a shiver of discomfort at having abandoned her. But there was nothing she could do about that for now. Better to focus on where she could make a difference.

'Did you ever think of reporting the assault? If Joe raped you, Cara, he's committed a serious offence.' The words rang uncomfortably in the room. Ronnie wondered if she had played the wrong card. Jules Mayer wouldn't have let it come out like that, raw and shocking.

But Cara seemed grateful that the words were out there. 'I appreciate that, I mean, I know it's an option, but I'm not sure what it would do for me and the family. You're probably going to say it would make a difference to other women, that maybe Joe has done it again since, and I could have stopped that, but there's a limit to what you can do, a limit to what I'm prepared to risk.'

Cara was wiser than her years. Ronnie thought back again to her conversations with Serena on the pros and cons of pressing charges for the sexual assault she had endured as a teenager. The circumstances weren't always as simple as they looked, and not many women felt comfortable reporting a sex crime, even with good evidence.

'OK, I hear you.' There was a moment of understanding as Cara raised her eyes to meet Ronnie's.

'Thanks. I appreciate that. And thank you for listening. It feels better getting it off my chest.'

Ronnie stood to find a bin for her biscuit wrapper and pulled open a likely-looking kitchen cupboard. It was divided into general rubbish and recycling, and she had just dropped her rubbish when she caught sight of something that jolted her memory. She bent down to look at it more closely and turned back to Cara. 'I know this sounds odd, but that Highland Spring bottle, do you know where it came from?'

Cara didn't seem surprised at the question. 'It must be the one Dawn came home with on Wednesday. We don't buy bottled water. Seems daft when it's literally coming out of the taps.'

'So it's the one they gave her? The guy who took her?'

'Yes, I expect it is. Why?'

'OK if I take it?'

'Go ahead.'

Ronnie pulled on a glove and placed the bottle in a plastic bag, then she took her leave, thanking Cara for the chat and telling her she would do absolutely everything in her power to bring her son back home.

CHAPTER 13

When Ronnie arrived at Hemingway's that night, Susie was waiting for her at the bar, cocktail in hand, already chatting to a man. She tapped her on the shoulder. 'Hi, Suze, I would say sorry I'm late, but I think I'm actually early.'

'Ronnie!' Susie spun around from her bemused companion, then back again with a heartfelt 'sorry, I'm going have to abandon you' and pulled Ronnie into a hug. 'Soooo good to see you. Pull up a pew. I'll get you a drink.'

As Ronnie took her coat off and dragged a stool over, Susie was all questions.

'How have you been? What's happening in your life? I want to hear all about your holiday, all about work. I saw the news on TV today, it's so shocking about the abduction. Has there been a ransom demand yet?'

Ronnie waited till all the questions had landed before answering.

'Well, where shall I start?'

Susie turned to the bartender, whose eye she caught with enviable ease. 'Can we have another of these please? Thank you.' She turned back to Ronnie and took both her hands in her own. 'I've missed you! Tell me your headlines.'

They had developed a new way of catching up since their respective jobs had taken up more and more of their time. Their outings together might be brief, with either of them being on call or just exhausted and ready for bed, but this way they would get to the bottom of the main stories in each other's lives, rather than reveal a major chat-worthy event just as one of them had to leave. Each would begin with three headlines, related to personal life, work life and what Susie called 'mad crazy thoughts'. 'It's so important that we don't stop dreaming,' she had said, the day after their get-together was interrupted by an aggravated robbery across town. 'We need to make sure we don't sink into the muddy swamp of the day-to-day. Let's promise to always make time to talk about the stuff that we will probably never do but makes us happy to think about.'

The barman placed Ronnie's drink in front of her and they clinked glasses with aplomb.

'This is a very welcome beginning to the weekend.' She took a sip and let the warmth flood through her system.

'You deserve it, DS Delmar, I'm sure. Now, fire away.'

Ronnie sat back. 'Actually, why don't you start? Let me get my front page in front of the editor for final comments.'

Susie didn't need much encouragement. 'Work first then. I'll get it over with.' She turned her glass in her hands and a shadow crossed her face for a second. 'Obviously, I can't talk about the actual work. Client confidentiality. But I can tell you we've had some serious stuff going on.'

'I'm sure. You're on the front line when it comes to helping people recover.'

Susie's face was uncharacteristically serious. 'Some of the stuff we're dealing with right now, adults with PTSD from abuse thirty years ago. It keeps you grateful, that's for sure.'

'I know what you mean. Gives you perspective. But it must make you pretty angry, I imagine, hearing what people have gone through.'

Susie inhaled deeply and let a long breath out. 'Especially at the hands of the people who are supposed to look after them.'

Ronnie took another sip of her cocktail, thinking how much she preferred chasing the perpetrators than poring over the psychological damage they had wreaked on their victims. But right now, serious Susie needed steering back to a less depressing conversation and there was one sure way to lighten the mood. 'So, any hot guys in the office that have caught your eye?'

'Well, there is one actually, but it would be totally against the rules . . .' A smile returned to her face as she launched into a fuller answer. Ronnie was grateful for the thinking time and for the warm glow spreading through her as the alcohol did its job. The transition into discussing Susie's love life was welcome. With an office romance out of the question, but with her head turned, she had finished with the young man she'd been dating for the past month and had immediately arranged dates for every night the following week. She wasn't one to do things by halves, so it was no surprise that she would take the all-guns-blazing approach, but Ronnie secretly doubted it was the right way to go about it. Surely she needed a cooling-off period before diving back in?

'You've got to meet them to know if there's chemistry. No point chatting and texting for ever. You know as soon as you walk in the room whether there's anything there or not.'

It made sense, Ronnie supposed. 'Do any of the new ones have any money in the bank?'

Susie had a habit of finding herself paying for everything from the outset, as her dates pleaded poverty after being taken to the cleaners by their exes.

She winced at the question. 'Not entirely sure, but then what should we expect? Where there's a divorced man who's still solvent, there's a woman who hasn't done her job properly.' Despite never having been married, let alone divorced, Susie seemed to know all the rules.

Ronnie eyed Susie with mock suspicion. 'Simon's not exactly on the breadline. You saying I didn't do my job properly then?'

Susie rolled her eyes. 'You know what I mean. You know I never mean you. You are my idol, Ron, I need to be much more like you in life. Pursue things doggedly to the end, stop flitting about, and stop worrying about what people think.'

'It shouldn't be that way though, should it? Nobody should be taking anyone to the cleaners.'

'But they do, because often they're angry, especially if they've been cheated on, and adultery is the most common reason for divorce in the UK, *and . . .*' She paused for effect. 'Most adulterers are men.'

'But Suze, and let me tell you, Serena has been re-educating me on this, so I've been challenging the old narrative, but bear with me. Adultery is a two-way street, so we need to stop pointing the finger at the one who strays, don't we?'

'You've been Serena'd, that's for sure. Well done, girl!' Susie clinked her glass with Ronnie's. 'I like this. Do I detect the first green shoots of emotional breakaway from Simon?'

'Well detected,' Ronnie said, 'but it's taken me a while.'

'And now you think divorce should be go out with what you came in with and shut up whingeing?'

'Not exactly. But surely we've gone beyond handing everything over to the wife? I mean, what happened to going out there and getting a job? Simon and I split things fifty-fifty, and I just get extra cash for housing the kids.'

Susie lifted her hands in surrender. 'You're right, and that's how it should be, for sure. I'm just saying that we aren't there yet, from my experience.'

'So I'm worried now – what are your mad crazy thoughts if dating a new guy every night next week wasn't one of them?'

Susie's expression turned from despondent to triumphant. 'I'm going to do another degree. Part time, alongside my job.'

'You're what? You just said no more flitting about! And you've already got a PhD for God's sake.'

'I know.' There was a twinkle of pride in her eyes. 'But this is something new, something I have always been fascinated by, and it's so topical now.'

'What is it then?'

'Gender equality, diversity and inclusion.'

There was nothing quite like Susie's raw enthusiasm for life. If only you could bottle it and spray it on every morning, the world would be a happier place. Her *joie de vivre* had its roots in academia – she had been an A* pupil, excelled in the police force and had gone on to qualify as a psychologist. Ronnie shook her head, imagining what it would entail doing a degree alongside a job that took all your waking hours.

'I'm exhausted just thinking about it. Where do you get the energy?'

'Oh, you know, we all have the moment when we realise life's too short to hang around. I just can't stop saying yes to things.' She stirred her ice with the straw. 'But now it's your turn. Go backwards.'

'Go what?'

'Start with the mad crazy thoughts. Tell me an outrageous idea you've had recently. I mean properly mad, not just buying a sixty-five-inch TV.'

'Well . . .' Ronnie hesitated. She hadn't planned to share the idea that had been germinating in her mind. 'Don't jump on this, Suze; I mean, I know you will, but don't go over the top. I might not do it. I haven't decided.'

Susie inclined her head. 'Go on then.'

'I'm going to get back on the dating scene. It's like the big crazy dream *and* love life all in one headline.'

'Well, I'm pleased to hear it. I think it's a great idea.'

'That's all?'

'I thought you didn't want me to go over the top. I'm giving you my most measured response here, damn it!'

Ronnie patted her arm. 'Thank you, it's noted and appreciated. I have no idea where to start looking, but I'm sure you can fill me in on the pros and cons of all the latest apps. Slightly dreading it, but if I'm emotionally detaching from the ex, finally, I need to put my money where my mouth is.'

'Well, who knows, you may be pleasantly surprised.'

Susie seemed satisfied, so Ronnie took her chances and changed the subject. She gave brief updates on the public version of the Buckley case and the basic facts about her encounter with Ruth Jones. It was when she mentioned Ruth's sudden disappearance that Susie stopped her.

'Hang on. That's weird, isn't it?'

'Well, I thought so, but then plenty of women withdraw their testimony when it comes to acts of violence. That's partly why we end up with so few convictions.'

'Fair enough. But to run away mid-interview. Something must have spooked her.'

'And to vanish like that. I mean, it's pretty difficult to get past the whole of Halesworth's staff without anyone spotting you, I'd have thought.'

'So, you think she's a seasoned escape artist? Goes with the territory, I suppose, fleeing domestic violence. How long had they been together? Did she say?'

'Hardly any time, two or three dates, but it was when she went round to his place that he attacked her, from what I could gather. Shame she didn't give us his surname, let alone an address, and there's no record of her in hospital. We're going back to her place on Monday so with any luck we'll get to the bottom of it then. But we haven't got long. Lydia doesn't want any more time spent on it, so she's taken me out of the picture. Talking of which . . .' A familiar figure had just come through the door and was heading towards them. 'Here's our DC – maybe soon to be *DS* – Munro.'

Baz weaved his way through the clusters of drinkers and sidled up between the two women, rubbing his hands and eyeing their empty glasses suspiciously. 'Ladies, may I get you both a drink? You look like you could do with one.' He lifted Susie's glass. 'What was that? Leaf soup?' Then, sniffing it, added, 'Ahh, with rum. Leaves with rum. Delicious.'

'It's a mojito,' laughed Susie, slapping his arm, 'and yes I'd love another, and so would my friend here. And *then* . . .' She looked at Ronnie for approval, which she didn't get, and carried on regardless. 'And *then* we're going to find Ronnie a boyfriend.'

Ronnie hadn't planned to share her main headline with her DC, but then what she was divulging here was hardly state secrets, and Baz was already signalling to the barman, so the revelation hadn't exactly stopped him in his tracks.

She gave Susie a look while Baz ordered three mojitos.

'Oh go on, what's the harm in telling him?' Susie inclined her head in supplication. 'He might even know someone suitable.'

Drinks arrived and glasses clinked in a multilingual toast. '*Na zdarovye*,' said Baz. Ronnie countered with '*Salud*,' and Susie tried her hand at French

'*Bon appétit*, or something like that. I can't keep up with all you guys.' She looked imploringly at Baz. 'Baz, say something in Russian, not just cheers, something more substantial. I *love* the sound of Russian.'

Baz obliged with something he translated afterwards as being *I prefer my borscht without cabbage.* 'It's what we used to say to Babushka, on the rare occasions she came over here and tried to cook for us.'

Susie tapped a finger on the bar. 'Did you know that apparently the Russian cosmonauts took freeze-dried borscht into space? They're obsessed with the stuff.'

'Susie's about to start an MA in diversity and inclusion,' said Ronnie by way of explanation. 'So this won't be the last you'll hear of her wise words on race and nations.'

'Good for you!' Baz raised his glass to her. 'I think it's something we need to be much more aware of. The press are all over the police these days for the slightest indiscretion.'

'It shouldn't be like that.' Ronnie frowned. 'I mean, you shouldn't feel like that. If there's a reason to arrest someone that holds up under scrutiny, then that's good enough.'

'But it never is,' Baz said, before she could go on. 'The police have blood on their hands, every time. If you look at social media, they're racist, misogynist, homophobic, you name it.'

Susie put down her glass with a thump that announced her passion for the topic. 'But they *are*. I don't mean you personally, Baz, but the institution, most institutions, probably, have these elements, but the police especially. And unconscious bias is unconscious, so there's no point in denying our guilt when it comes to prejudice. Acknowledge the fact that it's there, and work together on fixing the problem.'

Baz smiled. 'I've missed you, Susie Marshall.'

'You mean you'd forgotten what I was like.' Susie gave him a look that a hungry lion might give an injured wildebeest.

Ronnie was wondering how much of a role discrimination had played in the life of the Buckleys, and whether things would have gone differently if they hadn't felt that the world was against them.

'OK, so fixing the problem in the Buckley case means winning back the trust of the families from the estate who have been let down by the authorities in the past.'

Susie was desperate to interject. 'And what I want to know is did that teacher release a little boy into the hands of a stranger just because of where he came from?'

Baz let it sink in. 'So, what you're asking is would she have done the same with another white child who lived in a posh house? But how would she know where they lived?' Baz looked puzzled.

Ronnie gave him an amused look. He had all this to come one day, the joys of toddlers. 'Oh, they know.

Someone's been round at some point, preparing them for nursery in the early years, or you just find out when the kids draw their houses and families. There are ways of finding stuff out, and children are famous for oversharing, aren't they? Remember show-and-tell?'

'*And*,' interrupted Susie, 'it's not just social prejudice in schools. They have these cultural diversity days but who's in charge of the proportional representation of different cultures and faiths? I bet they don't do a session on traveller culture, or Mormons or Jehovah's Witnesses. There are loads of groups that get really bad press and no airtime in the classroom.'

'The Jehovah's Witnesses are apparently the most persecuted community in Russia,' said Baz. 'Imprisoned regularly just for praying. They're seen as an extremist cult over there. Another reason why I'm over here. Not because I'm a Witness,' he added, alarmed. 'Just that there's so much intolerance.'

Susie laughed. 'You were worried we thought you might be a Jehovah's Witness. Doesn't that just prove everything? We don't want people to think we belong to one of these groups – that means we have categorised them as somehow not worthy, doesn't it?'

'No race or religion is historically blameless.' Baz looked from Ronnie to Susie and back to Ronnie, serious now. 'There's a huge backlog of sex abuse cases in the Catholic Church. They've always claimed to deal with these guys in their own ways, but in the end the truth comes out and their reputation is trashed. Same with that group that was in the papers, Pilgrims of something or other, was it?'

Susie seemed to flinch and looked down into the ice melting in her glass. Ronnie, meanwhile, pricked up her ears. New cults meant new traps for her children to fall into. She could just imagine Tilly coming home one day, or not coming home, and thinking she'd found the answer to world peace. Then again, if Eddie was kidnapped by the Moonies, he probably wouldn't even notice, as long as they had a games console.

'Anyway, best off as an atheist. Much safer.'

Susie looked perturbed. 'Some people don't have any choice if they're born into it.'

But Baz hadn't finished. 'But then, just like with everything else, we need to remember that all these crimes are committed by individuals. We shouldn't tar them all with the same brush, should we?'

Susie drained her drink. 'Baz, you have to take collective responsibility.' She shook the ice in the glass. 'You lot. I'm not sorry I left the force sometimes.'

Ronnie exchanged glances with Baz. Their procedure-driven lives were being given a proper hose-down by their ex-colleague.

Baz looked at his phone. 'I gotta go. Seeing Amber at eight for dinner.'

'Where did you two meet again? In a bar, wasn't it?' The argument was forgotten and suddenly Susie had a twinkle in her eye again. Ronnie knew what was coming next. 'Perhaps our friend Ronnie won't have to go online after all.' She glanced at the barman and back at Ronnie, who slapped her in exaggerated horror.

'I'm only thinking about what's best for you, Ronnie.'

'I know, and like I said, I'm on it.'

CHAPTER 14

Saturday. Ruth counts back the days to make sure, but they are beginning to merge into one. It's ironic that she wanted to hide away, be on her own where they couldn't find her, not even the police, but now she's trapped whether she likes it or not. She feels for the hatch one more time, traces the edges with her finger and feels for the tiny ridge that she can almost lift. There's a fraction of a second when she thinks she's done it but then she's lost it and a bit more nail has broken. She sucks her finger, tastes the dust and closes her eyes in defeat.

She reminds herself how much she likes being quiet. Quiet is where she can think. Quiet and dark, no distractions from her thoughts, but when she lets thinking take over, she's back at Mill Farm, and her mind is flooded with the horror of it all. Her stomach heaves with anxiety and vomit rises in her throat. She reaches for the pills that she always keeps in her pocket, to calm the terror of the memories. She must ration them because she doesn't know how long she will be there. She must be strong, think strong things, focus on a bright future for when she gets out. She's only been locked in for a few hours. She's had worse.

Perhaps it's a punishment from God for trespassing, for crossing the line. The words send a shiver down her back. Does God exist? She isn't sure, even now. Sometimes she longs for the certainty of the past. Being sure, one way or the other, must be better than the purgatory of not knowing. If you don't know, if you don't have faith, you don't belong, and she wants to belong. She always wanted to belong, but she was different. She was singled out, held up as an example of exactly how not to be.

She wishes there was another pill you could swallow to properly delete your memories, because what's the use of them when all they bring you is shame and regret?

She tries to remember her last phone call with Martha. She was at the reservoir, walking the trail from the car park to the highest point where you can see from Wakehurst and West Dean to Halesworth and beyond to the South Downs. On a clear day you can even see the sea. She likes that spot because of the fusion of natural and man-made, of past and present. Mill Farm to wind farm. It works somehow. It makes sense. She picked the place she wanted to be, but Martha picked the time, as usual, when Nate and Esther would be out, when she was alone in the house with just Rex and the coast was clear to make contact.

It was sometime around her birthday, she remembers now. Not her actual birthday, because they'd never celebrated it. Martha probably didn't even know when it was. But it would have been sometime around then because Ruth mentioned being asked by Madison for her date of birth and that Madison had said, 'But that's today – happy birthday!' and seemed astonished that Ruth would be at work rather than painting the town red. Martha had laughed and said, 'She sounds like a nice boss,' and Ruth had agreed.

She talked with them on FaceTime for what must have been twenty minutes. Rex showed her the new henhouse and the pig pen that had been turned into a goat hut, and she asked how he was doing at school, which made him excited enough to go and get his books to show her his marks. They talked for long enough to forget the time, and then the line was cut. Ruth's first thought was that she'd lost the signal, but it seemed odd because it was always perfect at the top of the hill by the wind turbine with the four blades. It stood among its three-bladed companions like the odd one out, like Ruth saw herself in the world.

If it wasn't the signal, then it must have been Martha's phone running out of battery. She didn't text after, but she might have forgotten. They had talked for long enough after all. And Ruth couldn't text her. It wasn't safe. That was the first rule. *Wait for me to get in touch with you.* Nate couldn't know she was alive, let alone in phone contact, so timing was everything.

Ruth doesn't want to use her phone any more in case they are tracking it, getting closer to her with every second it's connected. She switches it off, then keeps checking it hasn't somehow switched itself on again. As children, they were told by Nate and Aunt Esther in no uncertain terms that the mobile phone was only good for emergencies, if you were lost, you'd run out of petrol, not for idle chit-chat and the demon internet. God would have something to say if they started messing about with the worldly wide web. Whatever she thinks now, however much her thoughts have changed in the past ten years, she can't just cast off the messages of the past. Somehow, they have crept into the crevices of her brain and hidden there, solidifying like cement.

There were other things that have a similar hold over her. As well as letting her birthday slide by unremarked, she pretended to visit family at Christmas and hoped nobody noticed her sitting at home watching black and white films and eating pancakes. The pancakes were from the old days too. She'd tried to remember the recipe for Aunt Esther's Finest, the ones she served up before they went to Assembly on a Saturday. Ruth and Martha would race to finish first, licking syrup off the plate afterwards and looking up pleadingly at Aunt Esther hoping for seconds. Ruth's pancakes were OK but not nearly as good as she remembered.

She thinks about those early years of her life and feels tears pricking behind her eyes. A longing for Ma and Pa, with the kind of desperate need intensified by years of absence.

'It was God's wish. They should have been spreading the Word, but they chose to abandon the flock,' Nate had said as he wheeled his suitcase into the hallway of Mill Farm. 'They crossed a line. One day you'll understand what that means.'

Ruth was thirteen and Martha was ten when Nate and Esther moved in. Fifteen years had passed and they still didn't understand.

CHAPTER 15

Ronnie was more than grateful for Simon taking the twins off her hands on Sunday. The files on her desk were full to overflowing, the fridge was empty apart from a few cans of Fever-Tree tonic and washing was piling up next to the machine, which whirred unhurriedly with the latest load of sports kit spinning slowly in the round window. Serena would be happy to do the shopping, and probably the cooking as well, but she couldn't become completely dependent on her. Other single parents managed to hold down jobs, and it wasn't as if the twins were little and needed supervising all day. A trickle of guilt found its way into her mind, pushing to open the floodgates, and Ronnie took a moment to mentally seal the gap. This was no time to dwell on her inadequacy, real or imagined. A child was missing.

With every day that went by, she felt an increasing sense of dread about what might have happened to Liam Buckley, and she needed to prove to herself, and to Lydia, that she had really turned over every stone in the search. Uniform were out there combing the area, taking statements from everyone who had even the most tentative of connections to the Buckleys or to the school, and now there was the issue of Joe Buckley, whose true identity had muddied the waters of an already complex situation. Was Dawn involved in getting his son back to him? Had she invented her own kidnapping to divert suspicion, or was she a willing participant, paving the way for Joe or his representative to abduct her grandson? It was possible that the agreement might have gone wrong, the deal broken, and instead of meeting his biological son for an afternoon of bonding in the park, he had absconded with him. Was that the real reason they only contacted the police the morning after? She called Jules, who answered on the first ring.

'Sarge? Has something happened?'

'I'm just putting a plan together, but there has been a development that rather changes things.'

'What kind of development?'

'Joe Buckley . . . is Liam's biological father.' She drew a spiral on the notepad in front of her as she spoke, whirling outwards until it filled the page.

There was silence for a second before Jules spoke again. 'I didn't see that coming. That changes everything.'

Ronnie shared her thoughts. It was well within the realms of possibility that Dawn Buckley felt compromised by the family dynamics, and it wasn't out of the question that she'd want Joe to see his son, maybe even get him back if she didn't approve of Cara's parenting skills. Perhaps Joe was offering her a role in his care and a better home than a trailer. Maybe there had been a falling-out between the brothers and Dawn had taken Joe's side. If that was true, then Dawn needed to keep herself out of the picture, while she collected Liam as usual and went somewhere to wait for Joe to collect him. She could have 'arranged' her abduction to remove her from suspicion while Uncle Joe did the collection. It was all feasible, and all needed consideration.

Jules exhaled deeply when Ronnie had finished. 'So if the whole plan was to let Joe back into Liam's life, that would explain why Liam went willingly. It was either Joe or Dawn waiting in the playground.'

'That's certainly possible.'

Ronnie went through the witness statements online for the third time. Linda Carter had been visiting her elderly mother at a care home on Wednesday afternoon. The family of the boy who sat next to Liam in the back of the class were at pains to deny any hint of bad blood between them, except that Liam had been trying to copy his work and he'd got fed up with it and hit him, and Liam had hit him back.

Eddie shouted a goodbye before slamming the front door behind him and Serena appeared with a mug of coffee.

'A whole day of freedom for you. Make the most of it.'

'I wish,' said Ronnie, sitting back and taking the mug from her. 'I don't think I will feel anything like a sense of freedom until we're closer to the truth of what happened to this poor kid.' Liam's face was on the screen, snuggled next to his mother's in a laughing embrace. It was a portrait photo they had used for the appeal, alongside his school photo from the year before. In that one, his expression was serious and unsure, the traces of a smile unable to make the full journey across his little face. Ronnie remembered those photo sessions from her own schooldays, being marched up one at a time and told to smile, think of your favourite sweeties or imagine getting your favourite toy for Christmas. The smiles they produced were never the real thing, but they stared out from frames on the mantlepiece for years afterwards nevertheless.

'What are you thinking?'

'I'm thinking everything,' said Ronnie. 'Everything and nothing. I have to keep all possibilities in my head, follow every clue, every hunch, logic and instinct, and now, thanks to you Seena . . .' She gave her sister a nudge. 'I'm trying to challenge the narrative as well, to interrogate every assumption we make to ensure I'm not missing something.'

'Like what, for example?'

'Like the narrative that every family is a family – in the normal sense – like everyone has the same agenda, like they agree what's best for Liam, that the Buckleys are solid and supportive of each other. Shall I go on?'

'No, sounds like you're on it to me. And all that with a ticking clock.'

'I know. I can't give up hope but I need to be realistic. The chances of finding him alive are getting dramatically lower by the day.'

'You can only do your best. You can't be expected to second-guess the workings of a criminal mind that has clearly done a good job of removing a child without a trace. If they have done their job properly, you won't find him.'

It was the kind of brutal truth she didn't often hear from her sister, but it was what she needed.

'I need to be better than them, whoever they are. I *am* better than them. I'm trained for this. I have the experience. I know how these things work.'

Serena shrugged. 'OK, but don't beat yourself up about it. It will only make you ill. I'm going out. I can collect the kids from Simon's later if you like.'

'That would be great. I said five-ish. He's got something on this evening, so it's earlier than usual. He's taking them out to lunch.'

Serena nodded and pulled the door closed behind her.

Ronnie was only halfway down her to-do list when the phone rang and pulled her back from her mental exploration of all the scenarios that could have led to the disappearance of Liam Buckley. She had only come up with half a dozen and it was five twenty already. Time had flown.

'Seena. What's up? Have you got a puncture or is Edward too big now to fit in the tiny back seat?'

There was a pause that made her regret her flippancy.

'Tilly's not here.' Serena's voice sounded flat, the voice of someone who has delayed passing on the bad news until the last possible moment.

'What do you mean, not here?' Ronnie sat up straight, heart pounding. It didn't make sense. They had left together that morning, or had they? She remembered only hearing Eddie's voice saying goodbye.

'She didn't come. Simon said she texted him and said she had too much homework and a big physics test on Monday.'

Ronnie was on her feet now, heading for Tilly's room. She threw the door open but there was no sign of her, just what looked like the entire contents of her wardrobe spread over the bed and carpet.

'She's not here either. Did Eddie tell Simon she was at home with me?'

There was some muffled conversation on the line and Eddie took the phone. 'Sorry, Mum.'

'Sorry for what? What have you done? Where is she?'

There was a sigh on the other end. 'She said she was going to the library early to work. I didn't believe her. She was wearing make-up and stuff. But I didn't ask because I just thought it was better not to know, then I'd have to lie or piss somebody off.'

Ronnie hesitated. There was no point in doing what she wanted to do most at that minute, which was to shout *What the hell were you thinking?* because at this point it was still possible Tilly might even be at the library. She thought quickly. 'Get back here as soon as you can with Auntie See. I'll try and find where Tilly's got to.'

Eddie seemed relieved. 'Thanks, Mum. I'm sure she's OK.'

'She'd better be.'

Ronnie was dialling Tilly's number within seconds. It went straight to voicemail. She left a message, then phoned the library, which was closed. She sent a text, a WhatsApp and an email, each one saying *Where are you?*

Eddie says you went to the library but it closed at four. She took a deep breath and exhaled until her lungs were empty. *Think.*

Serena and Eddie arrived with muted voices and the front door closed softly this time. Eddie looked at his mother hopefully for an instant, then, seeing her face, his own fell in response.

'No news then?' Serena leaned on the worktop. 'What now? Where could she be?'

'Her phone's going to voicemail.'

'So she could be on another call?'

'Or it's run out of battery,' suggested Eddie. 'My battery's always dead by lunchtime.'

'I think we shouldn't panic,' said Serena, one hand on Eddie's shoulder.

'Don't tell me we've all got to sit down and have a cup of tea,' said Ronnie, her voice shaking.

'Actually, that's a really good idea.' Serena went to the cupboard and took out three mugs, then a fourth. 'She'll be home in a minute, you'll see.'

Ronnie sat on a stool at the kitchen island and scrolled through her phone contacts for any mention of Tilly. She could start with Daisy Elliot, who had been promoted to best friend since the holidays. She'd know where Tilly was.

'Hello?' said the voice that answered, like an alien recently arrived on earth and unfamiliar with mobile phones. Nothing new there. The twins hated answering calls from numbers they didn't recognise.

'Daisy, it's Tilly's mum, Ronnie, here. I'm just wonder-ing if you know where she is, because she was supposed to be at her dad's today and didn't go.'

'Err, no. I mean, she's not here if that's what you're asking.'

Daisy would make a good politician, avoiding the question expertly.

'Do you have any idea where she might be?'

'I haven't heard from her today.'

'What about yesterday?'

'Snapchat, Insta, the usual, but I didn't see her or actually talk to her.'

Of course not, why would they speak when they could post heavily edited photos of themselves instead? Ronnie bristled with frustration.

'So what about the social media posts? Can you see where she is in them?'

Daisy sighed, as if Ronnie was the most hapless techno-phobe she'd ever met. 'Even if I could, it wouldn't necessarily mean she was there. You don't always post photos of now on Insta. Yesterday there was one of her and Jake on the beach. I remember because the tagline was something like *nothing's sarong with this life*, or some other terrible pun.'

'What about Snapchat? That's always stuff from right now, isn't it?'

'Yeah, s'pose. But the pictures disappear, so I can't send you them.'

Ronnie swore silently. It was like getting blood out of a stone, as her mother would say when she and Serena were cagey about what they'd been up to. She shut her eyes tightly and tried to imagine what it might be like to be in Daisy's shoes. She might just not appreciate the urgency and her loyalty to Tilly was too strong to allow her to share everything she knew. But Daisy wasn't dishonest. In all probability, Ronnie just hadn't asked the right question yet.

'Daisy, do you have any way of finding her on your phone, like an app that shows where she is on a map or something?'

'Find My Friends? Find My iPhone? Do you have those?'

'I don't. I probably should have, but do you have anything like that?'

Daisy exhaled loudly, as if she'd been found first in hide-and-seek. 'Well, I suppose I could check Snap Map.' She sounded like a bored call-centre clerk.

'Yes, yes please, if you could. Thank you.' Ronnie's heart fluttered with anticipation. There was some button pressing on the end of the line. 'Whatever you can check, please check it.'

'I'll send you a screenshot. Looks like she's in north London.'

'North London?' Ronnie looked up and caught Serena's eye. Eddie was slinking out of the room. The picture landed on her screen in seconds. A small cartoon icon that must represent Tilly was grinning at her, wide-eyed and heavily made up, from a location somewhere in Hampstead. Thirty miles away.

'Must have gone to see Jake,' said Daisy.

'Of course.' Ronnie's stress lifted with relief that she hadn't been brainwashed and abducted by a cult, and then a surge of anger took its place. 'But why the hell didn't she say where she was going?'

Daisy seemed taken aback at the sudden change in mood. 'I don't know . . . maybe she thought you wouldn't approve? I don't tell my mum where I go all the time.'

Ronnie resisted the urge to say something challenging back. She needed Daisy on side. 'Can you do one more thing for me and send her a message on Snapchat or Maps or whatever it is, saying to call me straight away? Or something like that. Don't make it angry. I just want her home.'

Daisy must have complied because the phone rang two minutes later. Apparently Jake's parents had gone out for the day and he had invited her over. Tilly figured it was better to make up a work excuse than tell the truth and thought she could get away with it. Ronnie couldn't resist the obvious rebuff.

'You do know what job I do, don't you?'

'Sorry, Mum, I really wasn't thinking, and Dad usually brings us home at seven, so I was going to leave here soon anyway. I can be on the Tube in literally five minutes and home in an hour and a half.'

'No. I'm coming to get you. Stay where you are. Text me the address.'

A long drive through Sunday-night traffic with all the roadworks and bus replacement services clogging up the route was the last thing Ronnie wanted, but it gave her the chance to distance herself mentally and physically from the questions hanging over her head and, at the same time, to give some thought to her role as a mother. Her instinct was to blame herself completely and utterly for the fact that Tilly had gone AWOL. She'd clearly failed to teach her the values of honesty and consideration for others. But if she stood back and looked at the events through a different lens, Tilly was doing her own thing, forging her own path through life and prioritising what she thought was important, without, in her view, inconveniencing anyone else. Who did she get that from? *The apple never falls far from the tree*, Baz might conclude.

Jake's house was a four-storey terrace complete with the kind of cosy basement kitchen and raised ground-floor reception Ronnie used to love staring into during her days working in London. The sight of families gathered round kitchen tables, cooking meals, putting up Christmas trees, reading in the window seat, snuggled up watching television, filled her with a curiosity that bordered on envy. It wasn't that the houses were particularly beautiful or expensively decorated, it was more the way that their occupants used the space, performing their daily tasks like a live art installation, an exhibition of the modern family at work and play.

Ronnie stood for a moment outside the front door before knocking the big brass knocker, and breathed in the warm evening air, pretending for a second that she was coming home to a different house, from a different job, and that all this was hers. She could have chosen a less demanding career, one that made motherhood a joy and a pleasure rather than a duty she struggled to fulfil and a stick to beat herself with.

She knocked. Three hard raps that meant business. There was a scamper of footsteps down the stairs and the fumbling of keys and locks before the door opened to reveal the two errant teenagers, smiling in what may have been vain hope for clemency, or the satisfaction of a well-spent afternoon. She didn't dwell on which was more likely. Jake gave Tilly a hug goodbye and handed her a bulging bag of files.

'I'm sorry. But we did actually do a couple of hours' work.'

On the way home in the car, Ronnie took her chance to lay down some ground rules. Amid Tilly's pleas to be allowed *just a bit of freedom, Jesus!* they came to an agreement that Ronnie would have access to her whereabouts on an app of her choice.

'It's not as if I can see what you're doing on there, or even who you're with, just gives me some reassurance, and as you say, I only know where you last logged on, so it's not exactly a live trace.'

Tilly sighed and the conversation was done, until Ronnie raised the issue of contraception, at which point Tilly shouted: 'No, Mum, we are *not* having that chat. I've been to all the sex ed lessons. I probably know more than you do.'

And Ronnie didn't disagree. Perhaps it was time she changed that.

CHAPTER 16

'Sarge, a word?'

It was Baz. Ronnie beckoned him into her office, which wasn't more than a cubicle since the refurb, but offered a certain level of privacy she was grateful for.

'What's up? Did you check in with Ruth's work this morning?'

'She's not at work, and not at home either. Hasn't called in sick. The van's not outside her house or anywhere else in the vicinity.'

Ronnie sat back and drummed her fingers on the desk. This wasn't the outcome she'd been expecting.

'Damn. What about her phone? Can we find out when and where it was last used?'

'We can, but . . .' He looked conflicted. 'You know Lydia's position on this. She's convinced Ruth's off on a jolly and will be back when she's good and ready. Might have had a heavy weekend, doesn't want to get caught over the limit on a Monday morning.'

'She doesn't drink. That I do know.' Ronnie's heart sank. It was the same old story of comparative collateral damage. 'OK, so if she's a missing adult, she'll be low risk and low priority, but when it comes to the work van, that puts things higher up the list. They report it missing and she becomes a suspect in the theft. We can't just ignore it.'

Baz made a face that said he didn't want to give her the bad news. 'I asked what they wanted to do about it and they seemed pretty relaxed. The woman who runs the place seemed to be high on happy pills. Said give it a few days. There aren't any tools in it and worst comes to the worst they report it as stolen and get the insurance.'

'Err, I hope you weren't condoning insurance fraud, DC Munro.'

'No sarge, of course they didn't say that, and I didn't suggest it, but I'm just saying that's probably what they're thinking.'

'They won't get the insurance if they handed the keys to the thief.' Ronnie realised that was a presumption, but it made sense. 'So, where's she gone, our Ruth Jones? And more to the point, where's the man who hurt her? Because I refuse to believe the two aren't connected. I want him found.'

'I'm sure you're right, sarge. We'll see what the boss says. Meanwhile we're looking for the van but it could be a long way away by now if it hasn't been seen since last Wednesday. What news on the kid?'

Ronnie looked heavenwards, as if praying to some new god – the god of lost children. 'Day five, and we have basically nothing.'

Baz frowned and rubbed his chin. 'Must be torture for the family.'

'Worse than torture. I don't think his mother has slept or eaten since it happened.'

'Is there hope, do you think?'

'We're ploughing through CCTV and endless statements by parents who aren't quite sure from one minute to the next whether they saw Liam at all that day. The camera footage is worse than useless, even at the school gate, it's all umbrellas and hoods and even the children are indistinguishable from each other. The rain is literally lashing down. We've had a few calls come in since the TV appeal, but nothing that has delivered, yet. Didn't help saying there's going to be a reward but the amount hasn't been decided. Nobody's going to come forward until they know the prize money.'

'Any ransom demand? That's one way of pre-empting it.'

'Nothing.'

'Five days. It's a lot.' Baz swallowed hard. 'Statistics aren't good.'

'Let's not go there. Not yet.' There was a pause as they both let their unspoken thoughts run their course. 'I have a hunch that the grandmother is hiding something.'

'The one who was kidnapped to clear the way?'

'Yes, I'm trying to piece it together but there are so many missing parts, and someone isn't being completely upfront. I'm formulating a theory but it's not ready for sharing just yet.'

'Well . . .' Baz turned to go. 'Good luck, sarge. I know you'll find him.'

Ronnie smiled. 'I am very grateful for your confidence in me. And nice to see you out on the town on Friday night. Did you have a good weekend?'

Baz turned back, one hand on the door frame, or the frame where the door should have been if there'd been one. 'Oh, you know, B&Q, bit of gardening, a takeaway, Netflix. Very domesticated these days. How about yourself? Any progress with your latest idea?' There was a twinkle in his eye that told Ronnie he wasn't talking about police business.

'Ah, you mean the dating?'

'I'm sure you'll be snapped up in seconds, sarge, if you don't mind my saying.'

He flushed slightly as he spoke, as if his brain was failing to put the brakes on what he was saying and it had all gone out of control.

Ronnie smiled, trying to shrug off the embarrassment rising in her cheeks.

'Thank you for your confidence. I just hope they give me time to decide if I want to be snapped up.'

'Sorry sarge, I didn't mean . . .' He was blushing properly now and shifting awkwardly from foot to foot. He was hopeless at hiding his feelings, which Ronnie found endearing and amusing at the same time.

'Don't worry at all, Baz. I'm sure I will handle things better than that time we are both probably remembering.'

She couldn't handle them much worse than that, she thought.

She sat back in her chair, twisting a pen between her fingers. A new idea, loosely based on that one, had only started forming in the few minutes they had been speaking, but during that time it had taken root and grown into a plan. The confirmation of Ruth's disappearance had sealed her wavering resolve.

'Anyway, I'm going to give it a go. But don't go buying confetti just yet.'

The office was filling up. Phones were ringing. Blinds were being pulled down to shut out the low morning sun. The force worked to a routine, obeyed the rules, couldn't be seen to step out of line. The reprisals for professional wrongdoing were considerable and life-changing, so anything bordering on questionable had to be kept well under the radar. She couldn't let Baz in on her plan, even less Jules. This was something she'd have to do alone, or lose her job.

Jules Mayer wrenched her from her reverie, tapping on the half-wall that separated Ronnie's office from the rest of the team.

'Coffee, sarge? I'm just going down to the flat-white machine.'

The machine had been a controversial arrival at the station. The kitchen had been requisitioned by the reception staff, who claimed to have been sitting on each other's laps for want of space for the past two years. It offered a wide selection of hot beverages, according to the laminated notice on the wall beside it, but Jules and Ronnie had concluded that they all tasted like a flat white, even the tea.

'I'd love one.'

The contents of the Buckley file were spread out on her desk. Transcribed statements from all parties were open on different tabs on her laptop where they had been since the previous afternoon. She was deep in thought when Jules arrived back with the coffees and set them down on the one corner of the desk that was visible.

'Five days, sarge.'

'I know. Baz just reminded me. But given that they've combed the area and found nothing, let's focus on the fact we have no reason to believe he's dead.' Ronnie picked up one of the cups and took a sip. 'I just want to run through where we are and plan the next steps.' She put her cup down and sat back in her chair, swivelling left and right in rhythm with her words.

'A seven-year-old boy is taken from his primary school by someone he may or may not know, but they know him, or they have some way of identifying him and persuading him to go with them. The teacher, for reasons best known to herself, decides that the boy from the estate who now lives in a caravan can go home with a random stranger.'

'Sarge, we don't know that. It was just a mistake.'

Ronnie acknowledged her with a nod. 'OK, but just let's presume that unconscious bias is alive and well in the leafy suburbs.'

'OK, gotcha.'

'It's raining pretty hard, the other parents are concentrating on their own children, forcibly blinkered by hoods and umbrellas. Their children's testimonies are unreliable, and so all we have is an estimated time of departure of 3.20 p.m. Nobody saw them getting into a vehicle. Neither did anyone see Dawn Buckley being dragged at knifepoint into a black

Land Rover on the corner ten minutes earlier. It would be almost impossible for the driver of that car to dump Dawn at the reservoir and be back in time to abduct Liam.

'I'd say absolutely impossible. I've looked at the traffic reports and camera footage for that day and the weather definitely had an effect on the roads. Chock-a-block in the centre of town. The journey would have been a minimum of forty minutes, maybe forty-five.' Jules sipped her coffee, leaning in to search the paperwork for clues.

'Was Dawn sure about the time?'

'She said her phone died, so how did she know what time it was anyway?'

'It was based on when she left the site. Presumably there's a clock on the oven or some way she knew when to leave. Let's get more clarification on that. And find out if the woman in the car could have got out and collected Liam instead of going off on the trip to the reservoir.'

'Yes, sarge.' Jules was typing something into her phone. 'Hang on, we have something coming in from the traffic cameras now. Should download in a minute or so. And what else?' She pulled out a notebook and looked up at Ronnie for instructions.

'I keep going back to Dawn. Regardless of whatever Linda Carter has made us think, I don't think we can rely on her time estimate. It's pure conjecture as far as I'm concerned, and with no external corroboration we don't even know she was taken at all. What happened about the ANPR? Did you check for the vehicle on its *return* from the reservoir? If Dawn's kidnappers were the masterminds of Liam's abduction, they'd come back to finish it off, wouldn't they?'

Jules waved her phone in triumph. 'Yes, just heard back. They looked at the camera footage on the way back and bingo! We have a black Land Rover on camera coming into town, but only one person visible in the front, no passenger.'

'Where was it spotted?'

'On the high street, not far from the station, at ten past four.'

Ronnie put her head in her hands to concentrate. 'A long way past home time. Let's assume that the banging door wasn't the woman getting into the front at all. Dawn made an assumption based on nothing. The woman could have opened and shut the door for any number of reasons. And if she was blindfolded, Dawn couldn't possibly know. Which means . . .'

'Whoever it was could easily have gone into the playground to collect Liam.'

'Or if we're all wrong, and the female kidnapper did get in the front, then either she was crouching out of sight *or* the car we've got on camera could just be a car that Dawn remembered seeing and used to give credence to her story.'

'You mean if the whole thing was a lie? I mean, I share your doubts, as you know, but if she wasn't kidnapped, that raises so many more questions, like why she didn't collect Liam, where she went instead and why nobody saw her. And the driver of the vehicle on camera was wearing a baseball cap and glasses, as she described, so it's likely to be the same car.'

Ronnie exhaled. 'Baseball caps aren't a good enough ID for me. I know, it sounds as if I'm deliberately making it harder for us, but better than going down a blind alley.'

'So why *would* she lie about being abducted?'

Ronnie sat back and twisted her pen between her fingers, staring at the coffee, which was cooling fast. But she had to collect her thoughts before drinking any more of it. It was a deal she had struck with herself. Think first. Coffee later.

'So, I have one name in my head right now. Joe Buckley.'

'Ah, Steve's brother. The last family member to be dug out of the woodwork.'

'Where are we with him on the interviews? Because he needs to move to the top of the list.'

'We've asked him to come into the station to answer some questions. He needs to get the time off work, though, and he wasn't confident about how that would go down.'

'I don't care how confident he feels. He's coming in and I want to be there when he does. Because if he's involved, and Dawn is lying, then poor Lisa Blake is off the hook, and so are all the visitors to the school we have on our list.'

'Talking of which, I have the list here and there's nobody on it so far who was there at the actual time Liam disappeared. They'd all come and gone within the school day, apart from one, which we're following up. Just a surname, possibly a handyman coming in to fix a broken fence. The girls on reception weren't particularly helpful.'

'OK, so that line of enquiry is still ongoing but not looking promising right now. Let's hope we can talk to Joe

Buckley. And then we need to get back to the caravan to get the story straight on the reward, and also for another chat with Dawn.' Ronnie picked up a pen and scribbled on a pad in three bullet points: *Timings*; *slamming door*; *Prodigal son*.

CHAPTER 17

Ruth tries to lever open the edge of the hatch again, this time with the clasp of her hairslide, but the flimsy metal just bends back in submission. How did she manage to let this happen? Why didn't the hatch have a handle on the inside? She feels around in the dark for something else to use but finds only cardboard boxes of paperback books, clothes, plastic things she can't identify in the dark. A slice of light low down near where the roof reaches the wall does little to relieve the blackness. She thinks about Gemma and wonders what she's doing now. Soaking up the sun on a bright white beach, sipping cocktails, oblivious to all this. Her life is charmed. Ruth's was charmed once. But that was a very long time ago, before the accident and before the suitcases arrived in the hall announcing the arrival of their new guardians. Now, stuck here in the quiet and the dark, she has let all the bad back in. She fights it just a little longer because the thoughts aren't welcome and if she lets them fill her mind, she will drown. She forces herself to think about what's happening out there, whether the police are going to find her, whose side they're on . . .

With every passing hour, they will be getting closer. They will find her van first. They're good at that. Those cameras that stare down Cyclops-like from motorway bridges record the number plates of every passing vehicle, and stolen ones don't stand a chance, unless they take the back roads.

They'll have a team going through the footage, then someone will shout 'got it' and zoom in on the plates, then on the drivers. Maybe they have a database for face-ID. They'll track them down and get them to talk, probably throw them in a cell overnight, make them defecate in a stinking bucket in the corner.

That's what she had to do, in that cellar. And then in the cabin when they moved her because she'd tried to escape. She was a sinner, that much was certain, and would be punished by God in good time, Nate said, but earthly repercussions had their purpose too and he was more than happy to remind her of that and show her what he meant by it.

She had sinned, but if she repented, if she prayed hard enough, there was always the possibility of being welcomed back to the fold and being reunited with Martha and Rex. Nate came to see her every day to help her with her prayers, to remind her to be grateful for the chance of forgiveness. The door at the top of the stairs would slam shut, then there were his heavy footsteps with their promise of the punishment she deserved. As the key turned in the lock, she would take a deep breath and remember the most important thing, which was to stay alive, because one day, if God was good, she would get out of there.

It was hard to imagine that things could get worse, but after Nate found her in the coal bunker, a few precious seconds away from freedom, he made sure they did.

The bunker led from the yard to the cellar and was fitted with a metal lid with a sliding bolt on the inside. Nate used a special key to operate the bolt, which he kept in his pocket and brought out whenever a delivery arrived that needed to come through the chute.

One day, the key went missing. There was shouting and crashing around upstairs as he blamed Aunt Esther for washing his trousers without checking the pockets, Rex for stealing it to use it as a weapon for his toy soldiers. Ruth heard it all and felt sick with fear while she and Martha inserted the metal rod and turned it until it clicked and opened. Martha crept back upstairs and slid the key under a shoe by the front door. 'Have you checked your coat pockets, Uncle Nate?' she said. Whether he had or not was unclear, but he went to the coat rack, tripped over a shoe which had appeared from nowhere and shouted at everyone all over again. The key lay there, exposed by the wayward shoe, all innocent and shiny.

Ruth should have had the time to climb out and make her escape, but the delivery had already come down the chute and the tunnel was blocked. Too full of coal to let her pass through. Ruth tried to squeeze her tiny body along the narrow space between the coal and the roof of the tunnel but it was too tight. When Nate came down the stairs, he pulled her out by her feet and slapped her hard across the face. He made her stand in the yard to be hosed down, but at least it was fresh air, of sorts.

That's when he moved her to the cabin. He boarded up the window and left her with nothing but a crack of light and a Bible to read. She turned the pages, counting lines and words, found the chapter about her namesake Ruth, who received *blessings she did not merit*. Nate had made sure she knew that, but to her, Ruth had another purpose. She was the great-grandmother of King David. The mother of kings. Ruth thought about that when things were at their worst and she had given up hope. There were times when she wanted to die, so much that she'd rub her wrists on the wooden floor until the splinters made her bleed, then she'd tear at the wounds with her nails, willing the blood to come flooding from her arteries and bring an end to it all.

What Nate told Aunt Esther, Ruth never knew. She wondered many times whether Esther condoned the abuse, or whether she was genuinely oblivious and just relished the time when Nate was absent. She had mostly been a shadowy figure moving around the kitchen and the faraway look in her eyes said she was disconnected from everything going on around her.

The cabin had been Nate's workshop before it was Ruth's prison. A room inside a room, it had an internal door leading to the storage area, as well as an external one, both locked and bolted from the outside. Ruth supposed that with the right tools she could break her way out, but the chances of her laying hands on those were more than remote. She was grateful for the running water in the tiny basin and the single electric light, but there were no sounds of shouting from upstairs, she didn't get to hear the comforting voices of Martha and Rex. Martha wasn't able to visit her so easily. The daily tray of food would be brought by Nate or Aunt Esther and left just inside the door. Esther would avoid looking at her, head bowed, headscarf obscuring most of her face. Who knew what was inside her head, what secrets she kept?

There was no heating in the cabin, and in the first winter, Ruth got very sick with flu. There was no question of calling a doctor, and even less chance of hot soup and paracetamol. But that was the day that Martha brought an electric fire from the big house. Aunt Esther was hot on her heels, looking at her watch, never at Ruth. She'd clear her throat after a minute. Martha was never allowed to spend long in the cabin, perhaps in case she helped set up another escape plan.

'They let you bring that?' Ruth flung off her blankets in excitement.

'Of course. Uncle Nate only wants the best for you, Ruth.' She spoke her lines like a professional, and Ruth understood it was for her own survival that she stuck to the script.

'Please tell him thank you.' She looked at Aunt Esther with all the sincerity she could muster. 'It's very kind of him. I'll get well very soon now.'

He came to see her that evening to see how grateful she really was.

She can survive. Captivity is temporary. She lies down on the floor, stares into the darkness at what must be the ceiling and remembers how she used to draw patterns on it, use it as a canvas where she painted her imagination and took herself away from hideous reality.

She thinks about the little boy. Does he miss his mother? Does he think about her at night, when it's dark and the monsters come out? Will they find him and take him away or will things stay the same, the way they did for her until she questioned the Truth?

That was a many-layered word. Living in the Truth had turned out to be the very opposite, and what she'd seen in Finn's house was just another reminder that her whole life until this day had been – and still was – a pack of lies.

CHAPTER 18

Lydia seemed underwhelmed, to say the least, on hearing that Ruth hadn't shown up for work. She stopped flipping files shut and stared at DS Delmar and DC Munro, who stood before her, bearing unwelcome gifts of news.

'She's off sick? Not a crime last time I checked.'

Lydia's sarcasm spanned a whole spectrum, from barely noticeable to full throttle, and reflected her level of irritation, which today had hit a new high. Ronnie was glad that Baz paused before answering. It wouldn't do to send her over the edge at this point.

'She's not at home, ma'am, and we've tracked the work van to halfway up the M1.'

'She's stolen it?'

'Not even that simple. Pictures show two men in the front. It's more likely *they* stole it.'

'Maybe she's in the back, out of sight. They're in it together.'

'Or they've got her in the back, tied up.'

'Well, which is it?'

'We're on it now, should have some news for you shortly on that.'

'And Liam Buckley?' Her eyes switched to Ronnie. 'Five days missing and no leads?'

Ronnie straightened up instinctively as she delivered the current state of play, the frustrating lack of useful response to the appeal, ANPR results, the latest witness statements, the house-to-house and caravan-to-caravan, and the remaining key surname on the school visitor list that was yet to check out. 'DC Mayer's checking the neighbourhood CCTV to see if we can pick anything up, but it's the usual thing – a lot of the locals keep a camera up purely for decoration. Hardly any of them actually work. But—'

'Tell me you've got something.'

Ronnie delivered the news of Liam's parentage and its consequences to an astonished Lydia whose jaw dropped as it sank in.

'Needless to say, interviewing him is now top priority. But how did you get that out of her? Or was it DC Mayer?'

Ronnie felt a twinge of resentment that she shook off before it took hold. Lydia was right to assume she had Jules to thank.

'Actually no, it was me. Sometimes a one-to-one is an easier scenario for letting the truth out.'

Lydia pondered before delivering more of a telling-off than the congratulations she felt were deserved. 'Don't make a habit of it. You have a partner for a reason. Use her.'

Ronnie steeled herself once again and changed the subject. 'Yes, ma'am. Can I just go back to the question of the Land Rover? We think it's too far for Dawn's abductors to come back after leaving her at the reservoir, in time to take Liam from school, unless her timeline is wrong. Dawn said the woman in the back got into the front, but if she was mistaken, and the slam of the door was knife-woman going off on her own, she'd easily have had the time to do it. I'd like to proceed on that basis.'

'Good plan,' Lydia said, in a surprising display of support. 'With the Joe connection, Dawn should be our best bet as a witness. Can you get her in to do an e-fit?'

'Yes, it's in hand. And there's something else we might be able to use, further down the line.'

Lydia looked up, with a glimmer of hope in her eyes.

'We've managed to lift some prints off the water bottle Dawn was apparently given by her captors when they dumped her. Not a match for anything on our database but you never know what might turn up.'

'Good work. Keep me posted. I have to go to a budget meeting now.' Lydia ran her hand through her hair and it struck Ronnie that she'd never seen her do that before. It was a gesture that suddenly made her more human.

'Ah, the budget. Well, I can assure you, we aren't wasting resources, and neither are we cutting any corners. It's a tight ship you run, ma'am.'

Lydia forced a smile. 'Thanks, DS Delmar. I trust you to get this done.'

'I will. We're going to find Liam.'

Ronnie stood for a second, re-establishing her resolve to do as she had said. It was an easy promise to make, but their lack of leads was worse than frustrating. At least Joe Buckley was an avenue worth pursuing. And as for Ruth, Ronnie's plan would have to remain a secret for a while longer.

CHAPTER 19

Esther is standing over the stove, stirring the steaming gravy while the joint of beef stands ready to be carved. The gravy is thin and unappetising, so she adds brown sauce from the cupboard. It's out of date but it can't matter. Nobody ever got sick from old brown sauce.

Nate will carve the meat. But his meeting with the Elders is dragging on. She stops to listen, wiping her hands on her already grubby apron, but she can only hear the rumble of male voices, the occasional slap of the table, a muted growl of defiance. It's their second visit this week. Martha and Rex have been shut upstairs. They know they mustn't make a noise, especially Rex, and Martha will make sure of that.

She opens the oven and pulls out the tray of potatoes with the oven gloves that barely cover her hands. Nate says she can make do, so she makes do. She's careful, and if she makes a mistake, the burns on her wrists don't take long to heal. The potatoes are crispy, just as he likes them, but her heart is thumping in her chest because they won't stay hot if she takes them out now, and they will burn if she leaves them in there too much longer. She turns the oven right down and leaves the door slightly open. It will warm the cold kitchen, but Nate will see that and tell her it's a waste of money, because money is everything, the only thing he talks about or thinks about. She'll tell him the oven is off, just using its remaining heat to warm the room, but he'll want to know why she hasn't found something to cook in there as it cools, so perhaps she won't say anything at all.

Just then, the voices become audible. The door to the dining room has opened and the men are filing out, pulling on their coats and bidding Nate goodbye. Whatever they are discussing in there, their manners are always impeccable as they arrive and depart. Nate says they are God's people, his chosen ones, which would explain why he spends so much time in their company and is so keen to do as they ask. When they leave, he is always cranky and irritable, so she is grateful for the timing and for the potatoes being just right.

He opens the kitchen door, just as Esther is sliding the food on to a plate.

'It's roast beef. Your favourite.'

He carves the meat, slicing through the flesh with the knife he spends so long sharpening each Sunday morning. She would happily do it herself, but it's his way of releasing stress, or something like that, because once he sits down at the table, beads of sweat on his forehead trickling into his beard, he is back to his normal self.

She hands him a cold beer and he cracks it open with his teeth, takes a long swig and sets the bottle down in front of him.

'Shall I call the children?' Martha is hardly a child, but it's what she calls them and always will.

'Not yet. Martha needs to know what hunger feels like.'

'She disappointed you. You didn't tell me how.'

'It doesn't matter.'

'She shouldn't have disappointed you.'

He nods at her approvingly. 'You're a good woman, Esther. You know the difference between good and evil. The Lord will see that in you and you will be rewarded in heaven.'

She tries to smile, but heaven seems a long way off.

There is silence, apart from the clink of his cutlery and the chewing and slurping of beer between mouthfuls. Then he speaks.

'They want more money.'

Esther nods, because it's not the first time. She knows what the men come for.

'For the lawyers,' he adds, as if there was any doubt.

'How much?'

'Ten thousand.'

Esther stands still in shock. 'Can you find it?'

'Maybe. But that will be the last of it.' He takes a mouthful of meat and potatoes, dripping in gravy. 'There's a limit to the assets we can sell, and then it gets personal.'

'You mean, the house?'

'Everything. Every penny.'

Esther sits opposite him at the table with her smaller plate. He looks at it and then up at her.

'Where's your appetite?' His mouth is still full, and meat juices run down his chin as he talks.

'Not hungry today. I think it's the weather. I thought the rain would clear it but it's so warm and still.'

He shrugs. 'Suit yourself.'

She hovers between asking him more questions and staying silent. Which will he find less irritating? She settles for a quiet question. 'What are you going to do?'

He piles his fork high and answers before it goes into his mouth. 'Damage limitation. The Elders are worried there may be more of them out there, like Ruth.'

Esther's stomach lurches. She puts down her knife and fork and holds her breath.

'Like . . .?'

'Like Ruth.' He savours the words as he chews his meat, like he's chewing her, like he's chewing over the memory of her. Esther is transfixed and revolted at the same time

'But she died, in the fire.' Esther's voice is blank. She frowns at him to let him know he's not making any sense.

Nate regards her for a second as if assessing her in some way, as if wondering if she's worthy of the information that's on the tip of his tongue. He must have decided she isn't, because he begins to cram more food on to his fork.

CHAPTER 20

'Mum, you're so late. Lucky Auntie See made us fab dinner before she went out.' Tilly was draped across the sofa, too glued to her phone screen to look up, let alone get up.

Ronnie slung her bag on the island and broke off a corner of the crispy lasagne topping.

'Delicious. Where's your brother?'

'Gaming, of course. Have you been up to something exciting?'

'I wouldn't say that. And I can't tell you the details because you'll just go and put it all on Instagram or something.'

'You're probably right.' Tilly rolled off on to some cushions, expertly placed below as if by an anxious mother for a wayward toddler. 'You look distracted. What's up?'

'I've just got some work to do. I'll use the office. How was your day?' Tilly was right. She was very distracted.

'Oh, not so bad. The mock AS levels before Christmas are stressing me out though. Hardly any time to learn anything, let alone revise it.'

'Well, if you'd gone to the library as you said you had, yesterday—'

'I thought we were done with that. I've said sorry and you've got me on the tracker.'

'Fair enough. Anyway, you've got half-term to study.'

'Will you let me go and see Jake as well?'

'Of course. If I know where you are, it's fine with me.' Ronnie surprised herself with how reasonable she sounded.

'We talked about it yesterday.'

'About what? Half-term?'

'About whether we're exclusive or not.'

Ronnie thought she'd misheard for a second. 'You what? That sounds like until now you've been in an open relationship, rather than not in one at all.'

'It's between seeing each other and boyfriend and girlfriend, kind of thing.' Tilly turned her phone over and placed it face down on the table. 'About yesterday, Mum . . .'

Ronnie let a smile escape and planted a kiss on Tilly's forehead. 'It's forgotten.'

Eddie wasn't as eloquent or effusive when Ronnie went to see him in his room.

'Oright, Mum, whassup?'

It sounded all wrong, coming from him, but all his year group spoke like that these days. She was lucky it was *Mum* rather than *bro* today, but then she had liked *bro*, in a way. Made her feel like part of the gang.

'Nothing's up, just wanted to come and hear about your day, find out what goes on in that clever head of yours.'

'Clever? Where's that come from?'

'Well, you haven't taken your eyes off the screen or your hand off the controls. So I'm guessing that's a pretty clever multitasking job for a start.'

'Sadly not a transferable skill for maths and English.'

'It's only been a few days. You'll get back into the swing of it.'

He groaned. Ronnie couldn't tell if it was a reaction to her words or one of the on-screen enemies escaping his virtual clutches.

'So, any homework tonight? Can I help?'

'Done it. Auntie See made us do it before dinner. Said you didn't need the stress of bossing us about when you came home.' He paused his game and spun round, in time to see his mother's face break into a smile. 'I knew you'd react like that. You're such a wuss, Mum. You shouldn't be surprised that people care about you and want you to be happy.'

She nodded. 'You're right, I deserve it. Maybe I even deserve more.'

'Don't go getting ideas.' He spun back round to face the screen, which flashed into action, and soldiers were once again clambering over the rubble of a war-torn city.

'I'll leave you to it.' The momentary warmth had worn off. Each child was preoccupied with their world and it was time for Ronnie to take the next steps in hers.

The app wasn't easy to find at first. It was like googling one supermarket and ending up clicking on another that randomly appears at the top of the list. Sidekick was the name of a number of apps, and it was only the third suggestion that fell in the dating category. Ronnie poured herself a drink as the app downloaded, wondering for the umpteenth time that day whether she could or should go ahead with it. The stakes were high, but so were the professional consequences. Lydia's warnings about going it alone echoed in her head. She would have to take care to leave a trail that couldn't possibly expose her.

She texted Susie with the simple message, *I'm going online dating! What do you reckon to the Sidekick app?*

Her reply came back within minutes. *Don't interrupt my hot date! Yes, I've tried it, seems fine, met a guy on there once but didn't see him again.*

The trail was laid, but it would be safer to download a couple more dating apps as well, to make her intentions look more genuine. She spent a few minutes comparing the relative benefits of various others before remembering that time wasn't on her side. She needed to get swiping.

Opening the Sidekick app, she composed a brief profile. Thankfully, there weren't many compulsory categories to complete so she was able to be as vague as she liked. *City girl* she called herself, imagining herself a civil servant in London. From there, the details flowed almost too easily: grown-up children, golfer, sun-worshipper . . . She chose three photos that made her look younger than her age, and set her target age range to thirty to fifty because she had no idea how old Finn was. It took a matter of minutes to set up and in what felt like no time at all she was scrolling through photos of eager young (and old) men, a fair few of whom looked as if they'd lied about their age, among other things.

A left swipe – a rejection – would mean that the man wouldn't appear in her list of possibilities again. But to right-swipe on them all, in case they were him, might leave her with more options than she could handle. On the other hand, it would serve as a good explanation for the coincidence she was trying to manufacture.

The first picture was Geoff, forty-five, a grey-haired attractive man aboard a yacht, grinning broadly, presumably either at the wealth he had amassed or at the thought of all the women out there believing the boat was his. She dutifully swiped right, then moved on to the next. Russell, forty-two, dark and moody, thick eyebrows and a penetrating stare. There was another picture of him with two boys, presumably his sons, and another of him in shorts on a beach somewhere. He wasn't out of the question. She felt a smile creep across her lips. This could actually be fun. She hadn't predicted that.

She flicked through the profiles faster, finding a rhythm to her swiping that lulled her into a kind of meditative state. She could almost see how the teenagers found their screens so addictive. She was too absorbed to hear Serena's key in the lock, and her hand on her shoulder made her jump out of her skin.

'Hey, Ron, what's this? Is it what I think it is?'

Ronnie flipped the phone cover shut. 'Er, yes. I mean maybe, why not? I was just . . .'

'You don't have to explain!' Serena looked amused and delighted. 'I'm just going to put the kettle on. Fancy something? Or someone?' She winked and Ronnie frowned.

This must have been how the children felt when she joked about their online lives.

'I'm OK with my wine, thanks.' She stood up. 'Yeah, just a whim. About time, I thought.'

'Absolutely.' Serena peered into a box of teabags. 'Seen anyone nice on there?'

'A few possibles. Only downloaded it half an hour ago.' She drew her forefinger across the screen a few more times, like stroking a cat to calm her nerves. She'd just lied to her sister. Not exactly lied, but not been honest. It was hardly a whim, and if it was time for her to find a boyfriend, she'd be more upfront about it with Serena than this.

The blood pounded in her temples as she watched Serena make her tea. She hadn't even looked at the last ten profiles she'd swiped right on.

'Well, it sounds like you're a bit of a hit, from what I can hear,' said Serena as she disappeared out of the room.

Ronnie's eyes flicked back to her phone, which was pinging with notifications from Sidekick. *It's a match!* Geoff had liked her back, Russell too. She ignored their bland 'Hi City Girl, how are you?' intros and carried on swiping. After an hour, her index finger was aching and the faces had started to flash past in a blur. She silenced the pings and the messages mounting up in her inbox – *Hey City Girl, how about you show me around? Free to chat City Girl? Love the pics. Wanna meet?* She was close to giving up when a name on the screen in front of her made her catch her breath in shock.

Finnian, 37.

It was as if he wasn't even bothering to hide, as if he'd been lying in wait for her there, eager to meet her and take their adventure from the small screen into real life. He looked normal. Not like a violent abuser, but then they rarely did. His declared age looked about right. His only photo was a selfie in sunglasses. She wouldn't have looked twice in normal circumstances, but the letters of his name stood out like cavalry below the picture, a battle cry, a call to arms.

Ronnie drained her wine and poured another. A text from Susie announced that the date was only average and she was on her way home. Ronnie went to the balcony and took a few deep breaths of the still-humid air. *It will all be the same in a hundred years*. It had been her father's response to all problems, as if they could be swiped away like a finger across a dating-app screen. The idea was that nothing mattered as much as you thought it did. He had a point, and when she remembered his words, it calmed her. They were inconsequential beings on this planet, tiny cogs in a small wheel that was part of something they were never going to understand.

She sank back down on to the sofa. What had happened to her father, all those years ago? His boat had been found drifting but his body was never recovered. As Ronnie said to anyone who expressed surprise or shock, *Nobody's offering to dredge the English Channel to find the body of a missing window cleaner*. Her father's death was a mystery that refused to be solved. Ronnie's work in the police had in some ways been a homage to him. She might not be able to find him, but she could find other people. She might even be able to find Ruth Jones.

As if in answer to her thoughts, another message dropped on to her phone screen with stars and confetti saying *You have mail!* Within seconds, there was a text in her inbox.

Hi City Girl, nice to meet you. How's your day been?

Fine, just the usual. I've only just joined the site. How's it been for you?

Well, I guess I'm still here, so not that well, but I've met some nice people. It seems quite relaxed.

Glad to hear it. I'm Veronica by the way.

She'd given it some thought, and concluded it was easier to keep her first name and change the surname. She didn't want to be caught out not responding to a name that wasn't hers.

Nice name. Unusual. Mine's Finnian. No pseudonym, sorry!

Aha, I thought I'd start with a bit of mystery . . . So tell me a bit about you.

As he typed his answer, Ronnie wondered where the chat was going. Were they supposed to interview each other online about hobbies, children and jobs, or did someone offer to move to phone chat? Susie had said that she would go straight for the meeting – 'You know as soon as you walk in the room whether there's anything there or not' – and Ronnie didn't have the time or inclination for small talk. She took the plunge, hoping against hope that it wouldn't come across as weird.

So, do you want to meet up?

The thirty-minute wait for his reply felt like thirty years, but it came, Ronnie was relieved to find out, and not only was he happy to move straight to a real-life meeting but he suggested they go for a drink the following evening.

There's a quiet little gastropub in Wakehurst, the Fox and Grapes. Music's not too loud. How's 7 p.m.?

Ronnie was happy with an early drink, and relieved he hadn't said drinks in the plural, or even worse, dinner, because this man that she had just thrown herself at might be someone who attacked women like Ruth Jones, might be the catfish they had had complaints about, might even be the same man that had tried to spike her drink and take her home that dreadful night the previous summer. But this was work. And she wasn't scared of hard work, especially if it meant that women would be safer. Her fingers shook as she typed a reply.

Yes, sounds great. See you there.

CHAPTER 21

The next day, Ronnie could barely concentrate and it didn't go unnoticed. Jules asked her more than once if there was something wrong, if everything was OK at home, and Baz went as far as to ask her if that was a twinkle in her eye he could see. The Buckley case seemed to have come to a standstill, but Jules was following up on school visitors and brother Joe's alibi. With no further news on Ruth Jones, Ronnie felt more than a little downhearted as she arrived back at the flat and set her bags down on the floor. She checked her messages, half-hoping Finn had cancelled, but there was nothing except a series of party emojis from Susie surrounding the words *Keep me posted.*

She told the twins it was a work dinner with the new boss, and that Serena was in charge. Her sister's words of warning were delivered in whispers as Tilly and Eddie tucked into risotto.

'Be careful. I mean it. You never know with this online stuff.'

It was like having a second mother sometimes. 'I'm sure I can look after myself. I've been on dates before, you know.'

Serena looked flustered. 'Of course, but things have changed, there are some dodgy guys out there, and sensible women falling for them all over the place. How about I call in an hour or so, with some excuse about the kids, and you can tell me in code whether it's going well or not?'

'Oh my God, Seena, that's way too much to remember to do. I can't do talking in code. Trust me, I'll be fine. I'll text you when I'm on my way home.'

Serena seemed satisfied and gave Ronnie's hand a quick squeeze. 'Deal. Off you go then.'

The door clicked shut. Ronnie exhaled deeply and said under her breath, 'Right, Finnian, let's see what you're made of.'

The Fox and Grapes was a favourite haunt of the more well-to-do of the Halesworth area. Candlelit tables, snugly cushioned oak benches and a log fire crackling in the hearth were matched by inflated wine prices and an intimidating list of gins. Ronnie had been there with Simon on a couple of occasions: drinks to celebrate his promotion, their twelfth anniversary dinner. It struck her as a strange thing to be remembering as she scanned the bar and the seating area beyond.

He looked up from his pint as she came in. It must have been the rush of cold air from outside as the door swung closed. His face lit up as they recognised each other and he stood up to greet her. Ronnie felt a sudden flash of guilt at being there on false pretences, then reminded herself that all she'd done was swipe right on a photograph, which is what millions of people did every day, even in the police force. There was no reason for anyone to think otherwise.

She took in his features with the expert precision of a seasoned detective – committing each one to memory so accurately it could be recalled at a moment's notice to provide a description for a photofit. And what she saw surprised her. His photos weren't unattractive, but this man was an improvement on his online images. He was taller than she'd guessed, his hair was thicker and darker, and there was a peculiar connection she felt the instant their eyes met. She had always thought that when someone admired another person's eyes, it was because that person liked them back. There was something about mutual attraction that made the eyes the first target of the heart.

He lifted his hand in a small wave to spare her any uncertainty, and she smiled back, relieved that she wasn't going to have to proposition random men in search of him. She had dreaded the sequence of 'Are you by any chance . . . ?' leaving her open to their curious gaze for the rest of the evening: *I wonder how their first date's going . . .*

He held out his hand as she approached, then seemed to change his mind and leaned in to kiss her. A hint of floral cologne as their cheeks brushed left her momentarily lost for words and completely forgetting why she was there.

'I'm Finn, as you know. Good to meet you, Veronica.'

'And you. Sorry I'm a bit late.'

'You're not at all.' He was already summoning the waitress. 'What can I get you?'

They made easy conversation on the standard topics: where they were from, how long they'd lived in the area, their jobs and hobbies. Finn told her he worked in property, had lived in the centre of Wakehurst since moving down from north London with his parents twenty years earlier, had never been married despite a long engagement to a girl who left him for his best friend, and was a die-hard Arsenal fan. Their drinks arrived. A pint of bitter for him and a rosé for her. Then it was Ronnie's turn and she churned out a meticulously rehearsed set of invented facts, while staying as vague as possible about the detail, which she figured was fair enough on a first date. She worked in a busy government department, commuting in on the train every day, lived in a new-build flat overlooking Brookfield Park which she'd bought two years earlier when she moved up from Kent. Her childhood was spared distortion for the most part, as was her divorce, but the children were the hardest part to deny.

'I know it sounds weird, but I never wanted children.' It did sound weird, because those were words she had never heard herself say.

Finn seemed to believe her easily enough, or perhaps he wasn't listening. She had that feeling sometimes when talking to attractive men that neither of them was absorbing what the other was saying. You came away with a feeling of what they were like without much information about their actual life. You knew if you were attracted to them or not, but you couldn't say whether they'd been to university or what they'd seen last night on Netflix. He watched her talk as a lion might contemplate a gazelle grazing in a meadow. He wasn't licking his lips, but he might as well have been. She made a note to tell Susie that at their next meeting.

'So you've just joined the app. Weird timing. I've just come off it.'

'Oh!' Ronnie didn't know what to make of that. Was he trying to tell her that was normal procedure when you went on a date, or was this his leaving drinks? 'Why's that – or shouldn't I ask?'

He almost laughed, then seemed to think better of it. 'I don't know. Maybe online dating isn't what I thought it would be. I've tried it and it's time for a break.'

It was a sensible enough response, but all Ronnie could think about was where she fitted into things. Was he giving it one last chance tonight? If so, she didn't have long to find out what she needed to know. Yet, at the same time, she found herself enjoying his company, and not in a hurry to do what she had come to do. There was one voice in her head that said, *Enjoy yourself – you've done nothing wrong*, and another saying, *The whole point of this is to find out what happened to Ruth, so get on with it*. It was a battle that raged harder the more drinks he poured.

Ronnie hadn't expected dinner, but things seemed to be flowing so well between them she didn't want to break the connection they had. She pushed her sea bass around her plate, conscious that the adrenaline pumping around her body was making eating difficult, and the topsy-turvy feeling in her stomach wasn't entirely down to the covert role she was playing. Finn was reeling her in with his magnetic eyes and his easy charm, making her realise that for the first time in a long while she wasn't completely in control.

It was getting on for ten-thirty before she checked the time and pulled herself out from under his spell. She needed to bring things to a close one way or another before she forgot who she was and what she was doing there. But his eyes were still on her, making her melt inside, and she knew he could see the effect he had, by the faint smile on his lips.

He glanced up for the waitress and she was beside them instantly, and he was reaching for his wallet. 'This one's on me,' he said.

Ronnie put her hand on his arm. 'No, I insist on paying my half.' He let her do that, and they walked outside together. The night was refreshingly chilly, and she pulled her scarf out of her jacket pocket and wound it around her neck, protecting her body from his touch.

'Hang on.' He reached to detach it from one of her earrings. 'There you go.'

Ronnie smiled her thanks. 'Well, I should go. That was fun. Thank you.' Her words came out in a jumble and heat rose in her face. She was too unpractised in the art of dating for this scenario. She needed to go, but she couldn't quite tear herself away. Then he pulled her towards him and she smelled the scent of his aftershave as his lips touched her cheek.

'I want to kiss you, but I know I'm supposed to ask first.' His voice was a whisper.

Ronnie drew back, but not too much. Her resolve was crumbling, had crumbled already, and the wine had made her woozy. She shouldn't have had the second glass. She opened her mouth to speak but no words came, and now his lips were on hers. She should pull away, but the feeling was one she wanted to last. She drank in the feeling of skin on skin, the smell of his face, the warmth of an embrace which she had been too long without.

It was Finn that pulled away first. His hands were on her shoulders, his eyes still fixed on hers.

'Thank you.'

'I'm not sure what to say to that,' Ronnie said, flustered.

'Can I see you again?'

The words took her by surprise and she fumbled for a response. *Play for time*, she thought.

'I thought you'd had enough of this internet dating?'

'I can change my mind, can't I? What do you say?'

She smiled, despite herself. 'I'd like that.' The words came out faster than she had intended.

'How about tomorrow night?'

Ronnie was taken aback for a second. In deeper than she had meant to be. She'd been hoping for a chance to catch her breath before walking back into the lion's den. 'Why not?' she said brightly, silencing the voice in her head that was saying, *No, no, no.*

CHAPTER 22

Ronnie woke early, her heart pounding, her palms clammy. She must have been dreaming but she couldn't remember it. All she remembered was the kiss. She could still smell his cologne and feel his eyes looking right into hers. It was a new feeling, and a feeling she absolutely mustn't let take root.

She closed her eyes, tried to recapture a hint of where her mind had been wandering in her sleep. She rolled over to the middle of the bed, rested her head on the cooler pillows and stared through the window at the willow tree whose branches were just visible. She should get out of the habit of sticking to her side of the bed when there was no one on the other. Nearly three years since Simon had left and she still did it. Still hadn't gravitated to his zone, used his bedside light, put her book down on his table. It might have been symbolic of holding some kind of candle, of showing he still had a place at the table, as her mother would put it, but it was more likely just to be a habit she found it hard to kick. Right now, kicking it felt good.

Just then, a scene from the nightmare flashed into her mind. She was chasing someone. She'd chased a few people in her time, so that wasn't unusual, but who was she chasing? It looked like Simon. He was on the run, and getting away from her until two squad cars drew up in his path, and two officers leapt out. Simon turned around, but then it wasn't him at all.

Then it was gone again. She slipped out of bed and stepped into the shower, relishing the warm water on her hair and shoulders. She opened a new shower gel and felt the tension evaporate as she breathed in the fragrance of lavender. It was one of the luxuries of the apartment that they all had their own bathrooms. She let the children make whatever mess they wanted to in theirs and she didn't have to set eyes on it. The whole flat was a luxury, really. It had always been Simon's choice rather than hers. It was decorated simply and greyly, but it had everything you could wish for: speakers built into the ceiling, under-floor heating, huge windows and a utility room that could deal with the whole family's washing at once. Last year, all this had seemed wrong, too much, not hers, but the bad feeling had lifted over time, and as she dried her hair with a towel and looked around her, she found herself liking what she saw.

What had changed? Last night had been her first date since the divorce, but you could hardly call it a date, going online undercover to flush out a missing woman. Still, she felt somehow lighter, more carefree than she had done twenty-four hours earlier.

She checked her phone and felt a pang of disappointment that there was no message from Finn, then told herself off for even checking. What on earth was she thinking? What had she been thinking last night letting him kiss her? But then if it brought him closer, helped her find Ruth . . .

Find Ruth. She'd almost forgotten Ruth in the heat of the moment, the whole point of her escapades, still missing, for all she knew held captive somewhere dreadful for coming across something she shouldn't have.

Ronnie flicked on the radio and sang along to an eighties anthem as she pulled on her clothes. *Living on a prayer. Halfway there.* She hoped so, but it felt more as if they were still floundering around in the shallows of two impossible investigations. Then as the music faded, the two-minute news bulletin was hammered out by a voice that obviously hadn't pre-read the content and sounded as if she was announcing the line-up for a music festival.

'*Police are continuing with their search for missing seven-year-old Liam Buckley. Liam was last seen leaving school with an unknown adult last Wednesday. Following a television appeal by his mother, detectives are now following a number of leads and have asked for anyone who has any information to phone the dedicated line . . .*'

Jules called just as she was shouting goodbye to the twins, who were arguing over the last bagel in the bread bin. She put her on speaker as she took the lift down to the ground floor.

'What's the latest?'

'Joe Buckley has an alibi.'

'A good one?'

'Corroborated, but not cast-iron.'

'How's that?'

'He was at work, but the client was in and out, can't confirm he was on site the whole afternoon.'

'Could he have made it here and back in the time he had?'

Jules inhaled deeply. 'It's possible. Only just, but possible.'

'Any footage of his car en route?'

'Not so far, still checking the cameras.'

'Can you trace his phone?'

'I can do better than that.'

'Go on. Don't keep me in suspense.'

'He's coming in. Happy to cooperate with us.'

'God, I wasn't expecting it to be that easy. How's Dawn bearing up?'

'She seemed pretty flustered at the idea that we were getting Joe in for questioning, to be honest. I don't think I'm Miss Popular in that caravan just now. And that's putting it mildly. She actually told me to leave yesterday.' Her voice trailed off as the signal fell out and came back. The crisp cold air as well as the shock news that the police were no longer welcome took Ronnie's breath momentarily. If *Jules* had been told to leave, things must have been bad. 'But I think I salvaged it somehow.'

'So they are letting us back there?'

'I think they just needed a cooling-off period. And Steve's coming round finally. He's calling off his vigilantes, which is a relief, and he'll be there when we next go round.'

'Maybe now we're on to Joe, he doesn't have to go after him himself?' Ronnie thought aloud, taking it all in and making some mental notes. 'Have we picked up the Land Rover on any of the other cameras?'

'Yes, and it's more complicated than we thought. The one I was telling you about, with no passenger in the front, was reported stolen the day before the abduction.'

'Whose is it?' Ronnie wrapped her scarf more tightly around her neck, as if to protect herself from the next piece of information.'

'Belongs to a family from Sussex. Stolen from right outside the property.'

'Any connection with Joe Buckley?'

'None that we can see.'

'Get the team on to that next – check with everyone at the property it was stolen from, including visitors and staff, and see if there are any links with Joe and who had keys or access to the keys. And I'm still not done with the possibility Dawn is lying, so get uniform to go house to house with her and Liam's photo. People remember an adult with a child; we're more likely to remember a child if we're told who we saw them with.'

'You think it's a revenge thing, sarge? You're sure Joe or Dawn has something to do with it, aren't you?'

Ronnie thought for a few seconds. 'I suppose that is where I'm going with it, yes. But the alternative is too grim to bear thinking about. It's been a week now. Nobody lasts a week.'

Joe Buckley was nervous. Nails bitten to the quick and anxious glances around the room told the story for him. Ronnie introduced herself and offered him a glass of water, which he gulped thirstily.

'Thanks for coming in, Joe. We appreciate it.'

'Anything I can do to help.' His voice was quieter than she'd expected, didn't seem to match his athletic build. His expression looked strained, frown lines ingrained on his forehead, and there was something strangely familiar about his face that she couldn't place. It must be a family resemblance with Dawn, but Ronnie felt she'd seen him somewhere before.

'Can you tell us exactly where you were last Wednesday afternoon between 3 and 5 p.m.?'

'At work. I'm a roofer. I was doing a job out at Sheldon Lacy that day.'

'Can anyone testify to that?'

'Brian, the owner, he was in most of the day. They've spoken to him, haven't they?'

'He went out in the afternoon, apparently, unluckily for you.'

Joe hung his head. 'Nothing I can do about that. I didn't leave the house. Surely you can tell that by the amount of work I got done.'

'You work on your own?'

'Yes, sometimes. I was that day.'

'No one to hold the ladder for you?'

He met her gaze. 'They have scaffolding for that.'

'Did you have your phone with you?'

'Yes. I'm sure you've already traced it, haven't you?'

Ronnie smiled. Another amateur sleuth trying to beat her at her own game. 'When was the last time you saw your son?'

Joe closed his eyes tight, then opened them, blinked several times, looking up at the strip light above them. 'Two years ago. His birthday. Mum took him to the zoo. I met them there.'

'Did Steve and Cara know?'

'No. At least, not at first. Then Liam said something. Or drew something. He likes drawing. He drew himself with me and Mum, and Cara must have asked who the third person was because after that I got a visit from Steve.'

'What kind of a visit? Warning you off?'

'And saying if it happened again, Cara would report me to the police for harassment.'

'Did you harass her?'

'It was her way of saying that she wasn't done with me, that she still had something on me that she could use.'

Ronnie replayed his words in her head. So there was more to Cara than met the eye, and maybe she hadn't put the sexual assault aside, as had seemed to be the case when they'd spoken. She was using it as collateral to keep Joe Buckley at bay. Clever girl.

'And after that, you never saw him again?'

'Never.' Joe faced her now and met her gaze, steely-eyed and unblinking. Ronnie saw a different side to him. A gritty, determined side that made the hairs on her neck stand on end.

'How does your mother feel about that?'

'About what?'

'You not seeing . . . your son.'

The words had rattled him because he visibly recoiled. 'She thinks it's pretty unfair, now you come to mention it.

I mean, no one's asking them to tell him I'm his dad, but an afternoon out with Uncle Joe shouldn't be such a big deal, should it?'

'I suppose it depends on your viewpoint,' said Ronnie. 'But you'd say she was unhappy with the situation, I take it.'

'She's fuming.' The words came out before he'd had a chance to think, and Ronnie repeated them back to him. He squirmed in his seat. 'Not like literally, not all the time.'

'But she'd probably like to redress the balance between the brothers in some way, maybe be the one to restore justice?'

Joe sank back, his unblinking blue eyes piercing hers. 'You'd have to ask her.'

Ronnie waited a beat in case there was more. Joe eventually averted his gaze to glance at his phone.

'Got to be somewhere?' she asked.

'Well, if you're not going to arrest me, I'm done here.'

Ronnie fixed her eyes on him one last time, but he was impenetrable. 'How do you feel, Joe?'

He flinched. 'What do you mean?'

'About your son going missing. It's just that, you don't seem upset, that's all. I'd have thought you'd be beside yourself.'

Joe's eyes flashed with fury. 'Are you suggesting I took him? Or that I don't give a shit about who did? Because you couldn't be more wrong. I loved that kid. I have no choice but to keep my distance and find out what's going on in his life through Mum, who makes it clear she's in charge of when I see him, if ever.'

'You said *loved*.' He had used the past tense. She was sure of it.

'Like I said, I'm done here.'

Ronnie slid a piece of paper across the table to him. 'Just one more question for you. Do you know anyone from this address?' He peered at it before shaking his head.

'No, but that's not saying much. Who knows where anyone lives nowadays? We're all online. I don't know anyone's address off by heart.'

'A car was stolen from outside their house last Monday.'

His threw her a look that was seething with anger. 'I didn't steal it, if that's what you're asking.'

'I'm glad to hear it.' Ronnie stood up and went to the door. 'Don't forget, if you think of anything else—'

'I'll be sure to call you.'

It was a hunch at this point, but as she held the door open for Joe Buckley to leave the building, something told her that he was more of a pawn in his mother's game than a child-thief. But either way, both Dawn and Cara had been less than honest about Liam's contact with his real father.

When she relayed the interview to Jules, she was even more certain that Joe was a sideshow to the main event.

'What do you think? Any connections with the house where the Land Rover was stolen from?'

'No luck contacting the family. We sent uniform down there but nobody home.'

'Hmm, so what next?'

'I think we need to keep pursuing other avenues, but don't rule him out yet.'

'What have you got down the other avenues so far?'

'Actually, there is something.' A shadow crossed her face. 'If Dawn is telling the truth, then this might be important.' She leaned over the file on the desk in front of them and found the photograph of the pages that the receptionist had handed over from the day of the abduction. She tapped her finger on a name. 'You see this list? There's one visitor to the school we can't trace. I mean, he was booked to come in and do some work but they aren't aware that he ever showed up. Didn't sign in and wasn't registered in the book as having arrived.'

'What kind of work was he doing?'

'Something outdoors apparently, maintenance, which would explain why he wouldn't have signed in.'

Ronnie looked at the name. It sounded foreign but that meant nothing. 'Where's he from, what company? Can't we find him that way?'

'That's the problem, sarge. The school office staff are on a job share and this one has annual leave until tomorrow, but I'll get on it then, I promise. She should be able to give me more details on who it was that never turned up.'

'Or did more than turn up . . .'

CHAPTER 23

Every day Martha tries to think of a plan, but they all come to nothing, because he's made sure of it. If they ever leave the house together, which is rare, she's locked in the kitchen and cuffed to a long chain attached to the ceiling, so she can still move about and cook and clean but not quite reach the door. Even if she could reach it, she is sure it will be locked. They aren't taking any chances.

But more often than not they don't leave the house, or Nate goes out on his own and she's locked in her room upstairs, where she can hear Aunt Esther moving around in the kitchen and Rex calling her because he's hungry or wants to play in the garden before his allotted playtime. He hasn't been to school since the last phone call with Ruth, which must be two months ago at least. The phone was supposed to be for emergencies, she explains to Rex when he's sad that they don't see Ruth any more. She broke her promise, using it to make calls. He's taken it well, but then he had no choice, and he knows how to play the game. Thank God he knows how to do that. Sometimes she hears him crying. It's so much worse when she can't go to him, but she covers her ears, sings to herself and imagines what life will be on the outside, one day when they are found.

The house only goes silent if there's a knock at the front door.

When it happened yesterday, the persistent knocking and shouting 'police' and something about a stolen car, she willed them to go round the back and look up, to see the bars on the windows, to work out what was going on and break down the door. But they went away again, as they always did.

She thinks about shouting, beating on the window, but if nobody hears her, then life could be over, and not just for her. They've shown the lengths they can go to and there's no reason to believe they won't do it again.

It was only two months ago that things were so different. She and Rex had the freedom of the house and garden, she helped him with his schoolwork and worked with Aunt Esther in the kitchen. She fed the animals, washed and ironed, and even chopped wood for the fire. They went to Assembly together and prayed at home every night as a family, asking for forgiveness, for guidance, for mercy on their lost sister Ruth, who was taken away by a vengeful but righteous God, setting an example to all those who dared to challenge the Truth.

Once, Rex had asked what Ruth had done that was so wrong, and Uncle Nate had wiped a tear from his eye. 'One day, you will know. Trust in God and he will keep you from the same fate.'

The games she used to play with Ruth were what started it all. She drew a picture that set Nate's anger on fire, Ruth took the blame, because she said she was older and should have known better, and from then on, they were separated, with Ruth eventually being moved down to the cellar at night *for her own good*. Martha didn't know what happened down there at first, because she didn't want to know, but one day, when Nate emerged from down the dark staircase all sweaty and red-faced, with a glazed look in his eye, it dawned on her what was happening and she was sick at the kitchen table. Aunt Esther screamed at her, and she never raised her voice. It was as if everything was crashing down on the family all at once.

It was around then that she and Ruth were taken out of school. The head teacher came to say goodbye on their last day, wishing them luck at their new place and saying how much they'd be missed, but there was no new place, and if anyone missed them, they never said anything, or came looking.

The next milestone was when Nate made a new home for Ruth in his shed. The cabin, which was what he liked to call it, was a better home for Ruth than the cellar, or so she thought at the time, because there was ventilation and a crack of light between the boards on the window, and it was a new start of sorts. Her botched attempts at helping Ruth escape could be forgotten and from the day of the transfer, which happened with Ruth bound hand and foot in chains for good measure, Martha decided to do everything possible to regain Nate and Esther's trust.

In return, she was given privileges like taking meals to Ruth when she was sick with the flu. There was no chance of a game or a chat. But seeing her was enough. To know she was alive was to know there was still a chance. To ask for anything more was too risky, and someone needed to be there to look after Rex.

CHAPTER 24

'He must be gorgeous if you're seeing him again already.'

Serena was in downward dog, speaking upside down.

'He's not bad. That's all I'm saying for now.' Ronnie flung open her wardrobe and held up one blouse after another in front of the mirror. 'God, I hate my clothes. I can't do party. It's work or lounge wear, nothing in between.'

'This one is great.' Serena lifted an arm with annoying ease, balancing on the other, and pointed at the least party-looking top.

'OK, that will have to do then.' Ronnie could feel her nerves building as she did up the buttons. She draped a pashmina this way and that around her shoulders, then hurled it back on to the bed and pulled a fleecy jacket out instead.

'Kids need to get their sports kit ready for tomorrow. Don't let them tell you they'll do it in the morning.'

'Roger that, captain.'

Ronnie turned round. 'God, am I that bad?'

'Not all the time. But turn it down a bit for the date. You don't want to scare him off.'

Ronnie checked her phone. 'I'm late. Don't forget the sports kit.'

Finn had texted her just after 4 p.m. in the end, after she had started to worry that he'd ghosted her. He'd been at work, he said, and hadn't had a second all day. He suggested a bar called Delilah's that had just opened in West Dean and Ronnie had agreed with enthusiasm, and with an undercurrent of dread because she wouldn't have endless chances. She needed to find a way of getting past his seductive exterior, and she hadn't yet worked out how that was going to happen, even less how she was going to regain control of herself in his presence. Just the thought of him sent a rush of butterflies to her stomach.

When she arrived, he was nowhere to be seen. She checked the time; she was five minutes late. Had he already left, thinking she was a no-show? She ordered a gin and tonic and opened her phone, determined not to be caught looking worried. *It doesn't matter if he doesn't turn up. This was always going to be a long shot,* she reminded herself, but behind that thought was a nagging self-doubt. Had she given herself away and scared him off? She opened a news app and let herself be calmed by the dull stories of cabinet reshuffles and climate change debate that dominated the headlines. It must have worked because the next thing she was aware of was a tap on the shoulder.

'Glad you've made yourself at home. I'm sorry I'm late.' Finn leaned in to kiss her on the cheek. The five o'clock shadow was more pronounced than the night before, emphasising his rugged charm and making Ronnie's heart miss a beat. *Don't fall for this man*, her brain shouted, so loud she was sure he must have heard.

'No worries, I'm just catching up with the day,' she mumbled, lost for the right words.

'I'll just get myself a beer.'

By the time he sat down in front of her at their corner table, she had regained most of her composure. She raised her glass to him. 'Cheers, and so happy to have met you,' she said, wondering where on earth those words had come from. They didn't sound like hers.

'Likewise,' came his laconic response. She wasn't sure if she was imagining it, but there was a coolness about him that made her distrust his words as well.

'I was just looking at holidays online,' she lied, hit by a sudden brainwave. 'Not sure about you, but I don't get to carry any days over to next year, so I've got to use it up and there's two whole weeks left of my annual leave, apparently.'

'Sounds like a good problem to have.' His face was unreadable, but she detected a shadow passing over it, so she dug deeper. At least she was following the script now, rather than imagining taking him home with her.

'How about you? Where do you normally go on holiday?' It was a safe question, but when he gave the answer, the butterflies in her stomach were overrun by a rush of nausea.

'Spain, normally. I have family there.' He had already downed half his pint, she noticed. Something had rattled him. He was avoiding her eyes.

'Lucky you,' she said, moving down a gear in her eagerness. There was a change in him since the night before.

'You been to Spain?' he asked, with what looked like forced interest.

'Loads of times.' The question caught her off guard and she blundered through her answer, realising it was too late to go back. 'My dad's side of the family is from Andalusia.'

'Oh? You half-Spanish then? I suppose you can see there's a bit of Mediterranean blood in you.' He had livened up. Was it curiosity or suspicion?

She avoided the question and laughed. 'I suppose you see it when you're looking for it, but we're a pretty diverse-looking society these days, so most people don't even register it until they know.'

'Are you allowed to tell me your surname, then?' He leaned forward, eyes twinkling.

Ronnie ran her finger around the rim of her glass. 'I'll tell you mine if you tell me yours.' She was flirting and playing for time simultaneously. Meanwhile her mind raced through the names of tennis players and South American dictators, struggling for something that would sound right and that she could imagine living with.

'Macaulay. Finn Macaulay. And my father, as you might have guessed, is from Ireland.'

'Not Scotland? I thought . . .' She regretted the challenge immediately, but it went unnoticed.

'Yes, it's a Scots name too. So, are you at liberty to share yours?'

'Fernandez.' It was the right language at least.

'Very romantic.'

Ronnie blushed and jangled the ice in her drink, immediately wishing she hadn't, as Finn signalled to the waitress straight away and ordered her another. Then he turned to her with a smile.

'So it's Brexit schmexit for us then, Veronica Fernandez. The world's our oyster. We can elope to Puerto Banús, sip champagne on a yacht, watch the world go by.'

Ronnie's shock must have been written all over her face because his expression changed.

'I wasn't serious.' He moved back to let the waiter place the drinks between them, then reached across the table for her hand. 'Look, I know it's early days, but—'

'For a proposal, yes I'd agree with that.' She averted her eyes and took a sip from her glass, momentarily emboldened by the warm alcohol in her throat. She wanted to run a mile, steer the conversation back to safety, but she was so close now, so close. 'You don't actually have a yacht, do you?'

It seemed like an eternity before Finn answered. He sat back and regarded her with an expression that said *Can I trust you?* and then rubbed his eyes before leaning forwards again.

'Yes, actually I do.'

It turned out to be a share in a yacht with his brother, who rarely went out there. The family had built a place up in the hills above Marbella, complete with infinity pool and views to die for. Then they had moved back to the UK, leaving the place empty. Ronnie was transfixed.

'I can't believe they don't use it. I mean, what about your brother? Doesn't he want it?'

The cloud passed over his face again. 'We're not on such good terms, to be honest.'

'Why's that?'

'No real reason, at least not one I want to go into now.'

'Fair enough. Sorry for asking.'

'Don't worry, you weren't to know.'

The conversation had suddenly taken a depressing turn. Finn was looking at his phone, typing something and frowning.

'All OK?'

'It's my mum.'

'Maybe her ears were burning. What does she want?'

'What she wants, or what she needs, is money.' His eyes met hers for a second, as if trying to work her out.

'Money?' Ronnie wanted to ask *what for* but the words got stuck in her throat. Finn read her mind.

'We had a cash-flow problem in the business, nothing major.' He was avoiding her gaze again. 'She was investing in the new project, then wanted out.'

'Is that connected with your brother?'

He looked up. 'Yes, sort of. He bad-mouthed me to her, and now she wants out, which leaves me high and dry with the suppliers . . .'

'How much do you need?'

'Ten thousand, or thereabouts. It's not the type of money you can borrow off a mate down the pub.'

Ronnie nodded, didn't dare speak, because it was playing out exactly as Baz had said it had with the other women. This was actually *him*, the dating-app catfish who had taken cash off everyone who fell for his roguish charm and hard-luck stories, and she'd just proved herself to be no better than these women she had openly derided for their stupidity. She had been just as entranced as they had by his good looks and easy manner, the piercing blue eyes and strong shoulders.

A minute had passed. He was still typing furiously into his phone, as Ronnie deliberated what to do next. But seconds later, her mind was made up for her.

'Listen, Veronica. I know this will sound strange to you, as we hardly know each other anyway, so . . .' He stared into the dregs of his lager, shaking the glass gently to make the liquid swirl one way and then the other. 'The thing is . . . Oh Jesus, I'm really not sure how to say this.'

'Give me one minute, sorry.' In a second, Ronnie was up and heading for the loos before he had a chance to go on. She needed to make a plan. It was coming together, he was about to ask her for the cash and she hadn't even planned her response. She had been so sure it wasn't him, so taken in by the way he looked at her, that this had come as a shock. She needed to prepare herself. In the cubicle, she locked the door and sat down on the loo seat. *Think, think.* It wouldn't do to agree, offer to write a cheque on the spot, but neither should she express too much shock. She would need details on what the investment was for, the repayment terms, interest rate. It was a business chat they might even save for another day. It would mean dragging out the process, but if it brought her closer to finding Ruth, then surely it would be worth it. She flushed the toilet, washed her hands and reapplied her lipstick. She needed him to want to see her again. She needed to look like someone who might be asked out on a third date.

But the lipstick was wasted, as was the planned response, because when she arrived back at the table, there was a ten-pound note under his empty glass and Finn was gone.

He couldn't have made it far. She kicked herself for not knowing if he'd driven or not as she jumped into her Audi and started the engine. What had got into him? Her heart pounded with the thought of what the repercussions could be. She had sworn after the last time she wouldn't take risks with her career by taking matters into her own hands, but what had begun as a side hustle had become something else entirely. She had followed her gut again without thinking it through.

Dusk was falling as she pulled out of the car park, indicating right. It was a fifty-fifty guess, but going left only led to the industrial estate, and a few council houses that had escaped the wrecking ball when the new dual carriage way was built. The traffic was light. He drove a blue Golf Cabriolet. That was it. She remembered him saying he had a thing for convertibles – even in midwinter he liked the feel of the cold wind in his ears. Tonight was cooler than it had been. If his roof was down then he'd be easy to spot. If she could follow him to where he lived, even better. At least she'd have a clue about where Ruth had been that night.

She had almost given up when she pulled up at the lights on the edge of the village to find him two cars in front, indicating right in the filter lane. She glanced in the rear-view mirror and changed lanes to stay behind him. She knew these lights. The right-turn filter led across a level crossing. If the barrier came down between the two of them, she'd never catch up. The lights began to flash just as he was crossing the tracks, and the car between them suddenly slowed, indicating left to change back to the lane going straight ahead.

'Come *on.*' Ronnie willed the car to move, and edged past, just making it under the barrier before it closed. It was close. She'd taken a risk and her heart was pounding in response, but she had barely found herself safely through than she realised that the danger wasn't over. His car was parked at an angry angle, half blocking the other lane so she couldn't have driven past him if she'd wanted to. The crossing gate behind her blocked any possibility of reversing out.

The driver door opened and Finn was coming towards her. She wound down her window. *Show no fear*, a voice in her head said, but it was easier said than done. His face was like thunder. She recoiled, reached for the window button but his hand was on it, holding it down. His other hand reached inside the car, grabbed the collar of her jacket. She felt his knuckles on her neck.

'Why the fuck are you following me?'

'Why the fuck did you walk out like that?' She wrenched his hand off her and met his gaze, fury mounting inside her.

He leaned down and stared right at her with an expression of something between disgust and amusement. This wasn't the same man she'd let kiss her the night before. It couldn't be. 'Because I wanted to leave. It's not going to work. I don't want to see you again.'

Ronnie was quick with a reply. 'You could have just said so.'

'I don't have to do things your way.'

'You don't, but I'd like an explanation.'

He glanced at the road. No other cars in sight. No witnesses.

'I've changed my mind.'

'Again? You're getting good at that. Just tell me what's going on.'

Had she gone too far? The chances of finding anything out from him were dwindling by the second. She needed to change her approach, go gently. She looked him in the eyes with what she hoped was an invitation to open up.

He looked right back at her for a few seconds as if sizing her up, working out what her motive was, before releasing his grip on her collar and standing back, clasping both hands behind his head.

'Look, maybe it wasn't the right thing to do, but the last girl, woman, I went on a date with turned out to be a psychopath. I know it's us guys who always get labelled the troublemakers but she was something else.' He paused, as if he'd caught himself going too far, saying too much. The train thundered past before he continued. 'I'm sorry to let you down, Veronica, but we can't see each other again. Just think of it as trust issues or something.'

'Tell me about the psychopath.'

'Another time.'

'What happened?'

He spoke with his eyes on the level crossing. The train had passed and the barriers would go up any second. 'She broke into my place. I thought it was a burglar, we had a fight and she ran off. I hope I never see her again.'

The barriers behind them went up, revealing a queue of cars waiting to pass through. A second later, he was back in his car, engine revving into the night.

Ten minutes had passed by the time Ronnie turned into her designated parking space, switched off the engine and put her head in her hands. A huge wave of disappointment and frustration swept over. It was a failure on two counts, not just to seduce him but to follow him home, get his address, stand a chance of finding Ruth Jones. She had tailed him too closely, not given enough thought to what his own intentions might be. The last thing she had expected was to be dumped just like that in the middle of the street in the dark. On the plus side, she'd got him to admit there had been a woman in his life that had caused trouble – a psychopath, he claimed, but the term was so overused it was as good as useless.

She wasn't intending to tell Serena any of it, but she was still up and desperate to know how the date had gone. Ronnie fudged it and said he'd told her politely that they wouldn't be taking things any further. Serena was baffled.

'How could anyone turn down my stunning sister?'

'I know, it's hard to believe, isn't it?' Ronnie was grateful for the chance to make light of it.

'I suppose you're lucky it wasn't by text,' she offered.

'That would have been more normal, at least.' Ronnie poured herself a red wine. At least she had got herself a surname, if it was genuine, and she could ID him. There wasn't much else to crow about.

She went to the window and looked down at the park, where the wind was picking up, making the trees sway and flurries of leaves fall in the lamplight.

'Any news on the missing boy?' Serena ventured.

'We're looking at visitors to the school. There's one of them left to question. Then we're having a meeting with Liam's family in the morning. We need to get to the bottom of what's happening with Steve's brother.'

'I thought you said he had an alibi?'

'There's a chance he could have an accomplice. He's not stupid. He knows he'd be in the frame as soon as someone got wind of his role in the whole thing. If there's any way we can connect him to the stolen car that picked up Dawn, I think we'll be close.'

'You must be hoping he's involved because it means Liam's safely in the hands of family.'

'I suppose I am. It makes sense. And the thought that it was a stranger is worse.'

'Trust your gut, Ron. It's the only way.'

'But as Dad used to say, and as I have learned to my cost, sometimes gut feeling isn't enough.'

She spent most of the night tossing and turning, going over how she could have done things differently. She shouldn't have followed him. She could have just let him make his excuses over the phone. By the time he calmed down he might have thought up a reason for his departure, realised there might still be some hope of getting his hands on her money and there might still have been a chance of it working. Or had something happened to make him change his mind? What sleep she did get was peppered with aborted dreams, and she was grateful when her phone alarm sounded at seven the next morning.

CHAPTER 25

The caravan site was busier than last time. A handful of children were heading off to school, swinging book bags and rucksacks, and eyed Ronnie and Jules warily as they pulled up on the verge. The few parents among them seemed to be herding their offspring with closer attention than was normal. The fence that formed a barrier between the site and the rest of the neighbourhood was festooned with posters of a smiling, uniformed Liam Buckley flapping in the wind. A few curious bystanders were hovering in the street outside, who could have been press or just local residents. It wasn't obvious these days. Ronnie and Jules weren't about to publicise their arrival to anyone. It had been touch-and-go, but they had eventually been granted a visit, despite the change in the air since suspicion had fallen on Steve's brother.

Ronnie was scrolling through her phone when Jules switched off the engine. She could feel her eyes on her before she spoke, more hesitant than usual.

'Sorry for saying, sarge, but you don't look yourself today. Is everything OK?'

'Just a bit of a sleepless night.' Ronnie kicked herself for letting it show. She should have paid more attention to applying concealer. 'Can't stop thinking about Liam and the agony of days going by.'

Jules nodded slowly, seemingly unconvinced.

Ronnie slid the phone back into her pocket. 'I was just seeing if there was any news on Ruth Jones. Apparently they've found her work van.'

'I thought you'd done that, spotted it going up the M1?'

'Yes, and now they seem to have apprehended the thieves, or joy-riders, as they turned out to be. They stole it from Church Street in West Dean last Wednesday afternoon. It was left with the door ajar, keys in the ignition. They're arguing it can't be stealing if you don't break in.'

Jules smiled briefly, then fixed her eyes on Ronnie, who met her gaze with a trace of reluctance.

'You didn't want to take this case, did you, sarge? You're still trying to get back to the missing woman.'

Ronnie felt her stomach turn over in dread. Did Jules really believe her heart wasn't in it?

'Not at all. I'm giving this everything I've got.' She was. Officially, at least.

'But you'd rather we didn't have to choose, right?'

The words hit home with bullseye accuracy. Perhaps there was no choice but to give an honest answer. 'I completely understand that a missing child should always take priority over a missing adult, but I'd rather we were able to give the same resources to both, if I'm honest, yes.'

Jules had already got out of the car and slammed the door, or shut it, but Ronnie had heard a slam, so she followed her to where she stood leaning against the boot with her arms folded. One of the schoolchildren yelled something at another, who hurled a missile at him, to the amusement of his friends, but the fight seemed to subside as the group disappeared around the corner.

Ronnie's phone buzzed and she pressed the speaker button. 'Overton, what have you got?'

'Sarge? House-to-house have come up with something you need to see.'

'What is it? We're just about to go and talk to the Buckleys about brother Joe and his contacts.'

'Ah, well you might want to talk to them about another thing now.'

She checked nobody was in earshot. 'Fire away. DC Mayer is with me.'

'Right, so the girl who makes cakes for the café outside the railway station, called Pit Stop, she recognised our description of Dawn Buckley, said a woman matching that description was in there last Wednesday having hot chocolate with a boy of about eight or nine. She was on a delivery and waiting a couple of minutes for them to sign her forms. She said the boy seemed very excited about where they were going, and the woman was promising him things. She couldn't hear what. The bit she did hear was the woman telling him to shush, and that the car would arrive soon. He kept drawing things on the window, steaming it up with his breath and writing stuff, sticking the sugar spoon in his mouth and putting it back in the bowl, you know, messing about.'

'Did she see the car that arrived?'

'No, she wasn't there long enough to see them go. She didn't think anything of it, even after Liam was in the news, because it looked like a granny with her grandson and apparently only old men steal children from schools.'

'I suppose that's the kind of assumption that makes the public useless at detective work.'

'You're right, sarge.' He seemed surprised, as if she'd just explained for the first time how the water level rose when you got into the bath.

'Right, I suppose that gives us more to talk to Dawn about, although I'm inclined to wait until we have more before we do that. Have you shown the owner the pictures of Dawn and Liam?'

'The owner said she couldn't identify them categorically, way too many people coming in and out all day, but the boy looked about right and she thought the woman was wearing a fur gilet when she sat down. She remembered thinking it was a good thing she had been wearing a raincoat on top or she'd smell like a wet dog.'

'Nice image. Nothing else? No CCTV?'

'Nothing, and the table's been cleaned a dozen times since then.'

'What about the sugar spoon?'

'What?'

'The sugar spoon he was putting in his mouth. If the owner of the café didn't see what he was doing, it might not have been put through the dishwasher.'

'You're saying, his DNA . . .'

'Can you get over there and check it out?'

'Sure.' Overton hung up, and Ronnie thought aloud.

'Sooooo, perhaps we aren't done with you yet, Joe Buckley, if your mother's back in the picture. Suddenly we might be getting somewhere.'

Jules inhaled and seemed to hold her breath.

'You're about to tell me it needs careful handling,' said Ronnie, shooting her a look. 'I'm not going to mention the café until we get a DNA result. I promise to remain open-minded until we have hard evidence.'

'Good, because . . .' Jules was about to say something when she inclined her head towards the scene ahead of them. 'That doesn't look like someone who'd let a child suck on a sugar spoon and draw on the windows.'

Dawn Buckley was standing on the steps of the caravan, cleaning the front door vigorously with a cloth. Jules had a point, but Ronnie was already beyond it.

'Let's not let that cloud our judgement. Serial killers can be very good at cleaning up after themselves.'

The caravan door slammed shut again in response. But they were still some twenty metres away, so there was no chance of being overheard.

'Sarge! You just said you were open-minded.'

Ronnie ducked under a line of washing that hung between the Buckleys' caravan and another, less salubrious version a few metres away. 'That *is* open-minded, not making any automatic assumptions based on behaviour.' She checked to see that Jules wasn't misunderstanding her. 'Look, we aren't going to point the finger at Dawn or anyone else without the evidence behind us. I promise it will be by the book. We need her to come to the station to put together an ID for the Land Rover driver anyway, so with some expedited lab work on the spoon, we'll have our answers. Let's go and find out what's been going on. I'm looking forward to meeting Steve and finding out a bit more about what's behind this competitive relationship with his brother.'

The door opened before she had a chance to knock.

'You'd better be bringing some good news.' Dawn let them pass but her words stung Ronnie like wasps. She was wearing her fur gilet again and her face was the same picture of distrust.

Cara was sitting at the table nursing a cup of tea. She managed a smile. 'Help yourself, there's more in the pot,' she said, her voice barely audible, and they took their seats opposite her at the table.

'Is Steve around?' Ronnie asked. 'I was hoping to have a chat with him.'

Dawn groaned. 'What good's that going to do, exactly? If there was anything to say, he'd have said it.'

'He's on his way,' Cara whispered. 'He knows you're coming; he said he'd be here. He promised.' She didn't look as if she believed what she was saying, but they had time.

Jules poured them both tea and smiled at Cara. 'Thanks for this. Chilly morning out there. A bit fresher since all that rain, at least.'

Cara half-smiled back, but then her face fell into darkness again. 'I haven't been out, not for days. I feel frozen to the spot, paralysed.'

'I know.' Jules looked at her intently. 'You're doing so well. As you know, we're putting all our resources into finding your boy.'

Cara looked up at her with imploring eyes, while Dawn started on the washing-up.

'What's happened? What have you found out?'

Ronnie took over the reins to bring some positivity back. 'We are following a few interesting lines of enquiry and hoping they will bring some news very soon.'

Cara opened her eyes wide. 'What kind of news?'

Jules touched her shoulder. 'Only good news, Cara, there's no reason to fear it will be bad. We're making progress, proper progress.'

Cara gave Jules her best effort at a smile as Ronnie continued.

'As you know, we've talked to the teacher, to the parents and most of the children in Liam's class, as well as to almost all the visitors to the school last Wednesday.'

'Almost?' Cara looked half terrified, half hopeful.

'There's just one person who was booked in to do some work on the grounds who we're not sure turned up but that's in hand. We've also had officers going house-to-house, and, of course, there was the TV appeal, which generated a lot of publicity—'

'But no leads,' interrupted Dawn, scrubbing at a baking tray. 'You've achieved absolutely nothing, as far as I can see. I'm not sure why we ever even told you he was missing. Might have done a better job on our own.'

Ronnie exchanged glances with Jules, who adopted her unique de-escalation voice.

'I know it might feel like that, Dawn. I also know a lot of people don't have faith in the police. Every mistake we make is magnified a million times by the press, quite rightly most of the time, so we have a tough job on our hands regaining that public trust. But all I can promise you now, hand on heart, is that we are doing everything in our power to help your family.' She looked at Cara, then back at Dawn. 'We will not stop until Liam is found.'

Dawn looked almost taken aback. Her hands hung in the air above the steaming sink, bubbles of Fairy Liquid popping and dropping into the water like snow melting off a roof. 'Thank you,' she said. Then added, as a quiet after-thought: 'I'm sorry if I came across all huffy. I know you're doing what you can.'

Cara threw her a grateful glance, then her face changed. 'He's here,' she said, eyes on the door. 'Steve's home.'

Jules was up first, reintroducing herself, thanking him for being there and asking how he was bearing up, while Ronnie took a second to slide along the bench and get to her feet. It always felt like a disadvantage meeting someone when you were at a lower level than them.

When she turned to face Cara's husband, her blood turned cold.

As their eyes met, the pieces of a jigsaw puzzle she didn't know she was part of fell into place and the truth landed with a crash that made her heart stop. The man standing before her wasn't Steve Buckley at all. Or rather, today he was Steve

Buckley, but yesterday, last night, and the night before that, he had been going by the name of Finn Macaulay.

As the other two women looked at him for a response, Ronnie struggled to regain her composure. No wonder she had recognised Joe from somewhere. Their eyes were the same piercing blue and they both smiled more on the left side than the right.

Steve had quickly averted his eyes and was pouring himself a cup of tea from the pot. He set the cup down on the table, put his hands in his pockets, said he was 'up and down, you know, what did they expect'. His eyes darted from Cara to Ronnie and back again. He leaned against the worktop and addressed Ronnie directly.

'So what have you got? I hope it's good.'

She met his challenging gaze with all the courage she could muster. They had both lied, after all.

'Well, there has been a development we wanted to talk to you all about.' She left a pause long enough to bring the power back where she wanted it. 'It's about your brother.'

Cara seemed unsurprised. Dawn just raised her eyebrows and looked at her son.

'What about him?' Steve's expression was icy.

Jules took up the story, which gave Ronnie a chance to scrutinise Dawn for signs of discomfort.

'In view of the fact that Joe is Liam's biological father, we have questioned him in relation to the abduction.'

Steve's expression was unchanged, except for a twitch at the corner of his mouth. From Dawn, there was a sharp intake of breath.

'You can't arrest him. He had nothing to do with it.' Her eyes darted to where Cara was sitting, looking down at her hands. 'Cara? What have you told them? Cara?'

Cara just twisted her wedding ring and kept her head down.

Jules dealt with the interruption without batting an eyelid. 'Joe isn't under arrest. His alibi holds up.' She looked around to assess the impact of her findings but none was evident. 'But this doesn't mean he wasn't involved in some way. We're still looking into that.'

All three of the Buckleys were silent. Jules took it as a cue to carry on.

'The next issue was the vehicle used to kidnap you, Dawn.' She turned to Dawn. 'We traced it through the traffic cameras.'

'So you've actually seen this Land Rover on CCTV?' Steve asked. His eyes narrowed in distrust. Or it could have been fury that they weren't progressing fast enough. It was a normal reaction from any parent of a missing child to be frustrated. His boy had been gone a week and with every day that went by, the chances of finding him were shrinking. 'Surely you know who was driving it then? Don't you have face ID for situations like this?'

'No clear ID on the driver from the footage we've got so far, so as Dawn was the only person to have sight of them, we are going to need her to come down to the station to see if she can help us out with that.'

'What do you mean, an ID parade, like on TV?' Dawn looked alarmed.

'Not exactly. To start with, we need you to help produce an e-fit, which is basically a picture constructed out of the features you remember. It won't take long and it could make all the difference.'

Dawn looked at Cara and Steve for support. 'Do I have to do this?' She pulled her furs more tightly around her.

'If it helps find Liam, yes, Mum, you have to do this.' Steve's tone was authoritative, stern even. Then he turned back to Ronnie, who forced herself to meet his gaze. The discomfort refused to dissipate. 'Who's it registered to? Won't that solve the mystery?'

She summoned all her strength to answer him as normally as possible. This wasn't the time to let emotion get the better of her. 'The car was stolen ten days ago from an address in Sussex. Whether Joe had any connection to the family, we don't know. Police have been down there but there appears to be nobody residing at the property.' Residing? She never said *residing*.

Steve's expression hardened as he took it all in, and relief flooded Ronnie as Jules took over the questions.

'We were also wondering what you'd decided in relation to the reward.' There was no easy way of bringing that ball back into play, but Jules was the one for the job. 'Not that there's any pressure to do so of course.'

'No reward,' said Dawn quietly. 'I don't think we can put a price on our boy.'

Cara looked up at Steve, clearly needing his intervention, which she got. 'Firstly, that's not what we're doing here and, secondly, I don't think it's going to be your choice, Mum.'

Dawn stared at the floor.

'My parents want to go ahead with it,' ventured Cara, with a tentative glance at her mother-in-law.

Ronnie took a deep breath. She wasn't convinced it was the right route, but she suspected it wouldn't be her choice in the end. 'How much?'

Cara seemed to hesitate. She didn't want to tell Dawn. Ronnie let the question go.

'It's up to you whether you go ahead with it but, as I said, it can flood the lines with phoney calls, and make it harder to get hold of good information.'

'Can we do another appeal but together this time? Me and Steve?' Her expression was imploring, hard to resist. She took hold of Steve's hand and held it to her face, and Ronnie felt her insides turn over in embarrassment.

Jules exchanged dubious glances with Ronnie. 'I'm sure we can arrange that, if you're sure it's what you want to do.'

'It is. It's what we both want.'

'I'll make a quick call, see what we can do,' said Jules, stepping outside on to the veranda and pulling the door shut behind her.

Ronnie tried to imagine Lydia's reaction and decided it would most likely be a positive one. If the offer of a reward brought Liam home, then that would be a perfect ending. If it didn't, at least they would have tried. It would be a tough call to say it was categorically a bad idea.

Cara was rubbing her temples with her fingers. 'I can't stop going there in my head,' she said, almost trance-like.

'In the playground after school, imagining who it was that came for Liam, who he didn't mind running off with. I'm trying to see their face, but when I try, it just melts away.'

Ronnie wished Jules was there to say the right thing. 'Don't torture yourself, Cara. Whoever took him isn't going to get away with it. We will get there. I know it's taking a long time – every day must seem like too long – but we will get there.'

Jules came back indoors with a smile on her face.

'All approved. We'll send a car for you this afternoon, around 3 p.m. And Dawn, if you wouldn't mind coming with us now, we need to put together an e-fit of the driver, based on anything you can remember.'

Dawn nodded slowly.

'OK, I need to go back to work, but I'll be back here by three.' Steve's voice was stern, emotionless.

Jules was walking ahead to the car with Dawn when Steve caught up with Ronnie.

'What the fuck?' He turned to face her, fuming.

Ronnie drew back in surprise, then said with as much calm as she could muster, 'That's just what I was thinking.'

'You're *police*? What other lies did you tell me?' His voice was hushed, but furious. His hands clenched and unclenched at his sides.

'You're *married*. Doesn't that count as a lie?' She turned to face forwards. It was easier than watching fury sweep over Steve Buckley's whole being.

He ignored her question and responded with another. 'And you wonder why nobody round here trusts the police?'

Ronnie stopped and gathered her courage to stare at him, hating him for what he'd done to his wife, and what he'd nearly done to her. 'What do you think Cara would have to say if she knew you were looking for women online, seducing them with stories of yachts on the Med, charming them into handing over their cash before you leave them high and dry?'

'I never did that to you.'

'But you've done it to others, and you'd have given me the same treatment if you hadn't got spooked.'

'I didn't get spooked.'

Ronnie looked ahead to where Jules was waving from the car. She held up one index finger and turned back to Steve.

'What then?'

'That wasn't how it was supposed to go.'

'How was it supposed to go, exactly?'

He gritted his teeth, looked right and left and said, 'Can we talk about this later?'

'Yes, if you show me where you and your psychopath friend had your disagreement.' There. It was out. She held her breath for a second before daring to say her name. 'Ruth, wasn't it?'

His face lurched forwards towards hers. 'I don't have to tell you anything.'

'I wouldn't advise that,' said Ronnie, coolly. 'You're already good for an assault charge, and that's before we go into the other women you've duped. If I were you, I'd play ball, it might give you half a chance of seeing Liam again.'

'What do you mean?'

'I mean,' said Ronnie, stopping to face him, 'that when Liam comes home, he might prefer his dad not to be doing time at Her Majesty's pleasure. Do you understand what I'm saying?'

'DS Delmar, we need to head back!' Jules's voice could just be heard above the wind in the trees between them. Ronnie gave her a thumbs up.

'Tonight. Seven-ish. I'll text you the address,' Steve said.

'Thank you . . . Steve.' The name sounded strange on her lips. 'Your secret is safe with me. For now.' She didn't look to see his reaction.

CHAPTER 26

Ronnie had been right about it not taking long. The e-fit procedure was over in minutes, and Dawn emerged despondent with a touch of *I told you so*.

'It all happened so fast. I don't know how I was supposed to remember what the bloke looked like.'

It had been a long shot, but worth a try.

'Can I go home now?' She was pulling her gilet around her again, finding security in its snugness. Jules's phone beeped and she stepped out of the room. Ronnie watched her go, then turned back to Dawn.

'In a minute. Actually, there are a couple of questions I have for you. Something came up in the house-to-house and I wondered if you could help clear it up.'

Dawn looked up, nervous, then calm, as if checking herself, but Ronnie had spotted the first reaction.

'Have you ever been to a café by the station called the Pit Stop?'

'I know it. I have been there once or twice, yes.' Her face gave nothing away.

'When was the last time you went there?'

She paused to think. 'Must have been a couple of years ago. I was waiting for someone to come in on a train and I was early, as usual, so . . .'

Ronnie sat back, twisting her pen between her thumbs and index fingers. 'We have a witness who claims to have seen someone matching your description sitting in the window of that café last Wednesday, the day that Liam disappeared, with a boy of Liam's age.'

Dawn's expression changed to one of fury in a second. 'You what? But I wasn't there. I swear I wasn't there. You don't believe a word of what I've told you, do you?'

'We have to look into all the evidence, Dawn. This isn't a campaign against you.'

'Well you could have fooled me. How dare you even begin to think that a grandmother could steal her own grandchild. How could you?' Her hand came down on the table with a thump and Ronnie gave her a few seconds to let the fury subside before continuing.

'What if you were doing it for what you thought was a good reason?'

'What are you suggesting?'

'Like taking him to see his biological father. After all, Joe's your son, you love him and you want him to be happy. I've got kids. I'd want them to be treated fairly. I'd want them to have contact with their own children.'

'You'd want all of us stuck on the other side of town in a shitty tower block, that's what you'd want,' Dawn retorted. 'But some of us know how to stand up for our rights and won't be pushed around by people who are supposed to be keeping us safe. Now if you're done here, I want to get home. You've lured me here under false pretences, shown me a bunch of faces I've never seen in my life, just to throw this one at me. And I can tell you that everything I've told you is the truth. I had nothing whatsoever to do with whatever has happened to poor Liam. It wasn't me your snitch saw in that café window. And you'd best get out there and find out who it was.'

Ronnie watched her climb into the patrol car with Overton and replayed Dawn's words in her head, letting her assumptions fall away and her thoughts regroup in a new order. It was still possible that Joe had just wanted to spend some time with his 'nephew', but that didn't necessarily mean he'd go to any lengths to achieve it. Ronnie's conviction that she and Joe were collaborating on some level was fading.

Jules was back. By the look on her face, she had news.

'What is it?' Ronnie asked, blankly, 'Because Dawn has just flatly denied being at the café, and it has rather shaken my belief that she was involved.'

'Of course she's denying it. Since when do we just believe the suspect who says they didn't do it?'

'You're right. We don't, but there was something about the vehemence that I recognised as genuine. Don't ask me how.'

Jules nodded. 'OK, I get that, and we need to prioritise lines of enquiry on some basis, so if you're as sure as you can be . . .'

'I am, but it would help if we had something new.' She looked expectantly at Jules. 'Looks like you might have found it already.'

'Aha, you guess right, sarge. I have something for you. Look at this. They've found the untraceable man on the visitor list at Holly Lodge.'

Ronnie took her phone and pinched the screen to magnify the photograph. *Davor Kovac* meant nothing to her. But in the next picture was another name that she recognised.

Jules took the phone back and scrolled further down the screen. 'Apparently, they came to check on the planting of the sensory garden in the field that the school shares with the local park. It's the easiest way in to access the site, which is why he drove through the school to get there. That's the make and model of the van.' She showed Ronnie the screen again.

Ronnie often despaired of her brain's filing system, where words, places, scenes were stored away haphazardly, refusing to identify themselves when called for. But on this occasion the link came through loud and clear. The insignia on the van was the place Baz had visited, the people who had never had their van returned by Ruth but weren't in a hurry to report it. This changed everything and gave more credence to Dawn's assertion that she wasn't involved. The van that came to Liam Buckley's school on the day of his disappearance belonged to Madison's Nurseries.

Lydia was pacing the floor of her office when Ronnie tapped on the door. She appeared to be speaking on a conference call, and the voices were partially audible through the thin walls. *Running out of options . . . Protocol . . . Keeping costs down . . . Tightening our belts.* Variations on a theme, Ronnie thought. But in what context? Lydia motioned for Ronnie to wait outside.

Ronnie perched on a desk as phones rang and police officers moved about the open-plan office. It had undergone so many changes, even in the five years she'd been there, and each change was another cut in the budget. Losing the kitchen, then the report-writing room – what would be next? There wasn't much more they could shave off the current operation before it became unworkable. What this meant for her and Lydia, let alone Baz, Jules and the rest of the Halesworth team, didn't bear thinking about. If the station was closed, where would she go? And with Baz doing his sergeant's exams, where would *he* go, and where would that leave her in the resulting bottleneck?

Lydia was smiling now, through gritted teeth, nodding in defeat, saying, 'Yes . . . I understand . . . I will give it some more thought,' and then the call was over. She sank into her chair and waved Ronnie in. As cuts had been made over the years, Lydia's office had survived, like Dr Who's Tardis in the chaos of time travel, and shutting the door behind her made the stress fall from Ronnie's shoulders.

'Good to get in here just to escape the noise, or most of it,' said Lydia, reading her mind.

'Yes, but someone needs to be able to concentrate round here.' Ronnie wasn't sure if she sounded sarcastic. Should she clarify? 'Sorry, ma'am, I didn't mean—'

'Don't worry, you're right, someone does. Working conditions aren't ideal for the rest of you. How are you finding it?'

Ronnie was surprised by the question. Nobody, least of all Lydia, asked her how she was finding things. 'Fine. I mean, I have the luxury of cubicle-style privacy, so that's something, and I don't actually hear any complaints from the other staff.' It was almost true. Some of the uniformed officers would joke about how much snuggling up with detectives they'd be prepared to do to save space, but it was mostly harmless banter.

Lydia looked up. 'Thanks, DS Delmar, that's good to hear. I'm not sure how long that will be the case, however.'

'Something to do with your phone call, I'm guessing?'

'You guess right. There are plans to make more changes around here, and it's not going to go down well. Halesworth as we know it may not be long for this world.'

A chill ran down Ronnie's spine and she held on to the back of the chair in front of her. 'Closing down the station?'

'Not closing down, exactly, not yet. It's all to be discussed and negotiated, and I don't have a seat at the table, not one that carries any weight, at least.'

'Anything I can do to help?' Ronnie couldn't imagine there was, but it was worth showing willing, if there was going to be a priority queue for being thrown off the sinking ship.

Lydia gave her a benevolent look, and Ronnie wondered if this was a new side to her boss, or whether she'd been too blinkered to see it until now. Blinkered like the women Finn Macaulay had charmed into handing over their savings. The thought of him caused her stomach to lurch again and reminded her of the next task on her list.

'I'm sure that resolving our current caseload quickly and efficiently won't go unnoticed,' Lydia said, looking out of the window where the sky was still a heavy shade of grey.

Ronnie took it all in. The message was clear and unambiguous. 'Understood,' she said quietly. It was like being told to try harder when you were already trying your hardest. 'And on that note, the Buckley TV appeal is going out in half an hour so I need to get down there. They're announcing the reward.' She hesitated before asking Lydia if she'd care to join them. It would be a shame not to capitalise on the love in the room and make the most of the goodwill wafting between the pair of them, but then she didn't want to risk losing it. What if it evaporated the moment they stepped out into the hubbub of the main office and into the corridor? She wanted Lydia to stay as she was at this moment, not just her superior officer but her colleague, maybe even a friend.

She glanced at the time on her phone, just as Baz tapped on the door.

'Ah, DC Munro, can it wait a minute?' Lydia gave him a smile that was almost flirtatious.

'Actually, I do have some new information that he needs, so . . .' Ronnie looked from one of them to the other, unsure whether it was her place to contradict Lydia, and slightly troubled by the love in the room taking an unexpected turn. It hadn't occurred to her that there was chemistry between Lydia and Munro.

'How so?' Lydia's tone had already changed. 'Last time I checked, you were working on separate cases, and you were about to nail our Dawn Buckley for abducting her own grandson, pending the DNA result. And getting her to produce an e-fit. What happened with all that?'

'Only a very basic picture, I'm afraid. The visual was too brief, but, to be honest, we didn't expect anything. And she has absolutely refuted any suggestion that it was her in the window of the Pit Stop café.'

'Not surprising. But if you're convinced of it, where are you taking this next?'

'We haven't closed down the other avenues of investigation, ma'am. And it seems . . .' Ronnie's eyes were on Baz as he edged into the room, shutting the door behind him. 'It seems that there's a link between the two cases.'

'What? Between Liam Buckley and Ruth Jones?' Lydia seemed more irritated than pleased by the idea of a connection. 'How on earth could that be?'

'It was a bit of a surprise, to be honest. Davor Kovac, who works for the same company Ruth works for, Madison's Nurseries, was a regular visitor to the school grounds. They were setting up a sensory garden in an open space they share with Morley Park and he was due to come in that day for some regular maintenance work.'

'And did he come in that day?'

'His visit wasn't recorded, just booked in for 3 p.m., so within minutes of the time Liam was abducted.'

'But if it wasn't recorded, he can't have actually turned up, surely?'

'The visit might not have been recorded on the log – human error, maybe, or he didn't go via the reception area, *or* he may have slipstreamed another vehicle when the barrier went up. But before you ask, we have no CCTV for that entrance. The camera wasn't working. We're looking into sabotage on that. But with so many cameras out of action, it seems unlikely.'

Lydia's face fell. Baz stepped forward and leaned on the chair to get her attention, like a father promising a little girl a new teddy bear for Christmas. 'I'll get back over to Madison's. I had a feeling that all wasn't as it should be in that place. That Davor guy was hiding something, I was absolutely convinced.'

Lydia's face changed as she turned back to Ronnie. 'Well, your Ruth Jones isn't looking quite as saintly as she did an hour ago with this little revelation.'

Ronnie took a breath before composing her response. Lydia had a nerve sometimes, but she was the boss, and Ronnie needed to choose her battles.

'It wasn't her on the job. Davor was her colleague.' But her protests were useless. Lydia had moved on and was now looking expectantly at Baz. 'But we'll check it out of course, keep our minds wide open.'

'Now, DC Munro, shall we discuss your future?'

It was a signal for Ronnie to go.

There were new aspects of the appeal that were highlighted to the gathered press. Anyone who had seen the vehicle used to kidnap Dawn Buckley should come forward. Anyone with any sightings of this man or woman (cue grotesque photofits) who were believed to be driver and passenger in the vehicle should call the dedicated number. The reward for Liam's return was a hundred thousand pounds. Ronnie's jaw dropped and there was a gasp and a murmur from the journalists. It was hard to determine what a reward figure ought to be in any situation. You couldn't put a price on a life, and you had to start somewhere, but this was starting very high indeed.

Steve and Cara, their hands clasped together in full view of the press, presented a picture of unity and desolation. His words alongside hers made the room fall silent, except for the snap and click of cameras, until questions were invited from the floor.

After the appeal, the phone lines were rammed within minutes, just as predicted, and it would take days to check out each claim. Most likely, 90 per cent of them would be a waste of time and resources, but this was becoming the norm. It seemed that there were whole swathes of society who wanted nothing more than to watch the infrastructure they depended on fall apart before their eyes. How would those people feel if it was their child who'd been taken? And what lay at the root of the desire to misinform and mislead? Susie Marshall would say it was something about revenge for betrayal in childhood. Whatever was done to you, you were likely to go on to do to others. It wasn't a very cheery prognosis for the world.

Ronnie considered her plan to meet Steve that evening. Perhaps it was justified, given that her pursuit of Ruth now had a direct established link with the case she was officially investigating. It gave her some sort of legitimacy at least, and with every day that passed, especially after Lydia's grim forebodings earlier that afternoon, she felt more driven to do whatever it took.

She was perusing the statements of the most recent witnesses from house-to-house enquiries when Steve texted her with an address. *There's a Jacksons sign outside. Meet me there 7.45 and I'll talk you through it, but that needs to be the end of it.* She agreed, for what it was worth, and tried to quiet her thumping heartbeat as she pulled out of the car park and indicated left towards Wakehurst.

After a few minutes on the main roads, the GPS took her off down a side road and through a backstreet route she didn't know. As she drove, she noted landmarks and road names, and with every tick of the milometer, the voice in her head asking what on earth she was thinking became louder and louder. Eventually, she pulled over under a street lamp and took some deep breaths, reminding herself of what she was doing and why.

In her mind's eye, she had an image of the dishevelled, haunted figure of Ruth Jones, a frightened, cornered animal looking for help. It made her more determined and more wary in equal measure. If Steve Buckley was responsible for Ruth's injuries, then walking straight into his trap was nothing short of madness. She sent a quick text to Serena sharing her destination. *Just following a tip-off, if I'm not home by eight thirty find me here.* It gave her some form of relief to know someone knew where she was going, and she pulled out into the road with a clearer head and a braver heart.

It was almost dark by the time she arrived at Blyth Road. The house numbers were barely visible so she parked where there was a space and walked back the way she had come. They were 1930s semis mostly, with the odd gap, an undeveloped bomb site, and the occasional new-build standing out like a shameless impostor. Lights were going on in bedrooms – children being put to bed, while adults busied themselves in the kitchens, pulling the blinds for privacy as night fell. It was an idyll of domesticity and therefore, in Ronnie's experience, the perfect setting for a crime.

Jacksons estate agents had indeed planted their flag at number 11, which as it turned out was less of a house, more of a nameless flat building, the kind a child might make out of Lego, but less colourful. A pair of grimy windows faced the street and a pair of heavy steel doors at the front were padlocked shut and rusting badly. A scattering of parking spaces dominated an otherwise overgrown front garden, where a wooden sign lay broken and almost buried by brambles, its wording illegible apart from *Hall* at the end. A tarmac path, laced with cracks through which sprang sturdy weeds, led through a gate to another, less official-looking side door. There were lights on inside, but the frosted windows either side didn't allow her the luxury of seeing in. No doorbell. She raised her hand to knock and the door opened almost instantly.

Steve looked different. Taller, broader, or it may have been the padding of his jacket boosting his girth. He stood aside to let her in, and the strip lighting gave his skin a grey, pallid tone that reminded her of the mortuary. The week had taken its toll on him. It was no wonder he was coming off the Sidekick app.

'Nice place you've got here.' She swept the room with one swift glance. A kitchen, but in disuse for some time, by the looks of things.

'It's not actually mine . . . yet. I just run my business from here.'

'What business might that be? Catfishing?'

He gave her a look that said *that's enough*.

'Construction. Just the paperwork side of things.'

'So, tell me about what happened with Ruth Jones.' She let the words flood out. There was no more time to waste on small talk.

'We saw each other a few times. It was a mistake. I thought she was one of those women that was lying about their age. She looked older than twenty-eight, much older. I was thinking, like, forty at least. She was nice, but strange.

I mean, like someone had dropped her off here from another planet, or another time zone or something.'

'So you wanted to end it.'

'There wasn't much to end. You have to understand, Veronica, if that's your real name . . .' He put his face in his hands for a second. *'Fernandez* – wasn't it, that you called yourself? My heart wasn't in any of that stuff. I'm not that kind of guy. I love Cara. I love Liam.' He looked almost as if he was blinking back tears.

'Go back to what happened to Ruth.' His fake display of emotion only made her more irritated. Her hurt pride tried to surface but she pushed it back down with all the dignity she could muster as she looked around the room for distraction. The place hadn't been looked after in a while. The harsh odour of bleach barely covered the smell of drains and the overhead light buzzed and flickered. She pulled open the fridge door and shut it again, turning round to face him. 'Where were you when it happened, and what did you do to her?'

Steve leaned against the wall, arms folded. 'Like I told you before, she broke in. Must have been watching the place, which means she must have followed me here. Fucking nutter. I was on my way back to the site, but I forgot something and came back for it.'

'What did you forget?'

'Something I'd found when I was walking through the park. A cricket bat some kid must have left. It was chipped and stained, but nothing wrong with it. I thought I'd bring it home for Liam.'

'And then what?'

'I came back round the side, the same way you just came, through the gate, and let myself in. I could have sworn the door was locked before. It's not a good lock, but it just about works. And then I knew straight away someone was here, because you just get that feeling, or maybe there's a smell of another person. Something outdoorsy it was. Earthy. I'm not sure. But there was someone here, and I got ready to defend myself.'

'Who did you think it was? Who might be lying in wait for you here?'

'No idea. I mean . . .' He hesitated. 'You know about my brother, right?'

'You thought he might attack you?'

'Worse than that.'

'Kill you?'

'Or pay someone to. Quick way of getting my son off me.'

Ronnie turned and stared out of the bevelled window at the black night. This could all be a decoy, but then it made sense with the facts as she knew them. Steve's voice had shaken slightly, through lying or emotion, it wasn't clear, and she didn't want to believe him.

'He wanted you dead?'

'He'd made that obvious, a few times.'

'We were under the impression he'd made a new life for himself, didn't want any contact.'

'Did Mum tell you that? He's her son. She won't have anyone speak ill of him.'

It was a lot to process. Ronnie was almost convinced, and it would fit with the café theory, with Dawn collecting Liam and handing him over to Joe, but she needed more on the events of that Tuesday night. 'So you must have been pretty scared.'

'I picked up the bat and took a swing at them, at her. I didn't think at the time. She looked like a man, must have cut her hair. I hit her hard, she went down, and that's when I saw her face and realised. I lost my temper then . . . lost it even more. It was like my domain was being invaded and all I could think about was Cara finding out and everything falling apart.'

'Then you let her go?'

'I called an ambulance on her phone, then left.'

'You what?'

Ronnie let his words sink in. Ruth hadn't mentioned an ambulance, and to be fair, it was hardly normal behaviour for an assailant to call the emergency services to help the victim of their crime. The act of dialling 999 was almost that of a Good Samaritan, not a violent love-rat. But their hospital search hadn't thrown up any record of a Ruth Jones, which meant that she must have used a false name. But why lie to your rescuers, of all people? It didn't make any sense.

'How much time do you spend in this place?'

Steve shrugged. 'A fair bit because I'm doing it up to make it habitable for us. I use it for post because living in a caravan, it's pretty difficult getting taken seriously. Jobs, bank accounts, credit cards. You know.'

Ronnie looked back at the door she'd used to come in. On the floor next to it was a pile of unopened letters, leaflets, takeaway menus, the usual. She bent down and flicked through it.

'Looks like there are a few unpaid bills here.'

Steve grimaced. 'Yes, we're negotiating on all that.'

'How do you mean?'

'The sellers. They're in debt. Can't pay the bills. That's why I'm getting the place at such a good price. At least, it was supposed to be a good price.' His expression was pained. He blinked it away.

'You're moving your family here?'

'That's the plan. Raising the money was the tough part.'

'Hence Catfish comes into being.'

He closed his eyes, as if not seeing the truth would make it go away. 'Yes,' he breathed. 'I did try to get money off women. A couple of them. One did a runner. But the others, I mean, they offered it up on a plate. I didn't force them.'

'You might have told them lies to get them to offer it up, maybe?'

'Lying's not a crime, is it?'

'It is if you're deceiving people to get money off them.' She looked at her phone. There was a message saying *WTF??? I'm on my way.* She should make a move before Serena arrived and wreaked havoc. The situation was too delicate for an intruder just now.

Ronnie flicked through the letters on the doormat again. Looking back, she wasn't sure why she did it. Maybe the thought of her sister reconnected their spirits, gave her the urge to look deeper, look behind the narrative, because the story might not be all it appeared to be.

She put the pile of post on to the table. A few typed letters slid off and exposed the back of a folded newspaper, the *West Dean and Wakehurst Gazette*, that Ronnie was accustomed to putting straight into the recycling if it ever came through the door. And that's when she saw it.

The picture was as unobtrusive as it could get, a poor black and white photo with a message below it in capital letters that could just as easily have been an advert for gutter clearance or decorating services. But this wasn't a local trader looking for work. It was a plea for a missing person, and the face of that missing person made Ronnie's heart pound in disbelief.

Everything was beginning to make sense. The hospital alias, the sudden disappearance. Finn Macaulay wasn't the only person Ruth was running from. She glanced over her shoulder. Steve had disappeared into another room but she could hear his footsteps returning. She stuffed the newspaper into her bag. She didn't need to bring it to his attention just yet.

'Right, are we done here?' Steve was back, his eyes challenging hers.

'Yes, for now.' Ronnie followed him out of the kitchen door, through the side gate and watched him drive away in the dented Golf. To think that she had been as good as infatuated with this man only the previous day made a shiver run down her spine. How could her instincts be so incredibly off-kilter?

She was standing by her car when her sister arrived. Serena's MG screeched to a halt and she wound down the window.

'Ron, you had me so worried. What was this all about?'

'I'll tell you later. But I'm OK. I found out what I wanted to know, it just wasn't what I expected.'

CHAPTER 27

Ruth is hungry. She calms herself by thinking about life on the outside. But the last time she was on the outside was when everything went wrong. She's remembering Finn's house in Blyth Road. It's not a house or even a flat, but a cross between an office and a village hall. She's picking up the pile of post, but there's nothing addressed to Finn Macaulay. She's realising it can't be his house at all, that she's walked into a random building he happens to have just walked out of, and it's at that moment that she spots the newspaper, folded in half so the only visible part is the bottom half of the back page. But she'd recognise that face anywhere.

Have you seen . . .?

Have you seen . . .?

She pulls it out of the pile and the picture is larger than life. She's looking at herself, a photograph from ten years earlier. Someone's holding it for the camera. You can see his dirty fingers gripping its edges, one side of his face reminding her of what she left behind.

She blinks hard, refocuses, because it can't be who she thinks it is. From the part of his face she can see, she builds a picture of the rest of him. Behind those sad eyes that are tired of searching for her and appealing for help from the world is another man, a beast with a fiery temper and tiny dark pupils staring into her soul but not seeing her, not knowing her at all.

In the photo, her hair is long, straight, clipped back the way Aunt Esther always did it because it wouldn't please God to see worldly hair, hair that fell around your face in natural curls the way it wanted to.

And above it, capital letters shouting one question.

HAVE YOU SEEN RUTH JACOBS?

She realises her hands are trembling as she brings them up to her mouth, looking for the comfort of her fingers on her face, skin on skin, her own on her own, no one else's. Not his. She mustn't go back there in her mind, because she will fall down a black hole of infinite depth, but she needs to concentrate hard to keep away from it. Memories can flood through the tiniest crack in her resolve – memories of his heavy, sour breaths, the smell of sweat in the creases of his weighty body, almost stifling her as she turns her head away, tries not to breathe, tries not to think.

She is rigid now with the same stress she felt then, as he forced himself inside her, groaning, thrusting and with his hand grappling for her mouth to stop her crying out in pain.

'Nice girls don't do this.' His panting is heavy in her ear. 'So what does that make you?'

She forces her mind somewhere else, she's skipping through a meadow, making daisy chains, stroking ponies in the field, feeding the pigs the scraps from dinner, anything to remove her mind from what was happening. Then there's the climax, the roar that tears through her head, and the relief when he rolls off her. She can breathe again.

Sometimes she'd rather he'd killed her, because it was like dying a hundred times over. The only reason she survived is because of Martha and Rex, and the hope that one day it would be over and she'd be free.

Liberation had come at a price. The highest price anyone could pay, because it had to be that way. After Nate caught her trying to escape the first time and wanted to impose a harsher regime, smaller rations, fewer visits from her sister, it was Aunt Esther who pointed out that it was unlikely Ruth was going to make any serious attempt to leave Mill Farm. Ruth overheard them outside her door. Nate asked what on earth she meant and she replied:

'No one would leave behind what they love most in the world.'

Maybe she was right, because she had done exactly that, and found that freedom had the sharpest edges.

CHAPTER 28

Ronnie called Baz as soon as she was back in the flat. She had spent the journey home on the phone to the hospital checking the ambulance story and then composing a framework of white lies that would keep them both safe. At least that was the plan. Baz didn't need to know everything, not yet.

'Sarge, this is late for you. What's up?'

'Baz, something has happened, and I need your discretion.'

'OK . . .' There was the rustle of something on the end of the line. 'What is it?'

'Have you got a minute? I'm not interrupting?' Saying that, she realised that was where she should have begun, but her mind was a mess and her thoughts too jumbled to find room for politeness.

'Of course, just getting myself a snack. Fire away. Don't compromise my integrity though, sarge, will you?' His voice had a ring of humour to it, which made Ronnie's shoulders relax slightly. There was a munching sound, which brought what she was about to say back into the real world.

'You know I went online, dating apps and stuff?'

'Yeah. Any luck? Met anyone nice?'

'Sort of. Well, not anyone nice. That's what I wanted to share with you.'

The munching stopped. 'You didn't meet Catfish, did you?' There was an incredulous silence as Ronnie prepared to drop the bomb.

'I think I did. Tuesday night, then last night I saw him again.'

'Bloody hell, sarge, so why haven't we got the blue lights flashing? What's his name? Where does he live? And what's he done with Ruth?' The questions came firing at her like bullets, but Baz had no idea what was coming next, and she didn't want to be the one to break it to him. She wavered before re-establishing the context around what she was about to say.

'Listen, Baz, you know this wasn't intentional, don't you? I am still in shock, to be honest, that the first foray I made into the dating world sent me right to his door, not literally, but you know what I mean.'

His answer gave nothing away. Whether he believed her or not was best not known. 'Of course. I mean, it's a pretty massive coincidence, but I'd say you've stumbled on the best lead we've had yet. What's the story?'

'I ended up chatting to this guy, not paying much attention to his name, and then I remembered that Ruth said in the short time we spoke that the guy she met was called Finn, Finnian, but Finn for short, right? Well so was this guy. Even when it dawned on me, I thought there could be plenty of Finns out there. It's not necessarily the same one.' She paused, wondering how her white lies were going down, but Baz seemed to be waiting for more. That was a good sign. 'At least *Finn* is what I thought his name was, until this morning.'

'What, you woke up and he said he was called Brian?' Ronnie wished for a moment it had been that simple. She'd have to tell the rest of the story without letting him intervene. She didn't need his repartee just now.

'Finn, the man I met online and went out with not just once but twice, is not only the same one that assaulted Ruth Jones, but his real name is Steve Buckley.'

Baz was uncharacteristically silent for a few seconds.

'And I made him show me where they'd been when he hit Ruth, and that's where I found it, a missing-person notice in the *Gazette*. It was just a copy of the local rag lying on the doormat but Ruth must have seen it. And from what it looks like on the announcement on the back page, there are people out there looking for her.'

'Hang on a sec. Let me get this straight. Steve Buckley and Ruth Jones were an item?'

'Not exactly, but yes, something like that. She broke into what she thought was his home and must have seen the paper with her photo in it.'

'Do you *know* she saw it?'

'No, but the fact that she's officially missing makes everything a little more worthy of investigation. And the connection with Steve is another breakthrough. The assault was an accident. He thought she was an intruder.'

'They all say that, don't they?'

'He called an ambulance. It all checks out.'

'But the hospital confirmed no Ruth Jones had been in.' Baz sounded peeved, as if his homework had had a line drawn through it and *see me* scrawled at the bottom.

'She said she was called Martha Jacobs.'

Baz made a 'hmmm' sound.

'Anyway, there we go. That's my Thursday evening for you.'

'You took a fucking risk there, sarge, if you'll pardon my French.'

'I know. But it paid off. It's what we do now that we need to get right.'

'Of course. So, I imagine you want to call the number on the announcement. You've probably already called it.'

'Of course I haven't, Ruth Jones is *your* case. I wouldn't do that. Not without consulting you.'

'You didn't mind going out there undercover without approval.'

'It wasn't undercover. It was all above board. Weren't you listening?' Ronnie tried to disguise the panic in her voice. She couldn't let him think that, not for a second.

'Any reason you didn't share the news a bit earlier?'

'I needed to see the day through to its conclusion. I called you as soon as I knew what was going on. Can we talk about what we do next?'

'Of course. What do you suggest?' he added with a hint of sarcasm. 'I'm open to ideas; just like to be involved in them.'

'Thanks for your sense of humour. God knows I need someone with one of those to put up with me sometimes.' The words felt insincere but she hoped some false self-deprecation might draw a line under his doubts, if he had any.

'So what's the plan? Have you thought that maybe whoever was looking for her has found her, and that's why she's vanished?'

'I have, but if she found out in time, and there's a good chance she did, then she may have run for cover.'

'So Steve Buckley's out of the picture in terms of her disappearance?'

'I'm almost certain he wasn't involved.'

'On the basis of ambulance calling, you're probably right. Unless it's an elaborate triple bluff. So, what do we do? How do you want to go about finding the guys who are looking for her, when Lydia has categorically ruled it out and we're almost nine days into the search for the boy?'

'We go to Lydia and present the missing-person notice as a low-cost solution to one of our two big cases. We know Ruth's real surname, and we're about to find out who else is looking for her, and possibly why she's on the run from them.'

'Low-cost solution? You don't know that yet.'

'One phone call. I just think this is a gift of a development, like going up the longest ladder in a game of Snakes and Ladders.' She regretted the reference as soon as she said it.

'A game of *what*?'

'Never mind. Let's see what the boss says. I'll send you the number on the advert, see if you can find out where the phone is registered to. I'll be in a bit late in the morning. Need to do an errand on the way, so say nine-thirty?'

Serena handed her a camomile tea. 'To de-stress,' she said, as Ronnie sniffed it doubtfully. 'More effective than gin, they say.'

As she wafted back to her room, Ronnie took a tentative sip, acknowledged with reluctance that it wasn't bad, and contemplated their differences. Serena was calm in all situations, but that might be because she made sure she only existed in calm situations. She was never stressed, never in a hurry, she took care of herself and worked part-time in a job she loved, earning just enough money to finance her life. She was all yoga, mindfulness and meditation, whereas Ronnie was addicted to an edgier lifestyle. She was never happy unless she was out there fighting for something or someone, she rarely thought before she spoke and played hard and fast with the rules, treading a thin line between the permitted and the forbidden, always asking the question *Where does it say I can't do that?*

The two of them couldn't be more different, but Ronnie couldn't imagine a world without her sister. She only hoped her children would feel some sort of the same sibling closeness in the future. It wasn't going on now, as far as she could see. She pushed open Eddie's door, tapping on it to warn him at the same time.

'You OK? Sorry I was out again tonight.'

He spun round from his computer screen with a smile that warmed her heart. 'Hey, Mum, I got 80 per cent in the maths test today. That's the last big one before the mocks.'

Ronnie beamed. 'What did I tell you about being clever? I was wrong about that. You're a bloody genius.'

He basked in her praise, spinning left and right, throwing a pen in the air.

'Can I come in?' But she was already in, and picking things up off the floor out of habit, pulling the curtains closed against the darkness. 'I thought you'd be gaming.'

'Nah, revising for English tomorrow. Got to write about war poetry. It's actually quite good. Well not *good* exactly, but dramatic, makes you think.' He handed her a textbook, open at 'Charge of the Light Brigade', where he'd scribbled some pencil notes and stuck Post-its with commentary and analysis. Ronnie sat on the bed and read some of his notes.

'This is great. Looks like you've really understood it.'

'There's more.' He came to sit next to her and turned the page. 'I like this one.'

'In Flanders fields the poppies grow . . .' Ronnie felt a shiver down her back. 'I'm not sure *like* is the word,' she said. 'The brutality of war is a hard truth to look at.'

'I know, Mum.' He ran his finger down the lines. 'What about this, though? Doesn't it give you the chills?'

'If ye break faith with us who die, we shall not sleep.' She looked at him. 'Yes to the goose bumps. So, what do you take away from this one then?'

'A sense of responsibility. It's like a warning that we need to carry on the work of the soldiers who died, stand up for the freedom they fought for.'

'Sounds like a good rule to live by.'

'It feels like we've been thrown the chains that link us to the dead, it's like a duty we have to them. But a good one. That's why I do the Cadet Force. Feels like fulfilling a duty to everyone who fought before.'

Ronnie had always struggled with his passion for the armed forces. What made all sorts of logical sense didn't sit well with her emotionally. 'As long as you don't make a career of it. You may not come back in a coffin, but the mental health impact is almost worse. You hear about it all the time, and I don't want that for you.'

Eddie bounced back into his desk chair and spun back round to the desk. 'Right, I need to do another hour. Love you, Mum.'

His words, out of nowhere, jolted her like defibrillator pads on a crash trolley. She thought of Cara Buckley, who might never hear from her son again. She imagined Liam being collected and delivered to his Uncle Joe, the father who was never a father to him. Would Dawn go to such lengths to do that, putting herself at risk of a criminal record? What motive would Davor Kovac have to abduct a child? And why was Ruth on the run from the family that wanted her home? None of it made sense.

Tilly was on her phone when Ronnie popped her head round the door. 'Hey, Mum, I'll come and see you in a minute,' she murmured, hardly taking her eyes off the screen, and Ronnie went to run a bath, questions fizzing in her mind.

As she sank into the bubbles, she felt the weight of the world lift and float away. She closed her eyes and breathed in the steamy bath oil, letting her mind wander to a place of peace. Tonight, that place was the stretch of Camber Sands that they used to call Desert Beach. Half a mile from their seaside bungalow, it stretched along the coast as far as they could see, widening and narrowing with the tide, and bordered by sand dunes that gave it its name. She and Serena would make pretend journeys with camels and treasure, hiding from imaginary pirates in the dips and hollows, inventing stories about shipwrecks and smugglers, before piling back to the house, hungry and exhausted. It seemed like yesterday. But between then and now lay a real-life adventure, one they were only part way through, with her marriage and divorce, moving to the Surrey borders, and the death of their father that she still felt acutely every day. His face, his smile and his spirit were etched in her heart, and it was his voice she heard when she saw the words of the 'Flanders Fields' poem: *to you . . . we throw the torch; be yours to hold it high*. She would hold that torch high, whatever it took.

CHAPTER 29

Jacksons estate agents was conveniently situated at the end of a parade of shops in West Dean. Ronnie pulled up just as the door was being unlocked and waved to the girl in the window. She opened the door with a look of bewilderment as if she had been dropped from space into a role she had no idea how to play.

'Can I help you?'

She looked more in need of help herself, so Ronnie flashed her badge by way of explanation. The girl's expression changed to one of alarm. 'Has something happened?'

'Can I come in?' Ronnie asked.

'Of course, sorry.' Lights flickered on above their heads, blinds went up and a printer whirred into life. 'Please, have a seat.'

Ronnie obeyed, giving the girl a warm smile to put her at ease, but without success.

'Don't worry, we're not imprisoning estate agents today, you can relax. I just wanted some information on a property that's on your books.'

The girl's face transformed into a picture of content-ment. 'Gosh, OK, I just assumed, you always think police are only there to arrest you.'

'Too much Netflix?' She was another Lisa Blake. While Ronnie herself avoided police dramas like the plague, the rest of the population was soaking them up like sponges.

The girl laughed. At last. 'So which property is it that you wanted to find out about?'

'It's the Hall in Blyth Road. How long has it been on the market?'

The girl stood up and went to a filing cabinet. Pulling open one of the drawers, she flicked through some file dividers and withdrew a slim folder. 'Let's see . . . we took it on six months ago.'

'That's a long time, isn't it? No interest over the whole summer?'

'Some interest, but only from developers, and the asking price is too high, but the vendor won't budge, so it's just sitting there for now.'

'They'll have to budge eventually, won't they?'

The girl sighed. 'You'd think so. But it's a corporate vendor, an association or something, and they need the approval of the members to agree the price they sell for.'

'Does the name Steve Buckley ring a bell?'

'The surname does. From the news?'

Ronnie nodded. 'You're thinking of Liam, the boy who went missing. I was thinking of potential developers, won-dered if that name had crossed your path at all.'

She turned the pages of the file and shook her head. 'No, there's no Steve Buckley in here.'

'But they could be seeking a private sale on the side, I suppose.'

'It happens.' The girl was probably wondering where this was leading, but there was no need to pursue the Steve connection.

'So, who are the vendors?'

The girl looked uncomfortable. 'I can find out for you. They are getting rid of a lot of property all over the country apparently.'

Ronnie thought for a second. A mass sell-off was usually the sign of a financial crisis, debts to pay off.

'What was the Hall used for exactly?'

'Prayer meetings, social gatherings – although I'm not sure their definition of social gatherings is anything like mine. But then I shouldn't judge.'

The girl was warming up. Ronnie decided to take the risk.

'Ah, so some kind of Mormon cult thing, was it?'

The girl folded her arms and leaned back in her chair. Body language that said the questions had gone too far. 'I'm not sure about that. I just think they're quite a strict bunch, from what I can gather. Anyway, I really need to open the shop. I have a client coming in at nine fifteen.' She stood up, held out her card. 'If there's anything else I can help with, detective, please do give me a call. As long as you understand I have to respect client confidentiality.'

'Of course. But if you ever change your mind about that . . .' Ronnie gave her another of her warmest smiles and produced her card in exchange. 'There's mine, just in case.' In case of what, she wasn't sure, but you never knew.

In the car, Ronnie spent the journey to work mulling over what might be going on with the mystery vendors. Steve might be able to enlighten her, but at this point it was unlikely he would cooperate of his own volition. She needed to wait for the storm to pass.

Ronnie was just reversing into the only free space in the car park when her phone buzzed. Cara Buckley. She accepted the call and couldn't hide the hope in her voice. 'Hi Cara, any news?'

'Sort of. Yes. I'm not sure if it's good or bad. But Steve got a call last night from someone who has information.'

'What kind of information?' Ronnie tried to slow her racing heart. These things were all too often a waste of police time, some joker just wanting to lead them on a wild goose chase or imagining that the reward would be offered for a claimed sighting regardless of whether it led anywhere.

'They said, *she* said, she had Liam, and would bring him home, in return for the cash we offered.'

Ronnie switched off the engine, which was still running, and closed her eyes. Filled with a mixture of gratitude for Liam's life and anger that someone could remove him and have everyone searching high and low for over a week now, she massaged her temples and willed her mind to settle into some kind of calm. She couldn't be of any use unless she could think clearly.

'Have you got the number of the person who called?'

'It was withheld.'

'You said it was a woman.'

'Yes, he said she sounded nervous.'

'He didn't recognise the voice? It didn't ring any bells?'

'No, he said no.'

'What time was the call?'

'Late. Ten-thirty or something. I was asleep.'

Ronnie did a quick calculation. She had left him at Blyth Road around nine. 'What did they say? Did Steve agree to a handover?'

'Yes, tonight at the reservoir car park, but . . .' Her voice went quiet. 'He didn't want me to tell you. They said no police.'

'No police?' Ronnie repeated her words, hearing the echo of so many TV crime dramas. As if the police would ever let a kidnap handover go ahead without trying to intercept the abductor. 'I don't think that's an option, not now you've told me.'

'He can't know I've told you.'

'Don't worry. We'll be discreet.'

'What if they see you and they don't give us Liam?'

Ronnie reached for the right words and couldn't seem to find them. 'All I can say is this: whoever has Liam has committed a crime and will be punished for it, and if they aren't caught, they may well do the same to another family as they did to you. And as far as handing over Liam is concerned, if they get spooked and don't go through with it, it won't be because of us. Sometimes, the person either isn't holding anyone hostage at all, or they change their mind, try to extort more money out of the family. There are so many reasons for things not working out.'

She had done nothing to ease Cara's mind, but she hoped she'd made her realise that things weren't necessarily going to run as smoothly as she thought, and that a police presence would only be a good thing.

'Have you told anyone else?'

'Nobody.'

'Does Dawn know?'

'No. She'd be furious. She still hates the fact my parents put the money up. Says they're lording it over her, because she can't afford to help.'

Ronnie thought quickly. So this was further confirmation of her conviction that Dawn was innocent if she had no interest in the reward money. Or was it a double bluff? Was she feigning disapproval and secretly planning to pocket the lot and make a run for it? Her mind forced itself back to the scene in the playground, Liam running off happily to someone he trusted – Liam the little boy who drew messy pictures and misbehaved at the back of the class.

That was it. That was the connection.

'Cara, can you tell me if Liam wears glasses at all? I mean, how is his eyesight?'

'He's short-sighted, like me, but hates wearing his glasses.'

'Do you know why?'

Cara inhaled deeply, as if to steel herself to say what she didn't want to admit. 'He said the other boys laughed at him, took them off him and ran away.'

Ronnie considered this new information with a mixture of shock and understanding. Children could be incredibly unkind. But that would explain why Liam was easier to manage at the front of the class *and* why he might have mistaken whoever collected him for a family member, which in turn meant that it wasn't necessarily Dawn at all, but a total stranger who bore some uncanny resemblance to her, or to Cara.

'Let me call you back when I've had a think about this,' she said and swung the car door open. Today was going to be a busy day.

In the office, Lydia and Baz were waiting by the phone. Lydia was tapping her pen on the table.

'No luck on the trace, sarge. Burner phone.' Baz flipped open his notebook as Lydia dialled the number.

'DC Munro has briefed me on the situation. I think we're right to call this person who claims to be looking for Ruth.' She met Ronnie's eyes briefly before lifting the receiver.

Ronnie signalled to her to stop. 'Wait,' she said, looking at each of them in turn to get their attention. 'There's been a development.'

Baz was hard to read, but Lydia could barely conceal her delight at the news about the Buckleys' mystery caller. 'The end is in sight then,' she declared with a beaming smile. 'It's a surprise. I have to admit I was beginning to lose hope.'

'Who are her parents, that they can produce this amount of money in cash just like that?' Baz looked perplexed.

'Her father ran an online gaming website that he sold for a few million last year.' Ronnie had googled him after Cara had mentioned his name.

'Gambling? That's a red flag, I'd say.'

'Plenty of legal profit made in gambling,' said Lydia, who clearly didn't want the smooth path to resolution obstructed by a flag of any colour.

Baz got the message. 'So, no police? Or police?' He looked to Lydia for the answer, but Ronnie interjected.

'A discreet presence at a distance would be normal. But we have time between now and then.' She looked at the time on her phone. 'And we have some leads to follow. If we know who we're looking for, it's going to make chasing the abductor after the drop-off a lot easier. We might have an idea of where they're headed, and how they're likely to behave.'

Lydia nodded approvingly. 'I agree with you, DS Delmar. Shall we get on with this call? Not that I imagine it will tell us much.'

The phone rang three times before someone answered. It was a woman's voice, breathless, anxious, as if she shouldn't be speaking. The phone wasn't on speaker, but the voice was clear, if a little quiet.

'Hello?'

'Who am I speaking to?'

'This is Esther Jacobs. Nate's just coming if you wait a second.'

'Telling us her name just like that,' Ronnie whispered, eyebrows raised. Lydia nodded thoughtfully and wrote it down, underlined with a question mark and an exclamation mark.

There was a silence and a scuffle before another voice came on the line. 'Who's this?'

'This is the police, Halesworth CID, DI Lydia Burnett.' She looked up at Ronnie and Baz. He didn't need to know the whole team was listening in. 'I'm calling about the notice in the *Gazette*. I may have some information for you on your missing person, unless of course she's no longer missing.'

'Still missing, at this point in time. What information do you have?'

'Can we come and talk to you about Ruth? We think we may be able to help.'

'Can't it be done over the phone? It's a long way for you to come.'

'Where are you based?'

He seemed to hesitate. 'We'll come to you. Can you meet us at the café by the station at 2 p.m.? I have other meetings in town later this afternoon so it works for me.'

It worked for him. His words made Ronnie's toes curl, but Lydia remained businesslike.

'I'm sure we can have a useful exchange of information.'

She hung up and addressed them both, pulling out a notebook and pen.

'Can we take a moment to consolidate our position?' She didn't wait for a response before continuing, tapping her pen on the desk with each point she made. 'Ruth Jones first came to our attention as the victim of assault, but she's also wanted by these people who are suddenly very keen to find her after God knows how long. There's something about this notice in the paper and the sound of that Nate Jacobs on the phone that piques my curiosity enough to send you to see him. But Liam Buckley still remains our first priority at all times. This afternoon, DC Mayer's covering the Kovac interview. DS Delmar, you and DC Munro can take this one. See what you can get from Jacobs, obviously without giving away what you know. We need to keep our cards close to our chest. I want to know why he didn't take this to the police, and why this photo of Ruth is so old. It must have been taken at least ten years ago. If she's been missing that long, why didn't they come looking before now? Is she wanted for a crime we don't know about?'

Ronnie doubted that, but Baz just said, 'Right you are, ma'am,' in a voice that said he couldn't wait to get going.

'But don't let on that there's anything wrong with what they've done. We need their openness. As far as they're concerned, we have information they might want, not the other way around.'

The journey to the café was short, but long enough for Baz to give her the news she was least expecting. She had only wanted to make friendly conversation.

'So, how's the exam prep going? I bet you're looking forward to the big promotion.' She didn't dare take her eyes off the road to gauge his reaction. A removal van had decided to make a three-point turn at a point in the road where there were parked cars on both sides.

'You know I've applied to move away from Halesworth, don't you?'

'You've what?' Ronnie nearly rammed into the van in front of them.

'There isn't room for us both there, sarge. The DI has already made that clear.'

'She's what?' Ronnie couldn't comprehend any of it. The facts as she knew them had been tossed in the air and were floating down all around her like confetti.

'It's not a big deal. I'm happy to move.'

'But I don't want you to.' The words were out before she'd had time to apply the filter. 'We're a team, Baz, some of the time at least, when the boss allows it.'

'There's DC Mayer. We can't be a team if we're both DS.'

It was a lot to take in. 'Can we talk about it later? I might need to focus on how we're going to play this when we arrive.' She needed time to process what he'd said. It didn't sit well with her, but neither had the idea of there being another DS at the station. And in the background was Lydia's foreboding about the future echoing in her head. If DC Munro had safe passage out of there, what about the rest of them?

'What's the matter?' He was looking at her with a puzzled expression.

'Nothing. Nothing's the matter. Ignore me, Baz. I'm overthinking this. Let's concentrate on our next adventure.'

The café was almost empty. A young mother sat with a coffee in one hand, rocking a pram with the other. She glanced up as they came in, then down again. Waiting for someone, Ronnie thought. Her memories of early motherhood were all about snatches of human contact during the day, the sympathetic smile of another mother who knew what you were going through. At a table behind her, there was a glum-faced older couple, stirring tea and sinking their teeth into pastries. There they were – the past and the future. And no sign of Nate Jacobs.

Just as they had decided on a table at the back of the café, the door opened again. Two figures appeared, silhouetted by the daylight behind them at first, then gaining detail and definition as they came forward. The man was stocky, red-faced, greasy-haired, his once-white shirt straining across his middle. Behind him, almost invisible in his shadow, was a slight female figure wearing a headscarf and a long dark coat. It wasn't hard for them to spot the detectives among the scant clientele.

Ronnie beckoned him to her table and introduced herself and Baz by their names rather than ranks. It wouldn't do to alarm the other customers or give them reason to prick up their ears.

'Nate Jacobs, and this is my wife, Esther.' He indicated the thin woman at his side. 'Pleased to meet you.'

His expression said otherwise. He regarded them through narrow eyes, looking Ronnie up and down. He'd been expecting a man. He half-smiled at Baz, giving him what Ronnie assumed was a nod of approval for being the correct gender.

'Shall we have a cup of tea?' His words were all directed at Baz.

'A drink would be very nice.' Ronnie smiled, forcing him to acknowledge her as he pulled out a chair for her to sit on. His fingers, fat and stained with nicotine, left their impression on the cushioned plastic backrest. 'I'd love a flat white, if that's OK?'

'Just water for me,' Baz added, throwing her a suspicious look.

Nate turned on his heel and lumbered towards the bar. Esther headed off in the direction of the toilets. Ronnie riffled in her bag and pulled something out. Glancing over at Nate again, she was pleased to see that flat whites were still as time-consuming and complicated to make as she remembered.

'What are you up to, sarge? He'll only be a minute.' Baz looked perturbed.

'I only need a minute,' she replied, applying powder to the back of Nate's chair with a brush, then adhesive tape.

'Will that be all?' Nate was paying. He carried their drinks over on a tray, concentrating hard on not spilling anything while Ronnie affixed the tape to a piece of card and slid it into her bag. Baz wiped his brow and shook his head, as Esther appeared from the toilets.

Ronnie took her coffee and beamed at Nate. 'That's just what I needed. Thank you.'

Nate shrugged and took a slurp of his tea. 'So, what have you got for us?'

'As you know, we wanted to talk to you about your missing person. We came across your notice in the paper, and we think we may be able to help you find Ruth . . .' She hesitated, fumbling for the right surname. 'Jacobs.'

The couple looked at each other with expressions of worry, then back at their inquisitors.

'Can you tell us a bit more about who she is, and how she went missing? Is she your daughter?'

'Niece,' said Nate, hurriedly. 'We were her guardians.' Then, taking a breath and closing his eyes for a moment as if in prayer, 'We thought she was dead.'

Baz raised an eyebrow at Ronnie and turned back to Nate, who seemed happier talking to a man. 'How did you imagine she had died? And how did you find out she was still alive?'

'Her parents died in a car crash when she was thirteen. We moved in to look after the children but Ruth ran away from us and never came back. It was hard for the others.'

'What others?'

'Martha, her sister.'

Ronnie registered the name. The name Ruth had used at the hospital. Interesting.

'And Rex,' Esther added, ignoring Nate's stare.

'Who's Rex?' asked Ronnie.

'He's our son,' said Nate.

'You thought she was dead? Why?' Baz persisted.

'Because for years afterwards – must be . . .' He counted on his fingers. 'Ten years now, we never heard from her again.'

Esther gave Nate a look of confusion but looked away again when he glared at her.

'So when did you find out that Ruth was still alive?' Ronnie leaned forwards and looked at Nate, who had a knack of avoiding her gaze.

Nate leaned back in his chair and rolled his eyes. 'We found out when *Martha –*' he said her name with a lilt that showed there was no love lost between them '– was on the phone to her, when she thought we were out, and there was Ruth on the screen of her phone, alive as you like. Both of them had taken us for fools this whole time.'

Esther seemed to flinch as he said the words. Nate looked at her with a trace of something like pity and she reached for his arm.

'Where's Martha now?' Ronnie felt her hackles rise in response and tried not to let it show in her voice. 'Can we speak to her?'

'Why would you need to do that if you already know where Ruth is? All we want is to have her back in the family.' He gave Ronnie a sickly smile. She gave him one back. 'She's not well.'

'How do you mean?'

'She's not safe, out there in the world. She'll get into trouble.'

Ronnie gave him a look. 'What do you mean? What kind of trouble?'

Nate said nothing.

It was a moment she would remember for a long time, with two sides of the table needing each other's help but unwilling to give anything away. Nate was having to dig deep to keep his cool, and Esther's hand on his arm said a lot about their relationship as well as his character. Ronnie considered the balance of power. Nate and Esther wanted Ruth back home, and Ronnie doubted it was out of concern for the well-being of a long-lost niece. The information they'd imparted thus far was probably all she was going to get, which begged the question – why divulge anything? But there was more to Nate than he was letting her see, she was sure of it. And there were things she could tell him that weren't going to put Ruth in any danger, but which might satisfy them and earn her some information in return.

'We do have some information to share with you.' She tapped her coffee spoon on the saucer, as if to bring the room to attention, and ignored Baz's surprised expression. 'Ruth came into the police station just over a week ago.' Nate's eyes widened, then narrowed. Esther gripped his arm more tightly. 'She had been attacked by someone that we now know thought she was a burglar.' Ronnie scanned their faces for signs of concern about the attack but there were none. 'She was taken to hospital with head injuries, then ran away from the police station before the interview could be concluded, and it was then, or shortly thereafter, it seems, that she went missing.'

'She went to the police?' Nate's words cascaded from his lips in a torrent of ferocity.

'She'd been attacked. She'd come to report the assault.'
Nate's change in mood was palpable. She gave him a second to calm down before going on. 'But then she changed her mind, and then she didn't turn up to work, and hasn't been seen since.'

'I thought you said you knew where she was.' His voice was cold and monotone now.

'We know where she *lives*, but it seems she hasn't been home for some time.'

'Give me the address.' He was looming at her again, but Ronnie was unmoved.

'I don't think so.'

Nate stood up, his chair falling to the ground behind him. Baz threw an apologetic smile at the other customers.

'Well, I'd rethink that decision if I were you.'

Ronnie squared up to him. 'And why's that?'

'Because wherever she is, that's where you're going to find your missing boy.'

'What? What do you know about him?' Ronnie was knocked for six by the change of subject.

Nate smiled at the impact of his words.

'I only know the most important thing – where you need to look.'

It was a tactic Ronnie had seen enough times: spin the police a yarn about your secret knowledge that will have them eating out of your hand. It never worked. And it wasn't going to work today, but it might be worth humouring this old man, just for a minute.

'Why do you think Ruth has anything to do with the missing child?'

Nate was happy to sit back down and explain his theory, and did so at a leisurely pace, looking at her and Baz in turn, and occasionally at Esther for reinforcement he didn't get. Ronnie listened, with her mind elsewhere, running ahead. Something wasn't right in the room.

'Ruth was born and raised as a Pilgrim of Truth,' Nate began, as if telling a bedtime story. 'And then for no reason, one day she chose to abandon her faith and leave the community.'

'Without saying where she was going?' asked Baz.

'Like a thief in the night. Ten years later, we had no choice but to assume she had died, because who would leave their family, the people they love most in the world? We always thought there was something not right with her. And then we were proved right.' He paused for effect and took the next sentence at a slower pace. 'She's done this before, you know.'

'Done what before, run away?' Baz moved his glass and leaned over the table, clasping his hands.

'Ruth has *stolen a child* before.' Nate bristled.

Ronnie and Baz exchanged glances. Suddenly they were getting more than they bargained for.

'How did this happen, exactly?'

Nate seemed flustered for a second. 'That's in the past now.'

'This is Rex, the one you said was your son?'

Nate shook his head. 'You're not listening to me.'

'So, what happened to the child, the one she stole?' Ronnie had the bit between her teeth. Nate was taunting her now and she'd had enough of it. A plan was forming in her head.

Nate got to his feet and leaned across the table. 'Listen. All you need to know is that the girl is insane, and we need to find her so we can bring her home, where she belongs, so we can give her the care she needs.'

'But what happened that made her run away?' Baz stepped in, his voice echoing his frustration.

Nate spoke his next words slowly and deliberately, relishing the taste of each one on his lips but still refusing to answer the question. 'You find Ruth, she'll be able to tell you where you'll find your boy.'

Baz was staring at Ronnie in shock. She could see him in her peripheral vision but didn't take her eyes off Nate.

'But I think we're done here if you're not going to tell us where she is.' Nate pushed his chair under the table. 'And we'll just have to manage without you. If you've got anything useful to say to us, you have my number.'

'And if you have anything else to tell us, likewise.' Ronnie slid her card across the table. They had plenty to say, but whether they would was another matter.

CHAPTER 30

Ronnie had barely started the engine when Baz exploded with recriminations.

'What was all that about? You heard what Lydia said. Since when do we divulge all our covert operations to the general public, especially when we're both looking for the same person?'

'Calm down, Baz. I know what I'm doing.' She caught his expression as she turned her head to reverse back on to the road. 'There's no need to look at me like that.'

'OK, sarge, talk me through it.' He was fuming. Ronnie indicated left and took the first exit on the roundabout.

'All I told them was that Ruth had been attacked, that she'd come into the station. And did you notice their reaction?'

'Can't say I did, not to that specific thing.'

'Exactly. There was no reaction at all. You put an ad in the paper about your missing niece and then when you hear the girl has just been assaulted, you don't bat an eyelid. I find that weird.'

'You did it to test them?'

'I did it to find out how they really felt about Ruth.' She turned to look at Baz as the lights turned red. 'And I can categorically say they don't care.'

'What about that stuff about her stealing the child?'

'What about it?'

'Do you think there was any truth in it, that she'd stolen a child, that she was mentally ill? Should we be looking into it?'

'You can follow it up if you want, but I'm not sure you'll find anything.'

Baz turned to her, puzzled.

'There was something about the way he told the story. I have a feeling it was a load of crap. He was covering up something else.'

'What in particular made you think that?' Baz sounded pissed off. They had been handed a whole information pack on a missing woman and his boss wanted to dismiss it out of hand. Ronnie could understand where he was coming from.

'Firstly, why would he share that kind of information? It implicates him and Esther in the kidnapping of a baby all those years ago. It was made up on the spot. A last-ditch attempt to get us to tell him where she was.'

'It also might explain who has Liam, if Ruth is in the habit of stealing children. Shouldn't we take it seriously?'

Ronnie pulled over into the next-lane as the lights changed. It eased her frustration, gave her back a sense of control which had been rattled by their meeting with Nate and Esther. 'Not unless we have good reason to. Oh, and

I hope you noticed I didn't tell them the only information I'm absolutely certain *is* true.'

'What's that? I didn't think you thought anything was true, except Ruth Jones is languishing in some dungeon somewhere terrified for her life.'

'I didn't tell him that the reason Ruth went into hiding wasn't the attack, but the fact that she realised Nate was looking for her.'

Baz nodded and shook his head at the same time, as if agreement and disagreement were fighting it out in his neck muscles. 'So, unless this *good reason* to investigate Nate's information turns up, it was a waste of an afternoon, then, as far as you're concerned?' Baz was getting frustrated, and she with him for not getting it, not thinking like she did.

'It wasn't wasted at all. I have his fingerprints on record for a start.'

Baz put his head in his hands. 'He could have seen you and we'd have been thrown out on the spot.'

'But he didn't, and we weren't, and now we know who we're up against in our race to find Ruth. Personally, I don't fancy her chances if he gets to her before we do.'

'And he wants us to believe Ruth has Liam – why?'

'Lots of reasons. Planting the seed of distrust about her, making him and Esther out to be angels who just want her safe return, and to scare us into thinking he knows more about a case than we do.'

They had passed a few minutes in silence, each contemplating the tangled web they had before them, when

Ronnie's phone buzzed. Baz put Jules on speaker. Ronnie glanced down at the screen.

'Aha, DC Mayer, what news?'

'Sarge, I'm not sure you're gonna like this. We went to talk to Davor and Madison this morning, and the girl Eva who runs all the jobs. They have given us confirmation that Davor wasn't at the school that day. He was doing other jobs, and we have witnesses and some camera footage that backs him up as being elsewhere.'

'So they didn't arrive at the school, the job didn't get done, that's why there's no record in the school office?'

'Not exactly, sarge, the job did get done, but it was a last-minute switch. Ruth went there. She said she'd take that job as the previous one had cancelled and she was in the area.'

She paused, but Ronnie and Baz were too dumbstruck to speak.

'Ruth was at the school around the time of the abduction.'

'Ruth?' Ronnie's mind was a Jenga tower with one block too many removed, crashing down in slow motion. Ruth could pass for Dawn, at a distance to someone short-sighted, in the rain under a hood. It would have been easy. 'Of course.'

'*Good reason* just arrived,' muttered Baz.

Then Ronnie cleared her throat. It was time to take charge, even though the next thing she had to say went right against every instinct in her body. 'OK, Jules, the focus is entirely on Ruth now. Let's get a trace on her phone and a warrant to search her house.'

'And we have the DNA back from the sugar spoon in the café.'

'Go on.' Ronnie slowed the car to prepare herself.

'It's Liam.'

Ronnie and Baz looked at each other in disbelief. 'So, who was the woman he was with?' asked Baz, his hands clasped behind his head as he thought aloud. 'It sounded like Dawn, but now it sounds as if we're wrong on that.'

'It could just as easily be Ruth Jones,' said Jules. 'Now we know she was at the school half an hour earlier. We have to go on that assumption.'

'She wouldn't be able to take him just like that, would she?'

'Yes, I think she would. There's something Cara told me that makes that absolutely possible.'

Ronnie relayed her conversation with Cara about Liam's eyesight and was met with incredulity.

Baz was the first to speak. 'But even if he mistook her at the school, what about the café scenario? The delivery girl said she thought it was the boy's granny.'

Jules had the answer. 'To an eighteen-year-old who thinks anyone over twenty-five is ancient, yes, possibly, and anyone can buy a grey wig.'

'I suppose if you're on the run, it's probably second nature. What about the clothes? What was the woman wearing?'

'A pink faux-fur gilet over a purple top.'

'Dawn's outfit, but not exactly designer exclusives,' Ronnie pointed out. 'Easy to copy, and an easy identifier for a boy who can't see well.' Traffic was slowing in the inside lane so she pulled out to overtake.

'What else did you get from our new friends with their missing poster?' Jules asked.

'Nate Jacobs, Ruth's uncle, has only recently found out she's still alive. He caught the sister, Martha, on FaceTime with her, so she was obviously keeping the secret. They said Ruth had run away from home in some sort of mental health crisis and, having found out she's not dead, he wants to take her back, to punish her, no doubt.'

'Sounds bad. What did you think?'

'He's a slippery fish, doesn't give a monkey's about Ruth, and expects us to hand her over on a plate. He even suggested she had taken Liam. Said she'd stolen a child before and was crazy enough to do it again.'

'Oh my God, and with her driving the van as well. Maybe he's right?'

'Maybe he is.' Ronnie changed lanes again to slow down, her mind overflowing with questions. She had been so certain that the allegations about Ruth were completely unfounded, and now her conviction had been well and truly quashed by the emerging facts. How much could she trust her own instincts if they were so easily overturned? She drove the rest of the way in silence. Too many conflicting messages in her head. This was a case that could still unravel in a multitude of directions, and it was her job to find out which one led to the answer, before it was too late.

CHAPTER 31

The chains are too tight around Martha's wrists, and it feels as if the blood is draining from her fingers. Nate and Esther don't usually stay out together this long, even on the days they are hunting for Ruth. Today it has been hours, four at least, by her calculation, based on how far the sun has moved round. She thinks about Rex. He doesn't deserve this. He's a child still. She calls out to him. She doesn't know if he can hear but she calls out anyway, just in case. She hears nothing back, but she tells him it will be OK, that they will be back soon, that they will be fed. At least there's no crying today. She tells him to think about when they used to feed the animals together, asks him if he remembers the baby goats trying to eat his trousers. All this to an empty room, in the hope that the walls will have some compassion and will let her words pass through them to comfort him.

Rex is the reason she won't try to run. If she goes, she will have to take him with her, and she has nothing to offer him – no money, no place to stay. If she had made the move before Nate found out Ruth was still alive, then things might have been different.

Ruth. Poor Ruth. Where is she now and what must she think?

Martha still doesn't know what possessed her to let the call go on so long. She would always limit their FaceTime calls to half an hour at most, enough time to reassure each other that they were OK, to exchange news and sometimes, just occasionally, talk about a future when they might be together again. But this time she got carried away, she let Rex show Ruth all his school books, then he persuaded her to take the phone outside to show Ruth the new henhouse and the goats that ate everything in their path.

She saw Nate's face reflected in the screen before she heard his footsteps. They must have been so engrossed, he had managed to come up behind her unnoticed, despite his heavy thundering build and stinking breath. The shock of it hits her again now as she remembers it. The slap of his hand on the side of her face as he seized the phone from her. Rex's cry of pain as he was hurled to the ground. The phone was flung into the mill stream. In retrospect, that was a good thing, as Nate had no way of retrieving Ruth's number, but he'd seen enough. He recognised the wind farm with the mixed-blade turbines. He made sure Martha knew that. He said it would only be a matter of time before he found her now.

If she had hung up a few minutes earlier, she might still be unchained, she might be free to leave the house, feed the animals, breathe the fresh air and chop wood for the fire. But she took the risk, because every phone call she had with Ruth was a joy, ever since the first one. The one that came in from an unknown number, a voice from the dead, a phoenix from the ashes that said:

'Martha, it's Ruth.'

Then, because Martha was dumbstruck:

'I just wanted you to know I made it out of there.'

CHAPTER 32

It wasn't long before Jules was back with an update on the trace of Ruth's phone. It hadn't been used for the past week. The last signal had come from a mast near the police station on the previous Wednesday.

'That's not what we wanted to hear.'

Ronnie flipped the file closed. 'Where are we with the warrant?'

'As long as it takes. You know what they're like.'

'How are relations with the Buckleys?'

'Liaison's back in there with them now, keeping things calm, chatting to Cara about any contact they may have had with Ruth. Hoping to stumble on a reason that Ruth might have met them, or Liam, and identified him as a target.'

'That's a lot to find out, without giving anything away and causing alarm.'

'He's under strict instructions to ask open questions only.'

A thought occurred to Ronnie. 'So, if you've shown Cara a picture of Ruth, has Steve seen it as well?'

'Yes. Awkward moment if he really had been on dates with her. How did you find that out, sarge? I realised when you met Steve that something wasn't right.'

'That's a story for later. And I don't know if it's muddied the waters or cleared a path for us. You could see it either way. For Steve it must be a pretty shocking thought, though, that Ruth might be in the frame.'

'And not being able to tell your wife that the woman you had an affair with might have stolen your son.'

Ronnie let her words sink in and, with them, the realisation of their importance. How had she not seen it before? Was she so hung up on Ruth's vulnerability that she'd discounted the obvious?

'Of course. How did I miss that?'

'Miss what?'

'Revenge – the greatest motive of all. She finds out he's married with a child and punishes him in the way that's going to hurt him the most.'

Jules hesitated. 'I suppose, yes . . .'

'How did Steve actually react when he saw Ruth's picture?'

'I didn't want to examine him too hard for a reaction. But after a few seconds, when I managed to steal a glance at his face, I could see he'd gone pale, like he'd seen a ghost. Not as good a liar as we thought.'

Ronnie considered the irony of that, given what a brilliant liar he had been when it came to getting money off women he met online, but this wasn't the time for full disclosure on that point. A figure appeared in the doorway to rescue her from any comment. 'Ah, DC Munro is here.'

Baz nodded to Jules. 'I just thought we'd make a start on the fingerprints.'

Ronnie tipped the contents of her bag out on to the desk to find the piece of card. From among the receipts, notepads and unopened post, she produced what he was looking for, then looked again at the scattering of debris in front of her. She wasn't sure, even after going over things several times, whether it had already been on her desk or had come out of her bag, but she was staring at a newspaper cutting, screwed up and unscrewed again by the look of it. She smoothed it out as best she could so they could all read it.

FAMILY ESCAPE DEATH HOUSE FIRE

Ronnie held her breath as she read onwards. There wasn't much to the story, to all appearances. A wooden cabin in the garden had caught fire, the cause presumed to be an electric fire too close to the curtains. The shed was razed to the ground. Thankfully no one was hurt, the relieved home-owner was quoted as saying, but if the flames had reached the main house, things would have been very different. The photo was of a square stone building that looked like an Edwardian rectory, with bay windows and a heavy front door. The kind of place she might pore over on Rightmove, just a bit more spooky.

Baz read her mind and shivered aloud.

'Might be a nice place if it wasn't so sinister.'

'I'm not sure where this came from . . . did someone leave it on my desk?'

'It wasn't me, but maybe someone else did?'

'It wasn't there this morning. I'd have seen it before I left.'

'I can ask around.'

'Thanks, and while you're at it, can you look it up on the system and find out what happened?'

'I'll find out what I can and come back to you.' Baz and Jules left, leaving Ronnie with her head in her hands. It was another curve ball that had been thrown at her. She needed a break. Too many roads led nowhere.

Absently, she scrolled through her phone. Susie Marshall wanted to know if they were still meeting up that night because she was dying to hear Ronnie's romantic headlines after her online dating adventures. There was a missed call from Jacksons estate agents. Serena was asking whether she should cook dinner that night, and her mother wanted to check everything was OK. Her message sat below an attempt at a selfie that was just half her face and some blue sky. A last-minute holiday, a cruise around the Med with some sort of education element, which apparently meant on-board lectures by famous naturalists, she'd explained on the phone the day she left. Perhaps it was naturists and she'd got the wrong end of the stick. Ronnie smiled to herself. Nothing would horrify her mother more than being stranded out in the ocean with a boat load of naked people.

She typed a few quick texts back to them all and closed her eyes for a second. Sometimes you needed to take your mind away from the immediate problem in order to be open to the universe. That was another of Serena's nuggets of wisdom, but to Ronnie it sounded lazy and unjustified, so she kept it down to a few minutes. She checked on Snap Map and saw Tilly was in school, where she should be, and thanked the god of technology once again. Her phone pinged twice more. Eddie had got full marks in a French test. Ronnie's face lit up. Perhaps there was something behind all this to feel grateful for.

'Sarge?' She was dragged from her reverie by a familiar voice. 'Sorry to disturb your nap.'

'I wasn't napping.' As the words came out, she realised how stupid they sounded. 'At least, that wasn't the intention. So what did you find? Why have we been given the article?'

Baz made sure he had her attention before offering the answer to her question with a triumphant flourish.

'Because . . . this house is called Mill Farm, near Stoneybridge, and it's Nate and Esther's home.'

Ronnie let it sink in as Baz produced his iPad, which he placed on the desk in front of her. 'That's the fire report and we've got the postcode of the property – in the middle of nowhere by the sound of things. The construction of the barn that went up in flames was mainly wood, and there were cans of petrol stored nearby, so the destruction was almost total. The journalist was right. They were lucky they didn't set light to the whole pine forest next door, not to mention the main house. There was an electric fire in there as well. Must have gone up like a firework.'

'Right. I see.' She looked harder at the report on the screen. 'So, no casualties, you say?'

'No, everyone was accounted for. They were all in the main house. A storm in a teacup, maybe. The only thing is that the girl living there, Martha, was pretty screwed up by what happened, by all accounts. The police report had her in a hysterical state, saying it was all her fault.'

'How's it her fault? She admitted to starting it?'

'She said she'd brought in the electric fire the day before. She used to use the shed as a little getaway shack, it seems.'

'A woman-cave.'

'That sort of thing, yes.'

'But she survived the fire, they all did, so hysterics seems a bit extreme, doesn't it?'

'Maybe she thought she'd be in trouble. They also said, and this was just a curious PC who followed up on it, that Martha had to spend time in hospital and was only released weeks later by the psych ward on a cocktail of drugs.'

'Guilt is a destructive emotion,' observed Ronnie. 'And they could all have died, if it had spread. Perhaps it was that what-could-have-been kind of guilt.'

'Maybe. I can't imagine what else.'

Ronnie considered the facts. Ruth was being hunted down by people who had once been her guardians. A fire in her home, or next to her home, caused her sister serious psychological damage, whether it was guilt or something else. Was it Martha that started the fire? Only four people were mentioned as living in the house at the time. Had Ruth left before then, or was the fire the reason she left?

Baz flicked over to another tab on his tablet.

'Another thing – no reported missing babies from Stoneybridge. Nate was clearly lying about her abducting someone's kid.'

'None reported doesn't mean none happened. Teenage hidden pregnancy?'

'It's a possibility, of course.'

'You believe him?'

'Not necessarily, but if he's right, and if Ruth was on site at the time of the abduction, it's all adding up.'

There was a pause as they both let the new facts settle. Then Ronnie made a decision.

'I'm going to get to the bottom of this. I'm going down there.' She looked at her watch. 'There's plenty of time. I can be back by tonight for the meet.'

'Right you are, sarge,' Baz said. 'I'd come with you, but I've got something on this afternoon.'

'No, I can do this on my own. We don't want to raise the alarm by bringing the cavalry.'

Ronnie picked up her phone and scrolled down her recent calls before pressing redial. Jules answered immediately.

'I'm literally outside your office.'

'Can you pop in for a sec?'

Baz sidled out, pulling on his jacket, and Jules took his place in the seat opposite Ronnie.

'He looks nervous. What have you said to him, sarge?'

'Nothing at all. I just wanted you to do run some prints for me that I picked up this morning. Meanwhile, I need to get down to check out the Mill Farm place to find out what's been going on, in the hope that I can get a better picture of Ruth's life and what she was running from, maybe meet the famous Martha and Rex. I'll be a couple of hours, three max. Back in time for tonight's big event.'

'Won't they be there? Nate and Esther?'

'He said he had meetings all afternoon. I'm hoping that was the one true thing I've been told today. But I don't think they'll be there. Ruth might be.'

'Ruth? Why would she be there?' Jules looked shocked.

Ronnie closed her eyes to think. There were so many possibilities. This was just one of them.

'She's not at her house. When Baz first went looking for her, the neighbour said she sometimes went to her sister's in Sussex. We don't actually know that Nate and Esther still live there. We don't know where they live. But if Ruth has Liam . . .' She paused because the thought of it still seemed impossible. 'If she took him, what if she took him there? The last place on earth we'd look?'

Jules looked around for clues for an answer to the hypothesis. 'I suppose it's worth a try.'

'And if Liam's there, then there's no need for the meet-up tonight, no need to hand over Cara's parents' cash. It's just a hunch, but I feel I need to follow it up. What do you think?'

Jules nodded slowly. 'I see. But you shouldn't go there alone.'

'It's an hour away. I'll call for back-up if there's anything to report. If there's nothing, then I'll be back in plenty of time for the meeting tonight. I've promised Cara no police but I'm planning on breaking that promise.'

Jules gave her a doubtful look. 'OK, you're the boss. I'll call you as soon as we get a result on the prints.'

'And Ruth's work van, we need it checked for any evidence that Liam has been in it. Prints and DNA, as quick as we can get it.'

Ronnie's phone rang and Jules took her leave with a thumbs up.

It was Cara. 'DS Delmar, I was returning your call. If it's about the drop-off tonight, Steve is still adamant, no police. We just can't take the risk and I agree with him. So do Mum and Dad.'

Ronnie's shoulders slumped in response. Cara's parents with their online gambling business were about to hand over the cash, but to whom? Ruth Jones? It didn't seem likely, but then again, nothing had until now, or everything had, until it was knocked down five minutes later.

'OK, that's understood, as in I hear you.' She couldn't make any promises.

'So you won't agree to leave us to manage on our own?'

Ronnie thought carefully before answering. 'Actually, Cara, there's something else I need to ask you, which might mean we'll find Liam without you having to hand over the money.'

'What is it? I thought you'd asked everything there was to ask.' She sounded weary and Ronnie guessed she wouldn't be able to keep her on the line for long.

'Did you have any visitors to the caravan in the weeks leading up to Liam's disappearance? Or did you get approached by anyone, any strangers, cold-callers, sales people knocking on the door? Anyone who might have seen you with Liam who wasn't part of your normal day-to-day life?'

Cara sighed. 'I've just been through all this with the other officer. We don't have visitors, as a rule. There's not much room for dinner parties where we live. Why?'

Cara had interview fatigue by the sound of things. Ronnie needed to draw a line under the questioning once and for all and get a clear answer. 'The person I'm thinking about would be a woman in her late twenties, about your height, with curly dark hair and dark eyes. She might have introduced herself as Ruth, or she might have used another name.'

'I don't think so. Why? Do you think she has Liam?' Cara's voice had become jumpy. Ronnie wished there was an easier way of asking the questions without making her panic.

'It's just a lead we're following. But if you don't remember anyone matching that description visiting your caravan then we may be wrong in our assumptions.'

It was no use trying to find a link to Ruth if there wasn't one, but Ronnie didn't want to admit defeat. Ruth had been to Liam's school, was there at the time he disappeared, then disappeared herself on the same day, and she was on the run from a family who claimed she had stolen a child before. The day she'd come into the station, the same day Liam had gone missing, she seemed unstable, and Steve had called her a psychopath. She'd abandoned a van with the keys in the ignition and left her job with no notice or communication. But even given all that, if Ruth hadn't had sight of Liam before his abduction, and if he didn't know who she was, it was unlikely that even with poor eyesight he'd have gone to her. So how would she have persuaded him to leave with her without the teacher sensing something was wrong? They might be back at square one.

Ronnie was about to thank Cara for her time and say goodbye, but Cara stopped her.

'Actually, now I think about it, there was someone. I didn't give it much thought because it was a few weeks ago. I'd forgotten completely.'

'Anything, Cara, just tell me what you remember.'

'There was a woman, but she was wearing a headscarf. I couldn't tell you the colour of her hair, or her age. She was kind of ageless. You know? More weathered than wrinkled.'

Ronnie's heart soared. 'Right, so tell me about her. What else can you remember? How long did she stay?'

'She had a Bible and some leaflets, wanted to talk about God or something, and I told her we weren't religious. I tried to be polite, and she was very polite back. It was like the Jehovah's Witnesses, but they normally go around in pairs, like police.'

Ronnie smiled to herself. She needed to remember that. 'Did she leave anything with you, any of the leaflets?'

'No, I said she should save them. Dawn would have gone crazy if she'd found anything like that lying around. She'd say something like "Imagine if Liam got hold of it."' Her voice shook slightly at the mention of his name.

'Did she meet Liam?' It was a hard question, the hardest one she had to ask.

'Yes, Liam was there. It was just the two of us. Steve was at work. We'd just got back from football club and he was sitting doing colouring. She only saw him through the door at first, but then she asked how he was enjoying school and stuff and he went to get his new pens to show her and everything, so I ended up inviting her in for a cup of tea but she said she had to go.'

'Did she meet Dawn or Steve?'

'Not Steve, but Dawn was outside hanging up washing and watering pots. She's always doing something like that. She came in to wash her hands. I remember because . . .' She broke off, the way a child might when telling a story they suddenly realise will incriminate them.

'Because what?'

'When Dawn came in, Liam took off his glasses straight away. She left and I persuaded him to put them on again and I remember him saying, "The boys at school laugh at me in my glasses."'

So Ruth would have known that Liam's eyesight was bad. Ronnie needed one more answer. 'Is there any way she could be the woman in the photograph you were shown? The one from the newspaper, the missing person notice?'

The seconds it took Cara to answer seemed like minutes.

'Yes. I mean, it's possible. I can't rule it out, but I couldn't say definitely one way or the other.'

Ronnie let out a long exhale. It wasn't out of the question. The latest theory was holding water so far. 'Thanks, Cara. You've been great. We'll be in touch shortly if anything comes of this. And fingers crossed for tonight.'

CHAPTER 33

As Ronnie drove south-west out of town, Halesworth disappeared in her rear-view mirror until it was a dot in the distance. After a while, the grey walls of the suburbs gave way to green fields and hills, then back again as she reached the outskirts of Stoneybridge, where council estates clung to their urban roots with one foot in the countryside. The centrepiece, which must have once been the residents' pride and joy, was the bridge across the water that gave the town its name. The GPS directed her to the other side of town where the roads were narrower, bordered by high hedges.

Sitting in the next queue of traffic behind a black four-by-four in the midst of the Friday afternoon exodus, Ronnie's mind flashed back to the stolen Land Rover. What was the address it had been taken from that they had been trying to link to Joe Buckley? She'd shown it to Joe but hadn't given the detail much attention. She sent a quick voice note to Jules, who came back straight away saying the officers who had attended would get back to her with the address. Then, with a few minutes more on her hands, Ronnie went over the facts, as they now knew them to be.

She talked it through aloud, listing what was known, what was likely and what still remained a mystery.

Dawn had been first in the frame for Liam's disappearance, possibly covering for Joe, whose alibi and phone activity made him impossible to arrest. Liam was seen at the Pit Stop café with someone who was presumably his captor on the afternoon of his disappearance and that could have been Dawn, but was now more likely to have been Ruth, given that she was at his school at exactly the time he was taken. Whoever had taken Liam needed to have met him before, and if Ruth had visited Cara, then that would fit the story perfectly. Added to that, Ruth had a motive if she wanted to punish Steve for the way she felt treated by him. He had been cagey about where he lived, of course, because he was married, but if Ruth took that as rejection, who knew what reaction she might have had? It was looking bad for Ruth, and Ruth's backstory might shed some light on it all. But time was marching on, and Ronnie needed to be quick if she was to make it back in time for the reward handover. She indicated, glanced in the mirror and accelerated into the flowing traffic.

The postcode for Mill Farm showed it to be a short distance from the South Downs, and several miles from what Ronnie considered to be civilisation. It covered a relatively wide area of countryside, including some neighbours half a mile away. The GPS led her to their place first, and the elderly man that eventually answered the door had never heard of the Jacobs family. Frustratingly, the same happened with the occupants of the next house she stopped at. They were a young family, the father working from home and mother dressed up in Lycra ready to go running, or so Ronnie presumed. In fact, it seemed that none of them left the premises except by car, and the sportswear was a decoy. 'We only moved in a month ago, have no idea who our neighbours are yet,' the woman laughed.

Ronnie climbed back into the car and looked at the map on her phone. This was ridiculous, but on closer examination, it looked as if there was one more place to try. When she finally spotted a half-hidden road sign pointing right to Mill Farmhouse, she breathed a sigh of relief and swung into the drive. She was cutting it fine, but there was still time.

By now, the sky was darkening, and under the tunnel of bowed trees, the sudden change in the light caused her to drive straight through a pot hole in the badly surfaced road. She weaved past another three, gripping the steering wheel more tightly and wishing she was driving something more accustomed to dirt tracks when a deer leapt out in front of her, forcing her to swerve left and hit a boulder on the verge. She locked eyes with the animal, and a chill ran through her as it bounded away. In that moment, its fear felt contagious. She'd take things more slowly from here.

The track continued for another hundred metres or so before the house came into view – an imposing grey stone building, more intimidating than it had looked in the newspaper article, more derelict, and there was something different about the façade she couldn't put her finger on. The place was in darkness and silent as a graveyard. Ronnie wondered if it had been a wasted journey. All this way and she'd have to go back to the office with nothing to show for it.

She rang the bell and knocked on the door, not expecting an answer, and none came. Fat drops of rain began to fall and she took a few steps back and looked up. The ground-floor windows were barred vertically and horizontally, which seemed an excessive security measure in the depths of the countryside. The upper floor had vertical bars only, closer together and seemingly more recent additions by their colour.

As her eyes moved back to the ground-floor level, a woman's anxious face appeared at the window on the left of the main door, and it dawned on Ronnie what kind of security the bars were intended for. A hand went up, the other tried but was being pulled back by something. It was impossible to get closer to the window as a sprawling and neglected rose bush flanked by brambles blocked the way, but once she had got as close as she could, she held up her badge and shouted through the wind and rain.

'DS Delmar from Halesworth police. I'm a detective investigating the disappearance of Ruth Jacobs and a boy called Liam Buckley. Can I come in?' The face mouthed an answer and the head shook. A hand pointed to the front door and mimed a locking motion followed by a shrug.

Ronnie had to think quickly. By the age of the girl, she could be Ruth's sister. She spoke with exaggerated motion to see if the girl could read her lips. 'Are you Martha?'

There was a pause, a frown, then a vigorous nod after she'd repeated the question. Then the girl gesticulated wildly at the door, the window, the upstairs. Ronnie thought she saw the words on her lips. 'We're locked in.'

She wished Baz was there. What an idiot she was coming out here alone. She looked around for something heavy to break a window with, then remembered the bars that would prevent any attempt to break in. There was no enforcer in her car, so there was no chance of ramming the front door. But Martha was already waving at her, banging on the glass, mouthing, 'No, no,' and pointing downwards.

Ronnie looked down and couldn't see anything straight away. She kicked away the leaves and soil around where she was standing and looked up again to see Martha giving her the thumbs up. Grabbing a stone from the pile of rubble in the drive, she began scraping at the earth until she saw a square of wood, rather like a loft entrance from a landing, but leading down instead of up. She scraped at the sides, trying to find the edges and a way of lifting the lid. A makeshift plastic handle came away in her hand when she pulled on it, but the plank had moved enough for her to get purchase under one of the edges. She levered the stone under the edge and heaved. It hadn't been moved for a long time, that was for sure. As she lifted it up, beetles and woodlice scuttled away and a scatter of earth fell inside into the darkness.

Dark clouds were racing across the sky now, and what little light might have reached the yard was obscured by the tall pines that stood like sentinels around the land.

This was no time to go exploring dungeons, especially alone. Ronnie hesitated, looking back at Martha, who was making gestures with her arms that looked like an impression of a duck diving down into a pond. The window was steaming up with her breath and she wiped it away, then stopped and breathed on it again. She was breathing on the whole thing now and becoming invisible through the opaque glass. Then came the writing. She had moved to the right side of the window – Ronnie's left – and words appeared, hesitantly at first, slowly as she got used to turning the letters round, then more confidently. It was hard to read through the criss-cross of metal on the outside but gradually the words became clear. *Coal chute → cellar*. Ronnie pointed to herself and then downwards. Was that what Martha was asking her to do? Martha nodded, then pointed to her watch and started writing again. *They home soon. Please help.*

Ronnie stared at the words on the window, then shone her phone torch down into the chute. If this was a horror film, she would jump down there to find the trapdoor closing above her head, never to be removed. She looked back at Martha whose pleading expression was becoming desperate.

The wind was getting up now, and gusts of rain with it. Ronnie took a second to think, assessed the scene and came to a decision. It wasn't a hard one to make.

It's just a coal hole, a delivery bunker for something, she told herself. *It leads to a cellar, and that's how I'll get into the house. If there's a tunnel, it will be big enough to crawl through, or how else would they collect what was dropped into here?* It made sense. There was nothing to be afraid of. She shone her phone torch into the hole and there was nothing but blackness. She dropped a stone and heard the thud as it landed. It wasn't too deep. She could do this. She sat on the edge and looked up to see Martha's wide-eyed concern, just before she dropped down inside. It was a couple of metres at most. The landing jarred her knees but that was all. She felt around for an opening in the direction of the house. Each second felt like a minute. The air was thick with the dust that had risen as she hit the ground, and she pulled her jumper up over her nose and mouth. There must be a way out. She found it higher up than she'd expected. The tunnel opening was level with her knees rather than her feet, which made it easier to climb inside. The surface was rough and uneven, flakes of limestone came off the walls as she moved gingerly along, feeling her way with her hands. She hadn't anticipated the claustrophobia which was rising inside her. But there was nowhere to run to, not yet. She mustn't let it take hold. She pushed on, holding her phone in her mouth as she crawled along, reaching out for the end. It must be soon.

It came suddenly – something hard just ahead of her: cold, metal, heavy. She felt around the edge. It was secured by two bolts which she slid aside before manoeuvring herself into another position. Bracing herself for the impact, she kicked out hard, the soles of her boots ramming the obstacle into submission. There was a clatter of iron on stone and the smell of something rotten. She was in.

'Martha?' she called out, before collapsing into a coughing fit. The dust was everywhere, all over her clothes, in her eyes, in her throat. The smell was putrid and shocking. She shone the torch around. 'Martha, can you hear me?'

The ceiling was low and she followed it with one hand above her head while taking one step forward at a time. She found a wall and followed that to the right until it met another wall. A few feet further on, she found the door and a light switch.

As she flicked it on, she gasped, leaning against the wall to steady herself as her mind refused to comprehend what her eyes were seeing. On the opposite wall, two heavy, rusting chains hung above a narrow wooden bed. At the foot of the bed were two more. *Hands and feet.* The image refused to budge and she felt her stomach churn in revulsion. She dragged her eyes left. In the corner was an upturned bucket, and next to it a rudimentary crate with a small stained mattress inside and a scrap of a blanket. A makeshift baby's cot? Once it was there, she couldn't erase the thought from her mind. She swallowed the vomit that was rising in her throat and reached for the door handle, wrestling it open and pausing for breath on the other side. She needed to get out.

The space she found herself in was lit by a chink of light from above where a flight of broken stone steps led to another door. She staggered up them, pushed open the door and came out in a wide hallway where the air was even colder and damper than in the basement. A single lamp on a table by the front door threw a ghostly light

on the dark walls and above the lamp hung two heavy
overcoats, a scarf and something that looked like a dead
animal. Ronnie jumped, then took a minute to catch her
breath as she realised it wasn't a fox corpse but some sort
of furry jacket. She needed to focus.

There were two doors leading off the hall.

'Martha?' she called, coughing dust as she did so.

'I'm here, the door on the right of the front door as you
look at it.' Her tiny voice rang out. Ronnie tried the door
which was locked. There was no sign of a key anywhere.

'Stand back, I'm going to force it.'

It didn't give way the first time, but with a harder kick
just by the lock, Ronnie broke through. The door swung
on its hinges and the frame splintered where the lock had
slipped its moorings.

Across the room from where she stood, and with one
hand chained to a metal bar on the ceiling, stood a thin,
hollow-looking woman, bright-eyed but pale-faced and
scared. 'I'm Martha,' she said, unsurely.

'I'm Ronnie,' said Ronnie, 'and I'm going to get you out
of here.'

Ronnie undid her rudimentary shackles with ease when
Martha showed her where the key was. 'They put it just
out of my reach, like that's an extra punishment,' she said.
'They went out at lunchtime but haven't come back. They
said they were going to find Ruth, that the police were
going to take them to her.' Martha was talking fast, her
eyes darting around in fear. Ronnie pulled out her phone
to call for back-up but there was no signal.

'Do you have Wi-Fi?' she asked, looking around without much hope. 'I need to make a call.'

'They changed the password. I don't know what it is.'

Ronnie swore under her breath as her phone screen asked her for the magic code that would open up communication with the outside world. She tried *Jacobs family*, then *Nate Jacobs, Mill Farm, Mill Farmhouse* in lower and upper cases with no joy. 'Is there a landline?'

'No landline.'

Ronnie took a second to flick through the options in her head. Perhaps she could do without back-up for now. She was still trying to process the fact that Ruth wasn't here, hiding Liam. Another blind alley.

'Did Nate and Esther say anything before they left this morning? Any idea when they thought they'd be back?'

'They said to get ready for my sister to come home. Make something nice, he said . . .' She drifted off, looking around the room. 'But there's nothing here, nothing in the fridge apart from a lump of cheese. And I don't want her home. It's not safe here for her.' Her voice broke, but she pulled it back.

Ronnie looked around her. 'What happened here, Martha? Nate gave us some story that Ruth had stolen a baby and run away, never to be seen again. Missing presumed dead, until he caught you speaking to her on the phone.'

'He didn't tell you he tried to burn her to death in a fire?'

Ronnie gasped. 'The fire in the cabin?'

Martha's eyes glassed over. 'He had always wanted rid of her after Rex arrived. He would talk to Aunt Esther about the day Ruth was going away, he didn't know I was listening, or that I knew what he meant. She was never going to go away; she'd die before she left Rex.'

'Rex, their son?'

'Ruth's son.'

Ronnie's breath caught in her throat again. It was all making horrible sense now.

'Ruth and Nate?'

That explained the makeshift crib and the chains in the cellar. The thought of what must have happened there sliced into her mind and silenced her.

Martha's brow furrowed with worry like a lost child. 'He couldn't let anyone know, so he pretended it was their son, his and Esther's. Nobody knew them. The community just accepted it, but Ruth wanted her baby back. We always hoped, maybe one day . . .' Tears filled her eyes. 'Nate didn't trust us together after Ruth tried to escape the first time. First, he didn't let me go to her at all, and then later he only let me see her if Esther was with me, so we couldn't talk properly. I think he thought she was going to try something, or I was, and Rex was growing bigger.'

'That's why he set the cabin on fire?'

Martha nodded.

'But Nate thought she'd died, and there was no body to bury.'

Martha nodded again. 'That time is a blur for me. I was ill; they said it could be shock. I didn't know if she was alive or dead, but Aunt Esther told me everything had been taken care of, and I never asked what she meant. I didn't want to know. But I didn't want to give up hope. And then, out of the blue, I got a call from Ruth. She'd found my number in a chat room online.'

'How were you allowed on a phone, let alone chat rooms?' It didn't sound possible, but Martha had an answer.

'Those were the days when I had a phone and we had a tablet for Rex to do his school work on. The phone was for emergencies while Nate and Esther were out. There was only one number on it, and Nate trusted me not to go online for any other reasons than education.'

'Why did he trust you?'

'Because he made us scared.' Martha's eyes flickered with what must have been the memories of threats and punishments. 'He said he was watching us through the screen. We didn't know any better so we believed him, until one day, I thought I saw Esther shake her head when he said it and that made me think I could do it. I could try, just once . . .'

'And it went on from there.' Ronnie finished her sentence for her, imagining how it must have felt to take that risk.

'While I was supposed to be doing maths with Rex, I was posting things online using a code word I thought she might recognise if she was out there. That's how she found me.'

'Where is Rex now? How old is he?' Ronnie was bursting with questions.

'Nate keeps him locked upstairs, since he found out Ruth was still alive. I'll take you to him. He's ten, nearly eleven.'

Ronnie took the stairs two at a time, with Martha lagging behind, her frailty making her slow and breathless.

The key to Rex's room was on the ledge of the panelling next to his door. She unlocked the door and pushed it open.

The boy was sitting on the bed, huddled in the corner with the sheet around his face. His big brown eyes looked at her with incomprehension and terror.

'Rex? I'm here to help you. My name's Ronnie.'

'Martha, I want Martha.'

'I'm here, Rex. It's OK.' Martha stumbled in and took both his hands in hers.

'I'm hungry.'

Ronnie looked him over: pale, too thin, a shadow of what a ten-year-old should be.

'Let's get you something to eat, and I think I've got some energy drinks in the car.' It was a habit she'd got into in the Met, for the days when the schedule didn't allow a lunch break, but with suburban policing taking a slower pace she hadn't had much use for them recently. 'And then we need to get you out of here.'

CHAPTER 34

Ronnie was about to open the boot of the car when something caught her eye. She bent down to take a closer look, and her worst fears were confirmed. Her back left tyre was completely flat. It must have been the pot hole.

'Fuck,' she muttered under her breath. 'Fuck, fuck, fuck, fuck, fuck,' as if the word was a magic spell that was supposed to make the tyres reinflate. But there was no reason to panic. She kept a spare tyre and tool kit in the back like everyone else. She pulled open the boot and glanced around the other side of the car, just to check.

Another series of expletives burst forth. There was a second puncture on the right rear tyre, presumably caused when she hit the boulder to avoid the deer. 'Tell me this isn't happening,' she moaned into the wind. She needed to think fast.

There was no chance of making a quick escape with Martha and Rex, so the priority was keeping Nate and Esther at bay until that was possible. No point believing he had meetings later in the day. Nothing else he said had been true so far. She handed Martha the Lucozade cans. 'Take these and grab yourselves anything you can find to eat. And then I need you to do something for me.' She headed back into the house, with Martha in tow. 'You said there's no landline. Is there any other phone in the house that you know of?'

'There's a pager in the kitchen, for emergencies. You can type messages on it.'

'So, in theory, you could still reach it to contact Nate, even with the restraints he put on you? It wouldn't be suspicious if you used it?'

'Yes, just about, but I've never tried.' She picked up the gadget that lay on the worktop and inspected it.

'We need Nate to think you're still on side. I want you to message him to say the police have arrived outside and are knocking on the door asking for him. But that you're keeping down low and out of the way.'

'Won't that make him angry?'

'It will make sure he doesn't come home. Hopefully he'll think we want to talk to him about the whereabouts of your sister again, but he can call CID if he wants to have that chat. We just need him to stay away a little longer so we can get you out and secure the house as a crime scene.'

Martha looked frightened. 'I'm not sure. What if it goes wrong?'

'It won't,' Ronnie reassured her, trying to sound more convincing than she felt. 'You'll have to trust me.' She motioned for her to sit down at the kitchen table, where Rex was eyeing a greying block of cheese warily. The Lucozade would have to do for now.

'Martha, will you page Nate?' She took a knife and began chopping off the mould. Cheese was usually fine underneath – she remembered that from her student days.

Martha bit her lip and screwed her eyes tight shut for a second. A tear escaped and ran down her cheek. 'Yes, I'll do it.'

The message was typed and sent. Ronnie leaned across the table, her mind on something that was still taking shape as she spoke.

She stepped back into the hallway and took a closer look at the dead animal hanging on the hook. It was indeed some kind of jacket and it looked strangely familiar. Pinky-grey fur and no sleeves. It was just like the one Dawn had been wearing each time they had visited the caravan, the one someone had seen the woman wearing at the café. The woman who wasn't Dawn, or Ruth, if her new theory was right. The pieces of the puzzle began to fall into place.

She sat back down at the kitchen table and wondered where to begin.

'Martha, Rex, there's something else. It's not only Ruth that we're trying to find,' she began, looking from one pale face to the other as the two of them looked doubtfully at the cans of energy drinks in front of them. 'There's a missing boy called Liam who was taken from his school last week, and we think, or I think, that Nate and Esther may have been involved in his abduction.'

Martha's eyes widened, then flicked left and right as though she was trying to make sense of something.

'How old is he?'

311

'He's seven. He's in year three at primary school.' She looked at Martha. Something had changed in her face. 'Martha, do you think Liam might have been here?'

Rex looked at Martha with fear in his eyes. Martha's eyes dropped to the floor. 'I heard crying every day this week but I thought it was you, Rex.'

Rex took her hand. 'It wasn't me crying,' he said. 'I was being brave.'

Ronnie took a breath. It was falling into place, but she needed a few more minutes. The pager pinged with a response: *Stay quiet – keep out of sight and they will go away – we will be back tonight.*

Ronnie doubted they would. If she was right, by tonight, he and Esther would have the reward money and would be making a run for it. Whether they'd make time for a home visit to unlock Martha and Rex was unlikely, given what she'd found out since her arrival at Mill Farm. The current obstacle in her path was the phone signal, which was still flicking in and out randomly wherever she stood in the room.

'Listen, I need you two to stay here for a minute while I look for a phone signal.' Taking an umbrella from the stand, she switched off the phone and walked down the drive towards the main road, where she switched it on again. She couldn't do anything now without back-up. Martha and the boy were too weak to leave on foot, and even if they got to the road, Ronnie didn't fancy their chances flagging down a lift. She walked a few metres further, willing her phone to come back to life, and just as she rounded the bend where the pot hole had done its damage, the 3G symbol appeared in the corner of the screen. It was weak but worth a shot. She scrolled down her recent calls for Lydia's number.

The phone was answered before it rang, but she could only hear every second or third word. She filled in the gaps with what she could imagine Lydia saying. 'DS Delmar, what have you got? We couldn't get through but DC Mayer told us where you were headed so . . .' Relief flooded her in an instant. They knew where she was at least. She raised her voice to get the best chance of being heard.

'Listen, the line is very bad. I need you to send back-up. I've got two punctures. But I've also got news.' She paused, hoping they were still connected. 'It's them, it's Nate and Esther who took Liam.'

'What?' Lydia's voice sounded more afraid than incredulous. 'Is Liam there in the house?'

'No. I think he's with them. If they're on their way to collect the reward, he'll be in the boot of their car, unless they've locked him up elsewhere temporarily.'

She couldn't bear to think of Liam being so close to them just a few hours ago when they were drinking coffee at the café. But at least, if she was right, his ordeal would be over soon.

'The exchange is in under two hours. You won't make it back here by then.' It sounded like Jules's voice. She was right. There was no point in risking missing them at the reservoir. That operation needed to run smoothly, without the risk of late arrivals. 'At least they can assume they're looking for Nate and Esther now rather than Ruth.'

'Martha and Rex are in a terrible state. I didn't want to let them see how shocked I was, but they are both severely malnourished, so they're going to need a visit to the hospital. Hang on. I have something here.' Ronnie was already reading a text message that had popped up on her phone. It was from the lab. Her heart missed a beat.

Lydia cleared her throat. Her words came in threes and fours, and with fewer gaps, Ronnie could just about make out what she was saying. 'So can I just summarise where we are? There was a fire at Mill Farm in which Ruth was assumed to have perished. Neither the fire service nor the police were told about Ruth's existence, and with everyone accounted for, they closed the case. Nate assumes the fire must have destroyed all traces, although how he makes that presumption is still a mystery, because there would always be traces. Presumably he turned a blind eye, bulldozed the scene and built over it. Then Ruth turns out to be alive, and when Nate finds that out because of this phone call with Martha, he goes on the rampage, because as long as she's alive, there's a chance she'll blow the whistle on him.

'Meanwhile there's the Buckley incident, and Nate and Esther have now moved to centre stage there too. You can see how Esther might have been masquerading as Dawn in the café, and they may have been motivated by the reward money, but how would they have known about it, and how would they have managed to abduct Liam, without knowing him well enough for him to go willingly with them? How would they have known how to trick him like that? And can you explain how all that fits with Dawn's abduction?'

'Yes I can, just about,' said Ronnie. 'Cara has confirmed she had a visit to the caravan a few weeks ago from a woman that could have been Esther, Bible stuff apparently, and Cara introduced her to Liam. Dawn was somewhere in the vicinity at the time. If she was wearing her usual outfit, that solves that issue. Esther dresses up as Dawn. Liam *is* short-sighted, but won't wear his glasses. That also came out in the brief chat they had at the caravan. And we now know that it was Nate that drove the car that took Dawn away.'

There was silence on the line as Ronnie looked again at the message she'd just received. 'His prints, which I picked up this morning at the café, were a match for the ones on the water bottle that Dawn was given when she was dropped off. Nate was the kidnapper. He took Dawn away while Esther took Liam and he came back to collect them both from the café and took them back to Mill Farm. It fits.'

Their reaction to the news was inaudible as the line crackled and gave out, but Ronnie's phone pinged with a text as soon as she had hung up. Roadworks were holding up the back-up team.

Back in the kitchen, Rex and Martha were eating hunks of stale bread and old cheese as if they'd never seen food before. Ronnie opened the doors of the oak dresser opposite them and pulled out a tin of baked beans. Rex beamed and Martha's eyes lit up.

Ronnie was about to go back upstairs to take a look around when a pile of paperwork on the dining-room table caught her eye. She picked the first thing off the top, a closely typed document headed *Annual Strategy Proposal*. She flicked through the pages but nothing sprang out at her. It seemed to relate to funding for the most part, or the lack of. There was a set of accounts appended to the end, which at first glance looked like a miserable reflection of the organisation's finances. She turned back to the cover page.

Pilgrims of Truth. Founded 1987.

It was a long shot but, in her experience, people who changed their wifi passwords were never very imaginative. Most would opt for a version of the family name or address, and in this case neither of those had worked. She tried again with *pilgrims of truth* first in lower case, then upper case, with no luck, then with the date 1987 tagged on the end.

'Bingo.' The wifi symbol flashed into life.

Letting out the longest breath she didn't know she was holding, she typed *pilgrims of truth* into the search engine. There was an official website, a map of places of worship and learned articles on their teachings. On the next page in the browser there were links to web pages of local groups, with notices of the dates and locations of meetings. On the first site, she was invited to type in her post code to find her nearest assembly, and at the top of the list was Blyth Road Assembly Hall, 11 Blyth Road, Wakehurst. But directly underneath the address there was more. *This Assembly Hall has been closed due to unforeseen circumstances and is not expected to reopen. Click here to find an alternative.* The link led her back to the postcode page, and she entered her childhood postcode from their family home in Waterman Lane. Another address came up with the same notice of closure. Opening a new tab, she typed in 'closure of Blyth Road Assembly Hall Pilgrims of Truth' and the screen was suddenly full of links to blogs, chat rooms, help centres and, on the third page, a question that jumped out at her and made her catch her breath.

More sex abuse victims come forward. It was an article written for an online whistle-blower publication, called simply *LIES*, which declared itself to be dedicated to exposing hypocrisy in religious organisations. From what she could gather from a skim-read, there had been a series of historical sex abuse claims against the Pilgrims, beginning with an anonymous tip-off, which gathered momentum as more victims found the courage to speak out. The tip-off had come from the daughter of an abuser who wouldn't be named but gave the police the information they needed to kick-start the investigation. From there, the police operation had snowballed, and a cascade of litigation ensued. A lawyer called Alan Swinney had taken the bulk of the cases as pro bono work for the victims, but their assailants were swamped with mounting legal costs. The Pilgrims were forced to sell off their property, including the prized and precious assembly halls that brought the Elders and their flock together. The article concluded with a photograph of an estate agent's sign above an abandoned building and the words 'Would *you* buy it?'

She googled the name of the reporter, couldn't see any social media presence but did find other articles by him and links to case reports where victims of sex abuse were suing for damages years after the event, having been shunned by the Elders and told it was all in their imagination. The Pilgrims of Truth policy had been to investigate allegations internally without involving the police, and only then if there was a second witness to the events, which meant that the victim had to confront and accuse their abuser face to face. Ronnie read on until her heart ached with disbelief and disgust.

She flicked back to her home screen. Back-up was ten minutes away. She sent them a pin to show the exact location. There was another missed call from Jacksons. She pressed call back and the phone was answered straight away by the girl whose voice she recognised from first thing that morning.

'DS Delmar? Thanks so much for calling me back. I thought you needed to know after all. About the sale of the Assembly Hall in Blyth Road.'

'Thank God for that. Although, I think I know the answer now.'

'Like I said, it's a corporate sale. The group is called, hang on . . .'

'Pilgrims of Truth?'

'That's it. And the guy we were dealing with is called Nate Jacobs.'

'Yes, I guessed he was our man. What made you change your mind, may I ask?'

'It seems he's doing deals on the side, not involving us, so we have taken him off the books.'

Ronnie pulled out the fire report. 'Can I check his address with you? Is it Mill Farm, Stoneybridge?'

'That's it.'

If Nate needed a motive, then that was it. Nate wanted more money for the Assembly Hall than Steve wanted to pay, and getting the reward money from them would easily fill that gap. But to kidnap a child with no *guarantee* of a reward being offered was risky. A ransom demand was much safer. Why had they not taken that route straight away?

The back-up cars were a few minutes away now. Rex was still finishing his sandwich.

'Martha, I'm going to take one last look round the house, if that's OK.'

'There's not much left to see,' she said, following Ronnie up the stairs and pushing open one of the doors on the landing. 'This is the room Ruth and I used to share, before they . . . before she . . .'

Inside, there were neatly made single beds with bedside tables and a wardrobe. Small crosses had been carved into each bedhead, and the words *Here lies your pilgrim*. Dead flies littered the sill below a grimy window, its view sliced by iron bars.

'They keep me in here all day most days since the phone call.'

Next door, in what must have been Nate and Esther's room, there was a Bible at each bedside and folded nightwear on each pillow. A heavy wooden cross hung above their bed, and another on the opposite wall. Ronnie took it all in.

'Is this it? Any other buildings, store rooms, sheds?'

'The cabin was destroyed in the fire, nothing left of it. The goats live on that patch now. There's just the store room where you came in, down in the basement. Where Ruth slept . . .' Martha's voice took on a strained tone before she composed herself again. 'There's another room down there where Nate keeps all his stuff now since the fire.' They made their way back down to the hall, where Martha opened the door to the basement, switched on the dim light and started down the uneven wooden steps. 'Careful on these. They're worse going down.'

'What kind of stuff did he keep here?'

'Tools, petrol for the mower and the car. We're miles from the nearest garage, so he keeps some at home.'

Ronnie looked around her, at the door that led to the room she'd entered by, the one she never wanted to see again, and then at the other door, which stood ajar in front of them. 'And that's what started the fire?'

Martha nodded. 'He made me tell the police it was my fault, and he said we couldn't mention Ruth had ever existed, because she was dead and if they found out, he'd go to prison, there'd be no one to look after us and we'd all starve.'

'The petrol for the car. Is this the one that was stolen?'

Martha frowned and shook her head. 'I don't know about that. I thought they had gone out in it this morning.'

It was as she thought. Nate was driving his own 'stolen' car the day Liam was taken, and had been driving it ever since.

'Here's the store room.' Martha held the door for Ronnie, who covered her nose and mouth as the stench of fuel rose from the concrete floor.

'I see what you mean.' Her phone buzzed. Back-up was two minutes away.

'So where does he keep the petrol now?' She was looking around for signs of petrol cans, but there was none, just the smell of it.

Martha did a double take. 'Here. It's always here. Maybe they had to drive a long way, needed to take it with them.'

'Maybe.' Ronnie thought about it. Perhaps they were taking side roads and didn't want to be spotted by petrol-station cameras. She followed Martha back up the stairs, just as a sudden flash of blue light announced the arrival of the squad cars in the front yard.

Martha's face turned pale. Ronnie put a hand on her arm. 'It's going to be OK, Martha. There are some lovely people in those cars who are going to take you and Rex to safety.'

Martha just looked at her, blank-faced, and her hands began to shake. Ronnie sat her down on a stool in the hallway and crouched down to her level.

'I know this is hard to believe, but it's happening. Freedom is happening.'

'What if I don't want it? I'm scared to leave. I won't cope on the outside, not like Ruth did. This place is all I know.' She cast her eyes around the room, a haunted look on her face.

A sharp knock on the door made them both jump.

'Wait a second.' Ronnie opened the front door and stepped outside to talk to the officers, before coming back to Martha and taking her hands. 'I'd like you to try, for me. Just try, one step at a time.'

Rex was easier to persuade. He was already standing by the front door wearing a coat that was a size too small, his hair hanging over his face. Ronnie wondered how often he got to see the outside world. It was a miracle he wasn't afraid.

'Don't worry, Martha,' he whispered in a voice that wasn't used to talking. 'We can be brave together.'

Ronnie felt a surge of gratitude to him. 'That's right. We can all be brave together.' Then Martha was on her feet, reaching for Rex's hand as Ronnie opened the door wide. Outside, the blue lights had stopped flashing at least, and the sense of drama had dissipated.

'I want you to go with these nice colleagues of mine because we need you to be checked by a doctor, and we need to talk to the people who did this to you.' She touched the marks on Rex's wrist. His lip was trembling despite all the bravado.

Martha squeezed his shoulders as they both let themselves be wrapped in blankets by uniformed police officers.

'It's OK, Rex, it's all going to be OK.'

CHAPTER 35

It's cold in the boot of the car. Liam wants to stretch his legs but he can't unless he curls the rest of his body right round. It's like being a chick inside an egg, he decides. If he thinks about that, he feels better. If the chick can do it, so can he. When the time is right, he'll burst out and be free. But it's been too long. It must be time soon.

Someone has heard his thoughts because the jolting has come to a stop. He listens hard, but there's only the bang of a door, making the car shake with the impact. He's hungry and he needs the toilet. He hopes that they are getting him food, and thinks about the shepherd's pie his mum makes. It makes him feel a bit like crying, but then he remembers the brave chicks and his dad saying he had to be a man one day, and now was the time to start getting used to it.

There's another bang, another wobble and the car is moving again. Maybe they stopped at a shop to buy something delicious, or McDonald's. His mouth waters at the thought of a Big Mac. Mum wouldn't let him have them but Uncle Joe didn't mind. He let him have chocolate milkshake as well and made him promise not to tell. Liam is good at keeping secrets. The lady told him to keep this a secret too, where he'd been since they collected him from school that day. He must say he doesn't remember anything. It seems like ages since he was in the classroom but he doesn't miss it much. It's been better since they moved him and he can see what's on the board. Miss Blake is nice enough and always picks him when he puts his hand up, always lets him stay behind at break if he doesn't want to go outside. He wouldn't mind playing in the playground but the other boys are mean to him when nobody's looking; they call him names and say his parents don't care about him. Liam ignores most of it because Mum says it's just banter, 'water off a duck's back', she says, but it still keeps him awake at night. He's not a duck, or a chick, but he's doing his best to pretend now, so it's easier.

Another stop. He holds his breath to listen. There's no sound for ages, so he breathes quietly, just in case. He doesn't want to use up all the oxygen.

He's almost asleep again when it happens.

The boot opens. There's light, but not much. It must be evening or morning. He can't remember, but it's so exciting he doesn't care.

He uncurls himself and scrambles to his knees, hands on the frame as the lid rises up. It's one of those automatic ones because there's nobody standing there lifting it. A voice shouts something that sounds like 'get out' and he heaves himself over the barrier, flops to the ground and looks around him. There's darkness and something like torchlight. He panics. Has his eyesight got even worse since being stuck in the car for so long?

THE CHOICE

'Run towards the lights,' the man told him. He didn't know what lights, but he does now. There are car headlights through the trees. It might be Dad's car. Before he can even take it in, what's happened, the boot is closing again and the car is speeding away, sending up splashes of mud. He runs towards the lights, stumbling over tree roots and tripping over brambles, but they're already running towards him. Mum and Dad. It's a dream. It must be.

They wrap him up in their arms so tightly he can hardly breathe. Mum is saying, 'My baby, I can't believe it, I can't believe it,' and tears are running down her face as she puts her hands on his shoulders and looks at him. Now her hands are smoothing back his hair, looking at him with wonder and disbelief as if he's come back from the dead. Dad is behind her, being a man, not crying or anything, but there's something about his face that makes Liam think he's trying hard not to.

CHAPTER 36

Ruth is sleepy now. She has taken some pills for her headache. She was hoping they would stop her thinking, stop her remembering everything, but it's still there, just fading into the background. The pills have made her too tired to move so she can't escape it.

She hasn't used her phone because that's how they will find her, even though she's up in the loft, they will have a radar that locks on to the phone signal, they'll come to the house, knock the doors down and drag her out. But she needs to speak to Martha before the pills take her away, she needs to speak to Rex, just in case she can't speak to them again. It's been too long and life has been too difficult without the sound of their voices.

A clever person would have worked it out before but she hasn't been to school, at least not since Ma and Pa died, and she can't work things out like other people can. It takes her longer. But she knows what's happening now. Nate must have seen her on Martha's phone. That's how he knew she was still alive. If Nate knows she's alive, then Martha is in danger too. She wonders what Martha has gone through since they last spoke, but then her head thumps with fear and she bangs her fists on her temples, willing oblivion to take her away from the agony. Martha is in her head, her kind hands, her soothing words. She didn't deserve punishment. Ruth wonders if he's done the same things to her or whether he's found other ways.

Martha saved her life, although she never accepted that. With the stress of everything, she told Ruth that the doctors said she'd shut down her memory because it was too traumatic, but Ruth knows it was her that unlocked the door at the back of the cabin. She always knew where Nate's keys were. When Ruth crawled out into the undergrowth, she thanked not only Martha but every god in the world, in case the Pilgrims were wrong, which she was sure they were. She thanked the universe with her heart and soul. She didn't think about how she'd manage, where she was going, how she'd survive, she just crawled out of the door, praying her gratitude aloud in panicky gasps, and then ran for the woods. The pine trees were closely packed, but she remembered there was an opening where the low branches had been cut to make a path in. The pigs used to wander into the forest in the old days. Aunt Esther said they were foraging and it saved having to feed them as much as they'd have to otherwise. The pigs would eat them out of house and home one day, Nate used to say, but Aunt Esther never let him get rid of them.

Ruth had found the path and stopped to catch her breath. The bag had caught her eye because the light from the fire behind her reflected on its zipper and bounced back into her eyes. She bent down to see what was inside, her heart pounding. Pulling the zip open, she riffled through the contents. A pair of boots. A change of clothes. Some sandwiches, a purse with two ten-pound notes in it. Tears pricked her eyes because that's when she realised what her sister had done for her, and she'd had no choice but to leave her behind. Her heart had ached with the pain of it but she had forced herself to get back into the moment. Martha had risked everything so that she could escape. She couldn't let her down.

She wiped her eyes and pulled on the boots, took one glance back at the cabin, where flames were leaping skyward, and headed away from Mill Farm for the last time.

She walked most of the night before crawling in to sleep in a shelter made of branches tied with string, a camp left by children, lucky children who had freedom and a place to play.

The next day, she reached Stoneybridge but didn't dare stop. It was too close to home and she didn't know if Nate and Esther had eyes and ears among the locals. An old couple coming out of the corner shop gave her a strange look, but she just zipped up her hoodie and walked faster. On the edges of town, a car stopped a few metres ahead and a woman opened the passenger window to speak to her. For a horrible second she thought it was Aunt Esther, on her tail already under orders to bring her back to Mill Farm and God only knew what punishment for escaping. But this woman was different: she looked like Ruth remembered normal people from the outside, the teachers from school: well fed, with colour in their cheeks and neatly cut hair.

She had rings on her fingers and polished nails. She could be an angel or an alien.

'Need a lift somewhere?' She drummed jewelled fingers on the steering wheel as Ruth peered in and blinked, waiting for the mirage to clear, because it couldn't be real that someone might want to help. It must be a trick. Not Aunt Esther but her friend, someone Ruth might trust and whose car she might willingly climb into. 'It's a long road, wherever you're off to. Hop in if you like.'

She didn't think too long. There wasn't time. A quick glance back at the empty road and the thought of Nate and Esther on the hunt for her made the decision an easy one. She climbed into the back seat and whispered: 'Thank you. Wherever you're going will be fine.' She hadn't meant to whisper. It must have been the smoke in her throat and vocal cords. The thought of where she had come from made her stomach turn over in fear.

'I'm on my way to work. Brighton way, half an hour or so from here. That OK?'

Ruth nodded in reply, catching the driver's eye in the rear-view mirror.

'My name's Gemma, by the way. What's yours?'

Ruth said her name was Ruth Jones. She didn't think fast enough to change her first name, but the surname came to her in a last-minute rush for a little bit of anonymity. After that, they passed the journey in companionable silence until Gemma turned on the radio and some music Ruth had never heard filled the car with a cacophony of drum and guitar that hurt her ears.

With no instructions to the contrary, Gemma took Ruth right to the door of Open Doors, the refuge on the edges of Hove where she volunteered three days a week. 'Why not pop in for a cup of tea? You look like you could do with one.'

After two cups of tea and a cheese sandwich brought by another smiling woman with long grey hair, Ruth was shown a room where they said she could stay as long as she liked. They didn't make her talk about where she'd come from, but she couldn't hide the scars on her wrists, which told their own story. The other women asked no questions and let her be herself, whatever *herself* was. There was talk in the daily meetings of finding your identity again and building up your self-confidence, but Ruth was happy enough just being safe from Nate. Living in this community, it felt as if they had fled a common enemy.

After six months, she had gained enough weight to be off the danger list, she had learned to cook and use a mobile phone and Gemma suggested they might look at finding her a permanent place to live. In the same breath, she mentioned she and her husband were buying a new place a little further away in a village called West Dean. There was an annexe on the side of the house that might suit Ruth perfectly.

Gemma has helped her stay hidden, live the life she's lived until now, until the day she found the newspaper announcement with her own face staring out at her. Nate won't stop until he finds her. She knows that. She can't tell the police what he did because she has no proof and there would be no traces left of her at the farm. The cabin had burned down and he would have got rid of the dungeon in the house by now. What's more, who was to say Nate didn't have contacts in the police? He had always made a point of saying he had eyes everywhere, in case she ever *got any ideas*, and Ruth has never forgotten that.

Did fire delete all traces of a person? It must do, if Nate really believed she had burned to death in the cabin. She had always assumed that bones and teeth would survive any fire, but maybe she was wrong about that. Maybe she was wrong about everything, but there was one thing she knew for sure. Nate had made her have his baby and then he took the baby away from her. But it's not over. One day she'll get him back.

Her brain is foggy and she can't concentrate on any thought before it evaporates into another disconnected one. She switches the phone on and finds Martha's number because it's the last chance she'll have. She presses the number but the line is dead. The number doesn't exist. Her eyes are already closing, she's floating away. It won't be long.

CHAPTER 37

As Martha and Rex were bundled into squad cars outside Mill Farm, Overton got to work on changing the two wheels on Ronnie's Audi.

'Looks like you hit them pretty hard, sarge,' he shouted over the sound of car engines and buzzing radios – unnecessarily loudly, she thought. At that moment, her phone signalled a text had come in from Cara Buckley. It read simply *Liam's home* and a line of smiley faces and hearts. She took a moment to let herself relish the news before taking one of the officers aside. It was Jen Connolly, the one who'd gone with Baz to find Ruth on the very first day she was missing.

'How did the handover go at the reservoir?'

'Smoothly. They handed over the cash, left it where the guy could see it, he collected it and the boy was let out of the boot. No harm done to him but they're checking him over of course. Happy endings.'

Ronnie took it in. It felt like an anti-climax. 'Who dropped him off? Where's he been all this time?'

'Wouldn't say. They'll talk to him when he's ready. His parents didn't want him questioned until he'd settled back in. And the one who dropped him off—'

'Let me guess. A Land Rover?'

'Yes, but false plates, which they must have changed for others because they escaped pretty quick when they saw the Buckleys had company.'

'You let them get away?' Ronnie couldn't help herself. 'A man and a woman?'

Connolly shrugged. 'It was never going to be easy, if they wanted the boy returned safely. Lydia took charge of the operation, with DC Mayer and DC Munro.'

'And where is he now when I need him, that DC Munro?'

'Sorry, sarge, he wanted to be here but he had an appointment he couldn't miss.'

'An appointment? Now is not the time for a new haircut.'

'A hospital appointment, sarge. Antenatal.'

Ronnie stopped in her tracks. 'He's having a baby?'

'Yes, sarge. His girlfriend's pregnant. Sorry. Thought you knew. He's just called. Back at the nick now, ready for action.'

Ronnie had always painted Baz in her mind as a career-hungry ladder-climber with no domestic ties. How wrong she could be? 'Ah, OK. Sorry, I shouldn't have assumed.' She fought back against a twinge of *does everyone else know except me* and glanced at Martha and Rex whose anxious faces were watching her through the car window. 'We'll need medical checks on those two and full hospital security until we get hold of Nate.'

Overton gave her a thumbs up. 'Ready for you now, sarge. Go easy on your way out.'

She climbed in and revved the engine, setting the satnav to West Dean and calling Baz on speed dial.

'I was just about to call you, sarge. Presume you heard about the kid?'

'Indeed, and well done, although we don't have our kid-*nappers* yet, I understand.'

'Only a matter of time, sarge. They can't be far away and Liam's back home safe, which is a proper result. I wanted you to know that the warrant to search Ruth's house just came through, and there's something else. We've got some activity on Ruth's phone.'

'So we have a warrant to search the home of our suspect who is no longer our suspect.'

'That very one.'

'Well at least we can gain entry to the house if we need to. Where's the phone activity?'

'In her house, we reckon.'

'So not only can we get in, she can let us in herself.'

'That would be the best outcome, yes, sarge.'

'Meet me there in an hour. I might still count as a familiar face, and with everything we now know about her past, we might get the cooperation we need.' The traffic was slowing again, all three lanes of it. It was going to take her longer to get there than she thought.

'Yes, sarge, but don't forget, I've never laid eyes on this Ruth Jones. Can you send us a photo or something?'

They didn't have much more than the notice in the paper. She pulled over to ping him the screenshot from her phone. 'There you go. Should be with you now. Out of date but gives you a bit of an idea.'

'She looks familiar. I never forget a face.'

'An ex of yours, maybe.'

'Nah, not my type. I know I have seen this woman somewhere, but I can't place her.'

'The *Gazette*'s been stuffed through every letter box. Maybe even yours. Anyway, I need to get off the phone because we're on the move again, but there was just one more thing.'

'Yes, sarge?'

'I hear congratulations are in order. The patter of tiny feet and all that? I can think up some more clichés if you like . . .'

Baz laughed. 'Ah, thanks. Yes, a happy accident but we are thrilled. Slightly puts my career on hold, but then you'll be pleased about that, won't you?'

Ronnie felt herself redden automatically with embarrassment. 'What do you mean?'

'I mean, you didn't want me to leave the nick, move elsewhere, did you? Well, now it looks as if I won't have to. I'll stay as DC a little longer and you'll have me hanging around snapping at your heels for the foreseeable.'

She breathed a sigh of relief. 'Yes, of course. That is an added bonus for us all. But the most important thing is that you and Amber are happy, which it sounds as if you are.'

'Yes, although I'm sure we have no idea what's about to hit us.'

'Aha. You're right there. I'll see you at Lime Close. If I'm not there, go ahead without me.'

The journey took longer than expected, with another down-pour adding to the rush-hour traffic, but Ronnie could at least relax in the knowledge that Ruth seemed to be home from whatever adventures she'd been on. Now they knew something of the horrors she had escaped ten years earlier, her behaviour was beginning to make sense, and in a few hours she might even be reunited with her long-lost sister and the baby she probably barely remembered. When Nate and Esther were apprehended, which could only be a matter of time, there could be no other outcome than happy endings all round.

Her phone buzzed, bringing her back to earth. She put it on speaker. The traffic was at a standstill again.

'Sarge? It's me. No answer from Ruth's door.'

'Right, I'm a mile away, shouldn't be too long.'

'Great, and just to let you know a call's come in about a disturbance in the high street. Some hooligans put a brick through a window. They want me over there as I'm literally round the corner and uniform could be another ten minutes.'

'Roger that. See you shortly. I'll try the door again. Not sure we have a good reason to search the house now, except I need to know that Ruth is safe. Because as long as Nate and Esther are out there, I have a feeling she isn't.'

When Ronnie finally drew up outside the house in Lime Close, she opened the door to the unmistakeable smell of bonfires. Autumn was well and truly back on the scene, with all the memories its fragrance triggered, happy and sad, the full rainbow of nature's finest colours and at the same time, the ending of summer. The gates to the house and its miniature annexe stood wide open, revealing a vast magnolia tree and a web of red roses climbing the side fence. It was all too idyllic.

It was only as she approached the perimeter wall, and was within a few metres of the house itself, that the smell hit her. It was as if her brain had taken it on board and delivered a verdict based on the most likely cause. But this was no standard autumn bonfire. Thick black smoke was pouring through an open casement window, bringing with it the smell of fuel. Ronnie stood rooted to the spot for a second, trying to process what she was seeing. She pulled out her phone and called Baz, who answered, breathless, on the first ring.

'I'm literally seconds away,' he puffed. 'Uniform are on the case. Some homeless woman, on drugs they reckon, ran away without even trying to rob the place. Hang on, fucking hell, sarge.' He broke off and hung up as he turned into the drive. 'The place is on fire.' He took a few steps towards the house, then ran back towards her, his hands clasped to his head.

Overton, trotting behind him like a dutiful puppy, was already on his phone. 'Fire service . . . Lime Close . . . West Dean . . . Soon as you can.'

Ronnie backed towards the wall as things fell into place. 'It's Nate. He must have followed you here.'

'But I'd have seen him. There was no fire when I went to sort out the break-in around the corner.'

'That's when he must have done it. While you were distracted. The distraction was his work too. Esther could have passed for a homeless junkie throwing a brick through a window. He must have seen you arrive, then waited until you'd gone before doing his dirty work.'

'I'll get the enforcer,' said Baz, heading for the car. 'If Ruth's in there, she hasn't got long.'

'Not until we know where the fire started. It's too risky. Wait for the firefighters.'

Flames were visible now through the front window, leaping higher with every minute that passed, and more clouds of smoke were slowly finding their way out of the air shafts in the brickwork.

'Hang on. I've got it.'

'What?' Ronnie spoke without taking her eyes off the burning house. The fire service was taking an eternity.

'I've just worked out where I've seen that woman before,' he said, looking skywards as if in gratitude to a deity.

'Where?' Ronnie checked the time on her phone and shouted at Overton. 'Find out where they are – the fire station's only half a mile away, for God's sake.' She looked at Baz waiting for him to explain.

'Remember when I came here the first time, talked to the neighbour who said she was at work?'

'Yes, what about it?'

'It was her.'

'The neighbour?'

'Yes. The face in the photo you sent over looks just like the next-door neighbour I spoke to last week.'

'A minute away,' called Overton, as Ronnie stepped away from the front door, looking at Baz. Then, 'Watch out!'

Just as the fire engine swung into the drive, a section of the annexe roof imploded, folding in on itself to reveal the skeleton of joists and timbers where flames now leapt unfettered. Firefighters jumped down and headed for the burning building, ordering them out of the way. But Ronnie was still staring at Baz.

'That's where she is. You saw her next door. That's where she's been hiding all this time.'

She raced to the main house, rang the bell and banged hard. 'Ruth, are you in there?'

In an instant, Baz was behind her with the enforcer and the door burst open. The fire didn't seem to have spread inside but there was a smell of burning plastic and it was only a matter of time.

'Ruth!' she shouted, moving from room to room, but there was no answer. Kitchen led to dining room, to sitting room. Off the hall was an office, a downstairs cloakroom. The ground floor seemed to go on and on and the fire would make short work of the open-plan space. 'No sign downstairs.'

Ronnie took the stairs two at a time and searched the bedrooms, three of which had state-of-the-art en suites. Whoever's house this was wasn't short of money. But there was still no sign of Ruth. Ronnie shouted her name again and glanced up to see how the attic might be accessed.

There was a hatch on the landing. Taking a chair from one of the bedrooms, she climbed up and pushed it open. A ladder slipped neatly down and Ronnie's lungs were hit by the rush of smoke. She was about to brave the smoke and start climbing when a firefighter pulled her out of the way.

'You need to get out, DS Delmar. If anyone's in there we'll have them down in a sec. The ambulance is on its way.'

'Looks like both houses are linked at the top,' she spluttered.

'Got that. Now get out.'

She staggered down to the front door and burst outside, coughing too much to speak. Baz helped her to the car and they looked up from there to where the fire officers were now. If that was where Ruth was hiding, she didn't stand much of a chance.

The front door opened again. It was one of the firefighters with a woman in his arms, floppy as a rag doll.

'Is she OK?' Ronnie ran towards them, just as the ambulance swung into the drive.

'She will be,' he said, pulling off his mask as the paramedics set up the stretcher.

Ronnie leaned over her as she was lowered on to it. 'Ruth?'

Ruth's eyes opened, then closed. A paramedic affixed an oxygen mask to her face and gave the thumbs up to his partner.

'You've suffered smoke inhalation. But you'll be OK. We'll get you to hospital.'

Ruth's eyes darted left to where the firefighters were dousing the flames leaping from the annexe and her hand moved to her face to remove the mask.

'Don't try to say anything, wait till the doctor's checked you over.'

'Wait.' Her voice was hoarse, and barely audible. 'Nate . . .'

'Yes, we know. But he didn't get you.'

The paramedics slid the stretcher into the back of the ambulance, and Ruth reached out one last time, taking hold of Ronnie's hand and lifting the mask again with the other.

'He won't stop,' she whispered. 'Be careful.'

CHAPTER 38

Ruth wakes up with a drip in her arm and a nurse by her side, and her instinct is to pull out the tubes and run. But the nurse knows what she's thinking. She says, 'You're safe, it's OK,' and strokes her hand and her forehead, tucks the sheet in around her.

'Where am I?'

'Halesworth Hospital. There was a fire in the house you were found in. They said you must have been hiding from something, or someone, up in the loft.'

Ruth turns away, ashamed of everything. The nurse takes her blood pressure, tests her oxygen levels and puts the mask back on her face. After a few minutes, some people come into the room, first the lady detective whose name she can't remember. Then it comes to her. She's called Ronnie, which is a boy's name, but it suits her. Ronnie asks the nurse how things are progressing, whether she's ready for visitors. The nurse says yes, but nothing too strenuous.

She's never had visitors. She wonders who it can be, because there are only two people in the world she wants to see again. When the door opens again, the sight brings tears to her eyes, because here is one of them, wearing a hospital gown like her. For a second she thinks she has died and woken up in heaven.

Martha sits on the edge of her bed, holding her hands. Ruth opens and closes her eyes a few times.

'I can't believe it's really you, Martha.'

'I thought I'd never see you again,' Martha says.

Ruth tries to speak between shallow breaths. 'I know I've tried to say this before, but I owe you a million thank yous for what you did for me.'

Martha looks confused now. 'I've never understood why you say that. What do you have to thank me for?'

'Just saving my life,' she whispers.

Martha's face is serious. She leans forward and inclines her head, a frown furrowing her brow. 'I didn't save your life, Ruth, and I thought you were dead. I honestly thought you were dead, until that first time you rang.' Her eyes are blinking now. It makes Ruth want to cry too.

'It was so hard to find you online,' she whispers. 'Then I found these chat rooms where people look for their missing friends and family. Everyone used code names and I tried so many before I remembered what linked us.'

Martha smiles at her, the happiest smile ever. 'The king. Rex the king. I'm so glad you found us. I was so scared you were gone.'

'I miss him.' Ruth's breaths are shorter now. The nurse looks at her watch and puts the mask back on Ruth's face.

'You need to take it easy, young lady. Why not just listen and don't try to talk.'

Martha takes her cue. 'I've brought someone very important to see you,' she says. 'The king himself.' She gets up and moves away to make way for what must be a royal visitor.

The white door opens again and Ruth tries to take the mask off. The nurse says, 'Just for a few seconds, then it goes back on.'

He's taller than he looked on the video calls. He's a hundred times more real, and his smile is wider. His eyes are glassy with tears, but happy tears.

'Rex!' Her voice breaks as she says his name. She's never said it to him in real life before. They took him away before she had a chance to name him. She told Martha to choose Rex if she had any say in it, because Rex meant king in Latin, and the king was always the happy ending.

His warm hands are on hers now, touching her for the first time since they took him away from her. There are tears pricking behind her eyes as she takes everything in, and then he says her name and they are rolling down her cheeks.

'I thought I'd never see you again,' she whispers.

Then, taking one hand away to wipe her eyes, she looks at Martha and back at her boy.

'I think we have a lot of catching up to do.'

CHAPTER 39

It was only when her phone pinged with another missed call that Ronnie remembered it was Friday night and she hadn't replied to Susie about their plans for the evening. She climbed into the driver's seat of her car, texted back quickly and checked her other messages. Nate and Esther were still out there. Their Land Rover had just been found in the woods near the reservoir, so they were either on foot or had another car waiting. The latter was the most likely, but it was strange and frustrating that they had been so hard to trace. It should have been straightforward, but now it was dark and the officers out there didn't know anything about the vehicle they were chasing. A message from Lydia said she should go home after a job well done, but another sent just after that had come in from the front desk at the station: *Urgent package for you just arrived.* That was odd. Who would send her an urgent package on a Friday night after their two cases were as good as closed?

She pulled out of the hospital car park and headed back to the station, her mind reeling with the events of the day that had ended so differently for everyone. Ruth was spending the night in hospital, Liam had been reunited with his parents and Ruth with her son and her sister, who had already spent a couple of hours talking to specialist social workers. The story that was emerging was a horrific tale of ritual abuse, mainly sexual abuse in Ruth's case, but latterly imprisonment and neglect of Rex, and Martha had been the designated family slave, living with the threat that if she ever tried to leave, they would frame her for the murder of her sister. Nate told her he had done her a favour by not turning her in on the spot when the police came to investigate the fire, but that, in return, there'd be no mention of any sister.

Their evidence, as well as Ruth's, would provide the basis for the charges that Nate and Esther would face when they were caught. Word had gone out to forces across the country and to the border force to apprehend the couple on sight. Then, between them, there would be charges of kidnapping, abduction, unlawful imprisonment and arson, as well as historic sexual abuse and perverting the course of justice.

The officer manning the front desk was engrossed in something on his phone when Ronnie arrived. He handed her the package without a word. Her name was on the front and URGENT in capital letters.

'When did this arrive? Who brought it?'

'Half an hour ago. A guy in a baseball hat and glasses. I don't remember much else.'

She tore open the envelope. 'Don't worry. I think I know now.'

The photos had fallen out before she could catch them and scattered across the floor. She rushed to pick them up, but the only person waiting was a young man playing a game on his phone. Her heart was pounding as she sat down to flick through them. Some were hazy, but others had her completely in focus, leaning across the table conspiratorially with the man she now knew as Steve Buckley. Another one showed them embracing in the car park of the Fox and Grapes – whoever it was must have caught the split-second kiss by some stroke of fluke. Or not. Obviously not. This was something else, something planned, deliberate. Once again, pieces of the puzzle came tumbling into place. Attached to one of the pictures was a Post-it note that read: *Doesn't look good for DS Delmar to fraternise with a key witness. What will the boss say?*

Underneath it, another note said, *Meet me at Blyth Road 8 p.m. and you can have the rest.*

It would take her less than twenty minutes to get there. She'd just about make it. She tried Baz's phone, which was engaged, and considered calling Jules or Lydia but thought better of it. Her hands were tied. Only Baz had any idea she'd met Steve on the Sidekick app and she couldn't begin to explain the situation to the others without setting off alarms. This was no time to start jumping through official hoops. Once she was there, she'd secure his phone, delete the photos and call for support.

She jumped back into her car, reversing out of the space and heading straight for the main road. She drove in silence, drumming her fingers on the steering wheel, her mind flicking from option to option, making sure all routes led to the same conclusion. Surely Nate and Esther were in the frame for everything now, from arson to kidnapping to abuse and now blackmail. But the blackmail charges would involve more honesty than she was ready for just now. If Lydia was involved, she'd want chapter and verse on Ronnie's manoeuvres, especially with her track record of working off-grid. She was sure plenty of others had done worse. You read about it in the press every day, but that was hardly an argument she could put forward in her favour. She'd deal with the blackmail issue, and then they'd be sitting ducks, but it wouldn't do any harm to make the beginnings of a plan.

She tried Steve's number. It went straight to voicemail and she left a message asking him to call back. She tried Baz again but it rang out. She rang again. *Come on, you're not on paternity leave yet.* Still no answer. Jules's phone was engaged, which gave her an inkling of relief. She didn't relish the prospect of giving her exemplary DC the full picture just yet, and calling for uniform back-up would be to sign her own career death warrant. There was no choice. She'd have to manage this one on her own.

Once in Blyth Road, she drove past the Assembly Hall and back again, looking for a space. A light was on inside, and a shadow was visible moving around the room to the right of the main door, as if someone was laying a table.

She switched off her engine and took a deep breath, exhaling to the limit and waiting a second or two before breathing again. It was a tactic learned at antenatal classes years ago, which had done nothing to dull the pain of childbirth but worked well enough to calm the nerves in other predicaments. Whether she had ever been in a situation quite like this was another matter. *It is what it is*, Baz would say. *Fake it till you make it . . .* But idioms gave no comfort when fear was beating at the door of your soul. In a vain attempt at delaying the inevitable, she opened up Snapchat, and felt the tension evaporate at the sight of Tilly's avatar safe at home. She could do this.

It was a minute past 8 o'clock. She steeled herself, climbed out of the car and slammed the door. If anyone was watching, they'd know she wasn't intimidated.

One step at a time, she approached the entrance to the hall. No cars in the three parking spaces. They must have left theirs nearby, or been dropped off. She shuddered to think of who else might be involved in their escape. There could be a whole team of them out there, welded together by a misconstrued idea of religious faith and prepared to do anything to save a brother or sister in trouble. But there was no point in dwelling on imaginary scenarios. *The sooner this is over, the sooner I get back to my life*, she said to herself and pressed the bell with a decisiveness that might indicate the spirit of her arrival.

Within a second, there was the click of a lock and Nate Jacobs was standing before her, appraising her like an artist might take in the full glory of a finished painting. Ronnie's eyes scanned the hallway behind him. Nothing. What was she expecting?

'How good of you to come.' Nate gave her a flicker of a smile as he held the door open. 'Please go through to the meeting room. I think you know where it is.'

She'd only seen the kitchen the previous night when she'd challenged Steve, but Nate knew she'd been there. Her mind raced frantically to work out how that could be. Did he have cameras set up? Was he in the building at the time? The room Nate must have been referring to was a few metres down the corridor on the left, where a door stood ajar and a light was on inside.

'Go on then. What are you waiting for?'

No sooner had she stepped over the threshold than she felt the steely nudge of a gun in the small of her back. A sudden, unfamiliar wave of panic washed over her and she swallowed hard, automatically reaching into her pocket for her phone. But he was on to her every movement.

'Hands where I can see them. There's a good girl.'

She obeyed, looking straight ahead, calming her thumping heart with the flimsy reassurance of logic. He'd go to prison for life, on top of all the other charges. Then another small voice in her head said, *Perhaps he doesn't care. Perhaps he has another plan.* She flailed around to imagine what it might be, apart from his own suicide, and from what she knew about psychopaths, that would only happen once he'd put a bullet in her first. The adrenaline was in full flow around her body, but until the balance of power changed, there would be no chance of escape. To make that happen she needed to stay calm.

'Take a seat, detective.'

'I haven't got long,' she said with forced nonchalance. 'Let's make this quick.'

Esther was already at the table, her rough blotched hands clasped in front of her, eyes staring at the opposite wall. She looked up as Ronnie came in and it was hard to read her expression. Ronnie wanted to scream questions at her: what had possessed her to walk into a school and steal a child, to befriend the family so the boy would have no hesitation in running across the playground to her at home time? Why couldn't she have surrendered to the police after throwing the brick through the shop window? Where was her humanity? Where was her soul?

Nate pulled out chairs for them both, then a third.

'Are we expecting company?'

'Of course. You're not the only one with a secret.' He sank into his seat and glanced up towards the door and back at Ronnie. 'He'll be here in a minute.' The gun was trained on her now. She stared him straight in the eyes, her mind still working at breakneck speed to calculate what might happen next. She would stand even less of a chance against three of them, especially if the new arrival was armed. Nate tapped his fingers slowly on the table, narrowing his unblinking eyes. Esther's fingers tightened around each other, reddening with the pressure.

They sat in silence for a few more seconds before the side door opened and shut. Footsteps hurried closer and the meeting-room door swung open. Ronnie looked up and inhaled sharply. Of course. Who else?

'Steve, so glad you could make it.' Nate's eyes were still on Ronnie, triumphant now.

Nothing to fear. Exhale. Steve was on her side. He'd have to be if they were going to get through this.

Steve looked at Ronnie and Nate in turn, then his eyes fell on the photographs that sat on the table between them.

'What's this? I need to be at home with my son.'

Nate smiled. 'I thought it was time for a few home truths.'

Steve sank into his seat and slumped back, putting both hands on the table. 'I thought we were all done here. You've got the cash.'

Nate ran the fingers of one hand through the paltry strands of grey hair that barely covered his head and took a long breath, relishing the power he held over his prey. 'It might have been over, Steve. We might have seen the last of each other. With our signatures on the paperwork, this building would be handed over to you within days or weeks, and certainly in time for Christmas.' He looked around the room with the trace of a smirk. 'I wonder, where will you put the tree? And all those other worldly distractions that God despises. This place will be desecrated by your sacrilege.' His face darkened and his fist came down on the table. 'But unfortunately, we're not quite *done*, as you put it, because I need some reassurance. These pictures here . . .' he tapped a dirty forefinger on the pile, then swiped the first one aside, then the second and third, until they were spread out in a jaunty display of shame, 'should give me that, if we're all agreed?' He looked at Ronnie. 'And there you were, thinking you had it all sewn up.'

The look of shock on Steve's face told Ronnie everything she needed to know. She needed to think fast but give the impression she was thinking slowly. That might buy her time. 'So, let me get this right,' she said. 'You think that you can stop any prosecution by blackmailing us both.'

Nate said nothing.

With her best imploring look, she turned to speak to Steve, although the sight of him was beginning to revolt her. 'He's right that interfering with a witness would place me in an untenable position. I'd lose my job, my career in the force would be over. But with your evidence, that you were Finn Macaulay that night, not Steve Buckley, that I'd never met Steve Buckley at that time, we can deal with this.' She gave him a pleading look, because that's all there was now. 'Cara will understand. You needed money to rehouse the family. You were desperate. And nothing happened between us, or anyone else as far as she knows.' She stopped, expecting interruption or a challenge, but the men just exchanged glances.

Nate leaned forward and pointed the gun back at Ronnie, but with his eyes on Steve now. 'Nice try, detective, but I don't see him agreeing to that.'

'What do you mean?' Her heart pounded. She was still missing something. Steve's gaze was firmly downward. He let himself be discussed.

'Let me explain what I mean. Steve needed money, that's true enough,' said Nate, 'and so did I. I know you've spoken to Jacksons. You'll have read the papers. You know the predicament we find ourselves in, fighting legal cases brought by apostates. Our Assembly Halls are our treasured possessions, places of safety for our brothers and sisters. This is more than selling the family jewels. It's selling our souls. Steve would have happily bought the hall but couldn't raise the cash without going cap in hand to the in-laws, who despise him for not being able to afford to house his family in something more suitable than a leaky caravan, and he was just about giving up when we came to him with our idea. Weren't you, Steve?'

'Is that true?' It was hard to compute.

Steve put his head in his hands.

'You were in on this all along? You facilitated the kidnapping?'

Nate smiled broadly now. 'The male ego can only take so much bashing. Poor Steve was in a mess. Hardly surprising he agreed to go along with it. So I don't think he will agree to your little plan, DS Delmar. What will Cara say when she finds out her own husband not only led a double life, seducing other women online, but put her through ten days of agony thinking she'd lost her son, just to get his hands on her inheritance?'

Steve said nothing. Ronnie's phone buzzed.

'Give me that,' said Nate.

She took the phone out of her pocket, eyes still on her captor, and dropped it on the floor, kicking it away with her foot. 'Go and get it if you like. And please put down the gun. We can't talk if you're pointing it at me like that.'

He looked irritated for a second, then composed himself because the danger had been averted, placed the gun on the table and rubbed his palms together slowly, relishing each word as he pronounced it.

'You underestimated all of us I think, DS Delmar.'

Ronnie's head was pounding with self-flagellation. It made sense now, the troubled way Steve had looked at her, the calling it off straight after their meeting. He had reeled her in at Nate's suggestion. But how? And why?

'You came after *me*, specifically me?' She turned to Steve. 'How did you know I'd be on there?'

'I didn't.' Steve's voice was a whisper.

Nate stepped in to elucidate. 'He shared the pictures of the women he was planning on meeting, in case there were any deep pockets we could test, and imagine our delight when you popped up, detective. You walked straight into it. Nice fake name, but there are plenty of other photos of your real identity online. Nobody likes a bent copper.'

Ronnie calmed herself enough to focus. 'So, these photos, just leverage then? To ensure you and Esther enjoy a smooth getaway?'

'Just leverage.' He picked up the gun again.

Ronnie frowned. Something didn't fit, and the kind of leverage he was talking about was nothing compared to what he was up against. 'You can still be arrested for arson, false imprisonment, abduction and kidnapping and that's just for starters.' She stopped herself from mentioning the abuse. If he didn't know they'd spoken to Martha and Rex, he didn't need to, not just yet.

'But you won't be there to do it, DS Delmar. Your career will be tainted by these pictures, which can go straight to the press. And I have the support of Steve here, because even if he came clean to Cara about his philandering, my recordings of our conversations about Liam implicate him beyond doubt.'

Ronnie stared at Steve. 'You walked into your own trap. How did that happen?'

'It wasn't supposed to be like that.' Steve had found his voice.

'He didn't think things through, did you, Steve?' Nate was licking his lips. 'The photos were nothing, in the scheme of things. I needed the extra security.'

Ronnie felt a rush of disgust for him. 'They'd never believe you. The photos are fakes. Anyone can see that.' The words escaped before she could stop them.

Nate just shook his head. 'I reckon the police need to be squeaky clean these days. If there's even a sniff of corruption, I don't fancy your chances. You've been suspended for less before, I believe.'

How did he know? She put the question out of her mind. She needed to concentrate on dismantling his flawed logic, but he was on a roll now.

'Put the gun down. Please, Nate,' she said loudly. He would think it was her trying to re-establish control.

'You're like everyone else on the outside, aren't you? Just because of a few transgressions that make the headlines, you think we're all child abusers. You couldn't accept Ruth was insane and delusional. You were out to avenge her, and the missing-person advert was the answer to your prayers when it led you straight to me. You could tie up all your loose ends and draw a line under it. Poor Ruth, all those things that happened to her.'

There was a pause as he rolled his eyes, then looked back, pityingly, at Ronnie.

'Obviously, once we found out she was still out there, we had to get to her before she spilled the beans. You didn't want to tell us where she lived, so we gave you a reason to go there and we followed you. You couldn't fail to follow up a lead on the missing child. You and your buddy swallowed that hook, line and sinker, which was a gift to us.' He sat back, with a look that said victory was within his grasp. 'And then all it took was to say *Look over there* to send your junior scurrying off in the other direction, leaving the coast clear.'

'Clever. Very clever.' The mist seemed to clear before her eyes. In the heat of the moment, she'd forgotten she held all the cards on this one. 'Except for one thing. Your plan didn't work. Ruth wasn't in the house when you set the fire.'

Nate's jaw dropped, then he refocused and inclined his head. 'Expect me to believe that, do you?'

Esther was staring at him in shock. Were they both so sure it would be fatal, or had she not known about the fire in Lime Close? Presumably he'd told her to wait for him, just as he had the day they abducted Liam.

But Nate was on the back foot now and she needed to make the most of it. 'I think you have to believe it. Your prime witness is alive to testify against you. You have no way out.'

'And you have no evidence.' Nate said blankly. 'She's mentally ill. There's no way she could have escaped this time, and no way anyone will believe her any more than they'll believe a detective who had an affair with a key witness.'

'Who was conned into meeting a man she had no idea was any kind of witness.'

'Who went online to find one key witness and just happened to get snapped up by another. Don't try to get out of that one.'

Ronnie's head was pounding now. She could see her phone on the floor in her peripheral vision.

'The reward wasn't even on the table for the first few days. How were you so sure it would be offered?'

'Our Steve knows how to play things with his lovely wife. Gentle persuasion, wasn't it?' He smirked at Steve, one eyebrow raised. 'Or something a bit rougher?' He smiled a gap-toothed smile that turned her stomach. Steve had his head in his hands.

'What do you hope to get from this, Nate?' She was playing for time, but he was still taking delight in every word he spoke, pronouncing each one with hideous precision.

'We can slip away from this meeting unscathed, DS Delmar, your indiscretion gets brushed under the carpet. You've got Ruth, if what you say is true, but if she tries anything, my defence lawyer will say that the abuse was her imagination and she's just suffering from PTSD after her parents died in a car crash. As for Liam, we've already made sure he makes no mention of Mill Farm. The kid doesn't know where he spent the last ten days. It's a blur, but he's just happy to be home. Might get fed better, allowed to play outside instead of being chained up in the dark all day.'

Steve thumped the table with his fist but his face was still buried. Without that contact, she couldn't get through to him, so it was back to Nate. One last attempt to make him see sense.

'Nate, this won't work. The charges you're facing can't just be cancelled. They are more serious than that. It's not like your mother deciding not to press charges for someone stealing her geraniums. This is not negotiable. Surely even *you* understand that.' She regretted her tone but the words were out there.

Nate looked at his watch, then back at her, slightly rattled, or perhaps that was wishful thinking. He leaned right across the table so that his face was inches from hers. She drew back out of instinct. He knew how to make his point, take back the ground they were fighting over.

'I'm not asking much of you, detective. I don't imagine you've told anyone you're here, so why don't you just leave quietly, while Esther and I disappear? I have a fellow Pilgrim who has agreed to arrange safe passage for us out of the country. We just need a couple of hours to get to the airport. And in return, these pictures will disappear, just like us.'

So they did have a team behind them. Esther's face went pale, and it dawned on Ronnie once again that there was more, or rather less, to their relationship than met the eye. She thought about how Nate had reacted when Esther mentioned their boy Rex, her shock at the news of the fire a moment ago, and suddenly she wasn't sure whether Esther was quite the accomplice she had imagined her to be. Ronnie remembered giving her the card, the look of gratitude in her eyes, and then the anonymous delivery to the station of the newspaper article about the burned-out cabin. Was it a delivery, or had Esther slipped it into her bag at some point when they met at the café? She tried to catch her eye but, if Esther saw, she was doing a good job of pretending not to.

Agonising silence fell in the room. The overhead light flickered and buzzed. Ronnie closed her eyes to think. Nate clearly didn't know that they had rescued Martha and Rex. He had no idea of the level of evidence stacking up against him. It wasn't for her to reveal it now, either. It would only exacerbate his rage and she didn't need him panicking. She needed him calm and confident for just a little longer. He was waiting for an answer, but she could drag it out perhaps a few more seconds. Surely it wouldn't be much longer now. She cleared her throat.

'I can't promise anything. You know that.'

'Well in that case, neither can I.' He stood suddenly, sending his chair crashing to the floor. 'I was giving you a chance, but now these –' he indicated the swish of photos that still covered the table between them '– which are also on here –' he shook his phone at her '– will be on the front pages by tomorrow. The public will lap it up. Another nail in the coffin of our public servants.'

'Wait . . .' Steve was on his feet. 'You can't do that until I've had a chance to talk to Cara.' He glared at Ronnie. 'Come on, surely you can see it from my point of view? I've just got my son back. I'd lose him again. I'd lose my whole family.'

Ronnie's expression was blank, out of disbelief more than anything else, that Steve could be so unaware of his own role in it, that he could think himself worthy of sympathy when he had done nothing but lie and cheat.

'You can try to make her see sense if you like, but I haven't got long.' Nate looked at his watch again and frowned at Esther, whose fingers were gripping the table as if unsure whether to stay seated. 'I'm leaving in three minutes. What's your decision?' All eyes were on Ronnie, whose mouth was suddenly too dry to speak. 'Well?'

His answer came in the sudden screech of tyres on gravel and a slam of car doors. Nate looked up, alarmed, and made for the window, where a pair of blinding headlights shone hard through the slatted blinds. Ronnie took her chance and dived for her phone, hurling it at Nate's head as he struggled to refocus. He lost his balance for a second, fell sideways, losing his grip on the gun. Meanwhile, Steve was heading for the exit, but before he could reach it, the door flew open in his face and slammed against the wall behind. He staggered backwards, reaching out for support but only finding Nate, who pushed him to the floor.

'Armed police!'

Ronnie's heart leapt with shock and relief as the three officers burst into the room. It had been a vain hope that answering Baz's call before dropping the phone would instigate a response, but it had worked. She had been lucky, and no doubt someone would be reminding her of that very soon.

Nate had dropped the gun more in shock than obedience, and Steve was too stunned to protest. Ronnie read out the grounds for arrest – sexual assault, abduction, kidnapping, obstructing the police and wasting police time. It was a long list.

'And you'll need to hand over your phones.' It was a long shot, but tagging it on the end of the caution ensured they obeyed without a murmur. 'Open it,' she said, before taking Nate's. He reached out with his index finger and the screen sprang into life. Steve followed suit.

As Nate was bundled into the back of the car, Steve hurled some abuse at him, while Ronnie slipped back inside to retrieve the hard-copy photos and stuffed them into her bag. When she emerged into the parking area at the front, Lydia handed her a blanket. 'For the shock,' she said. 'It can get to you.'

Ronnie wrapped it around herself. Her teeth were chattering. Lydia might be right, and it was a good opportunity to clear up the last remaining traces of Nate's paparazzi work. She sat down on a wall and flicked through Nate's phone for the pictures of her with Steve, deleted the ones she could find and deleted them from deleted items. She scanned the last two days' messages as well, in case he'd sent them as attachments somewhere. Flicking back through the days and weeks, she saw blurred photos of Liam, unstaged and zoomed in, as if taken from afar. In one of them, his face was clear and smiling but partially obscured by a shoulder. Esther? It must have been taken when they visited the caravan. They needed to make sure they were kidnapping the right child, after all.

Steve's phone was clean. Ronnie's stress melted away as she joined Lydia, who was asking Esther questions. 'So . . . ?' Ronnie waited for someone to enlighten her. There was something they weren't saying. Lydia nodded, tight-lipped.

'DS Delmar, Esther has agreed to testify against her husband, Nate Jacobs, in connection with the abuse charges.'

'I'm very pleased to hear that, Esther,' said Ronnie. 'I imagine he can be quite persuasive when he wants to be.' That was an understatement, but enough for Esther's eyes to glisten with tears.

'It was you, wasn't it, that took Liam?' Ronnie asked, but it was a statement rather than a question.

Esther nodded. Her hands were shaking. 'I had no choice.'

'We'll see. In the meantime, unless my colleagues here have already read you your rights . . .'

It was a formality. What happened to her next was down to her solicitor and, with a good one, she should succeed in pinning the blame on Nate for coercion and get a reduced sentence.

Jules held out her hand to Ronnie and Ronnie clasped it in both of hers.

'Thanks for saving my life.'

'Don't thank me. Baz raised the alarm when you took his call and he heard what was going on. I think the mention of a gun within seconds was the clincher. I'd say it was pretty brave of you, going in there alone like that.'

'I think you mean foolish, but I had no choice really.'

Jules shut the car doors and threw her a grin. 'He didn't know who he was up against, sarge. He's a nasty piece of work, that's for sure. There was some bad stuff happening at Mill Farm and we have detailed testimony from both sisters, as well as the boy. Liam was vague about what happened. They probably threatened him to stop him divulging too much but at least he's unharmed. Cara's a different woman, as you can imagine, having him back home.'

'I'm glad to hear it.' Ronnie turned to go, then remembered the question that was on her mind, the one doubt she had that she'd make it out of Nate's hands alive. 'How did you find me so quickly? I realised I hadn't told anyone where I'd gone. I should have said something to give you a clue but my head was in chaos in there. Did you get a live trace on my phone?'

'We did, but when every second counts that's not always fast enough, so I called your home number. Spoke to your daughter, who was very helpful.'

'But I didn't tell her, either. Nobody knew where I was.'

'She found you straight away on some app tracker thing. Snapchat, was it?'

Ronnie reeled in realisation. 'Of course. She goes on there looking for me now, does she? I guess that's what you call questioning the narrative.'

'What?' Jules looked puzzled.

'Never mind. It's just that kids aren't as useless as you think, sometimes.'

CHAPTER 40

Esther is free.

She has been arrested and they say she will be probably be charged with kidnap and abduction but, even if she goes to prison, she is going to be freer than she ever was in the house with Nate.

She's waiting to hear what will happen next. They've found her a lawyer who is talking to the police. A detective has already told her she has a solid defence and might not even get a custodial sentence, because with Nate's coercive control she had no agency in any of it. Agency means the ability to make your own decisions, she said. In her interviews, Dawn had described her as gentle, even at the time of the kidnapping, clearly only doing what she did under duress, and Liam had said she was 'a nice lady, much nicer than my nan', checking to see that Dawn wasn't listening.

Esther is given a statement to read, but she has to have it read to her, because Nate never let her go to school. He has denied that, of course, and he's probably denied who she is as well. They must have thought something was wrong by the age difference, but maybe they haven't worked it out yet.

The police have been kind to her. They say this kind of thing happens a lot, but it rarely comes to their attention because people like Nate are so good at hiding it, and they make people like Esther too terrified to try to escape. She has never had any money of her own, gone out alone or learned to drive. She's just done what he's asked, every day of her life. She's thirty-two now, which feels very old, but the police ladies and the lawyer tell her there's a lot of life left to live and she needs to fight for it.

Then there's the fire at Mill Farm. They haven't asked for the details about that because Ruth thinks, and now everyone thinks, that Martha saved her life that night. Martha would have done, if she'd had the chance. There was no doubt about it, but Martha was asleep, and Esther would have been too, if he'd got his way.

She knew it was going to happen. He'd told her Ruth had to go. He took delight in telling her everything he had done and was going to do to her, to the point that Esther would be sick when he left the room. She lay awake night after night imagining how she could go to the police and tell them everything. But she never did. She couldn't go anywhere without him.

She never thought that he'd really go through with it. Maybe Ruth was becoming more of a challenge to him, or maybe Rex was growing up and questioning things. One day he'd be taller and stronger than Nate. Nate couldn't be looking forward to that day. Better to reduce the strength of the opposition before it got to that point. But she wanted to warn Ruth. All she could hope was that Ruth understood when she'd said, 'No one would leave behind what they love most in the world.' Ruth loved Rex most in the world. Nate would never believe she'd run away from him.

Nate had crushed up some pills and slipped them in their milk that evening. Esther had seen him do Martha's, then he did the same to hers and Ruth's, but she tipped them away when he wasn't looking. He was confident when he went over to the cabin that nobody was watching. So confident he didn't even bother being quiet when he poured the contents of the petrol cans inside the door of the shack and threw in a flaming rag after it.

But what he didn't know was that Esther had got there first. After he'd given them their hot drinks, and before he'd gone to set the fire, she disappeared upstairs and put some clothes in a bag, then slipped out of the door, saying she was delivering Ruth's milk, but the cup was empty. The key was in the back door of the cabin that led straight into Ruth's room. She unlocked it quietly, removing the key and throwing it into a bush. It would never be needed again. The key to Ruth's padlock was harder to find. She could hear Nate's voice calling her, telling her not to dawdle and that Ruth needed her sleep. Ruth ignored the mug Esther placed at her bedside. She just rolled over and turned her back. Esther hesitated, almost said something, then thought better of it.

'Esther!' His voice was louder now, and her hands were trembling as they felt along the ledge by the door. There it was. She flung the tiny key behind her as she left.

'Coming.'

She dropped the bag of clothes behind a tree just inside the opening to the woods and ran back to the house, her heart pounding in fear. At least she could feign tiredness and take to her bed and Nate would be none the wiser.

Martha and Rex slept through the worst of the fire, waking only when the wail of the fire engine siren made even drug-induced sleep impossible. By then, the cabin was nothing but smouldering rubble. The officers were happy with Nate's account of events and Esther, as always, said nothing to contradict him.

When she found the bag of clothes gone, she felt like crying with joy, and realised at that moment it was the first time she had ever felt true happiness. It was a miracle Ruth survived, but the universe must have wanted it.

The universe was a beautiful thing, and everything in it. When they talked about the Truth and prayed for their fellow Pilgrims in the Assemblies, Esther prayed to Mother Nature. Whatever Nate had done to her and to Ruth, Martha and Rex, she had always had a deep love for the natural world. The animals on the farm were her confidantes. She would spend hours sitting with the pigs, and when Nate got rid of them, the goats, who were almost as good at eating everything as the pigs had been.

Nate never took much notice of the animals. That was why she'd been able to convince him the pigs would have cleaned up any remnants of Ruth's body from the fire, that he had nothing to worry about from the police any more. He'd accepted it because that's what he wanted to believe, and he had always trusted her because she'd never given him a reason not to. The fire at Mill Farm was a triumph disguised as a catastrophe. Nate read her the article in the local paper and then told her to get rid of it, but she never had. She thought it would come in useful one day if she got the chance to show it to someone. It was unbelievable to think it was only yesterday that she dropped it into the detective's open bag under the café table.

The door to her cell rattles and opens. It's the lawyer that they sent to help her explain her side of the story. The guard locks the door behind him, but she can see the back of his head in the window. The lawyer is a bald, bespectacled man in his forties, and Esther smiles her best smile as he introduces himself as Alan Swinney and sits down next to her. She has learned to smile to cover up her nerves when she's feeling unsure, and she has never felt more unsure than she does now. But it seems that she doesn't need to because he's smiling too.

'I have some good news for you, Esther.'

'What is it?' She's almost whispering, in case she scares the news away with her voice.

The lawyer pauses. He must be scared too. Then he speaks, and it's as if he can't believe his own words. 'The charges have been dropped against you.'

Esther's eyes widen. He says it again, this time smiling with his eyes as well as his lips.

'All charges have been dropped. I know. It's hard to believe, isn't it?'

'Why, what changed their mind? I've done bad things. I know I have.'

'You may have been involved in bad things, Esther, but you weren't the orchestrator of the crimes that took place. Your life was controlled and restricted and you had no choice. Bringing that press cutting to the attention of the police was the first step to helping them find Liam, and his mother wants to show her thanks for that. It's her husband she's furious with.'

Esther's jaw drops slightly. She knows she doesn't deserve this, but the lawyer has more.

'And not only that, but taking that first risk, being the first one to talk about what was going on. That's why we have them now. That's why it's all over for Nate and people like him. Because of what you did.'

'What I did?'

'You helped someone. Do you remember?'

Esther remembers the old house, where she lived before she and Nate came to Mill Farm. The chains around her wrists and ankles. The crack of light that slid between the boards nailed to the window frame that gave her hope.

It was at their weekly visit to the Assembly Hall that she met Helen. Like Esther, Helen had never been to school. 'Dad teaches me at home,' she had confided in one of their whispered conversations. 'But I'd rather go to school. I think I'd make friends there.' Esther and Helen were allowed a few minutes after Assembly to sit and draw pictures in the playroom, under the watchful eye of an Elder who seemed to be too preoccupied by the newspaper to notice what they were drawing. Helen taught Esther a game called consequences, with pictures because Esther couldn't read. Helen drew things that made Esther's eyes fill with tears, because they had something in common.

'I remember,' Esther murmurs now to the solicitor.

'You gave her a phone number.'

Esther gasps as the memory lands with a crash in her head. She wrote the number down in yellow crayon where the sun should have been on her drawing. You wouldn't have seen it if you weren't concentrating. It might have looked like a scribble. But Helen knew it was more than that. Esther tapped her crayon on the sun and told Helen she'd seen a poster of a child crying and scared with the number written across the top. It must mean that children could call if they were in trouble. Helen nodded, tapped her finger on her temple and coloured in the sun properly. Esther always wondered what she meant by that but had just assumed Helen was saying she was crazy.

'Helen was the first one to come forward,' says Alan, his eyes on hers with a look of compassion she's never seen before. 'Thanks to you.'

After that day, they closed the playroom and said the children could sit in the car if they didn't want to talk to the grown-ups. Esther had no more contact with Helen or anyone else her age. Her life had carried on as it was, until they moved to Mill Farm, and Pa began doing the same to her cousin Ruth as he'd done to her.

Pa. It's unbelievable to think she'd ever called him that, but it was easy to stop, because it made her sick to know she was his daughter.

She forces her mind back to the present.

'Is Helen OK?'

'She's had a lot of therapy, and yes, she's recovering,' says Alan. 'When you get out of here, give this lady a call. Susie Marshall. She's treated other people who have been through similar traumas to you, with great results.' He hands her a card and she pretends to read it, but all she recognises is the *S* for snake and the *M* for Martha. She's ashamed again, ashamed of everything.

'I should have done something more, something sooner, to save Ruth.'

'It wasn't your fault, Esther. None of it was your fault.'

There's a knock on the door and the detective comes in. She smiles at Alan, then at Esther. Her eyes are kind. They make Esther's prick with tears.

'How are you holding up?'

Esther only manages a few words before she feels too choked to go on. 'It wasn't what it looked like . . .'

But the detective is nodding as if she knows that already. She touches Esther's shoulder, briefly, the lightest touch, and looks right into her soul.

'I know. Things so often aren't.'

ACKNOWLEDGEMENTS

Hurrah for my brilliant editor Rosa Schierenberg, to the whole team at Welbeck, and to my agent Sophie Hicks for bringing us together. Big thanks as well to all the writers and readers I've met through Twitter, especially all those who have taken the time to read and review *The Choice* despite dizzying schedules and Ben Nevis sized TBR piles (that's what they tell me anyway). To name but a few: Claire Dyer, Emma Christie, Fran Quinn, Marion Todd, Philippa East, Tim Logan, Simon McCleave, Caron McKinlay, Sarah Clarke, Jack Sutherland, Louise Mumford, L.V. Matthews, Clare Empson. You are all my best friends now. There is no escape.

Back in the real world, there's my long-suffering partner, Will, who watches so much rugby I have no option but to sit at my laptop all day. To my grown-up children Steph, Gina and Jude, who are sick of being listed in age order, and my rude brother Richard who is always the first to cast an eye over my initial draft and cross most of it out. On the plus side (and I needed one) Brian Simmonds and Kristian Baker at Surrey Police kindly shared their expertise in everything from phone tracking to interview technology, and Patrick Tawney patiently took me through the inner workings of the fire service, which seems to have changed a bit since Trumpton times. Libby Cavin is a PR genius who carries my books around with her to photograph in all her favourite Wimbledon haunts and knows how to use Canva which sends me into a flat spin. Almost equally helpful are my dog and step-dog for ensuring I get out in the woods once in a while. Many a plot twist has been hatched in the dingly dells of Wimbledon Common with Roxy and Suki . . .

Finally, a big shout out to you, my readers, for your online reviews (the good ones); for following me on social media, posting, sharing and retweeting my nuggets of wisdom; accidentally joining my email list and subscribing to my zany blog. You are the reason I do this. It's a tremendous privilege to have a place on your bookshelf and I will never forget that.

ABOUT THE AUTHOR

Lucy Martin is the author of acclaimed crime thriller *Stop at Nothing*, the first in the series featuring DS Ronnie Delmar – 'A switchback ride of a read' (Cara Hunter).

For Lucy, it's life experience that brings a richness to writing, and she isn't short of that. Drawing inspiration from multiple careers (lawyer, entrepreneur, teacher, songwriter, campaigner) as well as her own complex childhood, she is fascinated by the dark side of the human mind and what 'normal' people are capable of when pushed to their limits.

When not writing, she is mostly to be found playing Scrabble with a chilled glass of rosé in hand, or being dragged into the woods in search of squirrels.